THE COAST OF
DANGER

Shipwreck cast the three of them upon the wild, craggy Pacific coast—two men and a woman. Their pasts lay thousands of miles to the east—their futures lay in the unknown land before them.

From that moment the destinies of these three were intertwined in a turbulent, surging drama of striving and fulfillment, brutality and tragedy, love and lust, as each man carved his own road to money and power, and the woman used them both to satisfy her all-consuming desires.

Here is an epic saga of the West at its most lusty and brawling—and of the larger-than-life breed of men and women who made their own rules on the lawless frontier.

"Robust . . . earthy . . . great!"
—*Philadelphia Inquirer*

The Adventurers

by Ernest Haycox

A SIGNET BOOK

NEW AMERICAN LIBRARY

TIMES MIRROR

SIGNET TRADEMARK REG. U.S. PAT. OFF. AND FOREIGN COUNTRIES
REGISTERED TRADEMARK—MARCA REGISTRADA
HECHO EN CHICAGO, U.S.A.

SIGNET, SIGNET CLASSICS, MENTOR, PLUME AND MERIDIAN BOOKS
are published by The New American Library, Inc.,
1301 Avenue of the Americas, New York, New York 10019

FIRST PRINTING, FEBRUARY, 1975

1 2 3 4 5 6 7 8 9

PRINTED IN THE UNITED STATES OF AMERICA

Chapter—1

AN hour after announced sailing time the shore gangs still worked cargo aboard the *Jennie North* and the little groups of well-wishers on the dock, having exhausted their stock of pleasantries, began to grow restive. Prolonged farewells were unnatural, Mark Sheridan decided; it was best to say good-by and to turn quickly away. A man in an attractive fawn-brown suit sauntered along the deck and stopped beside him at the ship's railing.

"We're late," said the man.

"That's customary," said Sheridan, and considered the town he had rejected as a place of opportunity. Market Street ran up its easy pitch into a San Francisco which appeared to be taking some sort of shape after careless beginnings.

"A lively place," said the man. "Is it your town?"

"I thought it might be my town," said Sheridan, "but it's too late. The business chances are pretty well taken up. There's nothing much here for me."

"What would be for you?" asked the man.

"Logs—lumber," said Sheridan. "I'm from Michigan."

"Then you want Portland or the Sound."

"I'll look at Portland."

The man extended his hand. "My name's George Revelwood."

Sheridan gave his name and took the hand. Revelwood was of the smiling, easy sort who made something of an art of mixing, possibly too much of an art. He had a long dark face somewhat on the handsome side. His beaver was expensive, his cravat was a flowered pattern and on his hand a substantial diamond stood in the massive gold claws of a dragon-ring. It never occurred to Sheridan to inquire into Revelwood's business or destination; he had not that much curiosity concerning others. Instead he put his glance on a hotel hack running down Market at a rapid clip. He nodded toward it. "Somebody late. That's stretching luck pretty far."

5

"People who stretch their luck," said Revelwood, "usually come out fine. You can believe the world won't wait for you, in which event it probably won't. Or you can consider it will wait, and likely it will."

The ship's master, Sheridan observed, stood on a wing of the bridge and looked down upon the dock with a bearded, copper-colored face—a master of the taciturn type, bearing the air of strong displeasure; presently he swung about, came down the ladder and made his way through the crowd toward the gangplank.

"A lady," said Revelwood, and brought Sheridan's glance around to the hotel hack, which had reached the dock. The hackman stepped down and offered his hand to a single passenger, a woman; she, giving the ship a single moment of attention, turned her back to it and waited the hackman's recovery of her baggage from the back of the vehicle. She had light-colored hair and she wore a very pretty dress. Revelwood watched her with open admiration and interest. "For a pretty woman the world will not only wait, it will stop dead, it will turn over. Does lunch occur to you?"

Sheridan nodded and turned along the deck with Revelwood. He had a fore-and-aft view of the *Jennie North* as they went forward. She was a clipper-hulled vessel with three masts which could be hung with canvas in a following wind; otherwise the power came out of engines which passed through a big walking beam amidships to huge side paddles. He stepped through the door, Revelwood courteously insisting on his precedence, and descended a fan-shaped set of stairs to the dining room. It was a room of mahogany and yellowed ivory paint and crystal lamp brackets; but though the shape of luxury remained and the paint was fresh and the glasswork glittered, the original elegance had quietly vanished with the ship's youth.

Captain Powell, descending the gangplank, walked along the dock to the *Jennie North's* stern; he crouched and had a look at the waterline at the ship's counter, and rose and paced forward to the bow and had another look. His manner grew increasingly dour; his chin whiskers thrust themselves forward and his mouth, half veiled by his mustache, showed an in-pinching. He went over to the company agent superintending the freight load.

"She's got too much in her now," he said. "She'll take no more. She'll ride like a scow all the way."

Basler pointed to the freight standing on the dock. "If I don't load that, what'll the owners say to me?"

6

"The owners," said Captain Powell, "are doing well enough."

"You get a carriage, Captain, and go uptown and tell 'em that."

"I might," said Powell.

"And they might get another master, too," said Basler.

Captain Powell stared at the agent with his sharp-slicing glance. "What have you got left that's got to go?"

"Mill machinery for Teekelet," said Basler, and waited the captain's further advice.

Powell looked into the heat haze and made his private guesses on the weather. He wanted to say, as he had the power to say, that he would carry no more. Properly, he should have said that six hours before. "Well," he said, "put aboard the machinery—and that's all."

Mounting the gangplank, Captain Powell tried not to remember that the *Jennie North* was a tender, sluggish craft, strained by countless overloadings and started by too many heavy seas. He bowed to the owner's dividends when he ought to be remembering his two hundred passengers; he was afraid of his job. He walked through the scattered passengers on the deck, made taciturn and heavy-footed by his reflections. Looking upon him, the passengers thought him the very picture of rough and competent strength.

Rising from lunch, Sheridan found the *Jennie North* standing down the bay. The day was windless but the *Jennie's* speed created a small breeze and coal smoke began to lay its fine grit over the deck. Sheridan went forward with his cigar and watched the town drop back and for a moment wondered if he had been wise to discard San Francisco as a choice. A good deal of luck went into a career, but luck aside, he thought he was fifteen years too late for this country. The men who had come in 1850 were the ones who now in 1865 had collected the business ventures into their hands; the newcomer could only get the scraps they chose to throw away. He had left Michigan because he wanted no scraps; what he wanted was a country where the prime chances remained.

He finished the cigar and walked aft, past groups of people stationed at the rail, past acquaintances forming, past a game of deck horseshoe, past six young women sitting in chairs quite by themselves, accompanied by an older woman with a rough, raddled face. He drew his glance from this group rather suddenly. Near the stern he noticed George Revelwood standing before a woman in a

7

chair—the woman who had arrived late via the hotel hack. He intended going by, but Revelwood stopped him. "Miss Dale," he said, "may I present another ship acquaintance, bound also for Portland, Mr. Mark Sheridan."

She nodded, she smiled. Her eyes were hazel, her lips full-shaped at the centers, her hair was a light brown touched by auburn and the effect of these features was to create the impression of a character pleasing rather than determined. She wore a small hat atop hair swept away from her ears, and in her ears two pearl pendants gracefully displayed themselves. She carried a book in her lap, perhaps to read, perhaps to round out a fashionable effect. Meanwhile Revelwood kept his light conversation going. "We're all for Portland. Miss Dale has not been there. Neither have we."

"Will it be your home?" asked Sheridan.

"No," she said, and nodded toward two nearby vacant chairs.

Revelwood accepted the invitation more promptly than Sheridan. "Well," he said, "we shall all be pilgrims. My mother's first name, by the way, was the same as yours— Clara. She was from Ireland."

Clara Dale gave him her polite interest and, encouraged by this, Revelwood took care of the conversation while Sheridan sat idly by. Now and then the girl turned her glance to him and gave him a moment's smiling attention. It occurred to him presently that Revelwood scarcely needed assurance and, rising, he made his bow to Clara Dale and went on to the saloon. He found it crowded with the assortment of types common to any ship, any train or any trail—men in search of adventure such as he was, men selling goods, men on business errands, the usual collection of soldiers traveling to new stations, including one brigadier general, a few rough ones up from steerage, and an occasional man who bore no obvious label. They were a cheerful lot; they reached familiarity in short order, used strong voices, asked personal questions without embarrassment, and smoked enormous amounts of tobacco.

He had his drink and joined a poker game on invitation, and found himself waiting for the supper bell with a great appetite. Revelwood came in shortly before the bell and offered him a drink. They stood at the bar, Revelwood in excellent spirits. "She was doubtful of me until you came along. It's always easier for a woman to be friendly to two strangers than to one. You were helpful."

8

"I judged so," said Sheridan.

"Then that's why you left—to give me a better field?" Revelwood let go with a genuinely hearty laugh. "You're not so dry as I had guessed."

They descended to the dining room. The purser's seating arrangement had separated them; from a corner of the room Sheridan noted Revelwood at the captain's table. In a short while Clara Dale came down and took her place at the same table, the captain rising with gallantry and the other gentlemen following suit. It was an excellent setting for her; she wore evening clothes and her neck and shoulders were coral against the shining of the lamps, and the scene she made was very pretty. Her eyes searched the room and touched Sheridan. He bowed, and her head dipped in response and for a moment she held his attention; perhaps it was a bit of womanly coquetry; perhaps it was nothing more than a nice civility. She didn't look at him again, but he watched her and found pleasure in the watching.

The binnacle light was a small glow before the quartermaster; otherwise the wheelhouse was dark and the shape of the three men—captain, quartermaster and watch officer —was blurred. The horizons closed down and the California coast was a black suggestion four miles to starboard. A ripple of phosphorescence showed off the *Jennie North's* bows; a flat ground swell slowly raised and slowly dropped her. The captain walked to the barometer and lighted a match to read it; he tapped the glass with his finger and read it again, and pinched out the light. He stood behind the quartermaster. "Wind by morning," he said. "Northwest."

The second watch came up to take his watch and the first officer turned out with the captain's voice following him. "Ask the purser to step here."

The second officer took the first officer's corner, the captain stood silent with his thoughts and was nagged by his conscience. If the owners had known about the overload they would not knowingly have permitted it. But all owners were alike. They didn't want to know things like that. They put the responsibility on their agents and the agents, fearing their jobs, always crowded the line too close. It kept the conscience of the owners quite clear, for if there were disaster it fell on the agents. He should have refused the overloading.

9

When the purser came up, the captain said: "What's the passenger list?"

"Two hundred and twelve."

"Anybody the company wants particular attention put on?"

"There's a general. He's got something to do about shipping army contract stuff."

"I'll have him up for a visit tomorrow. Tell that madam to keep her six girls where they belong."

"They won't give you any bother, Captain. The professionals never do. When the doors start opening tonight, it'll be the nice ladies looking for a bit of fun away from home."

The captain murmured, "That's all," and freshened the light on his cigar; he stepped to the port wing of the hurricane deck and listened to the washing rhythm of the bow wave. The night, filled with shore smoke, was blind. He found neither sky nor foreground; the familiar headlands were gone and though his course was safe enough, he felt uneasy and decided to haul off. He spoke his orders through the wheelhouse door. "North by west." The wheelsman's small voice came back: "North by west, sir." The captain laid his arms on the hurricane rail. The owners were not unkind. They had children, they went to church; but they didn't see—they didn't want to see. "It's money, of course," thought the captain. "It makes 'em blind. Makes me blind, too, I suppose."

The morning seas came up from the stern, borne in by a strong sou'wester. The heat fog had dissipated and the violent surf broke against the ragged coastal bluffs, exploding into wild white spray. All that coast was sullen-dark with timber and the rain mist crowded it and boiled around it like live steam.

Sheridan walked the deck with little company and watched the deep-gullied waves run by. Wheeling gulls were flung up and down by the air currents; the wind held to its monotonous crying in the rigging. The army general and his wife tramped the deck for a while arm in arm, enjoying the adventure; he was a thin six-foot man with a goatee below a strong mouth and nose; she was scarcely more than five feet and still attractive—a spoiled woman with a clinging manner. During the afternoon Sheridan caught the eye of Clara Dale in the women's parlor, and, since gentlemen seemed permitted in there, he joined her.

10

She said: "Where are we?"

"I believe we should make the Columbia bar tomorrow afternoon."

She said: "I'm not fond of bad weather," and gave him a sober glance.

"Probably it won't last," he said. The parlor was crowded and the air too warm for his comfort. "Would you like a turn on the deck?"

She settled back into her chair. "I'm not adventurous, Mr. Sheridan." There was lightness about her face, a liking for luxury; her smiling glance had its faint inquisitiveness. He made his bow and left the parlor, and thought about her as he continued his walk. Maybe Revelwood was right about her.

Night came down with a fuller wind; the following daylight arrived in a roar. Sheridan braced himself against the washstand while he shaved. The *Jennie North* shook when the solid blows struck her; she moved slowly over, and kept rolling until Sheridan found himself waiting the recovery with some concern. He stared through the porthole and saw the ripped-up surface of the ocean directly before him. In this dining room, which had few people, he took his coffee and wanted nothing more.

"Where are we now?" he asked the mess boy.

The mess boy shook his head. "I don't know this coast."

The captain knew this coast very well. Standing on the wing of the hurricane deck in his oilskins—the wind and rain beating at his back—he searched for the great head which stood out as a sentinel for the Columbia's mouth. All night he had feared this coast and he had twice reset his course to pull away; now he had lost touch with it. Westward was only the gray morning gloom of rain and darkness. The ship took too much astern, she rode too heavy on a following sea. He said to the quartermaster: "Hard over starboard. South by west." Then he said to the first officer: "I don't think we've overshot Tillamook, but we'll work shoreward to have a look."

Coming around, the *Jennie* took the trough. She went into it heavily and lay solid there; and a great mountain ridge of water fell into her and buried her with its green avalanches. For much too long a moment the captain felt the inertness of the ship; then a second sea came aboard and the well deck filled and the port wing of the hurricane deck touched the lifting waves. The captain waited, hanging

11

to the high side of the hurricane deck; the ship rose and slowly swung into the seas. He called to the quartermaster, "Point east," and cupped his ears to catch the possible sound of surf breaking.

He knew this coast too well. North from San Francisco as far as the Sound lay a seafaring graveyard; there was not a ten-mile stretch of it without the bones of ship and men scattered on some rocky point or sucked into some reach of sand.

At noon he saw no land, nor smelled it in the wind, nor heard surf, nor noticed anything in the sea drift. Three soundings told him nothing; the mists drove in, the rains were blending strong. He took coffee and doughnuts from the mess boy and thus entered his fifteenth straight hour on the bridge. Now and then he thought of the owners, not so much in anger as in puzzlement. Why did men blind themselves knowingly?

Sheridan made one round of the deck and gave it up; seas reached up from the south, mountain high, and the coarse spray rattled like gravel against the bulkheads. He stepped into the saloon and discovered Revelwood at a game of solitaire, and looked on a moment and went out. He tipped his body to the pitch of the *Jennie North*, and spread his feet to the ship's excessive rolling. The captain stood on the bridge wing, both hands anchored to the rail and his shoulders thrown forward toward a land obscured by the black-swollen clouds and the wind-ripped mist. It was middle afternoon, the day even now dying.

Sheridan reached the aft deck and started back along the port side. The *Jennie*'s bow, slowly dropping, struck the water hard enough to throw him off balance. He seized a stanchion, and waited for the ship to come up again; unwarned, he found himself heaved forward with a violence that pulled his hand from the stanchion. He fell on his knees and, in this position, he heard the smashing, ripping sound of something solid on the *Jennie*'s hull. A hard, long shouting fled back from the bridge; passengers rushed from the saloon, from the parlor, from staterooms. A woman screamed. A wave raced along the *Jennie*'s side, its edges splashing aboard. He got to his feet and saw the passengers surge at him, cramped in the narrow corridor between rail and wall. They were struggling with each other for space; fear blackened their eyes and slashed strange lines into their faces. The foremost man hit him,

12

never really seeing him, and lashed out with his fists. Sheridan struck him in the mouth and knocked him back, but the pressure of the crowd came down on him and he turned and was shoved along the narrow space. When he reached the clear area of the rear deck he stepped aside and let the tide go by. He heard the queer, grunting, whimpering sounds coming up from the crowd; he saw women borne along in the stream, knocked from man to man, and fighting back with their fingers clawed out. A man went down and disappeared beneath the merciless stampeding of feet. Watching the stream spew out of the narrow deck alley-way, Sheridan saw Clara Dale jammed into the mass of flesh around her; she seemed to have no motion of her own, nor to be taking steps of her own. Her face had the common terror on it—that sleepwalking, drawn emptiness. He pushed his way forward, bucking the onflowing people; he turned his shoulder into the pressure, took hold of her, and got her aside. The ship seemed to slant more sharply. He had to brace his feet; he put an arm around her, hanging to the rail with his other hand.

She was dead weight; she was shaking violently, and her hands squeezed his arms with all the force she had. Revelwood escaped the stampede along the deck aisle and ran forward. The terror was on him, too, but even in stress, Sheridan noticed the man's wits were quick, for Revelwood's glance searched the deck and its scene of half madness, darting from place to place, from object to object, from hope to hope. Revelwood murmured through his swift breathing, "We've got to think of something." Sheridan shook his head; there was at this moment nothing to do, no way of working against the animal craziness around him.

The ship had struck a rock lying under the water and had been impaled by it. Having lost freedom of motion, it now became a target for the seas rolling out of the rain-mists. It shook under each mountainous wallop of ocean and swayed and ground itself deeper upon the rock; the sound of that came up from the bottom as a sudden groaning and clashing of metal. The seas, rushing aft, began to board the *Jennie* at midships and the deck turned into green mountain streams rushing down the slope.

A ship's officer worked his way aft from the bridge and the crew members were gathering, no less witless than the passengers. The ship's officer shouted: "Boat One—stations! Boat Two—come up there now." The crew members drove

13

through the jam of passengers and began to work at the lifeboat davits. One huge black man turned to face the crowd surging at the nearest boat. He shoved men away; he shook his head, not speaking. He shoved and shook his head.

Sheridan said to Revelwood, "Life jackets in that locker over there."

Revelwood turned toward a locker built against a bulkhead. He got to it and lifted its lid and reached into it for jackets; men suddenly saw the locker and stormed at it, and Revelwood disappeared in a sudden-fighting mob. A woman came toward the railing, holding the hand of a two-year-old boy. She looked out into the rain-fog, she stared around her, and her glance came upon Sheridan and walked through him as though he were a shadow; without warning she seized the boy and flung him into the sea. She cried and screamed at him and tipped over the rail, head foremost into the ocean.

Revelwood came back with his face bleeding, but with the jackets. The two of them got a jacket around Clara Dale, prying her arms temporarily away from Sheridan. The captain came aft to watch the crew work the first lifeboat around in the davits. He shouted, "You—ladies!" He seized them and pushed them at the lifeboat; he put his hands against the chests of men crowding in. The big colored man silently pushed them away, shaking his head and baring his teeth. The first officer came along to help; there was a sudden wild rush, men and women together, toward the boat. The captain snatched a gun from his pocket and leveled it on a crew member. He said, "Stand away there." The crew member reached out to knock the gun aside The captain flinched slightly and fired. He said to the first officer, "Take the boat away, Mr. Soames."

Revelwood said to Sheridan, "Let's get her on this boat."

Sheridan shook his head. "Not the first one. It'll swamp."

The *Jennie*'s slant steepened and the pounding of the rock continued to open her hull. The mizzenmast, footed into the bottom of the ship, swayed and plunged straight down through the ship. The mainyard, lying crosswise on the mast, slammed upon the deck, catching a man beneath it. Sheridan flinched at the scream and looked around. He saw the man pinned and squirming beneath the spar; he saw the man's gray face wheel from side to side. He turned toward the man and turned back, shaking his head.

The first lifeboat swung out with its women; the mate

14

crouched in the stern, shouting at the crew members at the oars, "Steady till I say." Other crew men hung to the davit lines, waiting out his call. The captain faced the first officer. "Soames," he said, "tell them if they hadn't overloaded us, this never would have happened."

"Let go!" shouted the first officer.

The davit lines were released. The lifeboat dropped into the curling seas, rode a moment on the crest of a wave and then began to work away. The oarsmen dug in, the mate shouting, "Now—now—now." Suddenly the watching crowd broke through, reached the rail and began to jump into the boat, smothering the oarsmen. A wave lifted the lifeboat, flung it against the *Jennie's* hull and cracked its ribs. The bow flipped up, and a following wave knocked it over, men and women spilling into the water. Sheridan watched their heads bobbing; he saw the unpinned hair of women streaming on the green surface. He saw them disappear.

The captain said, "Boat Two, boys." Then he lifted his voice against the crying, against the wind, against the boom of water and the wrenching and the smashing of the *Jennie North*. "I'll kill the next man who rushes a lifeboat! Women, there! Travis, swing it out."

"This one," said Revelwood.

Sheridan shook his head. "No use." He had seen something else. A whole section of the aft deckhouse, torn free from its bolts, slowly shifted on the deck as the *Jennie* swayed; it rose stiffly when the seas came aboard. He reached down to unlock the arms of Clara Dale who hung on with her senseless grip. He shook her shoulders. "We're going to get ashore." He took her around the waist and moved along the deck toward the drifting section of the deck housing. Revelwood went with him, but presently stopped. "Do it quiet," he said, "or they'll swamp that thing too," and then he turned back toward the second boat now filling.

Sheridan half carried Clara Dale across the slanting deck; he was foot deep in water and loose objects struck him in the shins as they were carried by—preservers, chunks of timber, doors, luggage blindly brought up and blindly abandoned. The deck housing had lodged near the rounded stern rail, and moved uneasily up and down, ready to break away. He got to the yard ropes as a sea broke aboard and smothered him. Clara Dale struggled in his arms and he heard her choke as the seas dropped away;

15

the sharp cold paralyzed his chest and the wind began to slice like a knife over his body. He crossed the yard and reached the deck section. He pulled Clara with him, and worked his way to a skylight. The glass hatch was broken; he kicked it aside and laid himself down beside the girl, and ran his arm through the iron rods of the skylight opening.

The second lifeboat disappeared over the side of the *Jennie* and there was again the flurry of men rushing to board it. He saw the black man, the captain and George Revelwood standing shoulder to shoulder, fighting off the attack. He had one thought then which he never changed: Revelwood was a *scoundrel*—but Revelwood was a brave man, and that covered everything. The deck crowd had thinned; of the three hundred souls on the *Jennie,* two thirds of them were now dead, and the rest soon would be. The madam stood with her girls around her, the general and the general's wife were apart from the crowd, arms around each other. Revelwood started over the deck, and then the *Jennie* trembled and a great explosion seemed to break her apart. She began to slide, and a wall of water tumbled over the rail, destroying the second lifeboat and scattering the crowd. Sheridan saw Revelwood bend his head and come on; the wave, reaching the broken deck housing, lifted it clear of the ship and flung it outward into the blind dark wastes. The last thing Sheridan saw on that deck was the body of a woman borne upward and outward by the wave, like a figurehead.

The deck housing was like a huge box capsized in the water; and on this Sheridan rode, one hand holding Clara, the other anchored to the skylight braces. Water rose around him, little ridges with separate saw-tooth crests etched against the leaden light. Spray cut him like knotted buckskin, and rain drove in furiously. A wave broke over the housing, its weight grinding Sheridan's crotch into the skylight frame; it snapped his head downward and he struck his mouth and chin against the wood. There was only a moment of feeling; the coldness of this water was an anesthetic—and he began to fear that the coldness would loosen him. The roar and the pounding diminished for a short space and he lost the half senselessness which came of too much crowded too quickly upon him. He felt the deck housing rise—the sensation like that of a cable car racing up a hill—toward one of the green summits. The summit faded before it reached him and he found

16

himself on a new crest formed beneath him, sliding downward into another valley; and at this point he first heard the sound of the surf on a beach he could not yet see through the mist and spray and twilight. It was suddenly loud and near, and fear came on him again when he remembered the violence of this surf.

He bent toward Clara Dale's head and shouted: "Don't fight against me if we capsize."

The deck housing rose up to the crest of a breaker, hovered there, and plunged. It went under. Again the pressure squeezed Sheridan and hauled at his arms and kicked him violently back and forth along the skylight frame. He lifted his head, seeking air; he took in a breath, half air and half water, and gagged it out. He lost his bearings; he felt tipped and turned and he was conscious of only two distinct things, the girl's arms gripped around him, and his own body wedged into the skylight frame. The skylight seemed to revolve like a turntable; he felt it strike bottom and lift, and the current rushed him on, and a wave picked him up, tipping the skylight. He could not be certain it would capsize but he knew that if he and the girl were caught beneath its weight they would be smashed; he released his hold on the skylight and threw himself into the water, still holding the girl. Instantly he was flung over. He touched bottom, and tried to right himself; he was knocked onward. He was crawling, his ears rang, and he felt himself lose the feeling of this earth and its life. He touched again and lay still a moment, with the beach waters boiling around him and the roar behind him. He got on his feet while the surf came hip high around him. When it turned outward he walked on until he could walk no more, and dropped. The next time the surf came it was only a shallow eddy. The girl seemed dead.

He felt disappointed, but he didn't really care. He pulled the girl a dozen yards forward, and lay out on his side and strangled up sea water; he sucked away at the air with greed. His hurt began to come at him faintly and from different sources. Rain fell in slashing sheets and the whole beach trembled to the impact of the great rollers beating against it. They day had darkened so much that he was able to see nothing toward the sea. On the landward side a low bluff skirted the beach and solid timber seemed to run inland.

He sat up and pulled the girl across his lap and lifted her shoulders; her eyes were closed, her hair matted with

17

sand. Her dress was torn open around her shoulders, her face was marble-colored. He said: "We're ashore. Can you stand up?"

She kept her eyes closed but she spoke to him more distinctly than he had expected. She had come back from nowhere. "Yes."

She opened her eyes. There was no motion in her face, and her lips were hard to distinguish from the rest of her skin. She was shaken by a steady trembling she could not control. "I don't know," she said, "if I can live through a night of this."

He had his own doubts. The rain could make him no wetter, but the wind destroyed the warmth in him and sucked out his vitality. Nobody could stand this sort of exposure indefinitely. He stood up and pulled her to her feet. He said, "Can you run?" and gave her a push, and trotted with her toward the bluff. She quit before they reached it.

"No," she said.

When they got to the bluff he took her by the hand and pulled her to its summit. Before them was the dark, solid face of that forest which he had viewed from the sea, now further darkened by the oncoming shadows of evening, and faintly glittering with the rains lodged within it. "This will be better," he said, and pulled her into the timber.

The trees broke the wind and the rain lessened, and this contrast was so great that for a moment he felt warmer.

Pushing on—to keep in motion more than for any other reason—he struck what appeared to be an animal trail coming down the slope, and followed it over a low summit and down into a meadow lying at the edge of a lake. Beyond the lake the forest began again and marched off toward the darkest and loneliest mountain he had ever seen. To the right the lake worked its way out of sight, around a point of land; to the left it seemed to pass into a creek and at this point he saw a broken scaffolding standing in the gloom, perhaps some open-air drying device used by Indians. Next to it stood an odd-looking hut whose log walls started well below the ground level and whose roof was scarcely more than five feet high—a long and narrow structure with a bark and dirt top, more in the style of Indian living than white man's. The girl saw it as soon as he and began to run toward it.

"We don't know what's in that place," he cautioned.

"I've got to get inside," she said.

They came upon a blind side of the shack, and skirted it

and found a small doorway. He pulled her back and went ahead, she crowding against him. He stepped down and forward into suddenly rank odors. He stopped, braced against surprise, and waited for his eyes to grow into this darkness diluted by muddy streaks of light coming through the door and through the cracks of the wall logs. There were a few rocks grouped in the center of the place, the mark of a fire, and in one corner was a mound of something which, when he put his hand against it, turned out to be dead grass and small branches.

He heard the girl draw a long sigh. She said, "Could we get a fire started?"

"No." Rain and wind struck the cabin and far off was the boom of the surf. In this quietness he felt temporarily warm. But that was contrast rather than real warmth; they had relief from the rain and from most of the wind, but no way of escaping the raw chill. He heard water drop down from her clothes and from his own. He went to the corner and bent down to explore the pile, which was small brush and fern and grass, crumbling dry, which somebody had used long before for bedding; there was a strip of it all along the end of the cabin. He went along the wall, drawing it together and carrying it back to a corner to make a decent pile.

He said: "Take off your shoes. That leather never will warm up. Crawl into the hay."

"Help me."

He gave her a hand, turning her. She dropped heavily under his support. She sat crouched over, still badly shaking. She wanted to take her mind from her misery and she began to work at her shoe laces and to talk at the same time. "Do you think anybody else is alive?"

"I doubt it."

He went to the far end of the shed and turned his back to her. "I'm going to wring out my clothes. You'd better do the same thing."

He peeled to the skin and twisted out the water. He dressed again, leaving off his coat. He kept his back to her; he heard her stirring in the hay, and the shaken ragged way of her breathing. "Your friend," she said, "Revelwood—that's too bad."

"He was a scoundrel but he paid off for all his sins on the boat."

"I knew he was a scoundrel," She said. "You can come here now."

He heard the half panic in her voice, as though she were afraid she wouldn't last. He dropped and crawled against her and pulled the hay and fern and brush around them. The dust and the chaff got into his nose with its rank odors. He kept his hands to himself, but suddenly she slid her arms around him and pulled herself into him. Tremors ran steadily through her; they started at various places and worked along her body. They shook her, and ceased, and came again. She had left off her undergarments, for he felt her body beneath the single layer of her dress. A woman, he thought, was more realistic than a man. He swung his body over and put himself across her; they were two solid lumps of coldness together.

She said: "I've got to get warm, or I'll die."

"Am I too heavy?"

"No. It helps. I don't shake as much. People never know, do they? I didn't realize that nothing mattered, except to live."

The reaction was fully on her. She was filled with terror. He felt it in her, in her greediness to absorb some of his warmth. Her arms had the same tightness around him that they'd had in the ocean; she laid her face into the side of his neck. He reached back, pulling more hay around them and over them. He felt the first small warmness make its clammy sensation along his skin.

She said: "I didn't know I could stand so much. I didn't know anybody could."

"We'll get through it."

"Do you remember the nice old general and his wife? And those girls with the horrible old woman? It was the captain's fault, wasn't it?"

"I guess so."

"I'm sorry for them all, but not too sorry. That's the terrible thing. I can't feel it the way I should. I can only feel that I'm alive. I'm not as cold as I was."

She shivered less frequently; she released her grasp and pulled the hay around his back and took hold of him again. He felt softness come to her body. Her head rolled aside but he knew she wasn't sleeping; she was lying still, soaking up warmth and thinking her strange thoughts—perhaps the same thoughts that worked through his head. The scene on the deck grew sharp before him—its short disconnected scenes flashing across his view. He admired Revelwood again. Then he thought, "What happened to the captain?" He tried to remember where he had last seen the captain, and couldn't fill in the blind spot. There were a lot of blind spots.

She said: "I've discovered a bad thing. You hung on-to me, but I was thinking only of myself. I had no pity for anybody else. Most of us were like that. We would have killed in order to save ourselves." She stirred beneath him and put a little pressure in her arms. He rolled away from her. She came against him, her body over him. She pulled the hay closer around them. "I know I'm going to live. I know it, because I'm not as selfish now. . . . I want you to live too."

"We're all like that."

"You weren't. Revelwood wasn't. It's in people, or it isn't."

Warmth began to flow between them; it came out of their bodies and clung around them. The hay held it in and threw it back at them. He felt the increasing throb of the injured places on his body. His left arm, from wrist to elbow, seemed afire. He turned her over his body and swung, facing her. She came up into him again, readjusting herself for comfort. She was whispering, her mouth near his ear. "People believe so many foolish things. I won't believe them any more. I talked to a girl night before last in the writing room. She was going to Portland to be married. She had done without so many things, just so the marriage would be nice. What good was that to her?"

"People have got to fight for happiness."

"I don't want any more misery. Who knows when this will happen again? You can't trust anything. I'm almost comfortable now. Tomorrow I'll be miserable again, finding a way out of these woods. It's just today that means anything. When I get out of this, I'll never be cold again. I've promised myself that. This girl waited a long time for her man. She's dead. He'll grieve for a little while, then he'll marry somebody else. What good did it do her to wait and save her pennies and never look at another man? She missed everything."

A tree crashed and the girl, hearing it, tightened her arms against him. He felt heavy and exhausted and soon fell asleep.

He woke later to find the girl had crawled nearer him. Her lips were round and warm and full on his mouth. Her body was shaking so that he thought she was cold, but in a moment he heard her crying, and felt tears

21

dropping from her and running along his face. He pulled his head aside. He said: "What's wrong?" She shook her head and her mouth brushed his face and found him again. She wanted to be nearer; he pulled her in and held her. When she had enough, her head dropped down on his arm and they both fell asleep.

Chapter — 2

FROM the doorway Sheridan saw the dismal morning struggle in through the steady rain. Mist rolled along the earth before the insistent wind and above the mist lay choked dark clouds. A creek left the lake, turned a bend and ran out of sight toward the ocean beyond the hill. Clara Dale came back from the creek, both hands holding her hair. She gave him a short side glance and went on into the shack. He felt dull and exhausted and irritable, and so did she. North lay directly ahead of him, across the creek, and north appeared the only avenue of escape; both behind him and to his right—to the west—the huge black mountains blocked his way.

She came back to the door, her hair pinned down wet to her head. She said in a half-cranky voice: "I'm not attractive, am I?"

He smiled at her. "You're alive."

She shrugged her shoulders and looked down at her wrinkled partly torn dress. She put her arms crosswise over her breasts and she stared at the day with her mouth pressed down. She hated what she saw. "How far will we have to go?"

He shook his head. She watched him a moment. "Well," she said, "I got through one day and one night. I'll get through another. I think I'll never live for more than one day at a time." She caught sight of the great raw track along his arm, and her expression tightened. "I should wrap it."

"Let the rain wash it out." He went back into the shanty and got his coat. It was still damp but he put it over her shoulders. "That'll be good for an hour or two."

They turned back into the timber, found the trail and followed it to the bluff. Here, under the partial shelter of a tree, they looked out upon the ocean and saw no ship. "It must have gone down right after we got away." He ran his glance along the shore, to the driftwood lying well up from the tide marks. He saw the darker objects lodged in the driftwood and other dark objects half buried in the sand; he saw one bobbing in the surf. "Not as many as I thought," he said. "They'll be drifting in for a week. Some won't come in at all."

They dropped down the bluff and walked through the soft sand to the hard-packed beach, here turning north. The creek lay in front of them, meandering across the sands. He lifted the girl and waded over and put her down and went on through a steady-falling rain, the beach curving in and out of its coves before them. The wind blew behind them, the smell of the sea was exceedingly strong. He saw other black bits of wreckage scattered on the sand, and other bodies. He saw one body stripped, marble pale in the morning and he turned inshore to avoid it.

They covered one long beach, waited the falling away of the surf and ran around a rock ledge to another beach. This led them into a cove, and the cove trapped them with its low promontory, over which they had to climb. Near what must have been noon they were half the distance toward a huge head standing in the foreground, and at this point Sheridan saw something that resembled a trail opening through the timber. He turned toward it. They climbed a short sand bluff, passed a brief meadow spongy with water, and found a break in the trees; the trail went directly into the semi-darkness of the forest, and the forest rose up into bulky mountains.

"We'll cross over," said Sheridan.

She set her mouth—which normally had so little hardness—into the tightest, homeliest line and nodded for him to go ahead. He stepped before her, passing into the windy, droopy shadows. The climbing ground was quite rough and quite soft; around a bend, fifty yards on, Sheridan reached a short clearing which, taking the waters of a rain-swollen creek, had become a marsh. Here, sitting on a log with the completest air of human dejection upon him, was George Revelwood.

He was ill, he was at the end of his rope; that long narrow face was pale and strained and listless. "My God," he said in a voice meant to carry feeling, "are you alive?" He spread his hands before him. "I can't find a way across this swamp." Rain dropped from his face. He wiped it with his hand and seemed to be crying.

Sheridan broke his way through the brush, traveling along the edges of the marsh. Beyond sight of Revelwood

24

he came upon an area of old logs fallen over the creek. They made a bridge across the marsh to solid ground beyond. He called back: "Come over here."

He waited and heard nothing. He returned to find Revelwood still seated. The girl looked at Sheridan and shook her head. "He won't try."

"God damn you," said Sheridan, "get up and walk."

Revelwood stared at Sheridan with an owlish interest. "I'm tired," he said. "I was on my feet all night, trying to keep warm."

Sheridan reached over, hooked his hand under Revelwood's armpit, and lifted the man from the log. Revelwood offered him a momentary resistance, trying to find anger enough to fight. Sheridan set him in motion with a push, and followed behind. The girl brought up the rear. When they reached the logs Revelwood stopped. "I can't cross the damned things. I'd fall in."

Sheridan gave him another push, whereupon Revelwood gave out a dismal groan and painfully climbed to a log. He pulled his coat around his neck and wiped the dripping water from his nose. The log on which he stood ran out into the marsh, its lower end under water; but another log lay over it, providing further passage, and this in turn reached solid ground beyond the marsh. Too exhausted to have confidence in himself, Revelwood crept along the first log, climbed to the second with an old man's painful slowness and, suddenly aware of the marsh yawning beneath him, sat down a-straddle the log and completed the journey an inch at a time. He stepped to solid ground and put his back to a tree. Sheridan motioned the girl to go ahead; he followed, guiding her over.

Revelwood stared at the hill running upward before them. "How do we know where that goes?" The girl listened to him and turned her glance on Sheridan, waiting for his answer. He shook his head and nodded onward. She turned and started up the hill. Revelwood followed her.

Sheridan said: "How'd you get ashore, George?"

"The ship just dropped out from under me. I grabbed a plank."

The slope stiffened. The girl stopped to catch her wind and Revelwood again put himself against a tree; his nostrils flared out for wind and his pulse throbbed rapidly against the skin of his neck. The girl had assumed an almost brutal expression, her chin set, her mouth turned

25

down at the edges. In this manner, plodding on, and halting and plodding on again, they crawled up the mountain, stumbling over fallen trees, threading the vines which slapped them and drenched them, sliding backward in the rain-softened earth.

They came, long afterward, to the summit of the ridge and were lost in its thickness; but the way was moderately level and the girl reached into some new strata of endurance; she went on without prompting, taking the trail downward. Arriving at a break in the trees, she stopped and pointed into a small, stumpy clearing. Coming forward, Sheridan saw a house and a lean-to barn. A spiral of smoke came from the house and a cow grazed on a miniature side-hill meadow. None of them said anything; they moved slowly down the trail. A dog barked through the rain, a bell tinkled, and when they came to the edge of the clearing they found a woman in the yard watching them.

Clara Dale was first to reach the woman. She began to say something but the woman stopped her. "You're from the wreck. There's a man here already from it." She was a dark, grave girl and pity softened her eyes. She put an arm out to Clara. "You come in," she said. "All of you come in."

Revelwood said, "I don't believe—" and fell on his knees and tried to support himself, and collapsed on his side. An older man ran from the dilapidated barn with a boy and a girl at his heels. Sheridan stared down at Revelwood, knowing he ought to lift him from that wet earth, yet having nothing much left in the way of strength. Clara Dale stared at Revelwood woodenly. Then she lifted her eyes to Sheridan. "I'm stronger than he is," she said.

She turned into the house. The man and his two youngsters came up and the older man said, "I'll take care of this fellow. Anybody else coming?"

"No," said Sheridan. "That's all," and went into the house.

They had eaten and they had slept; now it was another gray morning, the wind at half strength and rain falling in lazy gusts. The survivors sat at breakfast—these three and a rough, short Irishman who had preceded them down the trail.

The story came out with no prompting from the man who sat by the stove with his pipe and interfered with his

26

eldest daughter Katherine's cooking. She was the mother of the Morvain family in place of the real mother who was dead. She was the eldest daughter, as silent as her father was talkative. The two boys, sixteen and twins, were Bob and Harry—the best hunters in the county. "Venison," said Morvain, "is a poor man's way of stayin' alive. Bear's not bad, but my family don't like it." The eleven-year-old girl was Suzie. There was a boy a year younger; he was Elgin, and looked nothing like the others.

The small kitchen was warm and filled with the close, keen odors of coffee, bacon and hotcakes. Comfort soaked into Sheridan and his vitality came back; and Clara felt well enough to smile. It was Revelwood who sat jaded and drawn. Katherine Morvain worked steadily from stove to table, possessing practical gifts which her father obviously did not have. Her hair, remarkably black, lay neatly over her head, her dress was smooth around a strong body, and a summer darkness lay on her skin. She observed Revelwood's lethargy particularly and filled his coffee cup again and paused over him. "You'd better eat. It's cold outside and you'll be driving ten miles through the rain."

Revelwood shook his head.

"I'll ride you into Seaside," said Morvain. "You can catch a wagon of some sorts on to Astoria. There's daily boats from there to Portland. But if you're tired, stay here longer. My house is open. What we've got is yours."

Katherine Morvain's glance touched her father with a small warning which he didn't see. "This coast is rough country," he said. "I've had three ranches along it in five years. I'd like to go on over to the valley and would of done it earlier if I wasn't deputy sheriff."

He was mild and vain and blind to himself; he believed himself a bigger man than he was. That, Sheridan suddenly decided, was what Katherine Morvain knew about her father. This family was dirt poor. The rough room showed it; the misfit barn, the sidehill clearing, the clothing of the children, the slackness of Morvain himself— these things showed it. Out in the rain stood one thin cow and out in the rain too stood a plow gathering rust.

"We'll move on," said Sheridan. "We're under great obligation to you."

Revelwood spoke one of his rare sentences. "This was as far as I could come last night. If the house hadn't been here I'd have died in that timber."

27

"I ought to know the names of the drowned," said Morvain. "I guess that's part of a deputy's job. Maybe I ought to go over to the beach and see what I can identify."

Revelwood said rather quickly, "Let the coroner do that. It's not what anybody would want to see who doesn't have to see it."

"Oh," said Morvain indulgently, "I've seen a lot of death." His face was smooth and entirely free of care. He had no knowledge of care, Sheridan thought; it would be his daughter who took the care.

Rising, Sheridan reached into his pocket for the wallet which once, during the shipwreck he had thought of throwing away because of its weight. He took out two double eagles and extended them toward Morvain. "Will you be good enough to take this? And if at any time I meet you again and you are in need of help of any kind, I'll consider it an obligation."

Morvain had enjoyed himself in the role of an open-handed host, and this offer offended him. "By God, no. What do you consider me? If you knew me better—as people around here know me—you wouldn't offer it."

"Well," said Sheridan, "any time you feel like hitching up, we're ready," and went to the yard. With a full belly and a night's rest he couldn't bring back the sharp edge of yesterday's misery, but some of it came back when he saw the dripping timber. Morvain walked to the barn. Clara Dale rose from the table and came into the yard. She said, under her voice, "Give me that money."

He dropped the two eagles into her hand. She stared at them a moment with a scheming warmth in her. "Could you afford more?"

He brought out his wallet and opened it to her.

She said, "Is that what you start with in this country, Mark?"

"That's all of it."

She bent her head, thinking. Then she said, "They need it so much worse," and took two more double eagles and turned back into the room. She said something and put the gold pieces into Katherine Morvain's hands. Sheridan noticed the tightening expression come to her—something like the cut pride her father had shown. Clara put her hand on Katherine Morvain's arm and said some other thing. Katherine Morvain shook her head; she held one gold piece in her hand and passed the other three back to Clara.

The Irishman came out and stood near Sheridan without speaking. He put his hands into his pocket and looked blankly at the timber. Sheridan said: "How'd you get ashore?"

"I don't know," said the Irishman. "Never will know, I guess."

"Bound for Portland?"

"We were," said the Irishman. "My wife and three kids went down with that ship."

Morvain drove the wagon forward and Revelwood and Clara walked from the house. Sheridan gave Clara a hand to the seat and climbed into the rear with Revelwood. They waited for the Irishman to join them but he stood still, looking into the trees. In a moment he said: "I'll be going back to the beach," and turned away at once with his mind made up.

Katherine Morvain brought out a blanket for Clara. "Wear it to Seaside," she said. The rain-mist put a crystal net over her hair. Her eyes, Sheridan thought, had a good deal of pity in them. She knew enough about trouble to feel what they'd gone through. He looked at the long, firm fingers and the lean body within the plain dress, and at the dark face with its suppressed womanliness and he thought, "Another ten years of this and she'll be broken." She wasn't now. He said to her, "Will you ever be in Portland?"

"It is unlikely," she said, and gave them a kind, softening glance. "I wish you all well." Her eyes touched Sheridan and he saw the distant Irish flash of warmth. She let it come through her self-control, and gave him as good an appraisal as he gave her. He sat still, appreciating it, until Morvain clucked the horses down the hillside to the road. Braced in the wagon bed Sheridan looked back to the girl; she stood in the light rain, and as the wagon entered the trees she lifted a hand and this sight of her struck him and stayed with him—she motionless in the dull day, posed against the impoverished clearing and against the shabby house.

Morvain took them to Seaside; for ten dollars a rancher drove them the twenty miles into Astoria, a wind-beaten village crouched on a lumpy clearing beside the Columbia. They put up at a flimsy caricature of a hotel and had some chance to improve their clothes at a general store. Toward evening they went aboard the steamboat *Western*

29

Wave, bound upriver for Portland, a hundred miles inland.

Katherine Morvain watched the strangers go, feeling the loneliness of their departure, yet glad that their eyes no longer saw the shabby poverty of this place. Bob and Harry had drifted into the woods with their guns, the only thing they cared about, or knew about. In ten years of moving from one wild hillside clearing to another they had known but one year of schooling; they were growing up to be illiterate men who would marry, breed shiftless children, and sink deeper into the mud—all the love and brightness and good usefulness which lay under the Morvain skin at last dying.

She turned into the kitchen. Suzie had already begun on the dishes. Elgin sat behind the stove, working out a box trap with a knife. Elgin said, "I want to go look for bodies."

"No, the cow's to be milked."

Elgin put down his trap and rose without enthusiasm. He was young and at that age all boys were lazy, but she feared he too showed the slack streak which was in his brothers. He needed a harness put on him and he needed school. She went about her work in deep silence, her mouth pressed together. She cleaned the house. The older boys came back for noon meal, punctual in that one thing, and were gone again. She put Suzie to sewing the edges of the ragged tablecloth. She laid out an old school reader on the table. "Elgin—one hour."

He said: "What's the good of it?"

She said: "Do you want people to laugh at you?"

"What'd they laugh for?"

"Because you couldn't talk right, and you wouldn't get a job, and you wouldn't have clothes. Didn't you notice how nice those men talked? They're the kind that travel around and see things. That's what we want. You study a whole hour."

"All right," he said and went slowly to the book.

She stood in the doorway with her back turned to him and felt the gloomy day press in around her and narrow her life to this drab muddy yard with its stumps, its half-fallen fences, its cow standing uncomfortably under a weeping fir, its sagged barn and manure pile steaming in the rain; there was not a hopeful sight anywhere. She crossed her hands over her breasts and her stubbornness returned. "There's hope for him. I've got to think of a way." She was ashamed of herself for pinning her thoughts so much on Elgin. Suzie needed to be thought of too, but Suzie was a different problem.

Her father should have been home long before, but she knew he would visit along the way, talking politics because as deputy sheriff he considered himself a politician; or talking about farming though he hated all chores, or just talking. He never knew that he was deputy sheriff only because no other man wanted a job that took time and paid nothing, and never knew that these roundabout people smiled at his shiftlessness. He lived in a little false world and was happy. Now, though, she read the signs of restlessness on him. He had stayed here two years, and that was longer than he had stayed anywhere.

She turned to the bedroom and put on a coat and went into the rain, walking around the house toward a small gulch which ran along the eastern end of the place. She remembered very clearly her mother's words when they had come here. Her mother, stepping into his hut—then dirty and long unused and overgrown with fern—had turned to her father with a soft, terrible outpour of feeling.

"Well, Morvain, each move makes us poorer. The next move we'll have nothing—we'll be beggars. But there won't be a next move. Bad as it is, I'll never leave this place. You couldn't make a go of it anywhere else—and maybe you can't do it here. But if there's any power in you to provide a living, you'd better bring it out now. We'll live here or we'll starve here. I'll not follow you another step, nor any of the children."

She remembered her father's blindly hopeful answer. "Now, Liz, you're tired. It'll be all right. This country's a fine place and we'll get along fine."

Her mother retorted: "If it's a fine place, find me something for supper!"

She followed the pathway through the overgrown bracken fern to the edge of the gully. A cedar fence enclosed a very small cleared plot with its single grave; at the head of the grave stood a board, worked slightly askew in the soft earth, its black lettering faded so that only her memory traced the inscription: "Agatha Morvain. Beloved Wife and Fond Mother. 1821-1864."

This was an infrequent visit for Katherine. She hated this damp, closed-in spot. There never was any sun on it, and the vines grew around it and crept through the fence and threatened to hide it. After the misery and unhappiness of life, it was hard to see her mother lying in this unfavored place. Katherine stood here with her downborne thoughts. She knew her father would soon bring up the subject of moving and now she was her mother's voice and ought to answer as her mother would have answered. Her mother, beaten down by the years of moving around, by the poverty and hunger always hanging over them, had given up her ambitions one by one until she had left but one terror—the terror of her children being hungry. For food she had surrendered all other hopes.

To Katherine food was not enough. She hadn't yet been beaten down that far. The sight of her older brothers turning shiftless, the thought of Elgin maturing emptyhanded and empty-headed, the knowledge that Suzie's bright sweetness would some day fade into the dullness of a drudge woman—this was worse than a lack of food. Thus, standing before the ragged grave, she knew she would not argue against her father when he decided to move.

She put her hands on the fence. She couldn't wish her mother back; her mother had been far too tired and nothing now would have made her mother any happier for living. But she wished she might have some feeling that her mother knew why they had to move. There was nothing so degraded as ignorance and poverty together. They had nothing, they had not even the certainty of knowing that this grave would remain. When she left this ranch, Katherine realized, she wouldn't return; the fence of this grave would fall down, the vines would grow over it, the headboard would rot away. Nobody would know, in another two years that anybody was buried here. The poor couldn't even keep alive the memory of their dead.

She turned away, so bitter that she was blinded. She stumbled along the greasy wetness of the trail and returned to the house. Elgin sat at his book, looking craftily at her from the corner of his eye; he hadn't been studying. Suzie sat near the doorway with her needle and the frayed tablecloth. She watched Suzie. "I want to fix your hair," she said, and went for the comb. It was pretty hair—light brown and silky in its fineness; she couldn't let it grow shabby and unkempt. She had to fight against that. She had to fight against everything.

Her father came home at supper time, made cheerful by the elderberry wine of the Thomas family, and sat down to his meal. "The Thomas boys said I ought to run for sheriff. Patton's not liked. He don't get out and visit people. I said I didn't know. Your mother was right about this country. It was good when we came, but the weather ain't the way it was then. The rain's soured the soil. We ought to be over in the Tualatin."

"Elgin," said Katherine, "pull your chair closer to the table and sit up."

"Winter's coming on," Morvain suggested. "We've got everything out of this ground we're going to get. Now's the best time, if a man's to move."

Katherine said, "I don't mind moving."

He was truly surprised at his daughter's consent. He said, bright and brisk: "Then we will. I was talking to the Thomas boys about the cow. They'll take it off my hands for thirty dollars."

She remembered her mother's fear about food—and a thread of that same fear played through her. "We won't sell the cow. That's milk."

Morvain looked at her with his uncertain impatience. "Lord, girl, we can't lug cow and tools and stuff clear across the mountains. The road's a terror."

She rose and turned toward the stove for the coffeepot; she brought it back and stood by the table. She saw that light, shallow eagerness in her father's eyes, and she saw the two older boys looking on with their alert attention. "What we've got, we've got. It's something. We won't sell anything. Not anything. We'll take with us."

"Katherine," he said, "there ain't room for stuff and us both in the wagon."

"We'll walk."

He was uncomfortable and irritable and she knew he already had made some arrangement with the Thomas people to sell. A little bit of money looked big—it made him feel rich. Already he was dreaming of a big ranch and shiny new tools; he was envisioning a lucky accident which never would happen. As far as his head was concerned he was no older than Elgin. He had broken his wife's heart and didn't realize it. He had pulled his family down, blaming the weather, or luck, or anything, but never blaming himself. He wasn't thinking of them. He was thinking of himself, he was dramatizing himself with his visions of some big strike, he was seeing himself large-

33

handed and influential in some new neighborhood. He lived in a golden world which nowhere touched the earth.

"Well," he said, "I sort of made a deal with the Thomas boys about the stuff. I wouldn't want to go back on what I said!"

"No. As long as we've got something—anything—we're not beggars."

He flashed a stung glance at her. "We never begged, girl."

"We've borrowed," she said. "And never paid back. We won't sell."

"I don't know what they'll say," he murmured. "I agreed to sell." He looked at her but after a while he looked away, knowing she wouldn't change—and knowing he could not force her as he had so often forced his wife. He wasn't pleased. "All right. Well, if we're goin' to go, we'd better not waste time. I'd like to pack tomorrow."

She turned to the two older boys. "In the morning I want you to chop away all the brush around Mother's grave. I want the sun to get into that spot."

Morvain said: "We'll come back once in a while and look after the grave."

She knew they wouldn't. The poor were never free to do the nice things. The poor couldn't afford to carry out the wishes of their hearts. She said nothing throughout the meal; she was searching for some way to carry this family out of the wilderness and lift it from its slow degeneration. People had used them, people had laughed at them, people didn't care—and should anybody care for the Morvains if the Morvains had no pride in themselves? "Who has the big saw?"

"Why," said her father, "I lent it to Jim Terry."

She nodded at one of the other boys. "You go get it in the morning, Bob."

"Well," said her father, again uncomfortable, "he's done me favors, and maybe he'd like to keep it. Maybe he thinks it was a swap."

"I'll go get it then," said Katherine.

Morvain said, "No. I'll get it. But it's such a little thing."

"That's all we've got," said Katherine. "We never had anything big because we gave away all our little things. Mrs. Burian's got our churn. You go after that tonight, Harry."

Chapter —3

SHERIDAN left his stateroom door open and, sitting in it with his cigar, watched the riverbank crawl through the closing darkness. The bruised spots on his body troubled him, and his slashed arm throbbed. He needed a long sleep, but he couldn't muster up enough enthusiasm to rise, shut the door and go to bed. All his life he had hated to go to bed.

He was, he decided, less sleepy than he was oppressed by being alone, and presently he rose and walked toward the saloon. But he saw nothing there to interest him, and continued to the parlor where he discovered Revelwood and Clara Dale. Sheridan pulled a chair forward, the three thus forming a group of their own in the parlor's corner.

"This is no place for people who have lost considerable sleep," he suggested. He felt extraordinarily close to these people and always would. Clara's dress had had some pressing and mending, though it was not the fashionable outfit it had been before, and she had taken a good deal of care with her hair; she was much as she had been on the *Jennie North*, softened by the comfort around her.

"George," he said, "what will you do?"

"No idea. I'm never much of a hand to worry over the future."

"Need any money to float you along?"

"I've got a little. I'll remember the offer, though."

"It's all in the lodge."

Revelwood gave him a glance which had none of the man's customary skepticism. "You know, that's true. A pretty exclusive lodge—Miss Dale, you and I, and the Irishman. The rest are dead and maybe I ought to feel sorry—and I do, but not deeply. I guess I fought too hard to stay alive. The truth is, it's hard for me to recollect now what some of those people looked like." He paused, he shrugged his shoulders. "They were important once. They're not now. Maybe we'll think of them a little. But

35

that will stop and then the whole thing's forgotten. We're alive. That's the only fact which means anything. True, isn't it?"

The girl said, "Yes." The two of them had the same way of looking at it. Sheridan shook his head.

Revelwood good-naturedly challenged him. "I'm surprised at you. What more can you make out of it?"

Sheridan moved his hands around in an empty gesture. "I don't know—never think much about those things." He smiled at his failure, and the smile took the rough edges from his face. He bent over, arms across his knees, his shoulders loose. His hair, dark and coarse, made a straight line across his forehead; his mouth was long and fleshy and firm, with a chin flat below and a long heavy nose above.

Revelwood said, "You'll learn," and rose. "I still feel battered. I need a smoke. Then I'm going to bed." He gave them his bow and left the parlor.

Sheridan said to the girl, "Do you have people to meet you in Portland?"

"No. I have an aunt in San Francisco. She had a husband. He deserted her years ago and came up here. He died recently, leaving some property. A house, I think. I came up to settle the estate for her."

"Then you'll go back?"

"Maybe." She watched him with her smiling interest. "Maybe not. I'm old enough to do almost anything."

"Do you need money?"

"Yes—for a while. Mark—you'll look out for me?"

"Both Revelwood and I will."

He noticed a slight change on her face. "Do you trust him?"

"Now that he's in the lodge, I do."

She shrugged her shoulders and rose. She moved over the parlor to the doorway, and paused there, looking back—and waiting for him. He joined her and walked down the deck with her as far as her stateroom. She opened the door but she stood outside to watch the black mass of timber and shadow along the shore. The wind held on and a light rain fell over the river. She was silent and her shoulder touched him; she reached for his hand and held it. "I'm never going to be cold or hungry again. Never."

She waited for him to answer, and swung her head to watch him; it was too dark to see her face or its expression but the strong current of feeling was in her voice, and in the grip of her hand. She said: "Will you light my cabin lamp?"

He went into the dark cabin and stretched his hand across the table and touched the lamp. She was behind him. She said: "If I'm alive, you're the cause of it." He turned around and saw her shadow against the open door. She went on in the same smooth, drawling voice, "I'd never go to George for help. You're stronger than I am, but I'm stronger then he is. He hasn't any help in him. You have. I'd come to you."

He touched the lamp, withdrew his hand and turned around and reached out to her. She had waited for that, and came to him quite readily. Consent loosened her and the wish to meet and please him was the cushion against which he lay. He thought, "She's too easy." Then he checked that judgment. The fight to stay alive made a difference. It had jumped them across the usual maneuverings of a man and a woman. They had missed love-making and they had missed marriage; they had gone beyond both of those things and yet had neither. She lay quiet against him, still waiting. He lifted his hand against the back of her head, holding it in, and kissed her, and stepped back and lighted the lamp.

"I shouldn't be seen in here," he said. "The news will carry to Portland—and you've got to live in Portland. Good night."

She was smiling, she was happy. When he passed her she caught his hand with a quick and warmhearted impulse. "Mark," she said, "don't trust George Revelwood too much."

"Why?"

"Just don't. Don't trust anybody as much as you do."

"Not you?"

"You kept me alive—so you have to trust me. But not other people. You like to believe in things—you don't see people's faults. Maybe," and she put something then into her glance he didn't understand, a shading or a warning or a request, "maybe you'd know me better, or any other woman, if you were a little bit of a scoundrel, like George."

He said, "Good night," and turned away. But she called his name and turned him back, and gave him a smile that had much tender wishfulness in it. "Sleep well," she said, and closed the stateroom door.

He went into the saloon and got a bottle and stood with his drink, thinking about Clara and feeling fine. Somebody said to him, "Join me," and he turned to see a gentleman considering him with a toothy, smiling interest. He was of the solid order, possessing a roughly handsome face—a short and square chin, a full mouth, brightly colored eyes and a crop of short-curled hair. He was a bulldog, Sheridan thought, a bulldog with a light disposition. "My name's Bogart—Charnel Bogart," said the man, and brought his lips farther back from his astonishingly white and massive teeth. "Join me?"

"Pleasure," said Sheridan, and gave his name. Bogart offered him a hard, brief handshake and motioned to the barkeep.

"I know you're from the wreck," said Bogart. "It's news aboard." He poured the drinks, saluted Sheridan and downed the liquor. "Damned brutal thing. The lady is remarkably fortunate. Related to you?"

"No."

Bogart put an elbow on the bar, stationing his other fist against a hip and continuing his attention. "You have business around here?"

"Looking for a venture."

"Well," said Bogart, "we all are. What's your liking?"

"Logs and lumber. I'm from Michigan."

Bogart nodded. He gestured with his hand. "Here's the greatest forest the world ever saw. Hundreds of miles of it. Monster trees. On the butts of some of them you could build a small cabin. A Michigan log, against this stuff, would be a matchstick. Actually."

Sheridan let the conversation fall; it was Bogart who revived it. "I should like to offer you and your party the service of my home."

"I can't speak for them," said Sheridan. "My private intention is to find a hotel and clean up. I'm obliged."

Bogart smiled, bowed and drifted away toward a corner poker game, and Sheridan, suddenly tired, turned toward his cabin.

He stepped from his stateroom in the morning to find the *Western Wave* tied at a river dock before Portland. The rain had stopped and the day was warmed by a sun somewhere above the fat and broken clouds which sailed low to a southwest wind still not entirely blown out. Light steam rose from the glistening rooftops and muddy streets

38

and vacant grassy lots, and this gave the air a thickness he felt on his face and in his lungs. The forest had once marched directly forward to the edge of the river; from this solid timber the town had chopped out its elbow room and now extended backward from the river a dozen blocks or more, there fading into occasional houses, little farms and rows of cordwood. It was a place of about six thousand people.

For hotel hacks stood near the dock and the shouted advertising of the drivers came over to Sheridan. There was also a small crowd of waiting people; he saw women crying.

Clara and Revelwood joined him and the three walked over the plank to the dock. A woman came out of the crowd to speak to Sheridan.

"You're from the *Jennie North*. Are there any more to come?"

"We saw one more man," said Clara Dale. "He stayed behind."

"What was he like?" asked the woman.

"A short man. Irish I think. He had a family on the ship. They were lost. I don't think anybody else survived."

"But of course," said the woman, half hoping and half arguing, "there might be others. You couldn't really know. There must be others." She looked at Clara Dale with what seemed like antagonism. "It wouldn't be fair for you people to live and all the rest not to. It wouldn't be right!"

Sheridan turned Clara Dale toward a hotel hack and handed her in; and these two, with Revelwood, were driven to the Pioneer Hotel. Sheridan registered and walked back to the street and for an hour was occupied with the buying of an outfit. Returning to the hotel, he shaved, put on his new clothes, and stood for a moment at the window which overlooked the main street of the town. Somewhere in Portland was the venture he was after. How did he find it?

He turned from the window and sat before the bedroom table. He found a pencil and he searched the empty drawers and located a half sheet of paper—an old sheet discarded by some previous tenant who had begun to write a letter. He turned over the page and wrote down the amount of money with which he had begun the trip; then he put upon the table the contents of his wallet and

39

the small change in his pockets. He began to itemize what he had spent. He bent over the desk, searching his memory. Meals on the ship. Drinks. To the Morvains. Expenses at Astoria and on the *Western Wave*. These he added and found he was short of the required sum. He sat back and searched for the missing expenditures, and could not recall them; he grew irritated with himself, he rose and walked a line back and forth over the room. He knew he ought to have more careful financial habits, but this small bookkeeping always annoyed him and he never was successful at it. He thought wryly, "Good intentions gone to hell again," and went to the desk and put down the missing sum under the caption of "Not accounted for."

Morning was a wonderful time. He lighted a cigar and felt his confident impatience and walked down to the lobby. Charnel Bogart sat in a lobby chair with a paper before him; he lowered the paper to discover Sheridan.

"Sit down," he said. "I have a notion. Might be a good notion." He was an abrupt man and seemed to want to rush directly toward a point. "You said you knew lumber. Can you run a mill?"

"How big a mill?"

"Small outfit in the Tualatin Valley. Farmers drive up and pick the lumber off the pile. Crew of five in the mill. It'll turn out ten thousand feet a day. Another crew in the woods—six men. All local farmers."

"I can handle it."

Bogart paused. He had an offer in his mind. He gave Sheridan a direct, full-open look. "How'd you like to run it on shares—half and half?"

"What's the matter with the man you've got on it now?"

"Been closed down," said Bogart. "Last good man went to the mines."

"Can you sell all you can cut?"

"Can't ever cut enough. This is young country. Everybody wants lumber."

Sheridan rolled the cigar between his teeth and looked upon this thick-chested man with the coarse-grained face with the features of a fighter and the light eyes of an adventurer. He took care of his appearance; his hair was well brushed, his gray suit was of the thickest and tightest weave, and his boots were freshly blacked. He wore no jewelry at all; his lips were meat-red. He was by no means

40

the dry and sober kind of businessman. He put on something for a show and there was a sort of lusty bull pride in the corners of his eyes.

"Half and half," agreed Sheridan. "But a guaranteed two hundred dollars a month regardless."

"That's all right. I'll guarantee you two hundred dollars a month. At the end of each quarter year we'll figure out the profits and give you what you've got coming over the guarantee."

"Let's figure the profits each month instead of quarterly."

Bogart paused on the proposition, and seemed less impatient than he had formerly been. He ended the doubt by saying, "I'll agree," and extended his hand. Sheridan took it. A moment later Bogart's glance lifted from Sheridan and struck beyond him. The smiling confidence on the man's face shifted to the keenest sort of interest and he said, "Your lady, Sheridan," and promptly rose from his chair.

Sheridan stood up, watching Clara Dale come. She kept her glance on him, seeming not to be aware of Bogart. In some manner unknown to him, she had completely repaired the disasters of the trip and looked now as she had on the *Jennie North*.

He said: "Miss Dale, this is Charnel Bogart."

Clara Dale now permitted herself to give Charnel a direct glance and flattered him with a charming smile. He bowed. He said, "I want to express my regrets at your misfortune. Possibly, as a Portlander, I may be able to offer you my services."

She said in a smoother voice than Sheridan had so far heard from her, "That's so very nice of you."

The effect on him was noticeable. He was a small man —not much taller than Clara Dale—but his shoulders were wide and his chest quite deep and through him flowed a touched-off electricity which caused him to stand straighter, to give him a springy muscular tension, and to put a flashing vanity in his glance.

She turned her glance to Sheridan. "I'm to find a lawyer who had my uncle's estate. His name is Deady."

"The judge," said Bogart. "Give me the privilege of showing you there."

"That would be kind," said Clara.

Bogart said to Sheridan, "We'll drive out to the mill tomorrow. Now, since you and I are in a prospect together,

41

I believe it would be good if you had dinner with Mrs. Bogart and me tonight." He looked at the girl and quickly added, "I should be most pleased to have you and the other gentleman as well."

She said, "It is nice of you," and thus implied her agreement.

Bogart dropped Sheridan a careless nod. "Tell your friend, will you? At six o'clock. It is on Fifth at Jefferson." With a gesture of gallantry he moved away with Clara Dale.

Sheridan now began a tour of the town. He saw Harvey Scott at the newspaper office. He discussed land with some real estate people. Out on Fourteenth and Stark—the last street in that direction before the town faded into stump land, woodchoppers' claims and Chinese truck gardens—he found a surveyor who enlightened him on the Tualatin and Willamette Valleys. When noon came he went into the Grotto Saloon on First and Pine for his first drink of the day, and had his meal at the Louvre. Later he walked a quarter mile southward to have a look at the Portland Steam sawmill, and still later he took the Stark Street Ferry to the east side of the Willamette and viewed the little settlement lying there. At five o'clock he returned to his hotel and discovered that Clara Dale had gone.

The clerk said, "Miss Dale left word that you are to call on her at seventy-nine Sixth Street."

This address, when he located it, was a small gray angular house sitting beyond a picket fence and flanked by other small gray houses common to the street. Clara Dale answered his knock. Revelwood had arrived earlier and seemed to be doing hard labor; he was in his shirt-sleeves and at this moment he carried a pot of glue and used it on broken-away sections of wallpaper on the front room wall.

"This was my uncle's house," said the girl.

It was a one-story house with four furnished rooms. The front room had a center table, a round parlor stove, a sideboard, a sofa and a set of chairs. Against the wallpaper, whose pattern was an ivory-toned Greek urn repeating itself in vertical stripes against a gray background, stood several framed pictures—one of which struck him at once; it was of a lighthouse throwing its yellow beam against a raging night.

"Do you propose to keep that?"

Revelwood said, "I'd keep it to remind me of my luck."

42

"I want it destroyed," said Clara Dale. "I don't want to be reminded. Misery goes through me when I look at those waves."

"The artist," said Revelwood, "drew on his imagination, didn't he? Raging seas don't look that bad."

"How much do you remember?" asked Sheridan.

"I recall going overboard," said Revelwood. "Somebody took hold of me and I thought I'd be pulled under. I had to fight the man away. I got hold of a door. Mind you, there it was, knob and all. Even the hinges. I hung to the knob. Next clear thing I was on the shore."

Clara Dale said, "We must not talk about it. I won't have it." She spoke with a short firmness, and Sheridan observed that she was literally turned cold from the thought. "Mark," she said, "take it down and throw it in the woodshed."

He removed the picture and carried it out through the kitchen to the shed. When he returned he found Revelwood in the rocker. He wasn't in the best of shape, according to Sheridan's eyes. He seemed listless. The girl stood in the center of the room, watching Revelwood with an air of speculation.

"Who's this Bogart?" asked Revelwood.

"I've got a deal with him," said Sheridan. "Running a mill."

"That's fast," said Revelwood. "You're a hustler. You keep moving."

For some reason the girl disliked Revelwood's remark. "I'd be dead if he wasn't that way and so would you."

Revelwood glanced at her, mildly surprised. "It wasn't an unkind statement," he said. "The pushers will get along while the rest of us end up in some slack eddy and go around and around until we sink." Some of his old cynicism made its appearance on his face. "You've got a weak point, though. You believe the game comes out well. You think men are honest. About this fellow Bogart—it was a pretty quick deal. How did he choose you?"

"Men are scarce," said Sheridan. "They've gone to the mines."

Revelwood was dissatisfied. "I know about these fast deals. I've had a lot of experience with men who work that way. Putting any of your own money into it?"

"No."

Clara Dale still disliked Revelwood's forwardness. "It's Mark's business, isn't it?"

43

Revelwood smiled in a manner that took the disbelief from his face. "We're all together, aren't we? We can't permit bad fortune to happen to any of us."

"What a nice sentiment," sail Clara, and forgot her displeasure.

Revelwood grew thoughtful. "There isn't much sentiment in me, but I am superstitious and I know in my bones that we three were picked out. We're tied together."

Sheridan said, "What will you do?"

The evasive cheerfulness returned to Revelwood. "I'll bide my time and get rich without work."

"That's what I thought," said Sheridan.

"Why, of course," said Revelwood coolly. "You both know me by now. I make my living from good people who lose their goodness at the smell of a profit. That's where I do my dealing. I'm somewhat of a specialist at it. I'll set up some small business and I'll make it appear that I have a very good thing. Sooner or later some sound citizen will think that he ought to have a share of my good thing. He will make me offers and I shall accept them. Then he will try to do me in." He stared at them, and drily added: "They always fail and I always profit. I teach men the penalty of dishonesty."

Sheridan let go with a long shout of laughter. "You're an honest scoundrel."

"You people know me. You've discussed me, haven't you?"

"That's right," said Sheridan.

Revelwood became wholly serious. "Nobody knows anybody else too well. We just make guesses. Well, a man of my sort seldom has real friends and a man of my sort, when he finds such friends, never hurts them."

"George," said Sheridan, "we're all in the same boat. We'll stick together."

"So we shall," said Revelwood.

The girl watched Revelwood with a rather close interest. Conscious of it, Revelwood turned his eyes to her and for a considerable time these two were engaged in a silent conversation which excluded Sheridan. They had—he definitely felt it—some common thing that Sheridan lacked. They understood each other, and they were aware of it, and thus he was pushed aside. Suddenly the girl broke the glance by turning to Sheridan. She put her hand on his arm with a certain restlessness. Her voice was un-

44

settled. She said to Revelwood: "Mark's the strongest of us. I'd always turn to him for help."

"I expect that's true," said Revelwood. "That's why I'd not like to see him done in by strangers."

"Or done in by anybody."

"Yes," said Revelwood slowly. "By anybody at all."

"We'll go for the rig," said Sheridan, and motioned to Revelwood. The two men moved down Sixth to Oak, and down Oak to a stable and waited there while a surrey was hitched up. Half an hour later the three of them were let off before a large, homely house painted brown which sat in the center of a half block on the south edge of town. Bogart met them at the door.

He had changed into a brown suit. His intensely black and wavy hair had been brushed and polished until it fell in a perfect wave across one side of his forehead. He carried himself to his full height and against the thickness of his torso his legs seemed small and curved. He was at the peak of his vital good nature; his affability was a warm gush of wind from the interior of the house. "Come in, my friends. This is my distinct pleasure—mine and Mrs. Bogart's."

Mrs. Bogart was plain and thin and smileless. She acknowledged the girl's name with a shift of her mouth and a smile that came and rushed away. She bowed to the men, and then her glance went watchfully back to Clara Dale. "Charnel, will you pour the wine before we sit down?"

Frequently in later days Sheridan thought of that dinner and felt strangely embarrassed by the showing he had made. They were five strangers sitting at a table and never in the course of the evening did they become more than that. Bogart carried the conversation along with his bullying vitality, he let no silence grow awkward, he kept his humor in play, he maintained his courtesy—and all of this he did with such force that the lamplight at last glittered on the fine moisture along his forehead. Revelwood, too, sensed the strain and drew upon his long skill to match Bogart's liveliness.

Otherwise it was a strange meal. Clara Dale, charming enough, did most of her talking in the early stages. Later she fell back upon a smiling silence. Mrs. Bogart sat at the foot of the table, her thin body stiff and correct, making no pretense at genuine hospitality. She spoke for the maid when the maid was needed. She reminded Bogart to serve when serving was necessary. She mentioned the wine. She said: "Mr. Sheridan requires more meat, Mr. Bogart." She said: "I'm afraid Miss Dale finds our table poor."

"I have not had much appetite since the wreck," said Clara. "The adventure left me unsettled."

"Adventures do. Mr. Bogart, will you offer Miss Dale more wine?"

Her barren courtesy had its vigilance. Behind the exact measure of deference she showed her husband was the clear impression of her own pride. She was not a pretty woman; in her spare body and lean frigid face there was no hint that she had ever been young. She was cold on the surface, but her eyes at unexpected times showed a deep-down heat. They were hard eyes to meet. They turned to Charnel Bogart and watched him with a heavy attention. They touched Sheridan and made him uneasy. They stopped on Clara Dale again and again and sucked out the meaning of this girl's presence; and the effect of that stare was to bring a greater chill to her face. Mrs. Bogart was a thousand years older than any of them.

Sheridan was glad to see Bogart rise at the end of the meal and lead them back to the living room. The cigars were passed and pleasantries were said. Charnel Bogart relaxed in his chair, and wiped his face with a handkerchief, and for the first time during the evening he permitted the conversation to go along without him.

Revelwood cast his glance and called upon his easy store of talk. "Do I understand there's not enough men around here?"

"The mines took 'em," said Bogart. "Gold is a bad thing. Raw gold. It drains a place. These men will drift back in a year or two. They'll be broke. They'll be out of the stream, out of the crowd—and maybe they'll never catch up. It's the old story. Potatoes and lumber and tinware will make a man rich. Gold dust will ruin him." There was silence again. Bogart stared at the tip of his cigar, shifted weight in the chair and nodded to Sheridan. "I'll come by the hotel for you about seven. There's a farmer near the mill. Name's Murdock. He'll board you reasonably. You'll have to recruit your crew from the neighborhood."

Mrs. Bogart was a stiff figure across the room. She had listened and her restless eyes had searched. Now she spoke to Clara Dale.

46

"You're here temporarily?"

"I came to close my uncle's estate."

"Then," said Mrs. Bogart, "will you be returning to your home?"

"I've not decided," said Clara Dale.

Sheridan, who had said so little, now rose and paid his respects to Mrs. Bogart. "I thank you for your kindness," he said. Bogart immediately fetched Clara Dale's coat and held it for the girl, his gallantry visibly glowing. Revelwood did his courtesies. Clara Dale gave Mrs. Bogart her smile. "I shall remember my first hosts in Portland with pleasure." Bogart opened the door and in another moment the three of them were out of the house and walking along the street.

When the visitors had gone, Bogart closed the door with a quick push and went across the room to the parlor stove. He opened the top, knocked the ashes from his cigar, and turned about. He laced his hands behind his back. He took no notice of his wife. She stood against a wall, watching him, beating at him with her glance, reading the signs upon him. She had darkened; the mask of scrupulous, chilly courtesy was no longer necessary to her and she let it go gladly.

"You found her attractive, Mr. Bogart?"

He gave her the shortest possible glance. "She is, apparently, a friend of Sheridan's. I need Sheridan to open the Tualatin mill. It's a good idea to be nice to her."

"Not difficult, is it?"

"I feel for her, Emma. The shipwreck was brutal."

"She's a wench. You know that."

He gave an irritable twist to his shoulders and met her glance. "How in God's name could you know that about a woman you've only met?"

She said evenly, "How could you know it so soon?"

"I don't know it," he retorted.

"Yes," she said, "you know it. You knew she was the moment you saw her. That's why you brought her here. She's a wrench at my table. To whom I was forced to be polite."

He let go with a short, noisy laugh. "I could have cut the gloom with an ax. By God, Emma, you were rude—it embarrassed me."

"Was it your intention for me to help you arrange an

47

affair with the woman? Your wants were plain enough. You were a bull—a bull in heat."

He snatched the cigar from his mouth and threw it to the floor. He walked past her toward the kitchen with a quick, bandy-legged stride. His face was scarlet; he swung his hating glance at her. She watched him and showed him her equal hatred. Her skin had turned sallow, as though from nausea, and her mouth was nothing more than a scar across her face. Her eyes had a staring roundness; she was trembling.

"There's always some goddamned evil in your head," he said.

She swung around; actually she jerked herself around and went up the stairs with a sluggish, aimless step, her hand striking the banister as she climbed. She went into her room and stopped there, enclosed by the room's darkness. Light came up the stairs to throw some small glow into the bedroom and to touch her eyes and to make them shine. She stood still. She was a shadow with shining eyes; she bent slightly forward, her muscles rigid, staring out of the darkness into the hallway. She hated Bogart, she hated the girl; and she hated and feared herself. She feared she was turning crazy.

They turned to Sixth and thus came to Clara's house, and found they had forgotten to put a fire in the stove. The house was cold. Sheridan found paper, built a fire and trimmed the damper. They stood around the stove.

"It was a dull evening," said Sheridan.

"Dull?" said Revelwood and stared at him. The girl, too, raised her eyes. "I'll tell you something," said Revelwood. "Your man is a crook. I've seen enough of that sort." He dropped his glance to the girl and spoke deliberately to her. "It wouldn't be wise for anybody to trust him."

"I'll watch for that," said Sheridan, not impressed. But Revelwood wasn't interested in his answer. He had his unfavorable glance still on Clara; she looked back at Revelwood and shrugged her shoulders.

"Perhaps," she said, "Mr. Bogart should take care of himself."

"He'll do that quite well," said Revelwood. "And those who play with him will regret it."

"Mrs. Bogart," said Sheridan, "was scarcely amiable."

48

"And let Mrs. Bogart also take care of herself," said Clara Dale with a greater force than was her custom.

"She was rude, of course," said Revelwood, still talking to Clara. It seemed to Sheridan that these two were arguing between themselves. He had lost the sense of this conversation. He was sleepy and he had his mind on tomorrow. "Even so," continued Revelwood, "she might have good reason to distrust her husband."

"I am not interested in what she thinks, or what he is," said Clara Dale.

"That's a wise conclusion," said Revelwood pointedly.

She displayed her annoyance at him, turned to Sheridan and put her hand on his arm, showing him a smile which seemed weary and wistful. "You don't look for the worst. You don't make things out of nothing. I wish we could all be that way."

Revelwood said with the sharpness still in his words, "Were we talking about that?"

"George," said Sheridan, "what are we talking about? I don't follow."

"George feels I may have encouraged Mr. Bogart's interest," Clara said.

Sheridan thought about the dinner and he remembered Mrs. Bogart's manner, and Bogart's flushed and lively face as he had placed the coat round Clara. He smiled. "I think Bogart may have caused his wife some concern in the past. I can see her possible concern now."

"You confuse me," said Revelwood. "I'm never able to make out what you see and what you don't see. But if you see this thing, what would you say to Miss Dale?"

"Nothing," said Sheridan and he looked down into Clara's face. He had first thought her to be a self-confident woman; that was the way she had seemed to him on the boat. He had learned more of her during the night ashore, and still more in the cabin of the *Western Wave*. He never saw her twice in the same way. He had been deceived by her smiling assurance at the Bogarts'. She had been hurt there, he realized—he saw the questioning and the uncertainty on her face now. At the present moment he felt only a resentment at Mrs. Bogart for the manner in which she had used Clara. "George," he said, "her business is not your business or mine, is it?" He looked around the room and shook his head. "But we shouldn't be here. This town's got eyes; and it might tell stories."

Clara, still with her hand on Sheridan's arm, gave Revelwood a look of small triumph, whereupon Revelwood turned out of the room without comment.

Clara looked up to Sheridan. "When will you be back?"

"I don't know."

The pressure of her hand increased on his arm. "Don't stay away too long."

"All right."

She waited for him to kiss her and he knew she wished it. This was something he couldn't unravel in his mind, this willingness a strictly good woman wouldn't have or wouldn't show. Yet he could not call Clara bad; he could not bring himself to believe it. Her warmth and desire came out of her—as she no doubt intended it should—and disturbed him; even so, the sense of evil was absent.

He said, "Good night," and crossed the room. At the door he looked back and noticed her disappointment and its suggestion of loneliness. Revelwood waited for him at the gate and the two walked back to the Pioneer.

Chapter — 4

BOGART and Sheridan rode away from the hotel at seven, threaded the stumpy clearings at the edge of town and struck a road which promptly climbed into a solid stand of fir.

It was a muddy and sunless ride through very rough hills. They met an occasional farm wagon, bound into Portland; at the summit of the ridge stood a gray farm house on the porch of which a very old woman sat paring a bucket of apples, a leathery brown toothless woman with black bright eyes who stopped her work to watch the wagon approach and did not resume work until it had dropped downgrade toward the valley beyond. From this viewpoint, when the trees occasionally broke, the valley lay nicely checkerboarded below, held in by hills to either side and running off into the western haze where other hills vaguely lay.

Bogart pointed westward. "That's the Coast Range—roughest, heaviest, darkest patch of country on the continent, I do think."

They left the hills behind them and moved into the valley flatness with its fields, its clumps of fir and oak, and its occasional farm yards. "Just about twenty years old—all of this settlement," remarked Bogart. "It's beginning to catch its second wind. Considerable building going on. That's why the mill will do good. A couple of towns off there—Hillsboro and Forest Grove—and some general stores scattered here and there that might grow into towns." He gave Sheridan an oblique cheerful glance.

"In a country like this you never know which way a thing's going to jump. Don't buy a farm. Don't buy property in these little towns. Find out what people want most. Then you go into the business of supplying that stuff to them. But don't stay in any business too long. If you're doing well, somebody will start competition, and pretty soon there's too many in the business. In a new country you hunt for chances that people don't see. You work it up for a while. Then you sell out before the cream's been skimmed from the pan."

They turned from the main road and took a lesser pair of ruts northward toward rolling timbered ridges five or six miles distant.

"There's plenty of chances still open," Bogart continued, "but a man's got to be clever. He's got to see when to jump in. Then, he's got to watch out that the big men with money don't freeze him out. Those fellows have the power. If you can get strong enough financially before they catch on to what you're doing, then they can't run you out. But if they do see what you're doing and move in before you're big enough to fight back, you'd better join 'em or take the offer they make you."

"Ought to be enough here for everybody," commented Sheridan.

"Business is business anywhere, and power's power. Same as poker. *The big stack wins.* If you're a smart player you can run *a few chips into a fortune.* If you're not smart, you'll end up broke." Bogart adjusted himself more comfortably on the buggy's seat. "The truth is, not many men can play the business game. Most men end up working for somebody else."

"There's some luck to it," said Sheridan.

"Oh, sure. If a man is in the right place at the right time, he's made. Otherwise he can work like a fool and get nowhere. But even with the time right, no man will amount to much unless there's something rough in him. If you've got too much tenderness in you, you'll go around in rags, preaching the brotherhood of man. The rest of the failures and misfits will think you're a fine, Christian soul and you'll convert them—as don't need converting. But the big ones, the tough ones, will drop just enough small change on your collection plate to keep you happy and they'll go right along getting richer. You'll save no souls there." He fell silent and he was quite thoughtful. Somewhat later he shook his head. "Every man will fall according to his own particular weakness. We've all got to defend ourselves against that."

Around noon the rig passed from the main valley to a narrow meadow lying cramped between timbered hills and arrived at a mill which sat close to one of the ridges. The side of the ridge showed earlier logging and a rough road came down this ridge to a log platform which, in turn, fed a carriage and a pair of big saws. Behind these saws was another saw for trimming, a small conveyor to carry away scrap, a deck for piling the cut lumber, a boiler and engine. All this, except the log deck, was roofed over. "This is it," said Bogart. He pointed toward a house farther down the meadow. "That's Murdock's place. He will be your saw filer. You can board there."

The Murdock place was a ragged, hard-scrabble sort of place. A bed stood in the yard for summer sleeping; a pair of hogs rooted through the small orchard, and chickens ducked under the house foundation and stirred up the dust. A woman came from the house at the sound of the rig—a young woman in a short-sleeved dress, with a darkly sunbrowned skin. She had pretty features turned heavy; her lips were long and her face had a lazy, bold insolence on it. She wore no shoes and suddenly was conscious of that, and looked down at her feet and raised her glance to Sheridan. She watched him quite closely.

"Your father here, Liza?" asked Bogart.

A second woman, middle-aged and heavy, came from the house. She made a dashing gesture toward the loose hair over her forehead. "Mr. Bogart—well now! You've come again. Startin' the mill?" She turned and sent a ringing cry toward the barn. "Murdock—it's Mr. Bogart." In a moment a man put his head around the barn, looked at the newcomers a long interval, and slowly moved forward, nothing but thin legs and thin arms and thin body. He seemed suspicious, or perhaps near-sighted; as he got into the yard the darkness of his face broke. "Oh, Bogart." Then he looked immediately toward his wife. "Dinner ready?"

"It is," she said.

"Well, then," said Murdock to the men, "get down and don't be strange."

"This is Mark Sheridan," said Bogart. His finger ticked off the people in the yard for Sheridan's information. "That's Murdock, that's Emma Murdock, that's Liza Murdock."

Sheridan nodded and dropped from the rig. The three Murdocks gave him a close regard, an exceptionally solemn and personal study, and the girl suddenly turned back into the house. Murdock said: "Whut for you're here, Bogart? Startin' the mill again?"

"That's right. Sheridan's the new boss."

Murdock let his head sag downward on its thin neck— a head which seemed too small on his long frame—and owlishly considered his boots. It was a sly mannerism which he completed by jerking up his head, as though to catch Bogart off guard. "He'll have to see Kerby first."

Bogart said, "You look fine. Everything been all right?" He nodded toward the bed in the yard. "You'll have to move that thing inside. Fall's here. Rain's comin'."

Out of his solemnness Murdock unexpectedly delivered a whooping laugh and a sharp slap of his hand against his side. "Woman and I got wetter'n hell in it last night. Come in to eat."

Sheridan stepped into a kitchen which occupied half the house and whose walls were covered by newspapers laid on with some sort of homemade paste. It was not an unclean room, but it was untidy. At one end stood an open fireplace with its crane and kettle of an earlier day and now obviously not used. A heavy iron stove took its place—something new and something ugly. The heat of it filled the kitchen and the smell of baking bread was very sweet in Sheridan's throat. A long row of tomato vines, loaded with half-green fruit, hung along the ceiling joists to ripen; a cot, with the quilts scrambled from former sleeping, stood in a corner; a side doorway gave Sheridan view of a pantry built around a well.

The table had been set for dinner and the girl, coming out of a bedroom with her hair in better order and shoes on her feet, silently added two more plates. Mrs. Murdock let the conversation flow on while she moved from stove to table. "It's been awful hot this summer. Murdock was sick a lot. I'll never pitch hay like I did this year—I'll get another husband first. Not that anybody wants me. That's the wrong of it, Mr. Bogart. A man can marry again, but who wants a woman forty years old? Sit right down. It ain't much of a meal but it'll hold you."

They sat down before Mrs. Murdock's idea of not much of a meal: steaks pounded and floured and fried and drenched in gravy, an enormous bowl of red beans laced with onions, green peppers and tomatoes seasoned hot enough to scald Sheridan's throat, potatoes boiled until their fluffy interiors burst out of their jackets, hot blackberry pie gently steaming through its open-work crust, sliced cucumbers soaked in vinegar and cream, spongy-fresh bread with a thick golden crust, a chunk of butter out of an oak-leaf mold, and all the accessories of corn relish, pickled beets, huckleberry jam, and a jug of milk on which the yellow cream lay an inch thick.

Mrs. Murdock said: "For just the three of us around now, it don't pay to cook. I've lost the knack of it. When the boys were all here it did me good to see the food go." She sat next to Sheridan, a fat and perspiring woman with her odors, a crude and slack woman with the brightest eyes and the reddest mouth and a full face that scarcely had a wrinkle in it.

Murdock sat stooped and he fed himself in glum silence. He appeared to be a gloomy man, yet out of this gloom came odd slivers of humor.

"When I marry next," he said, "It'll be a woman that don't talk."

Mrs. Murdock spoke promptly. "There's got to be some sound around here—and I got to make all of it. You're a mouse for quiet. And somebody's got to stand up for your rights, which you don't do. Anybody could run over you."

"Never did like to get roused," said Murdock. "Man never knows what his temper will lead him to."

"Well," said Mrs. Murdock, "it's certain you don't know. You ain't got one."

"And when I get my next woman," said Murdock, "she'll be young."

"I'm young enough," said Mrs. Murdock promptly. "You've got nothing to complain of." She planted her elbows on the table and looked over at her husband with a good-natured suspicion. "Who'd you see when you went to Forest Grove the other day?"

"Ain't sayin'," said Murdock. "Pass the beans, Emmy."

Mrs. Murdock said to Sheridan: "It makes him feel proud when I think he's seen another woman. If he saw one he'd run."

"Not too far," said Murdock, "and not too fast, either. I been thinkin' about that. I'm gettin' to be an old man and I ain't sowed no wild oats. It don't seem right."

"Ah," said his wife, "what woman wants you now, Murdock?"

Murdock pushed away his plate and dropped back against his chair, a born-tired man of unknown quantity and of fugitive wishes unexpressed. "Well," he said, "that's probably true. I looked good once. Don't seem long ago that I was chasin' gals Liza's age—and they was willing enough to be chased. Always hard for a man to understand he gets past lookin' good. He gets twisted and he works too much and his teeth go to hell and then he's old and not agreeable to look at. Beasts are different. There's that old Curly horse. He's twenty-two, but he's as good-lookin' now as he was when he was a colt. One day he'll lie down and he won't get up. But he'll look good right to the end. Ain't that way with men. I wonder why?"

Mrs. Murdock watched Murdock, and a kind of loose emotion came out of her and she said to him: "That's all right, Murdock. You look good to me."

"But," said Murdock, still with the other thought on his mind, "I wonder why?"

"Murdock," said his wife, "you think too much. Just take what comes."

"Why," said Murdock, "I guess that's what we all do. Maybe there's a man now and then who can make things suit himself. The rest of us ain't got that power. I suppose if I was a city man with money, I wouldn't look like I do. I think of that. But, hell, it's thinkin' that makes people feel bad. Might be better if a man wasn't born to think much."

Bogart said, "Where's the boys?"

"Gone," said Mrs. Murdock. "Tip's up in Montana. Ed, last we heard, was on a ranch in eastern Oregon. Reeves went down the valley a year ago. I don't know where. Ben, he left this spring to work in Portland, but we heard through some people that he took a sailin' ship out." She was thoughtful as she spoke; her glance went through a window and looked into the distance and saw something. But she shrugged her shoulders and brought herself back. "Well, they're gone."

"Ed," said Bogart, "I'm trying to remember him. He was pretty young."

"Fifteen," said Mrs. Murdock. "That's old enough. He licked everybody around here, so he can take care of himself." The group rose. Murdock stretched his arms over his head and gave out a great belch and walked, loose-legged and weary, toward the door. The girl, who had remained silent throughout the meal, now began to clear the table. She seemed shy; she was conscious of her hands and of her appearance. She kept her head down as she collected the dishes but when Sheridan left the room, she paused and followed him with her glance. Mrs. Murdock whispered: "Put on your other dress tonight—the tight one."

Murdock laid himself out on the bed in the yard for a

nap while Bogart and Sheridan got back in the rig and rode as far as the mill to inspect it.

"Who was your woods boss?"

"Sampson—at the end of this meadow," said Bogart.

"What've you been paying these people?"

Bogart brought a list from his pocket and handed it over. Sheridan considered it. "Higher than Michigan."

"We get more for lumber," said Bogart. "Other side of the sheet is the price list. When a man drives up here for lumber, let him show his money. You'll have to sell green until you can lay by something to dry. Same price though!"

Sheridan said: "Be sure you're here every Saturday night with money for the payroll—until I've got some money laid by from sales. We'll settle between ourselves the first of every month. What about this head sawyer? You've left something out."

"Just a sorehead. We had an argument. But he's had all summer to lay around and think about it. He'll come back." He brought out a cigar and lighted it and returned to the rig. "One thing more. You've got to push these fellows or they'll slack off. That mill ought to do ten thousand feet a day."

Sheridan said: "That's what you didn't say in the beginning. Your last foreman couldn't handle the crew. He got run off, didn't he?"

Bogart's great white teeth were exposed in his sudden smile. "Well, it was like that. The boy didn't know much about men. I can see that you'll do better."

"You said the sawyer's name was Kerby?"

Bogart gathered the reins. "You can handle him. The main thing is to push. You'll get along." He was friendly; he was taking the time to leave the best impression behind him. He clucked at the team and went away.

Sheridan closed the boiler valve and fed in enough water to make a quick head of steam. He started a fire and, waiting for his steam, he located a can of grease and filled the pulley boxes. He checked the lacings on the drive belts; he cleaned out the junk which had fallen around the saws and the track of the log carriage. He gave Kerby a moment's thought while he worked; there was always one bully boy in every settlement, and probably Kerby had pecked away at the former mill boss until the latter had lost control of his crew. No crew had any respect for a man who couldn't run the show. A boss did the bossing and if he couldn't do it, he took a walk down the road.

When the gauge showed him pressure he turned on the steam and watched the big wheel roll over. He got an oil can and went around to fill the oil holes, to lubricate the noisy crevices of turning parts. He boarded the log carriage and threw it into gear and rode it back and forth. He let the machinery run for half an hour, listening to the sounds which came in with an ear which had heard such sounds before. Then he turned off the machinery, stoked the firebox and watched the steam gauge creep up. When the safety valve popped, he noted the pressure, and opened the firebox door to spread the fire. He fed in a little more water and waited for the pressure to drop. The safety valve, he decided, could be set a little higher. Absorbed in his job, he didn't see the man with the huge legs and black felt hat come out of the road into the mill. The man stood by and watched him a full five minutes. Then he said:

"You the new boss?"

Sheridan looked at him. "You Kerby?"

"No, I'm Sampson."

"Can you get a crew for this outfit?"

"Sure," said Sampson. He came forward to lean against the carriage.

"We'll have to build up a week's logs before we start the mill," said Sheridan.

"We got a lot of logs down and bucked," said Sampson. "Never brought 'em in because the mill shut down quick." He was near fifty, with gray short whiskers and steady, staring eyes. He had enormous hands.

"All right," said Sheridan. "We'll start in the woods Monday and work the mill Tuesday. I don't want Kerby. Can you find another sawyer?"

"George Weed," said Sampson. He slid his hand into his pocket and came out with pipe and tobacco. He made a long-drawn ceremony of the pipe filling. He said in a mild it's-none-of-my-business voice: "Sure you don't want Kerby?"

Sheridan shook his head, and changed the subject. "Where are we getting these logs?"

Sampson pointed up the scarred hill. "Back there a mile. Bogart still runnin' this shebang?"

"Yes."

Sampson evidently had a comment to make, but he thought about it at some length and only said: "Likes things to move fast, don't he? I'll get your mill crew here Tuesday and you'll have logs till hell won't have 'em." He turned and went down the road at a chopping walk.

When the fire had died well down, Sheridan climbed the hill and followed the logging road back through an area of stumps, splintered fragments, silvered snags and wind-blown deadfalls; the quick fireweed grew here and salal and huckleberry and Oregon grape—and the humbly relentless wild blackberry. Clumps of vine maple flashed out a rich fall scarlet; the water-greedy alders stood in brushy thickness along the foot of the ridge where a creek ran. Beyond this logged land a thin trail took out into the silence and the never-ending shadows of a forest which had covered these hills since time began. The giant-standing trunks rose around him, broken by barricades of fallen trees interlaced like matchsticks and he looked down into a ravine of salmon-berry and devilstock where the deer should be drinking.

He sat on a log and felt the pull of those sweeping-away forest deeps; he smoked his pipe and rested with his lonely contentment, and at last rose and started home. After supper he sat down on the porch floor and smoked his cigar with a wonderfully sluggish nerveless feeling of well-being. The crickets were singing along the meadow, and in the evening twilight the hills showed their ragged silhouette.

The girl walked from the kitchen and went on into the yard, traveling without direction. He heard Mrs. Murdock let go with her little-girl giggle and he turned his head to look through the door. Murdock had a towel and a dish in his hand and Mrs. Murdock, swinging from her pan, dug into his ribs with her forefinger. Murdock made his irritable protest. "Quit it—quit it, Emmy." Mrs. Murdock's face so smooth in its fatness, was reddened by the stove's heat and her hair was a strewn untidiness across her forehead. She put her wet hand on Murdock's face and swung back to her pan. Murdock finished his dish and laid it down; he stepped behind his wife with idle slyness. He seized her around the arms and stuffed the towel inside her dress, down against her breasts. She broke his grip by the simple mass of her weight. She giggled and bore him backward, pushing her fingers into his ribs. He said: "Stop it, Emmy—dammit, quit."

59

The girl returned to the porch and sat down on the steps near him. She had avoided him, but now she wanted his measure and took it frankly. She was restless. Her arms were round, her hands were square and strong for a woman; there was a padded firmness and an insistent vitality about her, and his guard went up against the sensations she drove into him.

"I wish we were on a main road," she said. "People would go by. Nothing happens here."

"Where's the dances?"

"Down at Blossom Hill School. That's not enough. The other foreman went to Portland once in a while. You will too, I guess. Take me when you go. I like to eat in restaurants."

"Where's your friends?"

Her mind jumped across the things he said and went directly to what she thought he meant. "Oh, he comes around. You married?"

"No."

"I didn't think so. There's a married look. Even when a married man comes here and says he's not, I can tell."

He said: "Sounds like you've spent a lot of time on it."

Her answer was quicker and more rebellious. "It's not wrong to think about things like that. I'm alive. I've got to look out for myself. The preacher comes through here once in a while, talking about being happy. He's an old man. He's married. He doesn't have to worry about being young and losing out. He just doesn't know what it's like. It's all right for old people to go to church. It makes them feel good. It doesn't make me feel good. It makes me feel dead. I want to get out of here. If I were a man I could. What could I do in Portland?"

"I don't know. Maybe you could get housework. Or work in a hotel."

"The hotel would be fine," she said. She was silent a short while, darkened and embittered by her thinking. Her eyes regarded him with a closer interest; she sat still, yet her thoughts moved her against him. "If I had been born in town I'd had the chances other girls have. I wouldn't have to work in a home or a hotel. But that's all the chance I've got—to take the cheap and dirty work. Well, it's better than nothing. You don't know what I'm talking about, do you."

"I don't know," he said. "Maybe I do."

"You won't like it here. There's just old people around

60

here. The young ones get away—most of them. The ones that stay haven't any spunk. It makes me feel queer, like I'm lost. I want something to happen. I'd like nice clothes I could wear without getting them full of mud or dust. I want to get married. I want some fun. I want things nice." She bent forward to read his face in the growing dusk, and he saw the recklessness flash up. "Anything's better than nothing!"

"Maybe your folks wouldn't want you to leave."

She gave him a surprised stare. "Them? They don't care."

Murdock and his wife came out to the porch and sat side by side, Mrs. Murdock laying a gross arm around her husband's shoulders. He sat still, covered by his mild gloom. Mrs. Murdock's glance touched her daughter and Sheridan and a sly warmth flickered over her face.

"It's a relief," she said, "to sit down. There was a time when I didn't mind bein' on my feet. Lots of times I danced till the music just quit, and rode a long way home, and worked all next day and never felt tired."

"It wasn't a long way home," said Murdock. "You and your men just took a long time gettin' home."

"You ought to know," said Mrs. Murdock pointedly.

"Well, I guess I do."

"I never," said Mrs. Murdock in a melancholy tone, "got enough of it. I had lots of fun—but never enough. Ain't it odd? Folks never do. I wonder why."

"Well," said Murdock, "we live and we die. That's all. We live and we die."

Mrs. Murdock's dreaming voice went on toward the expression of something so heavily felt. "I was a crazy girl, like all girls. I wanted to get married, because I was afraid I wouldn't. I wanted to get married and have children. So I did. Now I'm an old woman and the children are mostly gone, and what's left for us? It don't seem right. The kids will get married and they'll do the same thing we did, and they'll get old, and their children will leave, and what have they got then?"

Murdock said comfortably, "You got a cryin' spell comin' on. I can tell. Your damned arm's heavy, Emmy. Somebody's comin' up the road."

It was a horse and rider jogging through the gathered blackness. The rider sent a shouted "Hello there!" ahead of him, and turned into the yard.

"Why," said Murdock in his strengthless voice, "it's Tom Bush. Get down, Tom. Had supper?"

"At Sampson's," said the man and dropped from the horse. "Ain't going to stay. Only wanted to say hello." He advanced to the porch. He bent forward to see this group and he said "Hello" to the Murdock girl, and stared at Sheridan. "I don't know you."

"That's Sheridan," said Murdock. "Bogart brought him out. He's goin' to run the mill. That's Bush, the sheriff."

Bush put out a firm hand, shook Sheridan's fist, and drew back. He was one of those elderly men who retain physical youth. He had a vital push in his voice.

"What brought you this way?" asked Murdock.

"Couple Indians got off the reservation. Supposed to be up here with a jug of whiskey."

"Now you know better," said Murdock, mildly. "If they had a jug when they left the Siletz, they ain't got it now. They drank it quick. Just go back near the reservation and you'll find 'em sicker'n dogs in the brush. Anyhow, let 'em travel. I don't like to hear of people herded into one place."

"Well," said Bush, "the government says they got to stay there."

"I don't believe in government," said Murdock, with a rare flash of conviction. "It ain't got the right to tell people what to do."

"Maybe you're right. How's things been?"

"We got the wild man back again. Came out of the brush last month, scared hell out of a girl, and went back to the brush."

Mrs. Murdock said: "Mrs. Pullman saw him once. He ain't exactly human. His legs are shorter than his arms and his face looks like a wolf."

"Where'd he come from?" asked Sheridan.

"Oh," said the sheriff, "he's probably a white man that likes to live by himself. Maybe sunstruck."

"You're just like any man, trying to make it seem less," stated Mrs. Murdock. "You know what's said about that Spanish ship bein' wrecked off the coast a long time ago, and one man surviving and living in the woods until he was no better than an animal, and him finally marrying a wolf, and this fellow now coming from that family."

"Oh, pshaw," said the sheriff, "such things can't be, Emmy."

"How do you know?" challenged Mrs. Murdock.

"Ain't possible," said the sheriff.

"Why ain't it?" pressed Mrs. Murdock.

Murdock came out of his silence to supply the answer for the sheriff. "Well, Emmy, it'd be awfully hard for a man to sleep with a she-wolf."

The sheriff let out his great, gusty laugh, and slapped his knee, and turned back to his horse. He climbed to his saddle; he sat still a moment, keeping the air around him. "First time I came up here was in the fall of 'forty-six, with Joe Meek. Wasn't a thing anywhere in this part of the county."

"You got a good memory for dates," said Murdock.

"I remember that one," said the sheriff. "Joe and I shot a buck and carried the meat along. Well, it turned a little ripe on us, so we got diarrhea. That's how I remember. It was the year of the diarrhea." He sat still, his mind sweetened by those long-ago memories which so readily came to him. "It was a fine country. It was like what a man thinks paradise might be. We were the first ones, and there's only one first time. Nobody will ever see this land like we saw it. Nobody had anything. Everybody shared what he had. Everybody knew everybody. It wasn't a state —it was a family. There wasn't such a thing as a stranger. Everybody belonged. Nobody locked their doors and when a man saw a cabin light down the distance he knew he was comin' home, wherever it was and whoever it was. It made everything mighty close and pleasant. I think there was more fun then than there's been since." Then, after a short silence, his voice faded out: "Or maybe it was because I was younger. Good night, folks."

They sat in silence, listening to his horse clopping down the soft road. Presently Mrs. Murdock heaved herself up from the bench. Murdock rose too, saying: "We goin' to sleep outside?"

"Bed's still damp."

"Why don't we put it in to dry?"

"Oh, the weather will dry it—if it don't rain again. Come on, Murdock."

Sheridan sat with the final fragrant stub of his cigar. The Murdocks were amiably bickering inside and Murdock's voice came out with its monotone protest: "Quit it, Emmy." The girl watched him from her side of the porch. He couldn't see her eyes but he felt them. She said: "It's lonely here. There's nothing to do, nobody to talk to. I hate being alone. I'm nineteen. I'm scared."

63

"What about that man?"

"I don't want him. It would just be moving to the other end of this valley and being alone there for the rest of my life."

"Where do I sleep?" he asked, and threw away his cigar and got up. She rose and passed into the house. He waited in the darkness, hearing her move around in an adjoining room. She lighted a lamp and came out of the room. "That's yours," she said. She stood near him, looking up. Her lower lip made a heavy, soft shelf against which her upper lip lay; he saw the brightening of her eyes, the rising of a thought—the shifting of an expression from uncertainty toward deliberateness. He walked into the room and closed the makeshift door behind him. He got ready for bed and blew out the light and pulled a blanket over him. The Murdocks were directly beyond the partition to his left. Mrs. Murdock giggled intermittently and Murdock's listless voice kept murmuring . . . "No, Emmy, Damnation. You're always foolin'." Suddenly the giggling ceased and the woman began to cry in long, snuffling gusts of sound. Murdock comforted her with his gentle exasperation. "I knew you was comin' on a bawling spell."

"Murdock—I'm old—I'm ugly."

"Oh, hell, Emmy, quit it. You ain't ugly, but everybody gets old. People got to take what comes."

"You think we really go to a better place when we die?"

"Preacher says so though I ain't so sure how much he knows about it."

"Oh, him. You know he fooled with the Hobstone girl."

"Far as she's concerned, the preacher got there late."

"Wish I could know I was going to a better place. It'd make this a lot easier. I wouldn't feel so bad for what we've missed."

"Well, think so, Emmy."

"Thinkin' so ain't so."

There was silence, Mrs. Murdock having subsided to a deep breathing. Out of the silence came Murdock's soft voice. "What've we missed, Emmy?"

There was no answer; she was asleep. It was Murdock who lay awake with his wonder, not the woman.

Chapter — 5

ON Monday the big oxen came down the hill with their logs; at seven o'clock Tuesday morning Sampson showed up with the men for the mill. They had worked here before and took their places without instruction from Sheridan. Sampson, however, made a point of introducing George Mead. "George," he said, "will take Kerby's place at the headsaws." Standing aside, Sheridan watched the deck crew roll the first log on the carriage. He said to the sawyer, "We'll cut two-by-fours and one-by-twelves," and observed the saws bite into the log. They were, as he had thought, too slow and left the surface of the boards too rough.

Sampson, who belonged up in the woods, found it necessary to inspect the underpinning of the log deck. He came back to Sheridan, shouting above the whine of the saws. "Ought to put new supports under there." Sheridan went out with him. Sampson filled his pipe and lighted it —and gave the road a casual glance. There was, Sheridan noticed, a man coming down from the upper end of the valley. Sampson drew a good draught of smoke into his lungs and leisurely pointed out what he thought the weaknesses of the deck. "Rotten under that support. Whole deck needs straightenin' so it won't tilt." He went gravely on, wasting this time while the single traveler marched forward.

He was a tall and wiry sort of a man with unfriendly gray eyes. He carried himself a little straighter and a little broader than was necessary—but this was because he knew he had the attention of the crew on him. Sheridan noticed the man's knuckles and the reach of his arms, and he looked again at the face with its loose, restless manner. Not much of a mind behind the eyes, he decided.

"Well," said Sampson with a surprise poorly carried out, "what you here for?" He looked to Sheridan and said, "This man was sawyer before. Kerby."

"What's the matter with me sawin' now?" asked Kerby. "You took the old crew back, didn't you?"

Sheridan had his back to the mill. He heard the machinery running but he heard no saw biting; the men there had quit to see how this would turn out. They knew there was a fight coming, and they knew he knew it. It was something everybody understood to be necessary, like a drink of water before sitting down to eat.

"That's right," said Sheridan.

"I always was on the crew. I heard nothing about coming back."

"No, you didn't," said Sheridan. He felt dry and lean inside and he wasn't certain how he'd come out. Maybe the man was faster and meaner than he appeared to be. He stood still, giving Kerby no opening. A little spiral of heat moved out of his belly and he began to grow deliberately angry. He didn't like to fight—he didn't like to be standing alone here with strangers around him, facing a man who intended to cut him up as much as possible.

Kerby said: "Sampson told me you didn't want me back."

"No," said Sheridan. "I don't want you around the place. You're a sorehead and you won't work. Anybody gettin' a day's pay from me has got to earn it." The crew had come up from the mill, meanwhile, and now stood behind him. He looked back and noted the impersonal curiosity in the eyes of these men. They wanted to see him fight, to see him cut and get cut; they waited for their entertainment.

"By God," said Kerby, "turn around and face me."

Sheridan looked quickly back, knowing he was in danger. Kerby wanted to waste no more time; he dropped his shoulders and he lifted his fists, one stretched half out, the other risen and drawn back toward his nose. He advanced a foot and he narrowed his eyes and squinted across the fist near his nose. He wasn't quite ready—he had not yet set himself to charge and Sheridan, realizing it, stepped in and hit him in the belly.

It was a belly tough as a board, but it gave. Kerby's wind belched out. Kerby's fist came down on Sheridan's nose and started up bright showers of light before his eyes. It destroyed his vision for a moment. He struck straight ahead of him, reaching Kerby and trying to keep the man off balance until his eyes cleared. He aimed for Kerby's face and watched the man step back. He moved on, got Kerby in the belly again, and reached out with a long swinging punch and missed and fell against the man.

He was struck rapidly and driven back. Kerby yelled and jumped at him and he felt his mouth crush up against his teeth, and his brain roared as the blows came on. He was hit in the crotch and lost his wind in the sheets of pain which flowed upwards, and then he was down on the ground, half out. He pulled his knees upward to protect himself from a kick he felt coming. It didn't come. He rolled over and rose and found Kerby waiting.

He was making a poor fight. Kerby had him whipped. He stood a moment, letting his head clear, and then, driven by the pure need to cripple Kerby, he jumped in again. He ducked Kerby's swing and came up and slammed one punch and another into the man's stomach. He lowered his head, he weaved aside. Kerby took a step backward, gathered himself and rushed in. He battered Sheridan's tipped-down head and his fist scraped along Sheridan's chin and nose. He hooked into Sheridan's temple, and then the blows came on again as they had before, out of nowhere, starting up the blaze of lights in Sheridan's brain. He felt them and he heard them, and could not stop them, and slowly he lost his sense of balance and went down.

He was swearing silently to himself. He was cold and had no fear; he was desperate. He got to his knees and looked around the littered soil of the log deck. He spotted a chunk of limb thick as a billy club and a foot long. He turned to place Kerby and saw the latter waiting with a long and pleased face. He got to his feet and walked over and scooped up the club and turned about. He walked toward Kerby, lifting and lowering the club in his hand.

Kerby's manner turned thoughtful. He watched Sheridan's face and he watched the club. He made a quick side step and started in, and drew back; he circled, he attempted short grabbing gestures toward the club. He pinned his glance to it and his eyes were half closed and he had a scheming, completely centered expression on him. He swayed half forward and half aside; he balanced himself, waiting his chance, and when he thought he saw it he reached forward with both arms. Sheridan, swinging the club upward and down, cracked it across Kerby's unguarded skull. It made a sound like the clapping of hollowed hands. Kerby bent at the knees and seemed to

67

gasp. He went down without trying to break his fall; he was unconscious.

Sheridan waited, sucking back the air knocked out of him; he touched his mouth gingerly with his fingers and was glad for the moment of rest. He stared at Kerby and suddenly turned away. He got a bucket and filled it with water at the boiler and brought it back and dumped it over Kerby's head. The man's shoulders flinched. He rolled over and he sat up, staring before him without seeing. He let his head fall and he shook it from side to side; he looked up again and saw Sheridan.

He said, "I had you licked," without anger. "What'd you use the club for?"

"I don't like to lose," said Sheridan.

"Hell," said Kerby, "it was just a fight. You shouldn't of used the club."

"When a man pushes at me," said Sheridan, "I'll use anything handy to level him off."

Kerby got up. He gave the men around him a short, sliding stare and looked away. "I'm a good sawyer as anybody," he said, and then Sheridan knew he had this man whipped. The crew knew it too.

"All right," said Sheridan, "it's your job. Mead, you go to piling lumber."

Kerby and the crew moved back toward the mill. Kerby went on ahead, not talking; the other men split and wandered to their places. They weren't afraid of him and they had no sympathy for him; he was the cock who had lost. Sampson still remained nearby, and he said, "Well, I'll get up to the woods. We can think about fixin' the log deck some other time. It ain't so damned necessary, I guess."

"All right," said Sheridan, and for a moment, watched the woods boss trudge up the hillside. He thought to himself: "I'll go into Portland this week and get new pulleys." The pain of the fight throbbed through him and he felt tired and somewhat sick. He couldn't show the crew any of this and so he walked to the mill and put in the day. It was a long day.

Chapter — 6

CLARA met Revelwood in the lobby of the Pioneer Hotel a little beyond noon and went with him to the Argonaut for dinner. She was in a gay mood, which he realized was the result of the clothes she wore. She had found a good dressmaker in the short time she'd been in town; her dress was a heavy mauve silk with a water-marked design, broken by dull gold insertions and lace-work. Her breasts, according to fashion, were crowded into prominence by the tightness of the dress and her waist was properly pinched in. On her head was a hat— scarcely more than a bit of scooped felt adorned by a raked feather—which achieved distinction by its slight tilt on her head and called deliberate attention to her hair —brushed and thick and throwing off a luster. She loved clothes and she loved strong colors. Her mood now was the mood of a woman who, well dressed, knew she was presenting herself to best advantage; it was a contrast to her frame of mind after the wreck when, hating her be-draggled appearance, she had been irritable with those around her.

He ordered and spent the waiting period in frank en-joyment of her presence. He had sharply exploratory thoughts concerning her. She was not the deepest of wom-en, though in the wreck she had displayed admirable for-titude. In her eyes, around her mouth and along those points of her face where character usually dwells, there was no indication of great emotion sleeping or fiery tem-per to be roused. Everything about her was soft warmth. She responded quickly to pleasant surroundings, she had a gracefully gentle greediness for the comforts of living; and since this was a thing he had turned over in his mind since first meeting her, he concluded that probably it was this love of good things, this dislike of discomfort which made it possible for somebody to corrupt her with less effort than would be needed for another woman. Yet she

69

had—and this was as close as he could put it—a distinct and charming flavor of her own.

She gave him a small white envelope which she had been holding in her hand. He drew out the folded page and read it:

> Miss Dale,
>
> May I have the pleasure of your presence at a tea which I have arranged for you? It will be at my house, four o'clock, Wednesday. In our town silks are considered proper for tea. I assure you that you will meet some of our best ladies.
>
> Your friend
>
> Delia Bogart

Had he not met Charnel Bogart's wife, he would have said that this writing, so straight and angular, was from the hand of an elderly woman. Rereading the note, he found interest in comparing the writing with the woman behind it. It was not fanciful and it was scarcely joyous; he saw Mrs. Bogart—her stiff manner, her dry face, her unpleasant mouth and her incredibly intense eyes—reflected truthfully in the penmanship.

"I don't know," he said, and was doubtful. "I don't know if I'd go if I were you."

"Certainly I'll go," she said. The note had pleased her.

"You realize she hates you. That was apparent the other night."

"Then why would she ask me to tea?"

He debated that in his mind while he poured the wine. He lifted his glass and nodded at her and sipped it. "Maybe she thinks her husband is interested in you."

She smiled. "That's flattery, George," and a light, dancing amusement showed along her face. "But, why would she invite me?"

"To find out if you're interested in her husband."

He said it in the same idle tone he had so far used, but he was more serious than the tone indicated. She continued her smiling. Her glance met his, not mocking him so much as fencing with him, and he understood that she would not give him an answer. "After all," he pointed out, "the man's married."

"I've not said I was interested in him," she said.

"Neither have you said you weren't. The truth is, you're impressed with his interest. You're thinking about it.

70

You're turning it around and looking at it from all sides. You think it innocent. It is, now. It may not be later."

"George," she said, "you have sharp eyes. You look very handsome today. The cravat is very good. You're rested. Your eyes aren't tired the way they were when you first came off the boat."

He said: "Coquetry with Bogart would be dangerous. He's not the sort of man to be led on and dismissed. You can't have your idle entertainment with him."

She grew graver, and slightly displeased. "I've said nothing about that, have I?"

"It's in your mind."

"There's only one thing in my mind," she answered. "I will never again be miserable or cold or forlorn. I keep remembering how many of those people on the boat believed everything would be all right tomorrow—how many of them were nice people, how many of them had plans. Now they're dead. They've all been cheated. I won't be cheated. I won't believe in tomorrow. It's too cruel."

He said: "I've done what I pleased and I've not particularly believed in tomorrow. I doubt if, in all my life, I've gone out of my way to be kind to anybody else. Do I look like a happy man to you?"

"I think you've had much fun, and not very much care."

"I'd trade my place for Mark Sheridan's any day."

An expression crossed her face. "Oh, but George, neither you nor I can ever be like him."

"How's that?"

"I think something was left out of me. Maybe it's courage. I can't face a lot of things. We're so serious, George. Let's not be."

"You're extraordinarily pretty," he said.

The compliment swayed her. She lifted her hand and gave him a straight, smiling attention. "You've had much experience with women, haven't you?"

"Some," he said.

"A great deal," she retorted. "You've been testing me. You began it on the boat. What did you see in me that made you think it possible to turn my head?"

He said, wary and gallant, "You were the most charming woman on the boat. I could do nothing else than to try to get acquainted with you."

"No, George," she said. "I know you better." She watched him closely, and there was a shadow of embarrassment upon her. "You were trying to—to capture me. I realized it. What made you think you could? What do I seem to reveal on my face? Do I look common?"

"My God, no," said Revelwood, and saw the inexpressible sweetness come over her. She had been troubled by the thought; it was deep in her pride. But she continued to press him.

"What do you see, then?"

He was too experienced to be caught in the trap. He shook his head. "I saw in you some of the things which are in me, I suppose. I mean, outside of being most lovely—which you are—you also seem lonely. You have some sort of a wish on your face. A wish not to lose the good things which go by us so fast. Not to have a dull life—not to be cast high and dry. Not to grow old without having something for it."

"Why," she said and was softly delighted, "you do know."

"I know well enough," he said. "But I have not got these things—not for all my trying. Nor will you get them the way you propose to."

"Why not?" she demanded.

The meal had come and they had been eating as they talked. An unusual thoughtfulness came to Revelwood, an unusual conviction got into his voice. "Most of life is plain drudgery and trouble. That's what we set up preachers for—to console us—to tell us that if we can just struggle through this one, we'll have a happy life later. Most of the fun comes, I think, when we've worked very hard for it. For a little while we know we've been honest, we've done what we should do—and we feel good about it. Then that fades out and we have to fight again. That's the point—we've got to work hard for any kind of happiness. It's no four-leaf clover we find accidentally. Nobody can get away from the penalties, nobody can find a short way to fun. There's only the long way to it."

She shook her head. "You're too serious tonight."

"You think you'll find the easy way. You think you're the exception. I thought so too. The trouble is, Clara, you and I are people not cut out for drudgery and dust. But that's what the world's made up of. So we don't belong. We don't fit in. In the long run we'll have a lot less happiness than the people who don't bother to look for it." He gave her a half-amused glance. "Maybe we're people who see too much. Maybe we see through the game

72

and don't want to play it. We ought to find a game that's better for us. But there isn't that kind of a game."

She said: "I'd thought your eyes were hazel. They're not. They're more violet—very dark violet."

He said: "I wish you'd listen to my advice."

She gave him a shrug. She was careless and completely certain of herself. "I shall go to the tea. Mrs. Bogart may dislike me—I think she does. I think maybe it was Mr. Bogart who asked her to give the tea. He's a domineering man. But I'll go. There will be some of Portland's nice ladies there. I wish to meet them. I wish to be invited to their homes."

After the meal he walked with her to her house on Sixth Street. She said: "I now have a housekeeper and may properly have you inside. I shall be back from tea around five. Do you want to come in before supper, just to know how I've made out?"

"Yes."

"We're all together—that's what you said. Or did Mark say it?" Her manner shaded slightly. "Have you seen him in town?"

"No."

She stood before him, her glance going beyond him toward the heavy hills west of town. She was for that moment thoughtful. Then the ready self-confidence returned and she gave him a smile and turned toward her house.

Watching her go, he realized she was still excited by the prospect of meeting the town's women at tea; Mrs. Bogart was actually giving her entry into the best social level of the town—and it meant so much to Clara that Revelwood realized she had never moved on that level before. Then he remembered that she had wanted to know what he had seen on her face to arouse him and he understood that this too was a part of her fear. She suspected herself of lacking quality. The tea, then, became one of the major events of her life; it offered her the chance to prove to herself that she did possess quality. Perhaps it explained her coquetry with Bogart. Perhaps, since he had displayed interest in her, she was using him as a means of gaining the genteel circle.

Traveling toward the hotel, he felt relieved to know that Clara was after all only playing the game any other woman would play in order to gain recognition among women of station. But he could not shake an uneasiness

73

from his mind. He remembered Mrs. Bogart's face so clearly, and could not believe her to be guileless.

Sheridan was in Portland that day. He had left the Murdock place not much later than three in the morning with the intent of reaching town for a long day's looking around, and was in Bogart's office at eight. Bogart was quick to see the scars on Sheridan's face.

"You've had a fight.".

"The one you expected," said Sheridan. "I want a new set of pulleys for the head saws. Your trouble lies there. They don't turn fast enough. They choke down on the log, slow up the carriage, and saw a rough board. I think I can get another five thousand feet a day from the rig."

"I won't spend money on machinery until we get something in the till."

"A couple pulleys is not much of an item. Where do I get 'em?"

"I suppose Dave Monastes could supply you." Bogart nodded toward the scars. "Kerby, I suppose."

"Yes," said Sheridan. "What about these pulleys? Do you agree, so I can go see Monastes?"

Bogart flared up with a mild irritableness. "Goddammit, Sheridan—why not tell me how the fight came out?"

Sheridan stared at Bogart. "I wouldn't be here talking business if I'd been licked, would I?"

The rebuke sat ill with Bogart and quite unexpectedly there was in this room a feeling of strain. Bogart said in a ruffled voice, "I compliment you."

"How about the pulleys?"

"No," said Bogart, "I'm satisfied with the mill's production."

"I'm not," said Sheridan.

"I don't follow that," answered Bogart. "All you've got to do is run the thing, and I'll worry about the rest."

"If I'm going to run it," said Sheridan, "I'll have to run it my style. Maybe you have forgotten that we're on shares."

"No point there," said Bogart.

"All right," said Sheridan. "No point in my staying on. You can hunt another foreman."

Bogart struck the desk a rapping blow with his knuckles and rose to walk the room; he thrust his hands into his front trouser pockets, stiffened his back and took up a turkey-cock striding. "I've no disposition to quarrel with you, Sheridan. Have I not got some rights in this mill?"

"Certainly. It's your right to hire another man."

Bogart paused and flung a glance at him. "Perhaps I can."

Sheridan watched him closely. "Be sure to pick one who can lick Kerby. Kerby's better than most scrappers."

"He's licked, isn't he?"

"I licked him," said Sheridan. "He'll stay licked as long as I'm around. If you get another boss, Kerby will have to be licked again."

Bogart took in the information and weighed it against his particular wishes. He jingled the silverware in his pocket; his mouth pushed together, assuming a bulldog stubbornness and his face was a fresh, ruddy red. He was irritated, but he was also cautious and when he had done his weighing he made a face-about in his manner and looked up at Sheridan with a smile. "Do your own figuring, don't you? It appears I cannot run the mill unless I find another man to whip Kerby. Therefore, having had trouble in that direction, I must work with the man who did it. Very smart of you."

Sheridan grinned at Bogart. "You'd be better off with some other fellow on straight salary than with me on shares. Go out and find your man."

"You need not grind me with the advantage," said Bogart shortly. "Go get your pulleys." He surveyed Sheridan, his vanity subdued by his business judgment. "You'll go a long way. I could wish only for a little more loyalty."

"You'll have all you require," said Sheridan.

"I took you on speculation," said Bogart. "It was an act of trust. Now you take me on trust instead. You have some doubts about me. It is a hell of an annoying idea." Then he burst into a short, unhumorous laugh. "Well, no doubt we'll get on. Certainly, you intend to get on. Remember, I did give you a chance—which is a great deal in a new country. Shouldn't there be some gratitude?"

"I got your mill started and I'll push it and you'll make money. So will I. That should be all that either of us require."

"I can tell you something more," said Bogart shrewdly. "You'll leave me, when a better chance comes."

"I will," said Sheridan. "But not without good warning."

"That's kind," said Bogart with irony. "I was the one

who gave you the advice to look to your own affairs and be tough. Do you have to practice the advice on me?"

"I had the notion some time before," said Sheridan, and left the office.

He walked down to the iron works and found Mr. Monastes, and was engaged there the better part of two hours. One of the pulleys he required was available; the other was not, but Monastes gave him some information which took him by wagon a few miles down the Red House road to a mill no longer in operation. He found the second pulley, made his bargain and put it in the wagon. The sight of the unused mill gave him a notion and he spent another hour with the owner, a lean and aging Yankee who was, it appeared, too near the competition of the big mills in Portland to make a profit.

"When this country was new," said the Yankee, "every man had a chance. For a few years it's fine—everybody's small. Then some men get bigger and then it's the same old story—the big fellow crowds out the small man."

"Maybe," said Sheridan, more for talk than from conviction, "we need some laws on that."

"Wouldn't do a bit of good," said the Yankee. "Never does. It's people. It's something in a man that won't let him be satisfied with just enough. If I was a big fellow I'd crowd just like the others do."

Sheridan returned to town and had his dinner. The Yankee's mill interested him—it was a possibility. Perhaps other and smarter men than he had looked at that mill and had seen nothing in it; yet there might be something in it which they had overlooked. He had no particularly long thoughts concerning business; he had not the time to make a philosophy for himself. So far as he had reflected on it, Sheridan believed a man should watch for his chances, push when he got them, and regard failure only as a temorary thing. Luck was a definite thing, but men made much of their own luck and he had no doubt of his own ability to do so.

Still thinking of this Yankee's mill, he thought it would be wise to look into the price of machinery, and he returned to Monastes. In the course of the conversation Monastes let drop the fact that there was another mill not operating over in the lower end of the Tualatin. The owner, it appeared, had died and nobody else in the district knew much about mills. There was a widow. Sheridan left the place, pleased with the uncovering of this bit of information, and since it was then about four o'clock he decided to look up Revelwood. He found him in an office around the corner of First and Pine, halfway to Front.

Revelwood was genuinely pleased to see him and for his part Sheridan found a good deal of comfort in the presence of this man who believed so little in the solid conventions and yet retained so much that was amusing. It was the scoundrels apparently who, packing none of the grave moral responsibilities with them and subscribing to no particular set of duties, could afford to be charming. There must, Sheridan thought, be something wrong in a way of living so upright that it made honest men dull.

"You have," said Revelwood, "been in a brawl. I take it you have had to knock somebody out of the road in your pursuit of fortune."

"The local bully of the woods. That's why the mill was shut down. The other foreman got run off."

"Which is the reason our friend Bogart dispatched you on the errand," commented Revelwood. "You understand that, I hope?"

"Yes."

"But you propose to continue the bargain with him?"

"Certainly. I licked the bully. He's my sawyer now."

"Of course you whipped him," said Revelwood in his dry way. "You're in a hurry and you won't be stopped. You'll probably make a million in ten years. Or, on the other hand, you may be dead. But watch out for Bogart. Now you know he's very sharp in his dealing. You think you can be more clever than he is. Don't believe it. No *honest* man is a match for a scoundrel."

"Why not?"

"The honest man sticks to rules. The scoundrel doesn't. No, that's only part of it. The scoundrel is so afraid of work that he uses his mind much more than the honest man. How do you like my shop? I'm in business."

"What business?"

"Real estate," said Revelwood, and shook his head at himself. "It is wholly honest, and wouldn't it be a damned peculiar thing if it turned out well? I walked around the edges of our town and put down a few dollars to secure five acres up where the woodchoppers are. I am going to sell it off in lots. If you were here tomorrow I'd show you a picture of the subdivision drawn by a very imaginative artist. I have sold four lots so far, enough to pay for the five acres."

77

"Why, George," said Sheridan, "that's fine!"

George shrugged it away. "Pays the rent and keeps my bar bill. But it is not my main venture. A prospector came in here the other day and sold me a gold claim over in eastern Oregon for one hundred dollars. He thought he had found a likely sucker and went out very pleased."

"What will you do with it?"

"I have found an essayer who says, on a sworn statement, that this gold vein—upon a little digging—is a major discovery. It is incredibly rich, so rich in fact I don't want the news to spread. I've only told four or five people." He gave Sheridan his smiling stare. "But you know how those things are. Good things always leak out. I suppose in a week everybody in town will know about it. Then somebody will come around and try to cheat me out of it." He got up, laughing, and put an arm on Sheridan's shoulder. "Let's go get a drink."

They crossed to the Grotto and stood in comfort at the bar. Revelwood looked well. His coat sat snug, his cravat was of black string against a hard white shirt, his waistcoat had a flowered pattern on a subdued side. He carried himself as a man of unhurried leisure, he was affable without familiarity, and his face, perfectly shaven and wonderfully smooth, had a fine close olive tint. His black hair, quite thick, made a loose roll against his forehead in the style of Franklin Pierce and this, with a pair of striking eyes which hinted at strong temper and yet flattered people by the directness of their interest, gave him an air. He had, Sheridan understood, spent much time on the perfection of this air. Several men nodded to him and he gave them back a better nod.

"Fully recovered from the wreck?" asked Sheridan.

"Occasionally I wake troubled. There was a woman on that ship who kept screaming. That still oppresses me. She died full of fear. I hope I may never die that way. Clara asked about you today."

"I want to see her."

Revelwood considered his watch. "We might walk over. She should be back from tea. A tea in her honor, given by Mrs. Bogart."

"I wish I thought so . . . Mrs. Bogart dislikes her."

They turned into Clara's yard to find a light shining through the front room window, and when they knocked, she promptly came to the door.

She was still in her mauve silk outfit; she had not yet

78

removed her hat. Against the light, in the softness of the light she was actually beautiful to Sheridan. The effect was so strong on him—so physically strong—that he realized he had missed her. It surprised him to know it for he could not remember having thought of her in the last few days. He said, "Hello, Clara," and waited for her smile to come out to him.

She didn't smile. Her face was preoccupied; she gave him an intent glance, yet one that seemed actually to be absent-minded. She took his arm and drew him in. "I'm glad you're here, Mark," she said. She turned from him. "I just got back. I've not even taken my hat off." Her hands moved up to her head, working with the fastening of the hat. She spoke over her shoulder. "I didn't stay for all of the tea. I left a little early. George told you where I went, didn't he?"

"Yes," said Sheridan. Revelwood had gone to a corner to stand behind a chair, his arms resting on its back; in this attitude he was watching Clara with a steady attention.

Clara turned and her glance touched each man and went skimming around the room. She moved restlessly, re-arranging the books on the center table. She lifted a chair, and replaced it. She walked to the wall and straightened a picture. Her mouth was troubled, her eyes were bright. She looked again at Sheridan and spoke in a tone meant to show interest. "Have you been busy?"

"Yes," said Sheridan.

Revelwood said: "What was the tea like?"

"It was quite crowded. I think there must have been thirty ladies there."

"Pleasant?"

"Yes," said Clara.

Revelwood pressed on with his questions. "Why did you leave early?"

"It was rather warm. I thought I would have a headache."

Revelwood straightened. "By God, Clara," he said, "what did she do to you?"

This was another Revelwood. It astonished Sheridan to see the rough anger rise up from a man so usually in-different, and, looking quickly over to Clara, he observed again the silent passage between those two people of things beyond him. He was still the outsider. Clara straightened under Revelwood's blunt question. She lost her restlessness, she abandoned the aimless little motions behind which she seemed to try to hide her trouble, and over her face came a rather subdued bitterness. With this unaccustomed hardness of character she was less pretty than she had been. Her voice was flat.

"She was cruel, George. Not rude—not impolite, but cruel. She asked me if I enjoyed her husband's presence. She asked me if I found you two agreeable. The other women knew what she was saying. She destroyed me. I'll never be asked in any of those homes." She stared at Revelwood, not at Sheridan; it was Revelwood who understood this best. Her voice dropped, still without tone; it was faintly unsteady. "She fixed me. You were right. She meant to do it. She did."

"We ought not to have visited you in this house," said Sheridan. "I'll go to Bogart and see to it that he speaks to his wife."

Revelwood looked at him. "You don't understand, Mark."

Clara shook her head at Sheridan. "No, it's done. I have my place now. It won't ever be changed."

"Clara," said Revelwood, so soft and untouched, "I wish you hadn't gone."

"Oh," she said, and shrugged her shoulders, "it would have happened sometime."

"I'll think of a way to make that woman suffer," said Revelwood. "I'll find the kind of a knife that will dig into her. By God, I'll take sleep away from her. I'll make her cringe until she's nothing but a shadow and a skeleton—and nothing but misery left in her. I'll find a way."

Clara said: "Don't bother." She watched Revelwood a moment and was plainly comforted by the sight of his anger. She had grown calmer. She turned her glance to him and he recognized something of the hollow, begging expression in her eyes he had noticed in the gray afternoon of the wreck—that lost and frightened look with all its emptiness and all its hunger. "George," she said, "would you go away? I want to talk to Mark."

It seemed to Sheridan that Revelwood displayed a surprised resentment, but he covered it soon enough and went to the door. He said to Sheridan, "Drop in on me before you leave town," and left the house.

Clara said, "I want you to stay for supper. I've not seen you. I've missed you."

"Will it be all right?" he asked.

She made a small gesture of indifference. "I have a housekeeper—and it doesn't matter now." She opened a door into the kitchen and spoke to the housekeeper and closed the door. She moved toward him, her glance brushing across his face with its light and kind and personal touch. "You've had a fight."

"I had to take care of the fellow who took care of the previous boss."

"You always take care of things." She came to him and put her arms over his shoulders. There was no hesitation or embarrassment in her manner; it was a gesture of old belonging and old habit, and she looked at his face a dragging moment and seemed to find relief, and then she laid her cheek against his chest and began to cry.

Her reserve, once broken, gave way completely and presently everything poured through the gap. She made no attempt to check herself. She said, "I'm not bad—I'm not different than they are," but he had trouble in identifying the words through the throaty spasms of her breath. She shook tremendously, and her fingers dug into his back and relaxed, and dug in again. "I'm—" She never got the rest of it out. She was crying in full, unlovely, passionate force. It was incoherent, shapeless tragedy spilling out of her; it was a great expelling of the nice things curdled by disappointment, it was such faith as she had—the warm wishes, the soft and undisciplined eagerness, the hope of belonging, the faithful respect of decency which none of her own lightness had ever really disturbed—it was all of this suddenly mixed with humiliation and destroyed self-respect; it was the final brutality of knowing she had been rejected. All of it came out.

He held her in and was stirred by a futile anger which found nothing to strike; he wanted to comfort her but he had nothing to say. He stood still, waiting the storm to blow over, but he knew something was happening to her that neither he nor anybody else could repair. Everything came out of her—nothing remained. He had never heard a woman cry with such unreserved distress. He felt it all along his nerves.

She relaxed, hanging to him with more weight and gradually bringing herself under control; and rather abruptly she turned from him, went into the bedroom and closed the door. He looked down at the wet spot on his coat lapel; he turned to the window and stood before it, staring into the gathered darkness of the street. He was depressed and he began to think of Mrs. Bogart, to wonder what cruelty there was in her to make this possible. It took a pretty powerful motive. Was this woman, so bloodless and unlovely, in fear of losing her husband to Clara? He thought about Bogart and he thought about Clara. The two of them had only met a week or less ago. Revelwood knew something about it, and had held it back. He had picked that up from Revelwood's manner. Whatever it was, there was no use asking the man. Revelwood had a close mouth.

The housekeeper came into the room to set the table. He turned to find her a small, dark Scotch girl rather frightened at what she had heard through the closed door. She looked at Sheridan with large hostile eyes, seeming to blame him for it, and went about the setting of the table. The room seemed cold, and he looked into the stove and found the fire burned out. He went to the woodshed for a load of kindling and wood; he got a piece of paper in the kitchen and built up a new fire. He was at the stove when Clara came from the bedroom. She had erased the damage except for a faint redness around her eyelids, and she had brought back her older manner. It seemed to fit her easily—the small smile, the lightness around her eyes the mouth. "It was bad, wasn't it?"

"Yes," he said. "Is it over?"

"Oh yes. Anybody can get over anything."

"No," he said. "I don't believe that."

"I'm tired," she said, and sat down at the table. He took his place across from her.

It was a good meal wasted. They sat back with their coffee, she in a long, long silence which he took care not to interrupt. She was going through all of it, reviewing it, remembering it, putting together the little pieces which she had before missed. It didn't seem a painful thing. In her tired and emotionless state she actually appeared to have some sort of detached point of view.

The Scotch girl cleared the table and again disappeared. He sat on the sofa with his cigar while Clara changed the cloth on the table and changed the location of the chairs. She came to him and, with a gesture of grace, she settled beside him. "I've missed you. Does the mill please you? Will you make a lot of money? That's what you want, isn't it?"

"Everything's fine," he said.

82

"Things work for you. I guess you make them work. Where do you live?"

"There's a farmhouse next to the mill."

She put her hand on his arm and sat silent. The man-and-wife feeling came back again, the close familiarity that was theirs. He remembered the night in the Indian hut and the memory of it grew very real and her soft shape beside him was a temptation. He had his close intimate thoughts of her and wondered if she thought of him in the same way.

"I wish you were in town, Mark. How would I come to see you?"

"Out Canyon Road to a little store called Bright's Orchard. Then turn right and keep going."

"You're always with me in the bad times. These were the worst I've had."

"It's pretty tough," he said.

"It's another wreck."

She said it so calmly that at first he missed the point. She had her eyes on the light dancing through the isinglass front of the stove and she seemed contented, but the delayed meaning finally got to him and struck him a rough blow. Then he knew what it actually meant to her and how great an admission of tragedy it really was. He closed his hand around her fingers. "I wish I could do something about it."

The comfort of his sympathy made her turn and lay her head against him. "I'll never again get inside a decent house in this town. I'm glad you're here. It would be a bad night without you."

"There ought to be a way of paying her back."

"Maybe that will happen."

"Are you going to stay here or go back to San Francisco?"

She didn't answer immediately. She lay quietly against him, but the stillness of her body was the give-away of a feeling going through her. After a long silence she said in the most matter-of-fact of voices, "I don't know." He got the idea he had displeased her; she seemed farther away from him.

"Where are your people?"

"My mother's dead. My father's married again. He's a dealer in hides and leather. I don't know much about them in the last few years. I've lived with my aunt. She's in Sacramento."

"Have you got a lot of friends there?"

She was silent again for a while. He got up and freshened the fire; when he came back to the divan she again rested against him, her hand searching for his hand. "Oh, they're all married by now. Do you want to know about me?"

"Yes."

"There's nothing about me," she said, "except that I have always wanted to be like my mother. I wish she had lived. Many things would have been different. She was a pretty woman. She always had a good time. Everything was so much fun to her. Never did I see her cross or solemn." She paused to think about that and to add a qualification. "Though I can see now that she must have been solemn when I wasn't around. She came from well-to-do people in the East and she had everything she wanted, a lot of friends, a lot of traveling—everything. When my father brought her West it was different. She had to work very hard. My father's friends were different —they were rough people, and sometimes my father wasn't kind. But she didn't show any of that to me. She smiled, as long as I knew her. Some people have a lot of quality, Mark. I have always wanted to be like her." Her tone changed and her question was carefully indifferent. "Do you think I ought to go back to California?"

"What will you do here? You're alone."

"Oh," she said carelessly, "let's not think of it."

She rested against him, the talk gone out of her. He nursed his cigar through the last of its fragrance and it occurred to him that except for the light and the warmth of this room, they were again as they had been in the Indian hut—two people crouched together for comfort in a hard world.

He had come to this house in good spirits; now he began to swing down a spiral of doubt which he had known before when his energy wore out or when he came upon cruelty he couldn't understand. These were the times when he saw himself in a jungle of a world through which people made their way as best they could but never with much kindness, never with much purpose. These were the times when the thought came to him that he was part of an illusion, that he was scarcely more real than a shadow on moving water. In such a mood he understood how Clara felt and was touched by the same pointless rebellion, the same questioning, and same madness, the same terrible

84

loneliness which lived with all human beings. This was why she had cried and had wakened him with her mouth pressed against him in the Indian hut; it was the aloneness that made her hold to him—this great cruelty of living which touched everybody. He turned his head and looked down at the slanted profile of her face. Tenderness came quickly upon him and swelled through him at the thought of the everyday brutalities against which she had no defense.

She felt his glance and shifted her head, watching him with a warming hope; her mouth was curved and receptive, and this moment's comfort brought back the hint of luxury to her face; and he felt himself then on the edge of a decision. He knew he wanted her and he thought she wanted him. He didn't understand what held him back—but some single restraining doubt did hold him back. They had met only a week ago, and maybe that checked him, or maybe it was the hint that it didn't matter to her how she went to him; there was that small curve of sensuousness along her mouth and that intimacy —or a wife waiting, of a wife silently provoking—in her eyes. The closeness was upon them and he floated indecisively within the closeness, finding it good and finding it hard to resist. A small guilt came over him for thinking of her as he did, and from knowing that she understood how close he was to hunger. She answered him definitely, the same expression on her now that had been in the cabin of the steamboat. He had provoked it within her and that was his fault. He drew back and got up. "No good for me to be here this late."

"Oh," she said, "it doesn't matter."

He walked to his hat. "I'll be back at the end of the week."

She rose at once and came to him. "Don't go yet. I don't want to be alone."

"I don't believe in holding grudges. But I'll find some way to pay off Mrs. Bogart."

"Never mind," she said. "She'll get paid off. I wish you were in town. I'd feel better."

"Good night."

She reached out and caught a lapel of his coat. "Mark —a little longer."

"Your neighbors will be watching," he said. "I shouldn't be here at all." He wanted to kiss her but he knew if he did kiss her, the ending would be bad. They were both defenseless tonight. He turned to the door, and opened it.

She stood in the center of the room, dark and let down, and she said again, "Another half hour, Mark. I think I'd be happy in another half hour. The house wouldn't seem so gloomy. Things would be different."

He said: "I'll see George before I leave town. I want to tell him to look out for you."

She said, without much expression, "He will."

"Good night."

She nodded and smiled; it was her best smile and left with him, as he walked away from the house, the strongest picture of her personality. He went down the street, still low in spirits.

It was near nine o'clock, with a long ride home; but he dropped into the Pioneer and found George in the lobby. Revelwood said: "Well, let's have a drink before you go," and led Sheridan into the saloon. They stood by themselves at the bar's end. Sheridan dipped his glass at Revelwood and downed his whiskey. "That will have to take the place of a night's sleep."

"Mark," said Revelwood, "she's fond of you. I had not realized how fond until tonight."

"I wish you'd watch out for her," said Sheridan. "It's been a bad thing."

"Naturally I shall," said Revelwood. He had a preoccupied air. "Everything changes," he said with unusual soberness. "I have almost no friends. I value your friendship. I hope you know that. What happens as time goes on, God only knows. We all change. We all get knocked around, and sometimes things happen to us we can't prevent. You understand?"

"You sound grave," said Sheridan. "It must be the weather. We're all grave tonight."

"Remember what I've said."

"I'll see you in a week," said Sheridan, gave Revelwood a touch on the shoulder, and left the bar. In another quarter hour he was homeward bound in the wagon with a vague starlight showing through the thin clouds above him. When he reached the foot of Canyon Road the great trees came down upon him and he passed into the black tunnel of that rough and lonesome road.

Chapter — 7

SHERIDAN reached Murdock's at two o'clock. Liza, having heard his wagon in the yard, rose to make him coffee to go along with a freshly baked huckleberry pie. He had not slept for almost twenty-four hours and he was dead-tired; but she wanted to be told about Portland. She had slipped on only a dress, nothing beneath it, and felt no immodesty in showing him the loose, free curving of her body beneath this scarcely adequate covering. She had the air not so much of having wakened out of sleep as of having lain awake waiting for him. She was restless, she was sullen and uncertain and aggressive from the bilked vitality within her. She didn't know how to handle herself, or him; she sat beside him while he ate, steadily watching him. She didn't smile, she didn't know how to smile her way into a man; she lacked that finesse. All she had was a pressing, ungentle insistence.

"I wish you'd taken me. You afraid of me, or ashamed of me?"

"It was too long a trip."

"I can stand anything. Anything's better than waiting here for nothing."

"I'll take you when I make a shorter run." He got up and turned toward his room. She came after him, carrying the lamp. She held it in the doorway of his room while he lighted his own lamp. He was afraid of her—considerably afraid of that raw, angular light in her eyes; what he saw there was the steady increase of a pressure which pushed against her with so much force that it made her cranky and half wild. He said, "Thanks, Liza," and waited for her to go. She gave him a glance, half of direct invitation, half of scorn, and swung away. He closed the door, undressed and got into bed. He listened a moment in the darkness hearing her move about her room, and he wished his door had a lock on it. But he was conscious of her and he listened to her settle into her

87

bed, and heard her hand gently touch the wall between and tap it. Then he was afraid of himself.

At seven o'clock he was at the mill to tally the preceding day's cut and to have a word with Kerby. "That's a good cut," he said. "We'll change over on the pulleys Sunday. I think that will give us another five thousand. I'll be gone for two days. Keep this thing running." He had no fear of Kerby's slacking off. Kerby was that type of man who, once whipped, became loyal to the man who had whipped him.

"Don't worry," said Kerby.

Sheridan set off in the light wagon, southward to Bright's Orchard—which was where the main Portland road passed—and then went in the direction of Forest Grove. The morning was clear save for an occasional thin cloud drifting sluggishly overhead, and the dryness of summer and fall gave the soil its sharp-distilled odors. Dust clung to the fern along the rail fences, the cut grain fields were amber against the stands of wood-lot timber, the cornstalks stood ragged and on all sides of this valley the low running hills exhaled a vapored blueness. Gently the earth rolled from meadow to brushy ravine, from pasture to pasture, onward over faint swells of ground, by the rectangles of farm yard and barn lot and section fence. He drove through the shadows of a covered bridge and passed a house sitting within a grove of young peach trees whose leaves were turning pale yellow. The house stood straight up and down, with nothing to break the front of it save two steps leading through a door; behind, half seen, was an ell which contained a summer kitchen and the usual milk house and woodshed. It was an angular, honest house, painted white—a spinster dressed neatly and too proud of offer seduction. He went through little cross-road settlements, each with its general store whose single room seemed to run back into darkness, with its blacksmith shop, its school and church, and its few houses scattered away. There was a seasoned fragrance on this land, and the quietness of a year drawing on. He went through Hillsboro.

A little sleep had freshened him, his thoughts were quick, his optimism restored. It was always this way; when depression came upon him he had sometimes strange fancies—like blurred images from a distorted glass—and he touched the edge of things he could neither name nor identify, unreal yet powerfully moving to him. Or, he was like a drunkard whose mind, released from restraint, saw himself and others about him in sharpest clarity, and understood himself as he never had in sober moments, and looked into the people around him with a perfect perception, hearing in their words the things they had not meant to say, and seeing in their eyes things so transparently true that he was startled. Those were the times when he was a loose giant knocking around a new world whose every view was new to his eyes.

But these were the deep moods that never lasted long, and from which he recovered suddenly and felt fresh and common and untroubled, and took on anew the things which seemed important, and struggled for them, and believed in himself.

Forest Grove was more than a crossroads settlement. It was the core of the upper valley, a town with streets and small business buildings and houses standing in considerable yards, each yard with a garden plot and a shed for a cow, a buggy and winter's wood. It was a pleasant town given to trees, not an old town—since no Oregon town went back much more than twenty years—but a town with a settled air, a far graver air than Portland.

He tied his horse and walked along until he discovered a print shop, and there he completed his errand, which was to have printed and distributed five hundred leaflets announcing the reopening of the mill at Murdock's. He inquired about the widow and her mill somewhere around here.

"You mean Colson's?" said the printer. "You take the Gales Creek road out seven miles or so."

Sheridan left town by the Gales Creek road, traveling west and north. The valley lay around him, coming closer to the dark coastal chain of hills which guarded the sea. He went along with his peaceful satisfaction, pleased with the scene. The road eventually came upon the foot of a ridge and went beside it. A creek watered these meadows and made them fertile, but the best of the valley was running out and the deep, rough forests were coming on. The farmhouses he saw made less of an impression— smaller, grayer, more carelessly put together.

He saw the mill across one of these meadows, and the scars of logging on the hill behind it. But the timber had scarcely been touched; it crowded the face of the hill and it ran on westward up and down other hills, so thick and so old as to make a country of perpetual shade. A low gray house sat near the mill, and another house stood a quarter mile away. He took a pair of ruts across the meadow and got down to find the kind of layout common to the country; it was like any small mill, built at the foot of a hill for convenience and cutting its ten thousand a day for local trade.

A woman stood on the porch of the nearby house and shaded her face to watch him. He crossed the yard and he said: "Mrs. Colson?"

She was sixty or better, with a dark, worn and peaceful face; she wore square, steel-rimmed glasses through which a pair of eyes considered him, neither to be outdone by him nor to be inhospitable to him; her voice had a tart kindness to it. "Yes, indeed." She wore a loose gray dress covered by a small apron and she slowly turned a thimble on her finger. Suddenly she looked beyond him to a white hen scratching in her flower bed and she said: "Shoo-shoo, or I'll cut off your head." She clapped her hands vigorously.

"I heard about your mill," he said, "and came to look at it. That's my business."

"Well," she said, "there it sits. It cost Colson a lot of money and ne never got it back. A sixty-year-old man's got no business working that hard. I told him so. It pleased him to work, like it pleases other men to drink."

"Would you want to sell it?"

"I really don't know," said Mrs. Colson. "It made such a terrible noise. But I wouldn't mind getting something out of it. You come from Forest Grove way?"

"Yes."

"Then you've had no dinner, and you're young and you look hungry. You come in."

He followed her into the kitchen, into the sudden strong aroma of apples simmering in a kettle. "Work's a habit with me, too. Dreadful habit. It's foolish of me to be puttin' up apple butter every year. But I've always done it and I suppose I always will. I can't bear to see anything go to waste. You'd go right ahead with the mill, like Colson did?"

"If I could find a crew."

She pointed down the meadow toward the farther house. "There's a man and two full-grown boys—and they ought to work. There's Odermeier beyond me. He used to work here. The Clancy boys did the logging."

"Who owns the timber?"

"It's some ours," she said. "But I think Colson was cutting in the government land."

"Did he pay for the government logs?"

She gave him an indirect glance. "That would be silly. It's just rotting away there. It's hard enough to get anything from the government, let alone give anything back." She moved about the kitchen with her short, quick motions. She searched her cupboard and her breadbox; she went to the pantry, she put before Sheridan finally a meal of cold chicken, graham gem biscuits, blackberry jam, butter and milk. She sat down across from him and nodded at the chicken. "That hen scratched once too much in my flowers. I warned her. That jam is this year's. What would you think of paying for the mill?"

He had thought about this since talking machinery prices with Monastes in Portland; and the woman before him seemed the direct sort. He said: "Fifteen hundred dollars."

She was placid in her chair. "Was that what Colson paid?"

"If he bought it new, he paid a good deal more."

She nodded. "He did." She watched him in a full, close way. "Young man, would you do me?"

"I'll make as good a bargain as I can, but I won't do you."

"Don't believe you would, either."

"If I run it and go broke, no harm's done—you've still got it. If I can get a crew I'll give you five hundred, and the rest out of the profit as we run."

"It will disturb the chickens, of course," she mused. "They didn't lay well last time it ran. The smoke got on my washing, too. Well, I don't know. I'll ask guidance."

"If you've got a man to ask—some man who knows about mills—"

She made a ticking noise with her tongue. "Men—men around here? They've got barely enough brains to guide themselves. When I ask, I ask the Lord. Always have. Always get an answer too." She watched him eat and was made happy by his appetite. She rose suddenly and went outside and he heard her scatting away the chicken in the flower bed. The room was neat as only an old woman with energy and spare time could make it; her kitchen-ware hung on a board behind the stove—each piece with its particularly fashioned hook, so constructed, Sheridan guessed, by the man who had been her husband. A small

91

breeze scoured the room and the apples made a bland, spicy odor around him. There was a picture on the wall, a Rock of Ages picture; and in a corner sat a worn rocker with a table beside it. The table held a lamp with a flowered chimney, a spectacle case and a man's pipe—these things laid out as if ready for use. Mrs. Colson's voice cried out cheerfully to somebody else down the meadow, "Now, then, I wondered if you'd come for the eggs. I can't bear to see 'em wasted. Oh, you didn't need to bring back that cloth. It's such an old cloth. There's a man here who wants—" She came into the room again with a woman following her. Sheridan, rising, felt a comfortable surprise come over him, and he smiled at this second woman and watched her sudden, intent glance cover him.

"I'm glad to see you," he said.

Katherine Morvain said: "Why you're here," and in her voice was a little girl's wondering melody.

She was thinner than he remembered her but around her eyes and mouth was the same driven-in composure he had so immediately noticed at the first meeting. Summer freckles still lay at the base of her nose, and her body had its straightness, its hardened roundness. She had almost smiled, and in that break he caught her off guard and for a moment saw the liveliness inside.

"Have you done well?" she asked.

"Good enough."

"Where is the tall man who was so sick and the pretty girl?"

"They're in Portland."

"She was nice."

Mrs. Colson stood aside, listening; her glance went back and forth, eager to read what was to be read, and wanting—as an elderly woman would want—to make as much of this as could be made, to speculate on it, to warm herself over it. Sheridan said: "It was the shipwreck off the coast, Mrs. Colson. The first house we came to was the Morvains'."

"My stars," said Mrs. Colson, "it's such a small world." She was intensely interested but even then her lively thoughts ran back and forth to other things. She moved to the doorway and stepped on a solitary ant crawling in. She came back. "Young man, you'd better stay overnight. Katherine, bring your people over to supper."

"That's trouble."

92

"I didn't say it wasn't. But doing nothing comes hard for one that's been lifelong busy. The Lord's got. His plans and maybe I did something that made Him leave me without Colson—though I do declare I don't know what it could have been. I hate bein' old. It's just waiting to die and sometimes it don't seem decent. We'll have beef—that quarter Obermeier gave me. We'll have new corn and peas. You come early and make that peach dumpling."

Sheridan went down the valley to see Obermeier, who turned out to be a sawyer. He climbed a ridge and found three houses in a pocketed meadow; these were the Clancys, three brothers, their wives and their pack of children living in a primitiveness that plainly suited them—in houses built like sheds, the outer walls holding tacked-up hides for drying, the doors mounted with deer antlers. The forest was around them, only a step away—and it was the forest which kept them where they were. The Clancys were long, dark and lazy men; they were men hard to know—secretive and self-sufficient, and silent toward him until they felt the weight of his words and were satisfied with what he was. They took time to consider his proposal that they work for him. They weren't eager for work; they had meat enough walking around the hills and the potatoes were waiting in the garden rows. They saw themselves through the winter without starving. They owed nobody and they had no itch for anything. They were satisfied. He put up his proposition and he let it go, adding no argument, knowing argument would only stiffen them. They were all stretched out in the sun, soaking up its comfort. It was the older of the brothers who seemed to make the decision for the three of them.

"Well—women might need some stuff at the store this winter. Little money might help. Guess we can work. Nothing else in the road."

It was like a concession grudgingly made. Sheridan said: "I'll talk to you again tomorrow," and left the Clancys. When he reached the crest of the hill—just before it dipped down into the valley—he stopped to watch the sun drop behind the western forest. There was, he thought, at least eighty miles of that forest between this point and the sea, trackless, lost in its own immense solitude; a great wild chunk of land through which probably no white man had gone; an enormous reservoir

93

of lumber without end. He felt good about it and his ambition lifted and he let himself think ahead farther than he usually did. This was a chance other men hadn't seen yet—this forest with its larger mills, and a railroad someday coming in; this was one of those original chances the first comers had missed. Or rather, the first comers were too early for it; maybe even he was too early for it, but meanwhile he was on the ground and he could work it small until the thing got big.

He returned to Mrs. Colson's and found the Morvains there. Morvain sat on the porch, comfortable and self-assured. He was heartily glad to see Sheridan and made a considerable racket of his greeting; "By God, if it ain't the man we saved. Well, we moved, you see. Ought to've done it a year before and I guess I would of done it too, except I hated to leave the neighbors. They'll have a hell of a time gettin' a deputy to do all the work I did free. People don't appreciate things like that until it's too late."

The two older boys, also on the porch, regarded him as they had before—with their narrow, faraway indifference; the small boy was out in the yard, walking a circle with his head down. He went into the house and discovered Katherine working up supper with Mrs. Colson. The smallest of the Morvains—the ten-year-old Suzie, sat on a chair chopping slaw in a wooden bowl. She recognized Sheridan immediately and gave him a broad smile. There was also a man sitting in the corner rocking chair—a man going robustly into old age, large of frame, yet spare-fleshed and with a remarkably smooth face dominated by a pair of large gray eyes.

"This," said Mrs. Colson, "is the Reverend—Hosea Crawford. What was your name, young man?"

"Sheridan."

Hosea Crawford gave Sheridan a practical and positive countryman's grip; his voice had a Yankee twang. "I don't know you, friend. New?"

"I'm running the mill at Murdock's. May run this one, if Mrs. Colson agrees."

"Murdock's?" said Hosea Crawford, as though he had recalled something he should not have forgotten. "I've got to get down there. The boys are gone, I recall. The girl—is she married?"

"No."

"She should be married," said Hosea, "I don't like to see marriageable girls wasted."

94

Mrs. Colson announced supper. The Morvain men came in with alacrity. The minister took the head of the table and, when everybody was assembled, he asked grace. There was no spurious supplication in the words; he spoke as though the Lord were within close listening range and as one with whom he worked on some sort of a familiar partnership basis. The brevity of the prayer indicated that he knew the exact balance between hunger and piety.

"Now," said Mrs. Colson, "this makes me feel a lot better. A full table's a wonderful thing. Ain't it a nice thing you happened in at the supper hour?"

"Amanda," said Hosea Crawford, "it was no accident. I came to the forks of the road at Bidwell's. I asked myself, Which fork do I take—left or right? I was needed in both places—but it came to me the need was equal, and when the need is equal, I always take the road where I'll find the best cook."

Katherine sat beside Sheridan, rising to fill the platters again, to pour the coffee, to bring on the peach dumpling. The silence was on her—the deep silence which seemed to Sheridan to cover repressed pride. She listened to the minister and she listened to Amanda Colson, but when her father talked—as he did often and with all the assurance of a man of learning and substance—her face grew slightly strained.

"You talked to the Clancys?" asked Mrs. Colson.

"They'll work," said Sheridan. "So will Obermeier. I need a few more."

"Well," said Mrs. Colson, "there they are," and nodded at Morvain and his two older sons.

"The mill?" asked Morvain. "Well, I don't know. I want to look over this country pretty well. I thought of going into Forest Grove and talking to the sheriff. I hear there's no deputy down this way."

"Deputy?" asked Mrs. Colson, and blew the notion out of the room with her tart observation. "We don't need a deputy any more than we need a cat with two tails."

"Well," said Morvain, "things happen—"

"Nothing happens," said Mrs. Colson decisively. "And it don't take a man with a star to fix it, if it does. I can shoot, and so can everybody else. Such a silly notion. We never had a deputy." Then she corrected herself and added thoughtfully, "Oh, yes we did once. Conover."

"Poor soul," said the minister.

"Well," said Mrs. Colson, "I don't know. He was fool

enough to interfere with somebody's else's business—instead of minding his own." It was sharply intended, but she cut the edge of it by seeming to be preoccupied with the things on the table. "Have some more meat, Reverend. Conover didn't have sense enough to run his own life, so he naturally wanted to run others'. Katherine, there's more cream in the pantry."

Mrs. Colson, it was clear, had made up her mind to do some missionary work on the Morvain men, but Sheridan had some doubt that Morvain got the point; he was pretty well insulated by his egotism.

As soon as supper was done the two older Morvain boys vanished into the darkness—wild hounds on some scent of their own. The preacher took to the easy chair, both hands laced across his full stomach. Sheridan and Morvain lighted their pipes; the young Morvain boy sat behind the stove and the women went at the dishes. Morvain got on a long story of his past years, making out of it a pointless sort of drama involving himself.

"Farming's the only thing," he concluded. "It ain't right that a man should work all his life for another man. If I ever find the right piece of land, I'll show some of these people what good farming's like."

The minister regarded him with a sleepy, steady interest. "Son," he said, "a piece of land is what a man does with it."

"You ever worked stump land?" asked Morvain with a trace of defensiveness.

"I have worked the stump lands of this life for forty-seven years," said the minister.

"I've thought of bees," said Morvain. "They don't require much labor. All you got to do is make boxes and see they don't swarm. One hive turns into four hives in a couple years. There's a lot of possibility in bees. Four hives makes twenty, and twenty makes eighty. It just goes on. I've thought a lot about bees."

The women, finished with the dishes, removed their aprons and joined the group. Mrs. Colson brought a rocker from her bedroom and settled herself in it, and sighed and was very happy. "I do enjoy company. A lot of people together always seem to make things go. A person alone just stands still."

"Why," said the minister in his easy way, "we were not meant to be alone. Out of the Ark the animals came, two by two, not one by one. This life is a chain of hands; and in heaven it is a company. Many men admire themselves as strong and able to stand alone against the world. But those are the men who live with their arms lifted against their fellows. They die in fear, and nothing remains behind them." He said it in such an easy, cheerful, disarming manner.

"It was best," said Mrs. Colson, "in the wagon train." She dropped an explanatory side remark to Katherine. "That was in 'forty-six. We were closer then than we ever were again. I do remember how much fun it was until the cholera came along. I guess we had a feeling we were all bound for the same thing. We've grown away from each other a lot since that day." She was silent, quite puzzled by the thought; she was trying to find a reason for it. "Well," she said, "maybe it was a little time when we had brotherood, and then we lost it. It's mighty easy to lose."

The minister got up. "Amanda," he said, "we're always getting it and we're always losing it. There would be no business for me if it wasn't that way. Now then, I'll ride on."

He put on an overcoat green with age and a formless hat which had suffered many rains, and he gave them the cheerful nod and turned from the house. Morvain went away, taking his meal for granted and giving no thanks for it, and the children slipped into the night. Katherine remained a moment. "It was a trouble for you," she said.

"A trouble I can endure," said Mrs. Colson. "You speak to your men."

"Yes," said Katherine. When she left the house, Sheridan walked with her over a meadow whose warm dry stubble exhaled so sweet a fragrance. The moon was hidden, the dark shadows seemed to break from the condensed blackness of the mountain and flow out upon its clearing. The Morvain house lights made a yellow beam before them; the crickets sang through the earth's massive stillness.

She said: "Do you want my brothers and my father to work for you?"

"Yes," he said, "if Mrs. Colson takes my offer."

Katherine walked on a distance before answering. "She will," she said.

"Have you been well?"

"Oh yes. I'm always well."

"It must have been a long trip inland."

"There wasn't much of a road."

She seemed not at ease with him, nor was he at ease. She offered him no opening; she used none of that idle talk by which a woman broke a road for a man. He felt again as he had so often before, some resolution or sore humiliation which would not let her be free. It seemed to him that she had her mind on other things even as she walked with him. He admired her; he had a great respect for her strength and for her silence which covered so much.

"You're doing well. You work very hard."

"I try to," he said. "I don't see any other way."

"No," she said, "I don't suppose there is any other way. It's nice to see things grow—to look out on something of your own and watch it get bigger."

She stopped before her house. He said, "How did you happen to stop here?"

"Somebody moved away. We're renting it, on shares."

"Well, you're out of the other place. That wasn't any good."

"There's a school here—that's important. We've got a second cow. We picked it up on the way over. The man who owned it was tired of taking care of it. He was foolish—he didn't realize how bad it is not to have anything. He'll learn, though."

The light of the house was behind her. Her face was shadowed and her voice had a subdued sadness in it; it had a tone like no other tone he could remember. She had fallen silent and seemed to be listening into the night. She turned her head and he caught the expression of her face as the light touched it—the unguarded naturalness which she didn't realize he could see. It surprised him to notice how much prettier she was when she dropped her reserve; her mouth was long and full and her face had a dreaming glow on it. It was the first time he had thought of her as an attractive woman, and the first time her presence physically touched him. She made a short turn to him, said, "Good night," and swung into the house.

He went back to Mrs. Colson's and found her rocking herself on the porch. She said, "Young man, you take that room off the kitchen," and her rocker made a squealing rhythm back and forth on the porch boards. "It's a lovely night. I smell smoke in the air. There's a fire somewhere in the forest. Won't be long till winter. I just sit here and wait for it. Then I'll wait for spring, so I can

98

set out my onions. Then I'll wait for canning season, and then it's time to wait for winter. A person's always waiting for something, till one day there's no more waiting. That's a good thing—the end of waiting, I mean. The older you get, the wearier it is to wait. Young man, I have had my answer. It came right sharp. You may start the mill."

"All right," said Sheridan.

"And Morvain and those two wild boys will work in it too," said Mrs. Colson.

Sheridan asked a question that had been on his mind during the evening. "You have children, Mrs. Colson?"

"I had four. They died when cholera came to the trail, in 'forty-six. All of them would have had their own children by now."

Chapter — 8

KATHERINE found her father and older brothers in the kitchen; there had been some talk between them. The boys watched her with an uneasy stubbornness and her father's manner was restless.

"That Colson woman's all right," he said, "but her tongue's too loose. Her husband must of been weak. Gave her too much freedom to say things that shouldn't be said."

She looked around the kitchen and her face took on its blank, stiff expression; she had the three of them to fight. "The neighbors are talking about us," she said.

"What talk?"

"Suzie and Elgin go to school with clothes full of patches. I guess they think we're shiftless."

"By God," said Morvain, irritably, "let them tend to their own affairs."

"When it starts raining," said Katherine, "they'll have no coats. They'll be the only ones without coats."

Morvain sat with his arms across his thighs; he looked down at his hands, his careless face clouded. It was, at that moment, a child's sulky face. "I can't do everything," he said. "They're not complaining. They'll get along all right."

"I need a crock to put up sauerkraut," she said. She looked around the room, at the stove, at the walls, at the floor. "If a neighborhood woman came in here she'd go back and tell all the neighbors we had nothing. She'd say the menfolk wouldn't work."

"We just got here," said Morvain. "It takes time to get started. I'm looking around. I'll see the sheriff this week. That deputy job pays something."

"I want a new stove to cook on," said Katherine. "I want dishes. I want a good buggy. I want things I can show the neighbors without being ashamed." She looked at her father directly. "I think he's going to open the mill.

I want you to take those jobs before somebody else gets them."

"A mill hand," said Morvain. "No, I won't be turned into a work ox."

"I want the three of you to get those jobs."

She saw her brothers exchange glances. They looked at their father, waiting for him to talk. This is what they had discussed before she came home. "No, Katherine," he said, "I won't do it."

"We've been eating off meat and potatoes Mrs. Colson gave us," she said. "It's charity. If you're so proud about common work, you're too proud for charity, aren't you?"

"We'll pay back," he said.

"I want you to go get those jobs," she said.

"Katherine," he said, "I'm a little old to be wrestling lumber twelve hours a day."

"Colson did it at sixty. You've got to work. The boys have got to work. If you make me ashamed before the neighbors I'll take Suzie and Elgin and go away. I'll show the neighbors you won't support the family. They'll laugh at you and you won't be able to stay here at all." She had worked herself into anger; her voice grew flat and tight. She did it deliberately, knowing that neither her father nor her brothers had any defense against this kind of quarreling. They hated her for what she was doing; she saw that in their eyes but she knew she could make them work. "You're not good for anything but hunting. I don't want people to find that out. I won't have it. I won't cook for men that won't work. Get your own meals, go beg your own food. I won't beg for you. If you're so proud, I'll go to Forest Grove and hire out in somebody's house. You go ahead and be proud. I'm proud too—but I'm not proud of three men living off other people. I don't want you to see the sheriff about a deputy's job. If you do, I'll go tell him you won't support your family. I'll—"

Morvain sprang up from his chair and shouted: "All right—all right, for God's sake, Katherine. If we got to work, we'll work. I don't know why you're so excited. We always got along."

"No, we didn't. We always lived off things the neighbors gave us."

"I did work enough for my neighbors," he retorted. "I always helped them."

"They laughed at you," she said, cruel because she had

to be. "They laughed at you because they could do you, and you didn't know it."

He gave her a surprised, terrible stare, for this was a thought that never had come to him. He had pride; he had enormous vanity, and his imagination was quick enough to catch the thing she said and make a picture of it, so that he could actually see his neighbors laughing at him. It was the one thing which could break him—this laughter; it was the one thing to crumble the egotism with which he surrounded himself. And, once broken, there was no other covering for him. He turned to the door, a poorer man in his own mind than he had been before. She had stripped him of his illusion and now he was what, in some deep recess of his mind, he may have always known he was. She had brought him face to face with himself.

He turned to the door. He put a hand on the casing and stared into the darkness, hating her as the boys hated her. He said: "All right, Katherine. You'd break a man to get your way."

"Will the boys work too?"

He looked back at the boys a moment. "If I can stand it, they can."

"Go see Sheridan in the morning," she said. "Before somebody else comes to him."

"All right," he said.

She was not through. She said: "If you work all winter, we'll have enough to do something. It will be the first time. All winter. I'll keep the money."

He had his back to her. He listened and said nothing. She said: "All winter?"

He swung and gave her a strange, strained stare. "My God, have you got no respect for any of us, or any trust in us?"

She drove home her last blow; all her long silence had gone into this and all her bitterness had stiffened her to it. "I want to be proud again. I won't live without it—the way Mother did."

He said in the quietest voice: "Your mother was contented with what she had. She never belittled us."

"She died a worn-out, brokenhearted woman."

He stared at the floor and his face was pulled together in a way that made it weak and small. "All right, Katherine, you needn't make it any worse. We'll work through the winter—if the mill runs." Then he said: "I'll sleep in the barn tonight." He was that low of spirit, but even so he made a little drama out of his hurt feelings.

She gave him no comfort; she wanted to destroy all of that self-delusion.

"You'll find it comfortable there," she said. "It's better than any house we've had for years." She watched him go; she watched the two boys slip away, anxious to be out of her sight. She said to Suzie and Elgin, both of whom had listened in shocked fascination to all of this, "Time for bed," and sent them into the spare room. Then she sat down at the table, facing the lamp; she turned the lamp lower, thinking of the kerosene it was burning away. She realized at once that this was a miserly gesture which had grown so strong within her that it had destroyed much of her normal pleasantness. Sheridan, she thought, saw her as an ill-favored woman and she rehearsed what he had said to her, and what she had said to him, and felt she had made a poor impression.

She was sickened by the scene she had created, but it had been long in her mind—and none of it was carelessly said. For, remembering back to her childhood, she recalled each move they had made, and each inevitable drop in possessions and she looked ahead with her frightened clarity and saw the family sink into ruin. Her mother had fought against it until, old and calloused, she had actually been glad to die.

Nothing could be much worse than it was, and nothing could make it better unless she destroyed her father's careless childlike egotism. She had weighed that very carefully against the future of Suzie and Elgin and the two older boys. Suzie and Elgin still had a chance. The two older boys had lost their school years, but she could hope to teach them to work.

Mrs. Colson would let Sheridan have the mill. Mrs. Colson, privately, had told her so. They would have three jobs at four dollars a day. There was seventy-two dollars a week, all winter long; it was more money than she had ever seen; it was a fortune, it was like opening a gate and going into a new world. She had a good, greedy feeling about it, a sudden covetous impatience born of the poorness which had been theirs for so long, and a kind of scheming delight in thinking of what the money would do for them. But with the delight was also a foreboding fear that this luxury, so near to them now, might suddenly disappear before they touched it. There was a stream of bad luck and missed chances and things done too late which carried poor people along toward the usual miserable end. This was the greatest of her fears and she had to turn her mind from it because she couldn't bear to look at the future. In the morning of course she would be stronger and then could weigh luck against failure. She had to think about it, since nobody else in the family would. The whole grinding weight of it was on her, and sometimes the weight was too much. Now she truly understood her mother's position.

For a moment she let herself think of her father, and felt sorry for him; it was nothing more than pity, actually, and not a deep pity. If his pride had to be destroyed in order that the rest of them might survive, it didn't matter too much. She got a looking glass and propped it on the table, and found a comb and brush; and as the one personal pleasure of the day she spent half an hour dressing and braiding her hair. She had to wake the older boys and her father early, so they could see Sheridan before somebody else saw him; and she had to be nicer to the boys so that they wouldn't take it in their heads to run away on their own. She had to keep them long enough to get money ahead. It was Suzie and Elgin she thought about most.

Chapter—9

IT was for Hosea Crawford a lovely night in which to be riding—a night with heaven coming down upon him and the feeling most strong within him that he was in close and private communication with his God. These were the roads he knew so well; and all the shapes and odors and sounds of night were familiar—the little rasping of small insects in the grass, the strong smell of fern and stubbled meadow, the sound of a belled cow riding gently across the distance, the occasional house light shining in the distant darkness—always reminding him of a soul glowing. Nothing so pleased him as to come upon a house, as the Colson house, and to sit awhile in the center of a group, listening to the common gossip, the rude humor and the old witches' tales in new form; to hear the cheerful rise and fall of people's voices, to catch from them the sound of weariness and comfort common to all, to bear witness to their moods, their inconsistencies, their strengths—to slyly observe the flash of sin in the face of beauty, to see the ancient by-play between a girl and a man, to enter into the vinegar mellowness of some old soul whose day was about done and who could afford to be natural.

The dust of the earth was his element and perfection was not much of a concern with him. People were human and they had work to do—most of it rough work; and in the dust and the sweat and the confusion of this work it was understandable that commandments would be broken. For all this Hosea Crawford had tolerance, and reserved the full thunder of this wrath for the weak who were mean rather than for the strong who erred.

He reproved himself for having displayed some vanity during the evening. It was a good thing to know, of course, that the fires of Adam had not burned out in him, yet it was scarcely fitting that he should have had a small twinge of envy at the sight of Sheridan walking out through the night with the girl. It actually was envy. Now, then, he had had his own young years and what more could he ask? "I do not take age with enough grace," he thought. "I must be more humble."

Then, as he always did on solitary journeys, he brought up a problem to discuss with himself, and the problem this night concerned Liza Murdock who ought to be married. She was ready for a man and she hadn't found him. He knew he ought to talk to her, but he realized it would do no good to speak of the difference between carnal and spiritual love to a woman who wanted love of any kind. There she was, ready. Who was he to judge her when she, pushed by the same force which broke the bark of a tree, found no one man she wanted, or who wanted her? That force would not stand still; as a young minister he once thought it would, but since that day he had married too many couples who had, as he well knew, made their marriage bed in the brush a little early. Those couples had done well as a rule; mostly they had turned into rather solemn parents, sometimes even a bit too sedate for his personal liking. Liza might come out that way. Then again she might not. As an old man whose own fires were so tamed that virtue was easy to come by, what could he say to her?

Maybe he ought to threaten her with hell-fire, but he at once rejected the notion. That was good enough for the high-flying revivalists who scared the wits out of a community and moved on, leaving to the regular pastors the job of bringing the flock back from the brush and briars into which they had bolted. No doubt she had sinned on more than one occasion, but she wasn't a bad girl. Married early she'd have been a mother, a church member, and would have supplied her chicken and salad at bazaars. She would still be the same Liza she was now, except for the license and the blessing.

He thought then of Sheridan living in the Murdock house and—knowing both Liza and the ways of single men—he clucked his tongue and felt a more immediate concern. Liza was not the kind of girl for Sheridan, not at all, yet it was the sorrow of things that Liza might, by a casual bedding down with this young man, commit him in honor to marriage. There was another problem in morals to trouble him. Was Sheridan morally bound to marry her in such event and suffer a bad mating? Or should he, having taken the delights of Liza, turn from her to Katherine? As a man of religion he had no choice;

106

but as a man of the world he did have a strong opinion on the subject. He evaded his wordly opinion, but it returned until he found it necessary to face it or be dishonest. "Well," he said to himself, "her lushness will fade and she'll be nothing but a drag to him, and he will hate her soon enough. That's as great a sin—indeed it is." He was distressed by the triumph of worldliness within him and grew irritable. "What's he doing in that house, exposed to the girl? Why doesn't he get out of there?" It was but a momentary flash of bad humor; jogging along at a comfortable pace, he speculated on Sheridan's resistance to Liza and concluded it would be rather a hard tussle. No doubt the devil was there and perhaps he ought to throw a private prayer around Sheridan to give him strength. His theology, he concluded, was not as sound and simple as it had been in younger years; what he saw was a young woman ready and a young man lean and restless as a hound, and these was nature in it as much as the devil. "Well," said he aloud, "God grant him fortitude," and so went peacefully through the night and at last rode late into Forest Grove and arrived home. He ate his bread and milk, gave his wife the gleanings of gossip, and went to bed and fell at once into sound sleep.

Chapter — 10

ON Friday, having spent three days to put the Colson mill into operation, Sheridan reached Forest Grove and made another deal with the printer for leaflets advertising lumber for sale at Colson's. Turning toward Murdock's he spent some time reviewing the venture he had entered. It was a riskier thing, of course, than the guaranteed certainty of the Murdock venture; he had given Mrs. Colson a hundred dollars and he had, the moment the mill opened, committed himself to a weekly pay roll. There would be a month's gap between expenses and income, to be covered from his own pocket. Some of his money from Murdock's would have to go into the Colson mill for a short period; but he had made up his mind that he would not make a practice of using one venture to carry another. Each one had to stand on its own feet and, if any venture began to fail, it was a better thing to drop it than to drag other ventures into it. He meant to take other risks where he found them. With Oregon only twenty years old, there were bound to be little things starting which would survive and become great things. Since no man was intelligent enough to forecast these, it became something of a matter of percentage; a man with one business had a certain chance whereas a man with ten pieces of business had ten times the opportunity to hit upon one which would flourish.

Riding down the road, Sheridan realized that he had noticed no stages along the way. There ought to be need of one between Forest Grove and Portland and perhaps this was something to consider. The thought of Portland suddenly made him remember Clara Dale and business went out of his head at that point. She walked in and out of his thoughts more and more, and she stayed longer when she came, and he realized that he was lonely for her, and that he had all this while been trying to make up his mind about her. She was easier than a good woman ought to be—and that was the thing he had tried to solve. Sometimes he had answered it by saying that they had been through too much to be like any other man and woman in courtship; they had missed the slow stages of getting acquainted. And sometimes he had answered his doubt by telling himself that she was a warmth-loving woman living in a world whose rules were set up by the cold-blooded. The argument went back and forth in his mind, but she was nearer and nearer him no matter how the argument went. She stood before him with a longing for closeness which was almost a promise in her eyes, which seemed to be telling him he would never doubt again when he took her.

He got home late in the afternoon and checked the mill-cut. He ate his supper, more than usually restless. A crankiness began to build up within him and he walked the roundabout roads of the valley for two hours or more to wear it off, and came home and went to bed. On Saturday he followed the small valley to its narrow head and came to a slatternly ranch cut out of the timber. There was a man here, a Crabtree, who had a horse and saddle for sale; and Crabtree had sons, one of whom watched Sheridan with a close and hostile attention. That, Sheridan thought, would be one of Liza's men, suspicious of any other man. He spent an hour dickering for the horse and saddle and rode away with his purchase. Bogart appeared that afternoon with the pay roll and went away soon, controlled by a close-mouthed bad humor.

He sat on the porch after supper and watched darkness flow along the hills, and was still restless. He knew he ought to be pleased with his luck, but his luck was a drink of water that didn't quench his thirst. There was something else—there was always something else.

He bent forward in his chair, hands over his knees. There was an answer, a form, a meaning, a feeling which once gotten would make a pattern for his life and give his days a meaning. He was sure of it and he was near to it. He sat still, like a man with a gun crouched motionless in the brush watching the shadow of a deer move inward through the starlight, not yet outlined but almost outlined; and so strong was the illusion that he tried to keep his mind still to receive the thing coming, but his mind could not be still; it made some false motion of its own and the answer which had been so close faded away. He reached for it and his thoughts strained too hard and there was nothing in front of him; even the sense of its nearness disappeared. He leaned back in the chair and struck his palm across one thigh. He got up with a tremendous disappointment and walked immediately to the barn to saddle his horse. He wanted Clara. He had made up his mind. It was after midnight when he reached town and too late to go to her house; he put up at the Pioneer, had a drink and went to bed.

Waking, he found he had slept well into Sunday morning, so late that the town's church bells were ringing. He called for a mug and a razor, and shaved. He crossed to the White House to eat the heavy breakfast which was necessary to him, oatmeal and ham and eggs and quartered potatoes fried brown and two cups of coffee. He left the restaurant with his cigar and walked through Sunday dullness; streaks of eagerness played through him when he thought of Clara—the strange fits and starts of excitement, of uncertainty, of diffidence which slowed him and sudden lusty impulses pushing him on. He turned through her gate in this frame of mind and rapped on the door.

Revelwood opened it—Revelwood dressed but without his coat. A half-surprised expression ruffled his face and disappeared; he got Sheridan's arm and pulled him in. "We've had breakfast," he said, "but there's coffee left."

Clara sat at the table, and when he failed to find the smile she always had for him, it occurred to him that he was something like an uninvited guest. It embarrassed him but it also irritated him. "George," he said, "is it safe for you to be taking your meals here? That's more gossip for Mrs. Bogart."

"It's safe," said Revelwood. "Sit down there." He went into the kitchen and came back with an extra cup and saucer.

That was a touch of freedom on Revelwood's part, Sheridan thought. He sat down. "I've had breakfast."

"Well," Clara said, "have coffee," and poured for him.

Revelwood took a chair at the table; he sat loosely on it, one arm carelessly hooked over the chair's back. He continued solemn.

Clara said, "When did you come in?"

"Last night late."

"You're thinner," she said, and he felt the strong personal force of her eyes. But it lasted only a moment. She looked at the table, engaged in side thoughts of her own, and her fingers idly touched the dishes and silverware, moving these things about. The silence went on a

110

considerable time without the freedom it should have had. Presently she lifted her head and glanced at Revelwood. He rose immediately.

"I'm going down to the hotel for some cigars. I'll be back in half an hour." He left the room without his hat.

"Nice of him to go," said Sheridan. "I want to talk to you."

She looked down at the table. "Did you come in just for that?"

"I wish I'd done it the other night."

"Oh, Mark," she murmured, and rose from the table, turning across the room. She faced the window, her back to him and her hands folded across her breasts. "Why?" she said. "Why—now?"

"Remember, I said I wanted to talk to you—the other night?"

"That was last week," she said.

"What's a week's difference?"

She didn't answer him. He got up, a coolness rolling through him. He said, "Turn around and tell me."

She turned around. She said, "If you wanted to say it, why didn't you say it then?"

"I don't know."

"I do," she said. "You were afraid. You couldn't make up your mind about me. You had to think it over."

"I have," he said.

"That was a week ago."

"What's the difference?" he asked.

"I'm married now. George and I. Last Thursday."

He turned back to the table and lifted his coffee cup and put it down. He said, "Why didn't the son-of-a-bitch stay here and face me?" He turned back to her. She came across the room toward him and put her arms on his shoulders. He stepped back from her, pushing her arms aside.

"He didn't want to see you when I told you the news."

"That's fine—that's a show of kindness."

"He didn't want to see it. Really he didn't."

"I made a mistake," he said. "I thought I saw interest in you. I didn't get it right."

"You got it right. You knew I was. In the cabin. On the boat. Here last week. You knew."

"But a week was too long. George used his time well. Would you have had me, last week?"

111

"Oh, yes." She searched his face for comprehension that wasn't there. "But when you didn't stay last week— when you went away, I knew it wouldn't do. George didn't change me. I changed myself."

He said, "I don't make anything out of that."

She shrugged her shoulders. "You weren't sure. You think you are now, I suppose. But—you're lonely, you've been working hard, you haven't seen a woman."

"I didn't come here that way."

She made a little gesture, and put her arms around him again. She waited for him and it seemed to him he saw everything there that had been there before, and when he kissed her, he thought he felt the same willingness. He drew back and watched the changes go over her face. "Why didn't you stay, then?" she said, and put her head against his chest, and was crying. "No, never mind. It wouldn't have mattered." It shocked him to realize that even now she was unhappy.

He said: "Do you know what you want?"

"Does anybody? Does anybody get what they want? There's no such thing. But I know that I can't help turning to you for help."

He put her away and walked over the room. He said: "What the hell did you marry him for?"

"Because," she said. "Because he's like me."

This one thing was the blind spot through which he could not see. She lifted her head to show him that willing intimacy which seemed to put him above other men. He turned for his hat, but she came over to him and touched his arm. "George will want to talk with you. Stay and have dinner. I'll have Jennie cook a good one."

"That won't do."

"It's no good for you to walk away and not come back. There's just the three of us and that mustn't change. Don't hate George. It's not his fault. And don't hate me, Mark. I can't have it. Where would I turn?"

"To George," he said. "That's where you ought to turn."

"How could I? I'm stronger than he is—I told you that before. If you don't come back, I'll come after you."

"With a husband on your hands?"

She shrugged her shoulders. "We were almost dead once and you kept me alive and I made you warm—and that's something marriage doesn't mean."

He said: "Have you ever said anything like that to George?"

"No."

"Never do it. Nothing could cut a man worse."

"I don't need to tell him. He understands. We both know what we have and haven't got."

He went back to something he had said earlier. "It was the week. The week was too long for you."

"No," she said, "we're not going the same way. That's what I realized—that's what the week did."

He turned to the door and opened it. Her voice came to him in a sharper way. "It can't be any worse for you than it is for me."

He left the room and walked down the street. He hadn't been in the house long, less than half an hour. The church bells were ringing again and people were moving toward church. The town air was thick with town smells and the day was dry and sultry. He went along Oak Street in the direction of the Pioneer, but he remembered that George might hunt him up, and he didn't want to see George, so he turned to Front and stepped into a saloon. He got his bottle and his glass and drank a pair straight and laid his weight against the bar. He tried to make something out of the scene he had gone through but he couldn't. Only one thing occurred to him. Clara and he were like two people who had been divorced; there was something between them still.

Chapter — 11

MARK was back at the ranch in time for supper and found a dozen armed neighborhood men in the yard. The Shottler family, living over the ridge in the next small valley, had moved in with the Murdocks for the night. The Shottlers were man, wife and one daughter around seventeen—she a pale girl with intense, round eyes and a homely mouth.

"It's the wild man," explained Murdock.

Kerby seemed to be the head of the armed group. Kerby said: "We'll keep two on guard here all night. Meet here in the morning and we'll get on his trail. Shouldn't be no trouble about that."

"It's the wild man," Murdock repeated to Sheridan.

They were unsure of what it was and they smelled danger in it and the glitter of hunting was in their eyes. The women were frightened—or at least Mrs. Murdock and the Shottler women were. They believed in the wild man's terror; it was a werewolf memory springing up from a very old place. "I won't sleep," said Mrs. Murdock. "Two's not enough to stay here and watch."

"I'll be here too," said Murdock. "So'll Sheridan. That's four. By God, he ain't bigger than four of us."

"I don't know. He don't make any noise. That's the wolf part of him sneakin' along. Lily said he didn't make a sound. Lily said he had a monstrous face—that's what I always told you, Murdock. She said his mouth was split wide and his teeth were terrible things. That's what I always said but you said no, such a thing couldn't be."

Murdock turned to Sheridan. "Lily here"—pointing to the big-eyed Shottler girl—"was walkin' out back of her place this afternoon. In the timber. Well, she didn't show up and her folks got worried and went after her. They heard her screamin'. She came out of the timber damn near dead for scared. It was the monster thing, or whatever it is. She was walkin' along a trail when it jumped out of the brush in front of her." He stopped and he scowled and he looked at the girl. "What'd it do, Lily?"

Lily Shottler wore a vacant, sly expression and her tone was the tone of a child going over memory work. "It had claws. Maybe it was a man. Maybe it was an animal, I don't know. It jumped at me and that's when I screamed and ran back. I heard Pa hollering, and so did the monster. It turned back into the brush."

"Whud its face look like, Lily?" asked Murdock in his mildly curious way.

"Like a man's, I guess. But not like a man's either. I don't know. I was terrible scared. I didn't see well."

"There, Murdock," said Mrs. Murdock. "Now you believe me."

"Well, by God," said Kerby, "we'll track it down in the morning. Ira, you stay with me here tonight."

The rest of the crowd wandered away into the twilight, homeward bound. Mrs. Murdock went into her kitchen to put the meal on the table, Mrs. Shottler following. Sheridan observed Liza Murdock on the porch. She stood with a shoulder slouched against the two-by-four post and she shared none of the fright of the two older women. She had her eyes on Lily Shottler and her expression was disbelieving. Lily caught Liza's glance but quickly avoided it. Mrs. Murdock shouted out of the kitchen. "Come in—come in. I got the meal on the table and I don't intend it should get cold while you talk nothin' out there all night."

"It's a funny thing," said Murdock in his idle way. "It's only women that see him. Seems he's smart enough to stay away from men, don't it?" He grinned at Sheridan, and he gave Lily an up-and-down look and turned into the house.

After the meal Sheridan walked through the shadows with his cigar, toward the mill. He moved around the lumber piles, scaling the cut with his eyes; the smell of the drying lumber—the heavy odor of sap drawn out by the warm day and warm night—was an unseen fog around him, a pleasant thing in his nostrils. The earth was dry, the air brittle, and the smell of smoke lay about him. From the log deck he had a view of the hills far across the valley and saw the corrosive-yellow glow of a timber fire. Behind him was the scuff of light feet traveling; he turned and saw Liza coming on. She stopped in front of him, close to him. She said: "I know why you don't take me to town. You've got a woman there."

"No."

"Then you're afraid of me."

"No."

"Then you don't like me."

"Yes," he said, "I like you."

She stood silent, brooding over his answers. "You've got a woman there," she decided. "Is she prettier than I am?"

He put his hand on her arm. Her body stirred at his touch and she lifted her head until he saw the dim flashing of her eyes in the twilight. He turned her about, saying, "Let's walk back." She dropped her head and walked silently with him.

The neighborhood men were in the yard at seven next morning. Kerby got them together and made his speech. "We'll cut up the logging road to the timber. Then we'll spread out and beat the brush. First man to sight tracks, let him yip. Lily said she saw this thing back on that old trail. We'll edge that way—but nobody go beyond it and get the trail all chewed up." He looked at Sheridan. "If you're goin', where's your gun?"

"You've got guns enough," said Sheridan.

They went over the short meadow, with Mrs. Murdock's half-screamed advice following Murdock, "Don't you get lost from the rest of 'em. Don't you do it." They scrambled up the rough hill, around the pitch-frosted stumps, through salal and vine maple and fireweed; they came to the logging road on the ridge and followed it, grouped together and full of talk.

"Too goddamned much noise," said Kerby. "Shut up—shut up."

When the logging road reached the solid timber, Kerby threw his arms out to either side, signaling for the crowd to spread, and the brush began to rattle and crack as men surged into it. Sheridan walked behind Kerby. Murdock, his breath hauling wind hard in and out, was behind Sheridan as they pursued the soft trail through the shadows. Kerby had his head down to read a sign. "There's Lily's feet and the old man's comin' after her—Shottler, I mean." Two hundred yards beyond, the hill having reached a level stretch, Kerby stopped. "That another set of tracks? Shoes? This creature wears shoes? He went rummaging into the brush, slapping it aside with his impatient arms; he halted and bent down. "Here," he said. "He must've

116

slept here, or waited here. Ground's got a sort of beaten look."

The other men came in and gathered around the beaten spot. Sheridan watched the little flickers of expression around mouth and nose, the keening and the quickening of their appetites. Murdock stood aside, tired from the climb and showing no great amount of interest, but there was a young man in this party—young Crabtree who had watched Sheridan with such close hostility during the purchase of the horse—who came to the beaten spot and watched others as they studied it.

Kerby went rummaging forward; he cut aside in the brush and he worked his way through it, and cursed at the vines. He came back, not satisfied. "We'll go toward Deer Creek Canyon. Spread out again. Yip if you see anything."

They left the beaten spot—all but the Crabtree boy. He stayed a moment longer, stooped over to read the ground. Then he rose full up, looked about him sharply, and trotted away.

Kerby walked through this with a spring-kneed speed. The other men were foraying through the trees, leaving the echoes of their travel behind them, calling back and forth. Murdock heaved out a painful observation. "By God, if anybody starts shootin', somebody's goin' to get killed. I'm gettin' old. It just came to me."

There was no more trail. Sheridan followed Kerby into a sunless reach of timber, over deadfalls, under the slanted archway of trees half fallen and lodged, through a dense patch of huckleberry higher than his head. Here and there daylight broke through as a single shaft of light in which dust turbulently boiled. They broke out into a knobby clearing made by some long-ago fire. Over to the left, a quarter mile or less, a shot faintly echoed, and was soon followed by a shot which rolled back in delayed, bouncing echoes.

"There," said Kerby, and clawed forward through the brush.

"That's mighty queer," said Murdock.

There was a second shot in that direction, and the underbrush crackled in a more lively way as men rushed toward a common center—downhill—through a swampy ravine's bottom, up another hill, over its summit to a breakaway edge. Everybody rushed this way and came panting in. Below them was a fire-swept flat cluttered with dead logs, and beyond was another hill. A third shot broke the clear morning quiet and suddenly Kerby pointed. "There he is."

On the face of that hillside, dark and small and wiggling, a man moved upward over the rough slope. Rifles came up at once to begin a potluck firing.

"How the hell you know it's him?" asked Murdock.

Kerby jumped in great stiff-legged surges down the slope, leading the crowd. Sheridan found himself fighting through the matchstick tangle of the logs in the flats, dropping farther and farther behind, and noticing that Murdock was considerably to his rear. He got to the foot of the slope about the time the guns began to shoot again somewhere at the top of the ridge. He dug in with his feet, pulling himself up the stiff pitch. He was stung on the hand by a wasp. Dust boiled up from the powder-dry earth and sweat began to roll down his face. The guns were still going off, one bullet screaming as it struck some small obstacle and went on.

Reaching the crest of the ridge he noticed the crowd in a semicircle slightly ahead. When he got up with the group, he saw the dense timber confronting them. They were shooting into this without much sense but, looking carefully into that darkness, he saw the edge of a body, or the motion of a hand behind a huge fir trunk, this marking the target at which they were all firing. Chips of bark sprang out from the tree as the bullets tore into it; the target disappeared behind the shelter of the trunk.

Kerby said, in a loud voice, "Jen—you start edgin' off to the left and I'll go the other way. We'll flank that goddamned tree. The rest of you don't move—and don't shoot at anything except that tree."

He hadn't gone more than ten feet when the human target behind the tree, no doubt hearing the strategy which was to uncover him, made a sudden rush away from the tree, angling deeper into the forest. Half a dozen guns cracked around Sheridan. He blinked his eyes at the sound of them, and for an instant lost sight of the victim. Then he saw the man, standing still with one hand propped against another tree. He had been hit and stopped. He could stand but he couldn't move. Another round of shots reached him and tore into him and fluttered him and shook him like a puppet; his arm slid from the tree and he dropped down.

Kerby said, "Careful now. Walk up slow." He pointed his gun at the fallen figure and he stepped on with flat-

118

footed care, approaching as he would have approached a buck he wasn't certain was dead. He stopped a few feet away and he waited; the others came behind, making a half ring around the body.

Kerby said, "I think the bastard's dead."

"Well," said somebody, "put another in him and he'll be damned dead."

"Naw," said Kerby and stepped on to touch the body with his foot. It gave to pressure, without flinching or reacting; then Kerby reached down, caught a shoulder and heaved the figure over on its back. He stared at it and stood up; he turned to the men around him with an off-guard expression on his face, an expression which might have been chagrin or sudden doubt. "Why, by God, it's a man."

It was indeed a man; a small man of around five feet four, with not much meat on his bones and weighing certainly no more than a hundred and thirty pounds. It wasn't possible to tell his age, for he wore a black, untrimmed beard which left nothing visible except a small nose, a button of a mouth and a pair of eyes which seemed hollowed out by either hunger or fright. He was a man, and nothing else at all; a small man who had turned fugitive or hermit. The bullets had all hit him in the middle body; his coat was black-speckled with the shot which had torn through him; and blood gently swelled through the holes.

Murdock was the last to come up, so winded he couldn't speak. He put a hand on Sheridan's shoulder to have his own look.

"Anybody know him?" asked Kerby.

Nobody said anything.

"Well," said Kerby, "that's the last women he'll scare." He looked around him as he said it; he said it without too much conviction, with defensiveness in his words. He met Sheridan's glance. "That's right, ain't it?" he asked. "I mean, you can't have something like that loose." Then he turned from Sheridan and said in his more natural way. "Well, we've got to get him out of here. That's goin' to be a hell of a job. A man on each leg and a man grab each arm."

Sheridan turned back without waiting for the rest, and made his way homeward. Murdock had also turned back and from the distant rear hallooed at him. "Wait for me, Sheridan." Sheridan disregarded the call and went on. It was late in the morning when he got to the Murdocks'. The women had heard the shooting and were all in the yard waiting for him.

Mrs. Murdock said: "What happened?"

"They got him," said Sheridan, watching Lily Shottler.

"What kind of a monster was he?" said Mrs. Murdock.

"Just a man. Pretty small—pretty thin."

"Then it's not the right one," said Mrs. Murdock. "They got the wrong one."

"No," said Murdock. "I guess they got the one you thought was a monster."

Lily Shottler said: "He had big teeth, didn't he?"

"No."

"They looked big to me!" Then she asked a quicker question. "Is he dead—did he yell or say anything?"

"Not a thing," said Sheridan.

"No," said Mrs. Murdock, "they couldn't of got the right one. The sheriff came by just a while ago. He started up there."

Liza watched Lily Shottler closely. The Shottler girl gave each one around her a quick glance and turned away. "I'm going home," she said and walked away.

It was another hour before the main party came into sight on the hill and straggled down its side, one group of four swinging the dead man between them, sometimes holding him up by his legs and arms, sometimes letting him slide. They dropped him in the road and stepped back, and all the group stood by. Another man presently showed on the crest of the hill—the sheriff on horseback— and let himself down. He called out: "You got him?"

"That's him," said Kerby.

The sheriff came up to the body. He bent in the saddle and took one short glance; he lifted his head. "You're sure he's the one?"

"Nobody else out there in them woods," said Kerby, his voice stiffening.

"Where's his claws, where's his wolf face, where's his fangs?" said the sheriff, quite softly.

"Well, hell, that was woman's talk," said Kerby. "But he must of been dangerous, hunting around for women like he was."

"His name," said the sheriff, "is Eb Price. He was a loony fellow with no harm in him. Ate nuts and raw wheat and didn't wear any shirt. Couple of years ago he

120

disappeared from Forest Grove. Just wanted to live alone. There's your wild man."

Nobody said anything. The sheriff ran a hand across his face and shook his head. He stood in great thought, looking from man to man. "Maybe you damned fools will learn there ain't any monsters in Oregon. You've all fired your guns—and from the looks of him I'd say you all hit him. That could go hard. There ain't an open season on men in this county."

Kerby said, "By God, he might of killed some woman sooner or later."

The sheriff let out a long breath. He said wearily, "I suppose that's the verdict that'll come out of this." He nodded at one of the men. "You go get your wagon. We'll take the body into Forest Grove."

"Why me more than anybody else?" asked the man.

The sheriff let all of his accumulated exasperation go into an enraged shout, "Because I said so," and stared at the man until the latter turned away. He remained silent until the wagon came up and the body was put aboard— his silence lashing the crowd with its effect; and still in silence he followed the wagon away.

The neighboring men had little to say; and one by one they broke from the group and moved homeward. Sheridan noticed that young Crabtree had left the party earlier.

Chapter — 12

THERE were no extra guests for supper, as Murdock pointed out. "I like neighbors," he said, "but then again I don't like a lot of people foolin' around. Well, Emmy, get the damned dishes done and we'll go."

Both women moved about the table to clear it and to take care of the dishes. Murdock sat waiting in his chair. As a sudden afterthought he mentioned the trip to Sheridan. "Emmy and I have got to see Brother Will the other side of Hillsboro. We'll be back sometime tomorrow. Liza can cook your breakfast." He changed the subject at once with his innocent mildness. "I got a bad taste from this day's business. He was such a little bugger. Nobody's to blame, I suppose. That's the funny side of it. Most bad things come up that way, nobody meanin' to do what they do, but gettin' snarled up and doin' it. Things—" He waved his hands around, seeking to give form to his thoughts and unable to do so. "Maybe if I had some sort of an education I'd know about this. I'm a dumb beast and so are my neighbors."

"You won't get a better answer from the educated," said Sheridan.

"Why," said Murdock, "there's an answer for these things, ain't they? Somebody knows, don't they?"

"I doubt it."

"Oh, no," said Murdock. "Somebody knows. Somebody's got to. It would be a hell of a world if there wasn't an answer to these things."

"Well," said Sheridan, "it is a hell of a world, isn't it?"

"That's for me to think," said Murdock. "That's for me —an old man knowin' nothin' and of no consequence at all. But it ain't for you to think. You're smart and if you don't think better than I think, it's a terrible waste of something." He got up and walked into the yard and presently Sheridan heard him drive up with the team. Mrs. Murdock scurried about the house with her last-minute confusions. "I want a jar of that honey to take, and a quarter of venison. Murdock, what'd you do with your nightshirt?"

"Damned if I know. Foot of the bed, maybe. Didn't you make the bed today?"

"I was so nervous," said Mrs. Murdock, running in and out of the bedroom. She put various things into a carpet-bag; she made extra trips back and forth to the wagon. Standing in the shadows of the porch, Sheridan watched them drive away. He went back to the porch and sat down, listening to the voices of the Murdocks ride the silent night, softer and softer. Murdock had a lighted lantern hanging from the end of the reach; it swung back and forth, yellowly glittering in the darkness. He heard no more sound—as though Mrs. Murdock were crying.

She was crying. She leaned up against Murdock and let the gusty wind stutter in and out of her. Murdock had to brace himself against her pressure. "Oh, for God's sakes," he said, with his mixture of kindness and irritation, "shut up."

"She ain't got anything, Murdock. Nobody comes out this way—not the young men. She ought to go to church down at the corner. She'd meet men there—but she won't do it. She don't seem to like the boys up in the hill."

"Well, she stays out with 'em."

"It don't mean nothin'."

"The hell it don't," said Murdock. "I ain't that much of a fool."

"Oh, that," said Mrs. Murdock, carelessly. "She's young and she's got to have her runnin' around—but she don't like them well enough to marry 'em."

"By God, she'd better like somebody well enough pretty soon."

"Well, it's Sheridan. She's got her mind on him. It'll work, too."

"Maybe," said Murdock.

"Don't you fool yourself. He knows when she's around. He's got blood in him."

"It don't necessarily mean marriage."

"With him it might. I want my baby happy, Murdock. Other girls are happy. Why can't she be? God, I don't understand it sometimes. We was happiest when we were younger and they were small. That was the good time."

"I kind of wonder about girls," said Murdock. "Do they all get men the same way? Ain't there another way to

123

do it? These Portland girls—do they got to let a man come in first before they get the man?"

"It's the same everywhere," said Mrs. Murdock.

They rode along in silence, Mrs. Murdock's emotional crisis subsiding to an occasional snuffling. She had relieved herself and become more cheerful. "I've seen him look at her. She'll turn him. That would be a fine thing for her, Murdock. He'll amount to something."

"Maybe," said Murdock. "Kind of tough on girls, I guess. Sometimes I think I didn't do enough. Maybe if I'd gone to work in Portland, years ago, we'd all be better off. Nobody knows about those things. Maybe the boys would of stayed around, too. Wish they'd write once in a while. Can't blame 'em for going. I went when I was young. But it's sort of hard not to know where they are. Maybe we'll never know. I guess we've got to say we've had our time with them, but the time's over. Seems like it might be different, but I suppose that's nature. I'd like to know though—if they're alive or dead."

She said with her sudden heavy-handed affection, "There's us, Murdock. That don't change."

"I guess it's the only thing," said Murdock mildly. "Well, I wish Liza well. I hope she does it. If she don't do it, I hope it don't trouble her too much. Kind of a cruel thing, when you stop to think of it. I mean the things people want and don't get. Must be an answer to that. I swear I don't know what it is, but there must be an answer. It can't be all blind, like it seems to be."

"Why, Murdock," said Mrs. Murdock. "You sound discouraged. Don't you get discouraged. I can't stand it."

Sheridan watched the wagon light dip and die in the distance, and heard the last sound of the wagon come over the distance like a spent ball barely reaching its target. The tremendously heavy stillness of the night crushed down on him, the bulky hill shadows squatted beneath the starlight, the small stirrings and sibilances rustled around him in grass and thicket. Liza had finished the dishes. He heard her steps go around the kitchen and stop. He listened for them to start up again, he knocked out his pipe and refilled it, and he sat back in the rocker.

She came out to the porch and stood at the break of the steps, turned away from him. She said: "That wasn't a wild man. Lily was up there with Clyde Crabtree. This man saw them and ran away. Clyde tried to catch him but

124

couldn't. Then Shottler hollered for Lily, and Lily was afraid the man would tell. So she screamed and made out that the man tried to attack her. Clyde got out of sight. Old Man Shottler didn't believe it was a wild man, either. He knew it was Lily and Clyde. That's been going on a long while."

In this summer-dry air the spice scent of dead-ripe grasses and pollen-heavy flowers grew stronger; and the smoke of forest fires touched the night with its disorder. The stillness was heavy on him, the shadow masses pushed in, and a rank, sweet wildness flowed down from the timber. She turned about to watch him; he saw her face in the house light's glow—the tension and the looseness alternately on it, the uncertainty and the boldness. Even in the shabby dress she was pretty.

"You do a lot of thinking."

"About the mill, I guess."

"Oh, that," she said. "What good's that?"

"Good for making money to live on," he said.

"No, you're not thinking about that. You're cranky. That's not from a mill."

"Maybe it's the little fellow I've got my mind on."

She said: "He's dead. Why think of him?"

"It was a cruel, dirty thing."

"Sure," she said. "But you can't make anybody better. They'll always be like they are—they'll lie for themselves and they'll cheat if it helps, and they'll do just what they please. You're not sad about it, are you? It doesn't matter. Think about yourself. They wouldn't think about you if you were dead. They wouldn't help you—they wouldn't care. You think Lily cares? She'll see Clyde again. Nobody cares about anybody. We've got to care for ourselves. We've got to take what we can. Who'll do it for us?" She stepped nearer and silently watched him.

He said, "Maybe."

A streak of triumph lightly ran over her face. The uncertainty left her and the awkward discontent left her. "A mill or people or money—what's that? It's not bad to think of your own self, to want a lot—or maybe just to want a little. I hate time going so fast. I don't want to lose what's good. People have got to think about that. It's awful easy to lose."

She waited for him to answer and, when he didn't, she gave her head a little toss and made a slow turn around him and walked into the house. He heard her go on to her room and close the door. He stirred in the chair and knocked the ashes from his pipe and filled it and smoked it through. The stars were silver-scattered clusters of shining, so enormously far away, so cold, so vacant of meaning. The earth around him held the smell of fall's decay. The sky was only unfilled space and death occurred among the obscure creatures around him in a thousand unknown unimportant ways.

He rose and went into the house. His lamp was on the kitchen table, lighted for him by Liza; he took it and went on to his room. He closed his own door and put the lamp on his table and sat on the edge of the bed to remove his shoes, but he straightened and reached for his pipe and had it filled when he saw his door opening. Liza stepped through, her bare feet making no sound. She closed the door and swayed back until her shoulders touched it; she put her hands behind her, the cotton dress lying like a thin bit of goods carelessly thrown around her.

She said: "I closed the front door."

He got up and reached around her to catch the knob of the door and open it and push her out. His hand slid along her waist; she swayed against his arm and flattened her back against the knob to block him. She stared at him with her lips parted, her face flushed and her eyes set knowing on him. He tried to push her aside but she got her arm around him and laid her weight against him and put her mouth toward his mouth; he swung his head but her mouth kept searching and sliding across his face. He hauled her from the door. She fought him silently and with an extraordinary muscular strength; she wrestled with him and turned him each time he started for the door. Her breath was hot and—prompted by a volatile rush of anger—she hit him across the cheek. He lifted her up and slammed her into the wall.

Resistance went out of her and she hung to him with her arms around his neck, a dead weight on him. She was trembling, she was out of breath. He stood still and as soon as his anger went away, he was greatly ashamed of himself for his treatment of her. She moved her head from side to side, rubbing it against his chest, and presently she met his glance and he saw that the unpleasant stubbornness had quite gone. What remained was a warm loneliness that reminded him of Clara. He had destroyed her confidence and he had brought her back to a kind of nothingness he hated to see. She was a human being with

126

no support, and when he realized it, his whole thought of her changed.

"Liza," he said.

She had been watching him and she had sensed the change. She waited a moment longer to be sure; then, prompted by the in-pull of his arm, she lifted her arms with a gesture of confidence—with a wonderful prettiness coming over her—and she put herself against him.

Chapter —13

THE fall season moved on with no rain. The dust of the roads was thinnest powder, the cut fields lay a darker yellow, and the dying ferns against the fence rails were brittle to the touch. Fire smoke stained the sky and the sun dropped over the western hills with a blood glow; moonlight was richest yellow, casting strange shadows upon the land. It was unseasonable. The earth waited for the due rains, the grasses needed it for growth, the hills slowly became tinder boxes for want of it; this Oregon land, living on the fatness of moisture, turned lean and infallow and cranky; and the roundabout people, accustomed to a soft air, were made irritable. The cycle was delayed, the rhythm disturbed. By night, here and there in the hills, the core of fires plainly showed.

Immigrant wagons began to roll along the country roads, having left Kansas and Missouri in April—the spent wave of greater migrations of early years. These newcomers camped wherever night found them and were a trouble to the settlers, now long in the country, who forgot the days when they, too, had sought for land and had camped where night found them. There was occasional thievery, and the talk was that the day of the unlocked door and the hospitable table was ended. Natives, satisfied with what they had, wished the country to be left as it was. There were people enough here now. More people would only spoil a comfortable way of life.

News came to the valley, passing from mouth to mouth, and made little ripples of disturbance and died away. The blacksmiths of Forest Grove fired their anvils at the news of Appomattox. The Navigation Company dropped handbills through the country, announcing its new palatial steamboats on the Columbia. Letters came back from the Idaho and Montana mines, written by Oregon men who had gone there for fortune; and some women, reading such letters carefully, began to understand that their husbands did not intend to return. There were infidelities in

128

the valley. Over by Iron Mountain a man murdered his wife and three children and the story grew into a comfortable horror tale for the lengthening evenings. A woman, coming to Forest Grove to speak on women's rights, found herself without lodging or means of travel. Apples hung fat and yellow on late trees; the cornstalks stood bare and the hunters ranged the hills for winter meat. One hunter accidentally killed another, but the gossip swelled again across the valley and a woman was mentioned. Hosea Crawford rode his rounds and preached his sermons, and ate his chicken dinners, and reassured the weak and found his pleasures in sitting by night in house kitchens, hearing the stories which never grew stale. Behind him lay the lengthening record of his travel, in weddings performed and prayers for the dead and baptism, and advice, and then listening privately to repentance; and sometimes he felt young and sometimes old, and he wrestled with his own conscience and had his doubts as other men did, and dispelled them with faith mixed according to his own recipe.

Somewhere in the world great things happened and great men died; but these events were far-away rumors which scarcely touched the valley. The boundaries of Oregon were the boundaries of the necessary world; what happened beyond those lines was of no importance. Somewhere the heathen sweltered and occasionally the Methodist or Baptist ladies, at the behest of their missionary societies, packed round barrels with cast-off clothes and sent them away, and were made happy by that act of practical goodness. But such places were on the under side of the earth, and what happened there could never happen in this valley. Let kings thunder and foreign artillery roll; it was all beyond the oceans. This land was untouched and untouchable. There was but one thing of common importance here at the moment; it was time for the rains to come and the earth to freshen. It was time for winter, for the lights to shine out on the gray afternoons, for houses to be close and warm; for this time had all the year's work been performed, the apples packed away in the barn, the crocks of meat and kraut put down, the vegetables layered between their straw and earth in the garden corner, the corn dried and milled, the flour sacked in the pantry, the barn lofts crowded. It was past time for the rains and for winter; people yearned for the time to come, so that they might feel the fatness and the comfort of their preparation for it.

Sheridan was in Portland only once during that time, and deliberately avoided Clara and Revelwood. His errand was to get from the postmaster some advice on the securing of a mail contract between the Portland and the Tualatin settlements. In Forest Grove he had found a man—Cray Jennings—willing to set up a stage line with him on shares; three experimental trips with a converted mud wagon had demonstrated the possibility of some profit, but a mail contract was the backbone needed for any stage line. On the strength of the postmaster's advice, Sheridan wrote Senator Nesmith in Washington, soliciting the Senator's aid.

He traveled south, out through Newberg and other little towns lying quiet and self-sufficient in the rich flatlands and between the low-rolling hills. Each such town had begun with some accident of situation. A ferry crossing had been the birth of one, or a grist mill, or a farmer doing a blacksmith's trade in his barn, or the crossing of two roads, or a church or a school, or the presence of some strong personality who had drawn other settlers toward him. However begun, each became the trade center and the social core of the roundabout district—to which people came to have their wheat milled, to buy or trade or swap at the general store, to visit the barber, the doctor, to meet the traveling dentist—to break the loneliness of the farm itself; and since the roads of this country were poor and money was a scarce thing and needs were not great, men seldom ventured farther than their neighboring town. Each town was the hub of the world.

These were the roads Sheridan traveled with his horse in the late dusty fall, across meadows dotted by groves of oak and fir and gray farmhouse groupings, over the soft folding of the dull green hills and through the sweet-smelling dampness of timbered stretches. All roads were bordered by the angular-marching rail-fence lines banked by fern and brush and dead grass, and out of these coverts game birds sailed low away at the sound of his horse's feet. By night he put up at whatever house was near and sat in the warm twilight and smoked his pipe and heard the neighborhood stories, and slept in one or another small spare room whose thin walls brought to him the murmuring and stirring of its people; and in early morning he rode through the strong, fresh smell of the earth and saw the faint glittering on the meadow grasses before sunrise, and heard the strident crowing of roosters from afar. Wherever he went, the stilled peace of the land lay upon him; nowhere was the voice of man or the machines of man great enough to break that overriding calm. By night the lights of a house shone lonely in the darkness; by day these houses sat as isolated strongholds under the sky.

Coming along the banks of the Willamette one day he saw a meadow surrounded by heavy stands of cedar, and an empty house and a shingle mill close by the edge of the river. There was a steamboat landing here, made no doubt for the mill, but the mill was idle and apparently had not been recently operated. From the nearest neighbors, a mile away, he learned that the owner of the land and mill had gone insane; there was a lawyer in Oregon City who knew something about it. Swinging homeward, he went by way of Oregon City—for the first time seeing the river drop forty feet over the great barrier of rock here—and had a visit with the lawyer, and took a new route homeward. Smoke came down the valley from a fire burning somewhere in the deep timber. Mrs. Murdock was nervous. Next day, passing along the Tualatin, he noticed the dark haze of smoke in the sky, and caught the sharper odor of fire. Suddenly, so low was the humidity, a dozen new fires had started in the hills. He put up at Mrs. Colson's and went over to the Morvains' for supper.

There was a fire in the ravine back of the mill, three or four miles away. "Some hunter set that one when he camped," said Morvain.

The youngest of the Morvain boys was not at the table; he lay on a cot in the next room. Going in to talk to him, Sheridan found him flushed and restless; there was a dull anxiety around his eyes. "What's wrong, Elgin?"

"Don't feel good."

"Where?"

"In my stomach!"

"You been eating too many apples?"

Katherine came in from the kitchen to stand by the bed. "No," she said, "he hasn't eaten anything for two days." She reached down and put her hand against Elgin's cheek and drew back. She smiled at Elgin, a sharp false streak against the soberness of her cheeks.

They ate in the lamplight. There was less brag in Morvain than formerly; he had been happier in his hours of vanity. The two boys, having eaten, went into the yard. Morvain followed them when he was done. Katherine put Suzie to her lessons and Sheridan helped with the dishes.

"Your dad talked of moving lately?"

"We won't move as long as the mill's running."

He said: "Don't buy here. Don't put your money in land—not for a while."

"Why?"

"This is the high end of the valley. The best land's farther down. Once in a while I see a bargain. When I locate something good, I'll tell you about it."

She said nothing. He gave her a side glance and went on wiping dishes, pipe clenched between his teeth. He had noticed before that she was thinner, and noticed it again around her face. The work of keeping a family of six people together kept her going early and late. She would hold up this family with her pride as long as her pride lasted; when that broke, she would break with it. She had the same dress she had worn when he first saw her and he guessed that she had saved most of the money the family had taken in. Standing by her he was conscious of her preoccupation, of the troubles and plans and swift ideas running through her.

Yet she seemed happier and when she looked at him, she smiled; it made a remarkable change on her face, lightening her and turning her younger. She could not be more than twenty-four or twenty-five, he guessed; and she was, without the dead seriousness, quite gracefully companionable. They finished the dishes and he stood in the kitchen with his pipe while she did the last chores, the putting away of things, the floor sweeping, the countless little movements and counter movements of house cleaning. She removed her apron and stood a moment to think of what had been done and what was to be done tomorrow; she spent a long moment at such thoughts and put them aside and looked at him. Her hair was a hard black; her lips relaxed and she gave him an attention unhurried by other things.

He said: "Good night for walking."

She seemed pleased at his thinking of her, and minutely self-conscious of it. Her hand went up to her hair and swiftly touched its edges as she left the house. They moved along the road which pointed toward the mill and turned left in the direction of the main county road.

She said: "Elgin worries me. Three days is a long time."

"Don't worry."

"Too many things have happened to my family for me to ever be easy about anything. I'm sure my mother often prayed that things would come out right. I used to see her stand silent and look through the window. I know she was praying then, but nothing ever came of her prayers—nothing I can remember—and when she got older I seldom noticed her do this. I think finally she wanted nothing so much as to die and to rest. I don't believe when she died she had faith in anything."

She walked beside him through the darkness, her head tipped toward the ground. She was lost in things past and the lightness had gone out of her. She murmured, "Each of us, I think, has just so much strength, and one ounce more is too much to bear. After that, nothing's ever right again."

He said: "This is a lovely night."

She looked up quickly. "I shouldn't be thinking such things, should I? Not when we're doing so well. Maybe people draw good or bad luck to themselves by thinking about it. But that can't be true, either, for my father's always thought of himself as growing suddenly rich. None of it's happened to him. It can't be that, can it?"

"Some of it must be," he said. "How else do you explain people—some doing well and some doing bad?"

"Oh," she said, "mostly thinking of one thing and working hard for it. Energy. The one thing I fear more than any other thing in my brothers is shiftlessness. Sometimes I think it must be in the blood, or not in the blood." She looked at him and shook her head. "I shouldn't talk to you like this. I've never done it before, to anybody. But I don't mind your knowing. It's a relief to say it to somebody."

She was in a mood to relieve herself of so many hard things long held within her. The bland, warm, smoke-acrid night had broken the reserve between them. She trusted him and drew close to him. He said: "You've got faith in something."

"It's not faith. It's a hatred of what we've been. I won't have it. I won't stay poor and shiftless. I won't see Suzie and the boys grow up without anything. I won't see them knocked about because they're ignorant. Bob and Harry are almost too old for school—it makes me sick to think of it, but they are. But they can learn trades—they can

133

be useful, Suzie and Elgin are still young enough and I mean for them to amount to something. I'd lie, cheat and steal for that. I'd do anything. There's just one thing I admire—strength enough to do what you want to do."

"Well," he said, "you've got that."

"I have now. My mother had it, too, when she was young. Then it got too much for her and she broke. That's what I dread—getting old and breaking."

"The worst of it's over," he said.

"I hope so. We're doing so well. Yet I lie awake nights wondering what will go wrong—because something's always gone wrong."

"You'll make things come your way."

She walked on with her busy silence, and stumbled on the dark road and caught his arm. The moment she righted herself she dropped her hand. "I want to go back to see my mother's grave. Do you think that would be such a foolish spending of money? I asked the neighbors to keep the brush cut down around it, but I know they'll not bother."

"It wouldn't be foolish," he said.

"I've turned too hard—I know it. My father hates me for what I've done to him. Bob and Harry don't like the way I make them work. Maybe they'll understand some day, but it's not good to know they don't now."

"I understand," he said.

"What a wonderful thing," she said with a wistful note in her voice, "it is to have people understand. You do. Mrs. Colson does. How terrible it would be if nobody did."

"Nobody was meant to live alone—to be cut off from everybody else."

"I wish I had more faith."

"It's a beautiful night, Katherine."

"You're calm. You always know what you want to do."

"No," he said. "I don't."

She turned her head toward him. "I never thought you'd ever have any doubt about anything. You'll be rich, you'll have a lovely wife. You'll live in Portland in a big house. That's the way I think of you. Whatever could make you doubt?"

"Most of the time," he said, "I work right along. Then there'll be times when I go down into some kind of a cave. Maybe my faith runs out too."

"Why should it? You're free. You can do whatever you please."

He touched her and stopped her. "Look up there," he said, pointing to the black sky with its stars faintly glittering. "What's a sawmill or a million dollars? What's scheming and sweating and dickering? What if all that turns out well for me? What have I got?"

"Why," she said, "that's only—" She quit on it and stood still, trying to see his face in the blackness. "That's only being alone." She swung back toward the house with him. "What ever happened to the girl who came ashore with you?"

"She married the man you met—Revelwood."

"Had they known each other long?"

"No. They met on the ship."

Her voice contained its tentative, cautious interest. "Had you known her long?"

"No. Same thing. Met her on the boat."

"She seemed nice," said Katherine, and waited for an answer.

The night filled with a sharper and sharper odor of smoke. Flakes of ashes drifted down from fires back in the timber, and a glow came out of the canyon behind the mill. "That's new," he said, pointing to it. Other red pillars rose across the valley in farther hills. Katherine stumbled again in the ruts; Sheridan took her hand and held it as they walked forward.

He said: "What's for you—not the family, but for you?"

Unexpectedly the question touched her humor and he heard her softly laughing to herself in the darkness. "I'm the same as a widow with four children. My prospects aren't good. Mark, it does help me to know you're not always certain. It always helps for the weak to know that even the strong can be weak, too."

"My God, Katherine, you're not weak. You're the strongest woman I ever hope to know."

She stopped dead and turned to him with a pleased expression. "That was so nice for you to say." She went on, still permitting him to hold her hand. He had warmed her so much that he felt it sweep out from her as a quick current of happiness; even her footsteps were lighter in the dust. She had forgotten her troubles for this short while. "That fire's bigger. There's been hunters in there all week. How do you stop a fire that big?"

"Sometimes a back fire. Sometimes a dirt trench. Some-

135

times you get out of the way and hope it dies. A good wind could whip it up and burn the whole country out."

"Have you been working hard?"

"I've traveled around a good deal."

"Another mill, or something?"

"If I find one, yes."

"It's energy," she said. "That's the big difference. Do you want to be rich?"

"I suppose so."

"I would. It would be comfortable."

"I guess I do. But I don't know why."

"Oh, that's simple," she said. "Because you're alive. You've got to go on, you've got to do all you can with your life. You've got to show yourself why you're here."

He said: "Makes it seem pretty good."

Her laughter lightly touched him and her hand stirred within his hand and her fingers resettled themselves against his palm. The fire was, he judged, five miles up the canyon, the glow of it spreading wider and wider against the sky. Turning by Colson's they walked in silence toward the Morvain house which sat in the jaws of the canyon; and here he felt the strong heat flow out of the hills. They stopped near the door.

"That thing's growing," he said. "If a wind comes up—"

She watched him with her smiling, permitting him to see the edge of her emotions as she had not done before.

Just as he took her by the shoulders, out of the house came Elgin's voice with its alarm: "Katherine."

She drew a breath, she grew tight, she swung away. "Mark," she said, "I'm afraid," and ran into the house.

Sheridan waited in the darkness, hoping she would return. A hardening heat swept down the canyon and the glow westward was bright enough to outline the ragged tops of the trees. That fire had gathered force by it own suction, a greater stream of air stoking the flames. He had not thought of it as a threat to him, but now he did, remembering the closeness of the mill and these houses. He continued to wait with his quiet impatience. He heard her voice in the house, and Elgin's, and her voice again. At the end of a quarter hour he realized she wouldn't come out; that little moment was gone. Turning, he walked to Mrs. Colson's and went to bed.

He woke with the feeling of oppression on him. An unnatural light came through his window, bright enough to show him the walls and the furniture clearly. He rose

136

and dressed and walked into the yard, finding Mrs. Colson there.

"It's going to be the year of big fire," she said. "That's the way the Indians remembered their years. Old people like me do the same thing. The wind's coming this way."

The Morvain house stood fully shaped beyond the mill. The Morvains had risen and were in the yard, their voices quietly riding over the distance; and neighbors were coming along the main valley road toward this spot. For the first time he saw the open flame of the fire in the canyon. Rolling chunks of smoke moved upward from the forest and broke apart to show the lean streaks of flame were creeping out from it, and burning fragments, borne on by eddies of heat, dropped in other places to start flash fires. A tree half a mile from the canyon suddenly broke into a sparkling brightness and became a solid wedge of flame. For the first time he began to hear the fire—the snapping and exploding of brush, the down-crash of weakened trees, the low and humming roar of air sucked in. A northwest wind had risen to drive it.

Mrs. Colson's chickens had gotten off the roost to peck along the yard. The Morvain men were walking forward, and the Clancys arrived with their wagon. They had detoured to pick up the nearby men of the valley. Obermeier, Sheridan's sawyer, was with them, and Lane Pickett, and three other men Sheridan didn't know.

One of the Clancys said, "I rustled up some shovels and axes. She's a boomer. She'll run like hell with the wind and she'll come right down here."

Mrs. Colson said, "We ain't that close to the trees, Jack. It won't come over the meadow grass."

Sheridan shook his head. "I've seen it happen in Michigan." He looked at Jack Clancy. "We'll have to make a try. There's that creek which cuts down the left side of the canyon. That'll make a line to stand on. We ought to plow six or seven strips across the upper end of this meadow. Can you rustle up any more men?"

Clancy said, "I'll ride down to Spring settlement and pick up everybody on the way." He turned back to the wagon and drove away.

"We'll hitch Mrs. Colson's team to the wagon and carry the plow up there." He looked at Morvain, "How's Elgin?"

"Oh, he'll get over whut's ailing him," said Morvain.

They hitched the wagon, threw in the plow and extra tools and took the road into the canyon. Not more than a quarter mile from the mill both the road and the meadow bumped against the brushy edge of the mountains. They threw off the plow and hooked on the team, Obermeier handling the reins. "Three or four dead furrows straight across ought to stop the fire creeping into the stubble. The wind will carry stray stuff and set the stubble going. So we need a cross furrow at a couple places on the meadow to check it. That's the easiest part of this. Up there"—pointing to the timber and brush of the hills—"is where we've got trouble."

Sheridan stood with his face toward the dense, flame-shot balls of smoke rising from the main fire—two miles onward more or less, he guessed. It had traveled three miles since evening and it would travel faster, now that it had gotten a running start. Breakers of heat and ashes struck him and the air grew rank with the cloying odor of those burning mountains. He watched Obermeier walk away, spraddle-legged between the plow handles. The ground came up under the plowshare in dusty chunks.

"We need wet blankets," said Morvain.

"As good as a match in hell," said Sheridan, and swung back around to consider the fire. Obermeier, having plowed two furrows, turned the team over to the oldest Morvain boy. The better thing, Sheridan thought, would be to make a stand farther up in the hills; waiting for the fire to come this far was waiting too long.

"Is there any break up in that timber?"

Bert Clancy said, "There's an old burn about a mile in."

"How wide is it?"

"Half a mile or so."

"We might stop it there, if the wind doesn't jump it across. There's not that much wind now."

Obermeier said, thoughtfully, "Might be, later."

"Might be," agreed Sheridan.

Obermeier shook his head. The eldest Morvain boy ran two furrows across the meadow and was spelled off by his younger brother. Another team and wagon came along the road from the mill, men riding in it and men walking beside it. A few others followed on saddle horses. Jack Clancy had fifteen men with him, and shovels and brush hooks and axes. These joined the group and stood around, staring up the canyon.

Sheridan said, "If we wait until the fire gets this far we'll be too late."

Obermeier, the oldest and the most cautious of the group, expressed his doubt. "That's all right so long as the fire's in front of us. But if she jumps over our heads, we're surrounded."

"That's right," said Sheridan.

"I don't like the looks of it," said Obermeier.

Each man studied it and each man made his own private judgment. Nobody said anything until Jack Clancy spoke up.

"Well, it depends on the wind. The fires in the crown now, but not bad. This ain't no time for a heavy northwest wind. It's a freak. It may die out."

"Maybe it will—maybe it won't," said Obermeier.

"That's right," agreed Jack Clancy. "Maybe it won't."

They were undecided. They stood still, self-wrapped in speculation while heat poured down the canyon and buffeted them with its invisible waves. The smell of the air was rank, scorched and woody; the lungs got tired of it and the nostrils were stung by it. Sheridan waited until he saw nobody was disposed to speak up; then he walked to the wagon and got a brush hook. "I'm going in," he said.

Jack Clancy swung at once, his own rough restlessness touched. "Well, to hell with it. Let's go."

The crowd broke and men walked to the wagon to pull out the tools. The younger of the Morvain boys came up from his plowing. There were eight furrows across the meadow, and if eight furrows weren't enough, nothing was enough. Sheridan said to the boy, "Unhitch and let the horses go."

Obermeier still remained in his tracks, undecided. Sheridan said, "If you think you shouldn't, don't do it," and turned to the wagon to get his shovel. He thought Obermeier had decided against it, but when he started up the trail he looked behind and saw the old man in line.

The sides of the ravine came closely down, crowding the trail against a small creek, and the massive first-growth firs towered above them, their branches interlaced to hide the sky. A wind played around them, hot and acrid. The party went silently on single file, one man coughing as he climbed and one man cursing as he slipped on the smooth stones of the creek.

The trail led up to a small bench, crossed this flattened spot, climbed a ridge and made a sightless turning ahead. Sheridan followed it, feeling the scarcity of good air. He was sweating and drifting ashes struck the sweat and made a thin coat of slime on his face. Turning a bend he saw a great hard glow of light down the narrow vista and he presently came out of the trees to face the ragged clearing made by an older burn. He stopped here, the other men coming up around him with their heavier breathing. They could go no farther. The fire was before them, great solid flashes intermittently leaping through the deep black rolls of smoke.

Sheridan said: "If it stays this way, I think we can block it here. It can't jump this gap."

"It can sweep around," said Obermeier.

"Well, we'll do what we can," said Sheridan. "Let's knock out a break along this line and back-fire the burn."

The crowd spread out, making a line along the burn at some distance from the lower edge of the timber; and, with Morvain electing to make himself a kind of overseer, a fire-break was begun—the brush knocked down—the duff scraped aside and the loose powdered soil scattered to make a break several feet broad. It was slow labor, it was miserable, oppressively hot labor. Somewhere in the forenoon of the day the wind rose and the main fire strengthened. It was time to try a back fire if they were ever to try it. Sheridan made a pile of loose, dry brush, and touched a match to it. He went along the line of dirt, setting off a series of such fires; by the time he reached one end of the line, the back fire had caught on at the other end and the figures of the workers there were shadowy in the smoke. The back-fire, fanned by the wind, burned to the edge of the break, and smouldered through the duff-filled dirt, and had to be stamped out; and now and then a small blaze burst up in the brush beyond the break. Eating its way steadily through the litter, the blaze stubbornly and slowly went against the wind, widening the protective strip. At one o'clock the wind was harder and hotter against Sheridan's face and he thought he heard the falling of a tree over the ravine on his flank. Obermeier sat on a log, shrunk down between his shoulders, a man turned quite suddenly old in his own mind.

Sheridan walked over to Obermeier. "Why don't you go back down the trail?"

"No," said Obermeier, "but I shouldn't of come. I know it now."

Sheridan heard a shout in the distance and saw men running toward a break of fire in the line. He turned and trotted over to join them. Nobody said anything.

Chapter —14

DAYLIGHT in the meadow was an unnatural dusk. The men had been gone for five hours and Suzie had started across the fields for school. Katherine took the kettle of water from the stove for the dishes, filled the wash boiler three quarters full at the pump, and put it on the stove. With all the smoke in the air, it was a bad day to wash. She started her dishes, working quietly. Elgin, restlessly awake during the night, had dropped into a turning, whimpering sleep. She quit the dishes a moment and stepped into the bedroom over him. The fever, still with him, had parched his lips; there was a darkness under his eyes and, even in sleeping, a strain on his face. It was an old and worried face. This was the fourth day of it without a sign of a break, and she knew then her fear was not foolish. She thought of everything she had done, and tried to think of something new. She could think of nothing; she returned to the kitchen. Through the window she saw Mrs. Colson coming over the field. She went out of the house.

"Elgin's asleep," she said.

"Oh, that's fine," said Mrs. Colson. "Good sign."

"No," said Katherine, "he's worse."

"Daughter," said Mrs. Colson, "you've had a hard life and you worry too much."

"I can't help it."

Mrs. Colson went into the house. Katherine stayed outside. She folded her apron around her hands, relieved by Mrs. Colson's presence and hoping that the older woman would see something she could not see. Mrs. Colson presently came out with the same light cheerfulness on her face, but Katherine, suspecting the cheerfulness, thought she saw small lines of pressure around Mrs. Colson's mouth. "He'll be all right," said Mrs. Colson. "He's young."

"Four days of fever's too much."

"In some things it don't break till seven," said Mrs.

Colson. "You got to get some soup in him." She met Katherine's eyes. "Girl," she said with a sudden positiveness, "you got to not worry so much."

"How do you do that?"

"Everything's for the best," said Mrs. Colson. "It had to be. What could we make out of all the trouble and sorrow and disappointment if it wasn't?"

"What can we make out of it?" said Katherine.

Mrs. Colson knew she wasn't convincing Katherine, and she searched herself and tried again. "Well, I'm old and it's all passed through me and gone away. I worried and I worked in my young days. Little things sometimes brought plain terror to me. Maybe you got to get old not to care any more. I'm clear on the other end of it, but you're just goin' through it. What you need most is a man to take it off your shoulders. I'm going over to Mrs. Prince's. She's alone and she's so flighty."

She walked away. Perhaps a hundred feet distant she stopped and made a half turn, inclined to say something more. She was very thoughtful, and she stood a moment as if to speak, but changed her mind and continued on. Katherine watched her go past the mill and the house and take the trail along the edge of the meadow toward Prince's whose place was beyond a grove of alder trees in the lower valley. As soon as Mrs. Colson had vanished behind the trees, Katherine returned to finish the dishes and to get at her washing. It helped to talk to Mrs. Colson; it always helped.

She lugged the steaming boiler out of the kitchen into the yard and set up her tub and began to turn out the clothes on the wash board; and while she worked she thought of Mark Sheridan quite thoroughly, going over his features, his voice, the signals around his mouth, the normal steadiness of his expression out of which, usually without warning, some flash of humor or unexplained sadness could so quickly come. He had a quick spirit, which she admired. He was very shrewd, he was restless; yet sometimes—and this drew her interest—he seemed to drop into discouragement. He was kind and ambitious; he liked women—this she sensed—and perhaps he had been in love before, which would explain his moments of discouragement; or, if not in love, maybe he had been close with women. Probably he had for he was a warm and optimistic sort of man.

She didn't know much about him, actually; yet he was

the man who could have kissed her if he wished. That was the new thing to her—that she was willing to be kissed by him. It wasn't love, she guessed. She didn't know much about love. If this was the beginning of love, it was a strange beginning, a groping around and uneasy feelings, and sudden thoughts rushing off and dying incomplete, and heated irrational daydreams and always a discontent or an incompleteness. She had thought of love as something which came upon a woman like the striking of a bell, so clear and complete—a roundness that had no uncertainty in it; she had thought of it as a sudden understanding which passed from man to woman, and perhaps a long talking out of what each was and what each wanted and what each disliked until the two thoroughly knew each other.

None of this had happened. The best she could say was that she wanted to be kissed by him. She worked steadily on the scrubbing board, throwing the clothes into the rinse water; her hair fell down around her face and she dashed it back with her soapy fingers. She straightened now and then to rest her back, and watched the immense pall of smoke closing out the western sky. The wind had strengthened and ashes were falling heavily on the yard. At the far end of the narrow meadow which led into the hills she saw the team and wagon standing, and this reminded her of Mark Sheridan and she went back to her work with him once more in her mind. He stayed with her until Elgin's short cry came out of the house. She turned from the tub and ran into the house.

He sat up in bed with his hands across his stomach. He was heavy-eyed and terribly sick. "It's here," he said, touching his stomach. "What's the matter?"

"Where—where there, Elgin?"

"I don't know—just there. It hurts too much. I want a drink."

She brought him a drink. She laid her arm behind his back to support him while he sucked at the water, and she felt the hot dryness of his skin. He dropped back and began to move his legs from side to side; an expression of painful terror came over his face and he turned on the bed and heaved up the water. "Katy—I ain't going to die, am I?"

"Oh, no."

"I don't feel good."

"Try to sleep," she said.

143

"It hurts too much. All over my stomach. I can feel it."

"What's it like, Elgin?"

"Like that boil I had. A big boil in my stomach."

She said, "Try to rest a little," and left the house. She was alone, and panic was on her and she started aimlessly toward the Colson house, and stopped and fought her way through a momentary blindness. She thought of a poultice for his stomach, she thought of something to make him throw up, her mind went vainly searching, vainly grasping for remedies. There was nothing to help her, and nobody to give her advice.

Looking up the small meadow toward the fire she noticed the Clancy wagon and team again. She began to walk in that direction and presently was running along the rough road. She reached the team breathless and she untied the horses from a tree and got in the wagon and drove it to the yard. Elgin was calling for her in his strained voice. When she went into the bedroom she found him sitting up with all the bedcovers thrown aside.

"Where you been?" he asked. "Where you been?"

"Just to get the wagon. I'm going to take you to Forest Grove to the doctor."

"What'll he do? He'll hurt me. I'm not going to die, am I, Katy?"

"No. He'll make you well."

She rolled away the quilts from her own bed and folded the mattress and carried it out to the wagon. She stretched the mattress along the wagon's bed and went back for Elgin. He wasn't much heavier than the wash boiler. He was fire-hot and he whimpered as she lifted him into the wagon. "Lie on the mattress," she said and returned for the bedcovers. He complained when she laid the covers over him.

"I'm too hot."

"You don't want to catch cold. It won't be long. Just two hours."

"You wouldn't be taking me there if you didn't think I was going to die."

"Elgin, don't be afraid."

She drove out of the yard, past the mill and down the lane toward the main county road. The wind was at her back, brisk and hot and thick with smoke, and when she turned into the county road she looked over her shoulder at the hills and noticed that the fire was running along

144

the north side of the ravine, circling the trail up which the men had gone.

The ruts of this road were deep, nor did the thick sheet of dust soften them. The wagon wheels dropped into them and the bed took the blow, and each blow hurt Elgin. He turned from side to side; he struggled to sit up, his body bobbing, but he hadn't the strength enough to support himself and dropped back again. She tried to keep the wagon on the edge of the road and at first she went carefully; then she grew afraid, remembering how far it was to Forest Grove, and she set the team on at a faster pace. She listened to Elgin's whimpering, slowing when he complained, driving faster when his complaints died off, and the conflict between her haste and her knowledge of his pain was like a saw going back and forth through her. She passed the Prince house and saw nobody there. Half a mile on she came to the turn-off road into the Pattons' and rejected the impulse to turn in, now knowing that there was no help good enough except a doctor's. The road swung beside a bluff and passed through the long tunnel of shade of an alder thicket. She whipped up the horses.

"Katy—it hurts."

"Try to stand it."

"I can't."

She slowed down, looking back at him. He had turned on his stomach and had lifted himself to his knees. He was trying to vomit, but nothing came up. He stared directly at her and seemed not to see her.

"Elgin!"

"Don't go fast," he said.

She held the team to a walk, watching the road for the worst ruts. Around the long bend, there was a straight stretch—a straight and lonely stretch running gradually upward over a small hill; at the top of the hill she looked forward and through the fire fog of early afternoon she thought she made out the little blur of trees and houses of Forest Grove in the distance. The team went more briskly down the slope, the wagon bed making a great racket. She looked back again and saw that Elgin had turned on his side; he was curled up and seemed to have fallen soundly asleep, so soundly that he was relaxed.

She let the team go running along, now and then using the brake when the wagon pushed them too fast. They came to the foot of the hill and entered another pocket of

145

alders. She didn't immediately see the sunken spot which crossed the road—the break made by some decayed culvert—and when she did see it she tried to pull in the team. The front wheels stuck hard and every nerve in her body stretched tight as wire as she waited to hear Elgin cry out.

He said nothing. She looked back and saw him lying on his back, both arms flung away from his body. His mouth was open and he stared at the overhead tree branches in so vacant a way that she hauled up the team and tightened the brake.

"Elgin!"

She climbed from the seat into the wagon bed. The team started on. She seized the rains and jerked at the mouths of the horses and cursed them, and tied the reins around the brake. "Elgin." She crouched in the wagon bed and lifted his shoulders and drew him against her. She put her hand on his heart. "Elgin." She shook him. She turned her body and sat down. She drew him into her lap, and looked at his face, at the lips turned slack, at his sightless eyes. His head rolled loosely. She put her arm behind it, gave him a long look and drew his face down to her breasts so that she wouldn't see it and all hope of every kind went out of her. Thus she sat in this shady stretch of road, three miles from Forest Grove, turned dumb and thinking of nothing in particular, holding her dead brother against her.

Chapter — 15

AT three o'clock in the afternoon, quite suddenly, Sheridan saw a great pall sweep overhead, pushed by the lifted vigor of the wind, and break into the timber which lay between this clearing and the valley below. That smoke, he thought, did not come from the original heart of the fire westward; it came from the north, out of the hills beyond the ravine.

The end man—that one nearest the ravine whom he could not see—now ran into view, stumbling as he ran; and other men, seeing his haste, dropped their shovels and brush hooks and ran with him. They came up, the touch of panic around their eyes and mouths. It was Bert Clancy who had first bolted; he bent over and laced both hands across his belly, as though cramped. Sweat had dried on dust and ashes until his face was like a dull clay mask. "She's going down the ravine. The heat hit me so hard I felt my clothes scorch. She's goin' horse fast."

"Obermeier—where's Obermeier?" said Sheridan. Then he saw the old man limping out of the onrolling darkness of smoke, and heard his spongy coughing. Sheridan said to Jack Clancy, "You and I'll stick with Obermeier. Anybody know another trail through the timber?"

Both Morvain boys started off together, one of them saying: "This way." Sheridan lifted his voice at them.

"Pull up. We're not in that much of a hurry."

"The hell we ain't," murmured Obermeier. "We better not be too slow."

Sheridan and Clancy walked with Obermeier; the other men struck away in some sort of ragged group which, as they turned into the timber, became no kind of group, each man working his way through brush, over deadfalls and around trees in a course of his own. The way was both downgrade and to the south, swinging from the ravine now blocked by fire. Heat came steadily in from that direction but as they turned more and more southward, Sheridan felt heat come at him from this quarter too. He

147

had no decent view of the land in that direction; smoke scudded and swirled through this forest, shutting him off, and all he saw was the immediate foreground, with the valley men working their way forward. Obermeier lagged and Clancy now and then gave the old man a short and impatient glance.

"Can't you walk it up?" he asked.

Obermeier's face had the thinness of great strain. He shook his head. His footing was insecure and when he climbed the heavy deadfalls he made a long, uncertain work of it. The wind-driven heat slid against Sheridan's face with a sharper touch and the air was thin—nothing in it for his lungs to hold; he found himself dragging the very bottom of his chest for breath, never quite getting enough. Both Clancy and Obermeier walked with their mouths open and Clancy, sensing something wrong, flung a hand around him loosely.

"It's jumped the ravine. It's in front of us."

Bert Clancy came into view, having retraced his trail. He made a motion toward the south, and moved off in that direction; he vanished from sight in the dark forest tangle. Sheridan reached a great tree lying diagonally on the earth, a walkway spanning a jungle of huckleberry and brush below. Clancy waited a moment for Obermeier and then, impatient, went ahead on the log. Sheridan gave Obermeier a boost to the log and Obermeier walked buckle-kneed along this natural viaduct and worked his way through the upstruck branches of the log and got on firm ground. Another valley man crashed into sight from the upper side, batting the brush away from him; he was hatless and his face was cut by the slashing vines. He ignored Sheridan and the others and moved recklessly on.

"No trail?" asked Sheridan.

Clancy said: "Missed it. Damned country's turned around. All I know is down."

They reached the slope of a ravine and made their way to the bottom, and sank ankle deep in the black mud of a sluggish creek hidden in the salmonberry and nettle. Sheridan turned to follow the ravine but Clancy shook his head. "No—that takes you back toward the other trail. Fire's there." He stopped dead and looked at the side of the ravine in front of him, and tilted his head and shook it. "We shouldn't of come in the first place," and began to scramble up the slope. Sheridan followed him, too dry to sweat, too tired to care. There was a small wincing sound behind him and the rattle of brush and when he turned he saw Obermeier lying face flat on the ground.

He slid back to Obermeier. He said, "Give me your arm," but Obermeier didn't stir. He put his hands under the man and rolled him over; it was like turning a thick piece of rope, loose and limp. He laid his arm on Obermeier's chest. From the top of the ravine's edge, Clancy called back.

"He give out?"

"He's dead," said Sheridan. He stooped over the old man, not feeling very much. His legs and arms were shaking and he lacked enough saliva to swallow. He got up and went to the bottom of the ravine and flattened against the scummy, stilled pool of water and drank, and sloshed his face back and forth in it until the water became a flaky mud. He got up and found Clancy still at the top of the ravine.

"Well," said Sheridan, "come on down. We've got to pack him out."

"Why?" said Clancy. "He's dead."

Sheridan boosted Obermeier to a sitting position. He knelt down and got the man weighted around his shoulders and he dug his heels into the soft, needle-slick soil and—slipping and plunging and straining—he reached the crest of the ravine's side. He had gotten to the bottom of his lungs and knew he couldn't get any deeper. There was a suction all through the forest and wind seemed to strike from each direction. The brush shook to it and the smoke flickered by him and rushed upward.

"We got no time," repeated Clancy.

"Let's go down the top of this ridge. I can't do any more climbing."

Clancy went ahead, parting the brush for Sheridan. He tried to hold the brush aside, but it slapped back into Sheridan's face. They reached a deadfall, whereupon Clancy crossed it and turned and took Obermeier and went on. Sheridan climbed the log and followed. He walked with his legs apart, slowed down by a terrible lassitude he couldn't overcome; his motions were erratic and the little ups and downs of the ground caused him too much work. Farther down the slope there was a lighter streak, and to his left a shutting of light and the humming of fire and the crash and spit and snap of brittle stuff igniting and falling.

149

Clancy, before him, swayed and came to a full stop and, with a great gesture of futility, he let Obermeier's body drop from his shoulders. He stood spent, his head drooped. He didn't look at Sheridan. He murmured something that Sheridan didn't make out and went on without saying more. He was trying to hurry. His leg caught in the brush and he fell flat on his face; he rolled and got up, and plunged ahead.

Sheridan stood over the dead Obermeier and passed the hardest, longest moments of his life. The slope ran downward through brush and trees, and now and then in the crowding smoke he thought he saw a yonder break which was the meadow. The fire was on both sides of him and the constant smoke gave him a feeling of sickness in his stomach; his lungs burned and he was brittle-dry, inside and out. He got down on his knees, groaning; he swore at Obermeier as he pulled at the man's unwieldly looseness. He stood up with Obermeier and bent his knees and got Obermeier over his shoulder. He braced himself and took short careful steps, watching the brush with a heavy anxiety.

He wanted to stay on the crest of the ridge but he slid a yard or more down the slope into the ravine and when he started to turn back he could not drive enough power into his legs to climb. Smoke followed this ravine as water would follow a trough; he worked his way, in fact, through a kind of flattened out chimney flue, carrying its acrid gases and forest cinders. His heart struck its loud, violent strokes against his chest and in his belly and along the sides of his neck. He saw nothing clearly and his nose seemed to be bleeding. He feared a log blockade in the ravine but against the growing light ahead of him he made out the canyon's slow widening. The ground seemed clearer and presently he discovered the flat meadow directly before him. A twenty-yard walk took him out of the canyon into the meadow's stubble. He walked another hundred feet to be certain he was beyond the fire's reach, and then he let Obermeier sag away and he bent down and touched the ground with his hands and slowly dropped to his side. The Colson house was considerably down the meadow; beyond the Colson house was a fresh bright stream of fire rising from the mill.

He watched the fire without interest. He was a piece of pulpy, low-celled life lying on the ground, expanding and constricting, making greedy sucking sounds, his thoughts shriveled and calloused and turned inward to himself with a dull attention to the exhaustion which cut off his wind and burned through his muscles like rheumatism. He had no energy to move, yet his nerves twitched at his muscles. He was a man who had swum too far out and now beat his way shoreward without the certainty of coming in; and for the second time in his life—the first time was when he lay on the beach—he was a spectator, listening to his own body struggle in the strange riptides which lay at the far limit of endurance. And, listening, he heard his body beat back and he felt himself come in.

Lying there, he saw the Colson mill become a skeleton outlined against a yellow-red plaque of flame. The fire, circling the burn, had raced down the ravine to the meadow. In a thousand outthrown bits of fiery debris it had touched off the dry grasses of the meadows and, sliding along fence lines and tinder-dry sheds and sawdust and lumber piles, it had come upon the mill. The Morvain house had collapsed to a last bonfire on the ground; the Colson house had not yet started but it too would go.

Men stood at a distance from the mill, idly watching. He got up and walked over to them. He looked around the crowd and he said, "Everybody accounted for?"

"Except Obermeier," said Morvain.

"He's back there in the meadow," said Sheridan.

"Well, it's too bad," said Morvain, "about him." He looked around him and he had to make some sort of statement, so he said: "Well, everybody's got to die."

One long ribbon of flame ran across the Colson yard and touched the porch and seemed to bounce away. They were all fatigue-drunk spectators watching the flame touch the house again, make a flickering run along the wall, and burst into a solid burning. Sheridan said, "Where's Katherine and Elgin?"

"Guess she took Elgin to the neighbors."

"My wagon and team," said Clancy. "It was up in that meadow. By God, I tied the team." He walked around the mill toward the Morvain house and he stopped to look along the little meadow leading into the hills. Sheridan, following, saw the meadow to be licked clean by the fire, the stubble turned to ashes. There was no team or wagon visible, and nothing on the ground to indicate carcasses.

"Somebody got it out of there," said Clancy.

Sheridan saw three saddled horses crowded into a corner of the big meadow, over near the county road—these belonging to some of the men who had come along to fight fire. He stared into the smoking pile that had been the Morvain house; nothing stood upright except the stove and three sections of chimney and two iron bedsteads. There was a washboiler and metal tub in the yard, both melted down. He made out the charred clothes in them. He walked over the meadow; he caught up one of the saddle horses and turned into the county road, following it toward Forest Grove. When he came to the Prince place he checked in, seeing Mrs. Prince on the porch.

"Where's Prince?" she demanded.

"He'll be along. Have you seen Mrs. Colson and Katherine?"

"Katherine went by about noon with the Clancy wagon. Elgin was lyin' in the wagon."

He pushed the horse into a gallop and went through the long tunnel of alder shade, seeing the wagon tracks freshly cut before him, and noting how these tracks ran irregularly from one side of the road to the other. He reached the long grade and pulled the horse to a walk as he went climbing on. Behind him, from this distance all the upper valley was covered with smoke.

At the top of the grade he saw a wagon and a team down at the foot of the hill in a patch of alders. The wagon had backed around until it sat across the road and the team fed on the grass of the road's edge. He saw Katherine seated in the wagon bed and—when he came up—he saw Elgin in her arms.

He got out of the saddle and he stood at the rear of the wagon, looking at her and at the boy. She looked back at him. He loosened the tailgate chains and let down the gate and climbed into the wagon. He took her arms from Elgin and laid the boy back on the mattress, and then he drew Katherine against him. He waited for her to cry but there was a stiffness in her body and she didn't cry.

He said: "How long have you been here?"

"I don't know."

"Do you want to go back now?"

"All right."

"The fire took the houses and the mill, Katherine. Maybe you'd rather go into Forest Grove."

"No—let's go back."

He laid a blanket over Elgin. He said, "Sit up in the front with me," and gave her a hand into the seat. He backed the wagon around and started it up the grade. She

152

put her hands into her lap, looking ahead with some kind of intentness and when he turned toward her he saw an expression on her face that was not what he had expected. It wasn't sad or any resemblance of sadness; it was a fixed bitterness. She was entirely alone and without faith in anything.

Chapter — 16

SHERIDAN returned to Murdock's two days later and found that Bogart had meanwhile paid a visit to the mill. "Yesterday," said Murdock. "He wasn't pleased to find you gone. The man ain't as neighborly as he used to be. What happened to your eyebrows? They're gone."

It was the first of the month, and time to make an accounting on the profits. Bogart had the records but Sheridan sat down that evening with his own privately kept set of books. He had his guarantee of two hundred a month; above that he saw another hundred out of the profits. That was not a bad thing for the first month. There ought, in the months to come, to be five hundred a month as a steady fact. Against that, the Colson venture was straight loss. He spent the better part of an hour at the Murdock kitchen table straightening his accounts and he had his gusts of irritation at the figures which would not balance, and his small glum moments when he saw himself not marching ahead; but when he was through with the chore, and when he knew exactly where he stood, he grew cheerful again. Optimism came easily to him.

He moved to the porch and sat in the smoky darkness. The moon stood round and red in the low sky; all along the western hills, across the valley, were the winking eyes of fires breaking out in the season's brittle dryness. Murdock and his wife had gone to bed. Liza came quietly from the house and took a chair beside him. She said nothing. She sat still and she waited for him and he felt the sudden possessiveness in her. All he had to do was touch her arm, and at his touch she would lay her soft flesh against him. She wanted nothing for it, no first gestures to make it reasonable, no words to explain it or cover it with the pretense of love or anything else. She was the nakedness of hunger that had no reason except to be satisfied.

He heard her slow, half sullen and half amused voice. "You're funny."

"Why?"

"Men don't act that way. Hot and cold. Don't you know what you want?"

"No. Neither do you."

"Yes I do," she said. "So do you."

"Liza," he said, "don't you hold off from men?"

"From the ones I don't like," she said, and asked him an offended question. "Don't I please you?"

"That's not enough."

She thought about it. "What more's enough?" She bent forward until he made out the mortal wisdom on her face, and he had the momentary feeling of being too young for her—such a feeling as had occasionally come to him when listening to Clara and Revelwood in one of their close conversations. In Liza's voice was a slow, cynical amusement. She thought that at last she understood him.

"You're just like other men. They've all got a guilty conscience when they run after women. So they try to make up a story about it. About how much they love a woman. You don't have to talk about that. I didn't ask you, did I?"

He said, "We're not just animals, Liza."

She caught his resentment, and tried to repair it. "I wasn't trying to run you down," she said. But her own experiences were too real to be thrown aside. "Make it out to be love if you want. I don't care. I just get tired of hearing men in the hills talk about something they don't mean. Maybe I don't know what love is. But if it's something real, you don't have to talk about it. Who made sin anyway? Somebody that was comfortable? Somebody old? I don't know. I know what's going to happen to me. I've got little choice. I'll marry somebody I don't much care for and I'll raise a lot of kids. Then I'll get old and they'll go away and that'll be all." Her voice had the old rebellion in it. She stared at him in the darkness, and her anger died and she touched his arm, whispering: "It's better not to ask questions."

He sat entirely still with the lusting presence of Liza still touching him and sending streamers of sensation through him; the desire was in him to turn and take her. He thought to himself, "No," and used his will to wipe out the image and the sensuous feeling of Liza beneath him and her broad mouth searching for his mouth. He shut his mind to it. He made a hard violent effort to put it

155

aside. There was a flashing side thought in his mind that perhaps he was a fool and that perhaps a good thing was good in itself for the moment it lasted. Down the road, past the mill, was the sound of a horse running in. He got up and he turned.

Liza's voice rushed at him. "You're a fool." She flung out her hand and struck him on the chest and swung and walked into the house. The rider came on at the same rapid cantering, aiming for the light of the Murdock house; but for a moment Sheridan, touched by the embarrassment of a man in such a position, turned to see Liza in the lighted kitchen. She stood by the table, her hands resting on it and her head dropped. Her face was morbidly dark. She hated him at the moment and could have physically injured him. She hated herself. Her shoulders were drawn up, her muscles were tense. She was a storm that couldn't break; it crazed her for this moment.

"House there," said the rider, wheeling over the yard. "Murdock's?"

Sheridan recognized that voice and swung around. "George," he said, "what's up?"

Revelwood dropped from the saddle and came to the porch. The fan-glow of the kitchen lamp touched him—his long face so handsome when shaven and smiling, now so unkempt. His eyes were glittering and restless, his mouth thin. There was a steel-flash of long stubble on his jaws; he appeared sickened and his clothes were wrinkled. He said: "I had hell's own time finding this godforsaken spot."

"Had supper?"

"No—don't want it," said Revelwood. He stood with one foot on the lower step and one on the porch level; he placed a hand over the higher knee and bent in partial rest, staring with a break of curiosity at Liza. She had come to the doorway and was framed in it. She said: "I'll fix you supper."

Revelwood straightened and removed his hat, and took her in with his practiced eye, and courtesy came quickly to him. "No," he said, "but my thanks for your kindness." He let his glance remain an added moment on her, and passed his attention to Sheridan, never so deep in his own troubles that he could not sense the relations of others. He said, "Walk down the road with me, Mark."

He took Sheridan's arm with a strange haste on him; he turned Sheridan and went out along the yard until he believed they were beyond hearing. Then he said, "Is she here, Mark?"

"Who?"

"Don't ask that," said Revelwood sharply. "Clara, of course. I can think of no other place. She'd come to you. She always said that. She's left me."

The first thought in Sheridan's mind was that she should have come to him. There was no sympathy in him at the moment for Revelwood—only a complete concentration on Clara. He wondered why she had disappeared, he wondered where she was and if she were safe and happy; and suddenly he wondered if there was another man.

"Why?"

Revelwood made a gesture with one hand. "You know her as well as I do."

"Been quarreling?"

"I've never lifted my voice to her. Maybe that was the trouble."

"I don't follow that."

"Well," said Revelwood with his ragged calm, "who does follow Clara? I thought I knew her, I do know some of her. Nobody knows all she is—she doesn't herself." He fell momentarily silent, searching for words. "Women want too much. They can't explain it to themselves. They want black and white at the same time. They want love but they want strength. They want to be sweet and pure— but they also want a hot tumble in the hay. The wind sings through them one way and cries through them another—and however it blows, that's how they want to be."

"Why did she leave?" repeated Sheridan. "There's got to be a reason."

"If you've got to have things explained, try to explain why she took me instead of you." Revelwood searched his pockets and found a cigar. The match burst against his face and light dug into the lines on his face. He flung away the match. "I never supposed I could give her much more than comfort. Maybe I was another damned fool man expecting it would grow into something more. I never believed such a thing until I met her. Then I went blind, the way any man does when he turns to a woman. But I always knew you could pull her away. You're sure she's not here?"

"No," said Sheridan. "Was there any other man?"

"I've thought of Bogart. But he's in town and she's not.

157

If there's another man—if he's led her into some damned miserable situation, I'll kill him. She makes a man think she's loose, but she's not."

"I'll go back to town with you," said Sheridan, and turned toward the Murdock yard. He saddled his horse and returned to the porch and found Revelwood ready to go. They rode on toward Portland, long silent. Revelwood obviously tangled in his thoughts, Sheridan methodically surrounding this news with his imagination. A great deal later he said: "Didn't she leave any word?"

"No."

"When did you miss her?"

"Two days ago. I've checked stages, boats, everything."

"It's too small a town to leave without somebody knowing it."

They turned into the main road at Bright's Orchard and rode westward. The moon shed its rouge-red glow over the land, and the shadows were stained with this redness and smoke-fog was a cobweb screen low against the earth. Late lamplight glittered out of farmhouse windows and a dog, sounding at their passage, tipped off the baying of other dogs one by one into the far distance. They left the valley flats and climbed upward over the rough shoulders of the hills behind Portland.

"If it's another man," said Revelwood, "I fear for her. He'll see only the easiness and he'll turn her into a cheap woman."

"Why should it be another man?"

"You know her as well as I do," said Revelwood.

"George," said Sheridan, "will you take her back?"

They climbed to the crest of the hills and passed downgrade into damp, wild-smelling jaws of Canyon Road. A light swung from the reachpole of a late-traveling wagon ahead of them and a sleepy voice spoke to them as they passed. A fire bloomed against the canyon walls farther along where a freight outfit camped. At the foot of the canyon they passed into scattered timber and gradually picked up the glow of Portland town. Not until then did Revelwood answer Sheridan's question.

"Yes," he said. "I couldn't do anything else. I can't help myself."

They rode along Tenth Street to her house and Revelwood swung from the saddle with a sudden eagerness. "Maybe she went on a trip. Maybe she's back." Sheridan, remaining in the saddle, heard Revelwood's first light knock on Clara's door, and the silence, and the second louder knock. There were no lights in the house. Revelwood searched the door with his key and went inside. Sheridan heard Revelwood's voice call Clara's name and presently he saw a lamp march through the house in Revelwood's hands. He sat still, closely thinking of Clara. She should have come to him. She had said she would, if she needed him. But she hadn't needed him—and that meant she wasn't alone. He should have hated her for her looseness but he couldn't. He was like George, knowing her and making excuses for her, but he realized now why she had married Revelwood instead of him. She had known that George loved her—she had captured all of Revelwood. She had not, Sheridan understood, felt that way about him—there was some doubt or some coldness or some reservation which had repelled her.

Revelwood came back to the porch. "No," he said.

"I'll put up at the Pioneer," said Sheridan. "I'll see you tomorrow." He rode down to a stable on Oak and left his horse, and walked on to the Pioneer and got a room. He lay back in bed, his thoughts plowing crisscross furrows. There was but one thing that his thoughts seemed to strike in their traveling. Bogart. Bogart was still in town, but that didn't mean too much. Bogart was sly, and Clara, going into an affair, could also be sly.

Directly after breakfast he found Bogart in the latter's office. Bogart sat with his morning cigar, the same restless, thick-chested man with his black hair tumbling down. He met Sheridan with scarce civility and made his complaint at once.

"You were not on the job when I came out the other day."

"Fighting fire," said Sheridan.

"I didn't hire you for a fire warden. You've been away from the mill a good deal, I find."

"The mill runs, doesn't it?"

"As well without you as with you."

"I gather you're still hunting a way to back out of the bargain."

Bogart's vanity was a volatile shallow thing and came up now in springing lines of distaste. He liked to drive but he hated to be driven. He sat there before Sheridan with his muscles expanding his small body to the bulkiest

159

possible inch, hating Sheridan for the kind of opposition he could not stomach.

"You've not kept the bargain," he pointed out.

"Your mill's running," said Sheridan. "It wasn't before. You're getting a better cut than you ever had. What's your complaint?"

"You've set up another mill behind my back. That's my time you're using for yourself. Are you fool enough to think I wouldn't find out?"

"I gave it no thought," said Sheridan. "It was none of your business."

"Why not?"

"I told you before. Your mill's running and making money."

"I also know that your mill burned. You've lost money on that venture. You need the job I gave you."

"I don't need a damned thing. I don't want to need."

"Oh but you do," said Bogart. "If you're going to stay in business you'll buckle to men that have got the power over you. You'll do it to stay in business. You'll buckle to me now, my friend—because I've given you a good thing and you've got to have it."

He rose and walked to a small safe in the room's corner; he opened it and searched a drawer and returned to the desk, placing thereon two small stacks of double eagles amounting to two hundred dollars. He put the money on his side of the desk—in such a position that Sheridan, accepting the money, would need to reach for it. "There's your month's pay."

"Plus a hundred and ten dollars," said Sheridan. "That's my half of the profit over expense."

"I told you that you didn't give me all of your time. You don't get anything more than the two hundred. There it is. Take it and go back to work. Or take it and get the hell out of my sight. No man can practice his smartness on me."

"We'll sign off right here," said Sheridan promptly. "But I want the extra share which was the bargain."

"You're a fool," said Bogart, "and you'll never amount to anything in business. A man's got to know when he's licked, and swallow the licking and go on."

"I won't work for a man who welshes," said Sheridan.

Bogart gave him an unpleased smile. "That's the squawk of a loser. There's your pay."

Sheridan said, "Then I'll take a little of your hide, Charnel," and started around the desk.

Bogart stepped toward the wall, thrust a hand into his pocket and came out with a darringer so small that his palm covered it. "I expected it," he said.

"Goddam you, put that down," said Sheridan.

"You're young," said Bogart. "You don't think ahead. You don't size up other men and figure what they'll do in a pinch. That's going to cause you trouble. I've studied you and I knew you'd do this. But you didn't study me, and you didn't know what I'd do."

Sheridan stood checked at the corner of the desk, watching this man with his extreme care. Bogart showed his satisfaction and yet his face was somewhat pale. The situation put him under strain.

"You realize," said Sheridan, "that I'll catch you somewhere."

Bogart shook his head. "You'll forget it. It takes a tougher man than you'll ever be to keep hatred alive. I can do it. You can't."

"No," said Sheridan. "I'll catch you somewhere. You've got that to worry about. You'll never turn another corner without wondering what's around it. You'll never wake up in the morning without wondering if its not the day you'll get that face broken out of shape past fixing up."

"That's talk."

"Remember," pointed out Sheridan, "I fought your man at the mill. I had a reason. I'll always fight when I've got a reason."

Bogart watched Sheridan, his gray eyes filled with flashing light. The weight of these moments wore hard on him. His mind was tough enough, but his body was the body of a middle-aged man, and the physical strain was more than he counted on. He took a step forward and he moved the two stacks of gold over to Sheridan's corner of the table, and stepped back. "Take it and get out," he said. "I can be proud too. You'll never get the extra share from me."

Sheridan took the money—noting the relief suddenly betray Bogart. He said to Bogart, "You've bought yourself a beating, Charnel," and turned to the door. Then he thought of the derringer in Bogart's hand—this derringer so conveniently ready—and it made him wonder rather suddenly if perhaps Bogart might have had the gun on him this morning for another reason. He turned back.

"You had the gun handy for me?"

161

"That's right."

"How did you know I'd be here this morning?"

Bogart looked down at the gun and restored it to his pocket. "I've been prepared for you a matter of days."

"I think," said Sheridan, "you've made a mistake."

He went down the stairs to the street, turning toward Revelwood's office. Revelwood wasn't there. He walked on to Tenth and saw the door of Clara's house open; he found Revelwood standing in the front room of the house.

"I've looked over everything," Revelwood said. "The neighbors next door know nothing. What did you find?"

"Nothing," said Sheridan. Walking uptown to this house, he had decided to say nothing concerning Bogart to Revelwood. It was entirely possible that Revelwood might, if he shared any suspicion of Bogart, go immediately down and face the man. Nothing could come out of that but somebody's death.

"Mark, you've got to give me a hand with this."

"Certainly."

Revelwood watched his friend with a momentary focusing of attention. "I know what she thought of you. You had more of her than I had. I know what you think of her. What I don't understand is why she took me over you. Do you hold it against me, Mark?"

"I did. I don't now."

"If she were your wife, would you hunt for her? If you found her, would you take her back?"

Sheridan checked the answer which so readily came to him. He had almost said that he would take her back, but that was the shallow generosity which came to anybody not hard pressed. He sat still, searching his way through uncertain convictions and it saddened him to think that in him still was a doubt of Clara and a doubt of himself. He said, quite slowly, "I don't know, George. A man can't answer a thing like that unless he stands in the place you're standing. I don't know what I'd say if I were you."

"Now," said Revelwood, and found some satisfaction in Sheridan's reply, "I understand why she took me. There's no doubt in me, and she knew it. She felt doubt in you. I didn't really catch on before."

"I'll see you later," said Sheridan and left the house. He walked along Tenth to Alder, and passed down that street toward the river. Paused on the levee, he watched the slow play of the water before him and he reviewed

Clara's reasons for leaving Revelwood and found no reason that pleased him. Had she deserted Revelwood because she regretted the marriage? He doubted it. She was not the sort to deprive herself of comfort and security because of remorse. She had known the quality of her affection for Revelwood before marrying him. She knew what she got and what she gave; she had pretty well balanced sentiment and practical consideration.

It went back to a man—the sort of man who reached into her and captured that formless hunger for warmth which was her strongest virtue or her deepest vice. But what man could, on so short a notice, come to mean that much to her? Bogart was the only one answering the description; and in Bogart's case there was an added reason which Sheridan had suspected from his first knowledge of Clara's disappearance—which was the desire to pay back the injury caused her by Mrs. Bogart.

He returned to Front and strolled south in the dry, smoke-stained heat. At Salmon he swung west until he got to Twelfth and skirted the Bogart yard. Through the front window of the house he saw Mrs. Bogart. She stared out at him and gave him no recognition—that stonelike face shocking him anew. He went the length of the block and circled it and came back along the pickets of the front yard. She still stood by the window and she gave him a second blank stare. He stopped, he loaded his pipe and lighted it and during the operation, he looked steadily at her; then he began another circle of the block.

The Bogart house covered half of the block, its yard running through from Tenth to Eleventh. Around on the Eleventh Street side stood the woodshed and carriage house and when he reached the carriage house he noticed the door to be open. Mrs. Bogart was inside the carriage house, near the doorway. He slowed his pace, looking about him, and stepped into the carriage house. Mrs. Bogart drew back to a corner; she placed her hands on her hips and looked at him with her enemy eyes.

"What do you want to say to me?" she asked.

"You know that Miss Dale—Mrs. Revelwood—has left town?"

"Everybody knows it."

"Do you know why?"

He had never seen any human being so filled with injury and misery and unforgotten spiritual wounds. The terrible

163

imagination within her quickened the flow of poisoned emotion. She said: "Are people talking?"

He put the question aside. "Somebody had to help her go. Was your husband out of the house any night last week?"

"What would you do to him?" she asked.

He couldn't make out whether the question came from fear or from hope. Evil things had lived in her so long that she had no power left to display an unmixed feeling. He felt sorry for her and he was afraid of her.

"Your husband and I have had an argument, over another matter," he said. "He understands I'll use my fists on him when the time comes."

She stared at the floor, and seemed to live through some brutal scene that fascinated her. "Hell ought to come to him on this earth," she murmured. "He was gone several hours last Tuesday."

"Do you know where he went?"

"He doesn't explain his business to me," she said.

He said: "That doesn't get us anywhere. Thank you, Mrs. Bogart.

"Are you giving up?" she asked, her voice unconsciously rising to a sharper pitch.

"No. I'll wait—and watch."

"I'll tell you something," she said. "He's leaving on the afternoon boat for The Dalles."

"I thought he didn't tell you things."

"I found out for myself by going to the ticket office. Will you go up there?"

"Yes," he said.

"Then I won't. If I went I'd kill her, and no doubt they'd hang me, and I won't let Bogart get rid of me that way. You'll break his face to bits but you'll quit there. That's what I'd like." Then she thought of the girl and her expression tightened into its unmerciful ugliness. "You ought to do the same to her, but you won't. She's made you blind, I can see. She made Bogart blind and this man Revelwood blind too. You ought to burn the skin off her face and leave it so men would cringe away when they saw it. But you won't."

"Mrs. Bogart," he said gently, "your husband must take his blame in the matter."

"My husband," said Mrs. Bogart, "is a stud horse. He's the vainest brute in this world and he has no pity for any living thing. I could endure him if he had pity. If you've

164

got pity it means you know what it's like to be weak and sick. He hasn't got it. He's destroyed me and wishes I'd die. I know it. All I can hope for is to see him weak and sick and to laugh at him as he's laughed at me and everybody else. That's what I live for. God made a terrible mistake in that man. Somehow I feel he'll learn to suffer. If he dies without learning it, I'll never believe in God."

She said it with a calm intensity and gave him one last hooded glance and swung away. He left the carriage house and strolled back to Front Street. He went up to his room in the Pioneer, and, lying on his bed, he made up his mind to tell Revelwood nothing. Revelwood was in a frame of mind to kill Bogart, which would of course be the end of Revelwood as well. It was a better thing for him to keep George in the dark, to follow Bogart to The Dalles on the morning boat, and settle the thing there.

He had no particular feeling of disillusion toward Clara. He tried to judge her but, as before, he could make no judgment stick. There was an excuse for her as there had always been. He tried, too, to understand his own exact attitude toward her. Was he in love with this woman, and was that why he went after her now? He couldn't get at the bottom of himself. He got up from the bed and went out for lunch and at two o'clock, standing at some distance from the Navigation Company's dock, he watched Bogart go aboard. Later in the afternoon he found Revelwood in the latter's office and only shook his head when Revelwood asked if he had found any information.

Revelwood shrugged his shoulders and settled back in his chair. His eyes were reddened from want of sleep, from strain, from excessive smoking; he rubbed them with the tips of his fingers and looked over Sheridan's head toward the windows. The light coming through the windows was unkind to him, thinning his jaws and weakening his chin and giving him a strange frailty. Here was a man, Sheridan suddenly decided, who had been perfectly in tune with his world so long as he had avoided strong emotions and strong attachments; but when these had cracked his shell and had gotten into him he was less of a man. He wasn't robust enough for heavy feelings. Revelwood brought his glance back to Sheridan.

"You've had some bad luck yourself. Probably you've lost your original stake. Do you need money? I've got some."

"No," said Sheridan. "I'll make out."

165

"You will," said Revelwood in a quiet, tired voice. "You'll not get weary. You believe. That's the thing. You believe in the fairness of men and the goodness of the world. You believe everything comes out right in the end. Well, probably it will for you though I wish you were more skeptical."

"Has it helped you to be skeptical?"

Revelwood considered the remark and shook his head. "That's right, Mark. I've believed nothing—and I'm no better off for it, am I? I guess we're all damned insects crawling around at the mercy of some careless foot. What are you going to do now?"

"I've got a shingle mill in mind, on the Willamette above the falls."

Revelwood gave his friend a small, soft smile and a gentle shake of the head. "Always pushing on." Then he darkened and grew inquisitive. "That woman out there at Murdock's. She's a lush wench. You mixed up with her?"

Sheridan shook his head and said a brief, curt "No." Revelwood watched him a moment and dropped the subject. They talked on in an idle way for a while longer, then Sheridan left the office. He had the afternoon to kill. He looked up the postmaster to discuss again the way of getting a mail contract for the Tualatin stage. The postmaster said: "You've written to the Senator?"

"Yes."

"Well, the Senator is beholden politically to one of the businessmen here. I'd go see Elijah Church."

Elijah Church kept his offices in the Moore Block, up a flight of uncarpeted wooden stairs that squealed beneath Sheridan's feet. There was an anteroom occupied by a single man sitting on a high stool before a desk, and a corner room austerely furnished with a walnut bookcase, a shabby desk, and a little stand on which stood a bowl of apples. Church was a New Englander, as so many of the town's businessmen were, spare of flesh, long-legged, neat and cool. He had a fluffy black beard fringing his jaws and his chin.

"I came to talk about a mail contract out in Tualatin Valley. I've got a stage line started—"

"Know about it," said Elijah Church.

"I've written the Senator asking his help. It's his power to recommend."

"Your stage line paying its way?"

"Just about."

"Well, it's fall and people ain't so busy out there. They can travel. Spring and summer they won't have time. Winter won't be good. You put much money into the venture?"

"Some. Not much. I've got a partner."

"I know Cray Jennings," said Church. "Best to be careful and move slow. Money's a hard thing in Oregon."

"That section can stand a stage service," said Sheridan. "Portland to Forest Grove doesn't make a strong showing by itself, but when you make a loop out of it, by way of McMinnville and Newberg, you've got something better. Could you put in a word for me with the Senator?"

"If I asked him a favor I create an obligation to do him a favor. Prefer to keep my bookkeeping on favors in good order." He swung a little and looked out of his window and small lines appeared around his eyes as he sat there. "I don't think you can do well. It's a slim bone you're picking. I won't help you now."

Sheridan returned to the street. There had been nothing warm in Church, and nothing particularly cold; nothing kind and nothing cruel. He was a common type of businessman in this country, his human instincts carefully divorced from his business desires; he had honesty in his business dealings but he saw to it that he was never maneuvered into an unprofitable position.

Walking southward along Front, and beyond Front to the river road, Sheridan placed himself beside Church for the sake of comparison. Church, he realized, never let sentiment sway his judgment. The keen flashes of emotion were not for Church. It caused Sheridan to wonder if he himself had the necessary bottom for business success. He worked hard and he thought he had a good enough eye to see the chances around him, but sometimes when facing a man like Church, he doubted if energy or foresight were enough. He had met some of the town's leading businessmen and he had noticed a common thoughtfulness on their faces and a certain toughness to be noticed through their courtesy or benevolence or affability. They had some kind of private formula. Perhaps it was the knack of discounting the optimism that made other and lesser men rush blindly on. Or, perhaps it was a much sharper sense of detail, or, perhaps it was a bargaining instinct; or a smell of the future or an ability to make other men work for them.

Far out in the country he turned back and, still with

167

these thoughts roving his head, he paced toward town—discouraged and yet driven by impatience. He thought to himself, "I don't mind a few failures, but I've got to know that there's some sort of destination." He could understand the kind of failure which came from error and laziness; what troubled him was the thought that even with hard work, experience and foresight, he still might fail. That was Revelwood's philosophy—that everything was blind luck, against, which no man had any defense. It was a poor philosophy. If there were no rules in the world and no rewards for the decent, it became a world without meaning.

He had supper and went early to bed. At seven in the morning he stepped aboard the *Daisy McGovern,* bound upriver to The Dalles, and in the late afternoon, having gone about a portage and taken a second boat, he reached the town.

It was a depot town, small but very active. Here the steamboats discharged their cargoes on the landing for transshipment over the portage road to the upriver boats; and freight teams, picking up their loads, moved east toward the mines and new settlements of the back country. The main street of the town faced the river and ran parallel to the landing, and houses straggled up the side of a hill which immediately began to rise from the river. It was middle afternoon and extremely hot; the air seemed dry and thin and he found himself walking rather slowly through an assorted crowd—obvious prospectors bound for the mines, townsmen, an occasional soldier, an occasional Indian, and now and then a woman.

He walked into a large frame hotel and found the bar busy. He had not eaten on the boat and so, with a whiskey in his hand, he moved to the saloon's steam table and made himself a rough lunch. Afterwards he returned to the lobby and got a room; when he signed the register he turned the page to the previous day's arrivals and saw nothing of Bogart's name. With the clerk's impatient eye on him he continued to run the pages backward. He had not much hope for finding Clara, suspecting she would not use her own name; but on the page of four days earlier he saw the small, immature signature of a Clara Dawson. He could not be certain, but he turned to the clerk.

"Is Miss Dawson still here?"

"No," said the clerk. "She's gone."

"Do you know where she went?"

"My friend," said the clerk, "a hundred people a day pass through here. I don't know where she went. Your room's Number Ten."

Sheridan went up to Ten. He stretched out on the bed and stared at a round rusty water spot on the ceiling, hearing the cursing of a teamster in the street directly below him. All this was rough country. A long way off to the east and southeast lay a few mining towns such as Canyon City and Auburn. Two hundred miles up the river was Lewiston, and over the Rockies, far off, were the Montana gold fields. The Dalles was the jumping-off place for these settlements and though it was not much of a town it had more comfort than anything beyond it. Clara, he knew, wanted nothing of that sort. Either she had turned back toward Portland or she was somewhere in this town.

He rose and brought up a chair to the window overlooking the street, and sat down. There was this one main street running beside the river, and a pair of streets cutting across it, from the river to the hills. The big mercantile houses sat shoulder to shoulder and at each of the street corners stood a saloon; slightly beyond this business center were the stables, the wagon parks and the corrals. Farther out, straggling without much pattern toward the limits of town, were the angular little dwelling houses beside their pathways or rutted roads. Board awnings sheltered the walks of the street from the driving sun, and the big wagons with their six- and eight-horse teams rolled by and threw a yellow, sparkling dust over everything. It was past four o'clock, and he sat in this barren, heated room and felt sweat dampening him, and watched the street like a patient fisherman. It occurred to him he was playing a strange part—a part he could scarcely explain to himself. He thought he was here to protect Revelwood, but he could not be certain that this was the honest reason. More likely he was here because he could not help it. Clara's fortunes had become his fortunes. He ought to be judging her harshly, yet he could not. He was not even sure he thought less of her.

A little beyond five o'clock he saw two people come from a house on the higher edge of town; they walked forward and when they reached the main street he recognized Clara and Bogart. They crossed over and disappeared directly beneath him into the hotel. They were, he guessed, coming down for supper.

169

He rose and stretched the kinks out of his legs. He walked back and forth in the hot room a matter of five minutes or more, returning to the window from time to time to be sure they did not reappear. Presently he turned from the room and made his way down the stairs. He crossed the lobby and got to the street and went directly to a hardware store opposite. He bought a gun—a .44 Colt—and he stood at the counter and packed the cylinders, powder, ball and wadding, and slid the gun inside his belt, underneath the skirt of his coat. Leaving the store, he strolled to the corner saloon and stood inside the doorway. The sun flared at the edge of the bald hills across the river, and sank and left a burning brightness in the sky; suddenly those hills turned from velvet amber to a wrinkled, ancient gray-brown, and a coolness more imagined than real touched the town. It was coming on dusk when Clara and Bogart left the hotel and returned along the side street toward the house. As they passed the saloon he had a moment's close view of them—Bogart with his flushed face, Clara half grave and half smiling; it was her old expression—that search for happiness strained with wistfulness.

He stepped from the saloon and turned its corner and waited again until they went into the house. He stood still, decided what he had to do; he walked toward the river, waiting for this dusk to settle into night. He reached the landing beside the river and swung around, keeping his glance on the house higher up the street, and his feelings got strong and made his thoughts jumpy. Bogart had pulled her into this dismal adventure and Bogart was the one to blame and punish; but as before, he visualized Clara's expression and he knew it was not entirely Bogart's fault. She had gotten into Bogart as she had gotten into Revelwood and into him. Maybe, by accident, God had formed her to be the unconscious image of those strange, hot dreams all men had; maybe she didn't know how she affected men.

The lamps of town began to wink and stars spread over the sky, quickening the blackness. He walked back through the heart of the town, hearing rough sounds rise out of the saloons, the brawling, the restless laughter, the stamping feet, the guttural, uneven run of talk. Heat came up around him exhaled by the overpressed earth and holding in it the ripe scent of dust and baked boards, of suppertime odors and whiskey and tobacco. He came opposite the little house and took a stand in the shadows. Light came through the drawn shades. Suddenly he stepped backwards; the house door opened and Bogart came out, closed the door behind him and walked down the street. He whistled quietly to himself as he went toward the main street and turned a corner. Sheridan looked at the house and at the vacant ground to either side of it; he crossed over and drifted toward the main street until he came to a warehouse; between the warehouse and its adjoining building was a kind of alley. He stopped here and stepped into its mouth and he put his back against the building wall, watching the corner around which Bogart had gone; he hadn't been there five minutes before a short and bustling shape came back around the corner. It was Bogart, still whistling. Sheridan let him go by, and stepped out of the alley with his gun drawn.

"Stop there," he said. "Don't turn."

Bogart halted; he stiffened in his tracks; he seemed to debate his course—and made up his mind and dismissed the thought of resistance. His voice was gritty with impatience and yet held a kind of rough amusement.

"You damned fool," he said, "I don't carry money around these streets at night. I've got ten dollars in my pocket. Get it and let me go. I'm in a hurry."

He thought it was a casual holdup. Sheridan, remembering from what pocket he had last seen Bogart draw the derringer, reached forward and patted that pocket. He felt the gun's small hardness; he reached into the pocket, got the gun and tossed it into the alley.

"Turn around, Charnel."

Bogart swung. He bent his head forward and gave out a short grunt. "That's you, isn't it, Sheridan?"

"Step into the alley," said Sheridan.

"Why don't you let a man alone?" asked Bogart. "You intend to shoot me?"

"No. Step into the alley."

Bogart's head swung, secretively searching the street for help. Men moved along the main street, not a hundred feet away, and close enough to be brought to this place by the summons of his voice. This was obviously in his mind.

"Charnel," said Sheridan, "I wouldn't shout. If you do I'll crack your skull open. You've got your choice in the matter—to have your brains scrambled or your face scrambled. I'll do one or the other."

"You're fifteen years younger than I am. That's a cold deal."

"You've hurt too many people. I'm going to teach you it won't do."

"Teach me?" said Bogart, his stubborn pride rising. "By God, you won't teach me anything!"

"Get in the alley."

Bogart murmured, "I misjudged you. You're a rank, sour damned fool. You're green. You're all mixed up in your thinking. You've got the face of a man looking down into the pit."

"Get into the alley," repeated Sheridan. "I won't tell you again."

Bogart had been testing him. Bogart never had been certain of his determination; but now he seemed to hear what he hadn't heard before and, with a little gesture, he went ahead of Sheridan into the alley, stumbled and stopped and turned.

"Mark," he said, "is it Clara, or was it because I didn't pay you your share from the mill?"

"I said I'd catch up with you."

"Then it's the money," said Bogart. "I'll pay you off and we'll forget it."

"No," said Sheridan. He put his gun back beneath his waistband and he measured the bulk of Bogart. The shadows were heavy and he saw nothing but Bogart's silhouette—a silhouette slightly swaying. Bogart's wind had quickened.

"Well, then," said Bogart in a changed voice, with a resigned and weary and somewhat saddened voice, "it's Clara. I guess I like you better for it. I had about concluded there was nothing but copper pennies in your veins. What good will you get out of this? You know how it is with a man and a woman. You've seen her. You know her. You've got your feelings about her. Well, I've got feelings too. Why should you care? She's Revelwood's wife, not yours. It's not your place to bring me to account."

"I blame you for her being here," said Sheridan.

Bogart gave out a short-breathing laugh. "You think she'd be here if she didn't want to be? She's not that innocent. She's the same as I am, the same as Revelwood. You're the green one, and if you were to see her tonight she'd tell you to go back to Portland and mind your business."

"Mind yourself," said Sheridan, and brought up his fists

172

and moved into Bogart's shadow. He hit the man in the stomach; he got a blow along the side of the face, he felt Bogart's arms reach around him and close in. He brought up his palms and jammed them against Bogart's face and broke the grip and sent Bogart backward. He marched on, feeling Bogart reach him with a swinging chance blow now and then, and in his mind he grudgingly gave this man credit for courage. Bogart was a scoundrel tough enough to carry off his part; he didn't break and cry, he wasn't a man playing a part and resigning it in distress. On the surface and below the surface he was one and the same man, and Sheridan admired him for it as he pushed forward and delivered his blows. He got Bogart on the mouth and again on the head. He drove Bogart against a building wall; and in that cornered place Bogart flung himself desperately into his own defense and was for a moment a chunk of fury. He hurt Sheridan twice, he tried to circle and break out of the alley; but Sheridan blocked him and knocked him back against the wall—and then Bogart was done. Halfheartedly and in exhaustion he tried to protect himself, and took his slashing in silence— until the time came when Sheridan found this a disagreeable business and was glad when Bogart slid to the ground and lay quiet.

He stepped back, waiting for Bogart to rise, and though he tried to hold his anger and his bitterness, he discovered he could not; and in a moment of perfect clarity, he recognized Bogart's position, and admitted the man's rightness to do what he had done. He couldn't feel any satisfaction from knocking this man around; it was dirty business.

He said, "I'm going to take Clara back to George on the morning boat. Stay away from her house."

He heard Bogart shift and stir on the ground, and groan. "You don't change me," Bogart said. "You can take her back but I'll have her again."

"If Revelwood finds you, he'll kill you. You're not safe in Portland."

Bogart rose painfully from the ground and was again a lumpy shape before Sheridan. His pride was out of him but his bull-like insistence remained. "Do you suppose I'd have risked my reputation and risked trouble with Revelwood by coming up here with her if I could have helped it? I don't throw away things for the fun of it. I had to have her. She's got into me, same as she got into you and

173

Revelwood. I can take her from either of you, and by God, I'll do it."

"Then you're a dead man when Revelwood finds you," said Sheridan.

"I'll take my chances."

Sheridan turned from the alley and went up the street toward Clara's house. Somebody had to be wrong in this business, yet how was he to blame Clara for wanting something better than she had, and who could say that Bogart was evil because Clara had stirred him? Maybe these people ought to be stronger, but there they were, just people.

He came to the house and knocked on the door and went in at the sound of her voice. It was a small house, the door opening directly into the front room. She sat in a chair and her mouth and eyes had an obscure smile, meant for Bogart; a smile ruffled by excitement. It went off her face at once; she stared at him, and then she relaxed and spoke with a dulled gentleness.

"What have you done?"

"I knocked him around a bit and told him to stay away."

A small outward expression of pain showed itself. "I don't mean to hurt anybody, Mark." She thought of something else. "Where's George?"

"In Portland. We'd better go back there in the morning."

She stared beyond him. She shrugged her shoulders. "All right."

"He'll take you back."

"Oh," she said, indifferently, "I wasn't thinking of that. Of course he will."

"You don't give him much consideration."

She made a gesture with her hands. "It doesn't matter. George knew what he was getting. He'll have to be satisfied."

"No," he said, "you've broken him."

She looked down and was oppressed by sadness. "Why does it have to be like this? Why can't people be happy and stay happy? Why is it that we're always making things worse when we only mean to be natural?" She raised her head. "You've not asked me why I ran off."

"Was it to get even with Mrs. Bogart?"

"Maybe," she said, "maybe not."

"Well, it's done. Now we've got to do something else."

She got up from the chair with a forced, awkward motion and walked over to him. She lifted her head and watched him a long moment and suddenly she put her arms around him and kissed him. "Never mind anything. I knew you'd come after me. Do you hate me—do you think I'm so cheap and low?"

"No," he said.

"If I were a little different, and if you were a little different, we'd never leave each other. But we're not. Now and then we have a wonderful moment—and that's all we'll ever have. Where will you stay tonight?"

"Here," he said.

"That's good. It's like the beach again—I'm cold, I'm afraid."

He said: "I'll stay in the front room."

"You know," she said, "there was a time when I was quite sure you wanted me. It was on the boat coming up from Astoria. But the evening I wanted you to stay and you didn't—when I came back from Mrs. Bogart's party —I knew you didn't."

"That's not right. I came to get you."

"You like part of me. You don't trust the other part of me. You can't help it. And there's nothing I can do about it. Neither of us can change. You'd have as bad a time as George is having. There's only one difference—I don't feel sorry for George but I'd cry to think I were hurting you. I'd cry—but I suppose I'd go on making things bad."

He stood silent, understanding that she hoped these things were not true, that she hoped he would break through his own uncertainty. She seemed to wait for some last change in him, some reversing of his mind which would dissolve his doubt. He turned away, failing her, and depressed by it. He said, "We'll be leaving at seven in the morning."

Chapter—17

WHEN they reached Portland he had one more strange insight into Clara, and again felt the power she possessed to change men. He said, "George will probably be at the office. Let's drop in there."

"No," she said, "we'll go to the house. Let him come to me."

"He's not the one who did the deserting, Clara."

"I'm not the one sorry for it," she said.

They walked up to the house on Tenth Street and found Revelwood in the kitchen cooking himself a noon meal. He heard them and turned with an attempt to carry off calmly. He came quickly out of the kitchen toward them.

"Clara," he said, "why didn't you say something when you left? Why didn't you leave some sort of word?"

"I thought you'd probably guess and let it go at that!"

"Did you?" He was pale and not in command of himself. He had been made physically ill by worry. "You ought to know me better. Who'd you go with?"

She continued to watch him with the same composure. "I'm sorry it's hurt you. I wish it didn't. I don't want to hurt anybody."

"Who was it?"

Sheridan said to her: "Better tell him. It will come out anyhow."

"Bogart," she said to Revelwood.

"God damn him!" Revelwood said. "He got at you. He turned you."

That touched her pride. "Don't be foolish. I made up my own mind."

"Men look at you, Clara, and they judge you wrong. They work on you. Well, I shall see Bogart."

She said: "Do you want me back?"

He ran a hand across his face, irritated and still unsteady. He was extraordinarily weary. "Of course," he said quietly.

"You don't have to take me back out of pity," she said.

Revelwood shook his head, showing something close to pain. "You don't understand, Clara. If I pitied you, it—it would be something else."

She did something then that Sheridan thought was unfair. She repeated her question, deliberately grinding the situation into him. "You're sure you want me back?"

"Yes," said Revelwood, very quietly.

"Then," said Clara, "don't talk about seeing Bogart. Nothing but trouble can come of it. I won't have you in more trouble over me."

Sheridan swung away, wanting to see no more of this scene. Clara's voice stopped him at the doorway and he turned to find her eyes showing him the warmth she had not spent on Revelwood. "If you'll stay, I'll cook something."

"No," he said.

"Where are you going?"

"Back to work."

"Will I see you again?"

"I suppose," he said and left the house. The scene stuck with him. Revelwood who once had been so confident he could make his conquest of Clara, was the broken one now. She was, as she had always said, the stronger one and though she was sorry for Revelwood, she had no real pity for his weakness. Now he thought he knew something new about her. It was strength, apparently, she respected, and for which she searched in men. She thought, perhaps, that Bogart had it but, traveling down the street, he realized that Bogart was no better off than Revelwood. Bogart, too, would be weakened by Clara—and she would eventually see it and lose her respect for him.

He walked into the Pioneer Saloon and, for the first time in his life he violated his drinking rule and put down three whiskeys though it was not yet quite noon. It was time to think of his own affairs. He had to go out to the mill and get his belongings, to go on to Forest Grove and see his partner in the stage line and then—because his interest came up quite suddenly—he decided to continue to Colson's and visit Katherine Morvain. Beyond that he had no plans. He felt dispirited. The liquor didn't loosen him.

A man said: "Your name Sheridan?"

He turned toward the speaker and nodded. He knew the man but couldn't place him.

"Cupples," said the man. "You remember? You were in Oregon City recently to talk to me about Breckman's shingle mill on the river."

"Yes," said Sheridan.

"We finally got Breckman's untangled. You still interested in that mill?"

"Might be."

Cupples nodded toward a corner table. "Let's talk about it."

For a short time Sheridan held his place. He saw himself in the back-bar mirror, rough and solemn, with a dry face held tight by an ambition that did him no good. This was what Clara had no doubt seen. It came stronger and stronger to him to refuse this man and do a thorough job of getting drunk, but the old stubbornness came up. It would not do to quit.

"All right," he said, and followed Cupples toward the table.

He reached Murdock's in time for supper, and at the table he gave them the bad news. Murdock said, "Well, maybe Bogart thinks he can get a cheaper man, but that man's got to lick Kerby. Where'll you go now?"

"I'm starting a shingle mill on the Willamette."

Murdock glanced at his wife who sat in unhappy stillness; he put his eyes surreptitiously on Liza who showed no interest. Murdock said: "You'll find something. People that want something usually find it. I can't say they're satisfied people, though. Or maybe what you find never amounts to what you figured, and so you got to look for something else."

"You think a man would be happier if he didn't want anything?" asked Sheridan.

"No," replied Murdock. "Things seem to hurt the folks that don't want anything just as much as those that do. I don't understand why it's so, but it seems to be. Anybody ever figure that out?"

"How would I know?"

"Well," said Murdock, "if you ain't got a better view of it than I have, what's the good of bein' educated?"

"Maybe I didn't get the right kind of an education."

"There more than one kind?" asked Murdock. "There's only one kind of ignorance, ain't there?" He watched Sheridan with his tired, kind face, and saw no answer to a question he seriously meant, and shrugged his shoulders and added, "Too damned much confusion. I ain't so sure there's any hope in this progress business. It just brings trouble. The preacher once said the more we know the longer we'd live. My question is, what for? A man wants a fire, a woman and a full belly. It ain't no easier to get those things now than when nobody knew anything. I ain't even sure about the medicine the preacher sells. It makes us out all sinners to start with, and we got to spend our lives worryin' about something we didn't worry about before." He stopped, he let out a great belch and his eyes grew dull with a comfortable fatigue. Then he said with a sly amusement, "You tell Kerby about Bogart? Kerby will run off Bogart's foremen till hell won't have it. That'll pay you back."

"No," said Sheridan. He rose from the table and walked out to the porch, with Murdock's voice following him.

"Always kill a skunk, or he'll spray you again. If education don't teach you that, it ain't no good."

Sheridan stood at the break of the porch and felt the stifling smoky air run up his nostrils; there had been so much of this smoke abroad during the past week or two that it seemed to have deposited a sediment in his chest. The earth was choked with a rolling haze and the heat of this unseasonable month had accumulated until it was a weight pressing uncomfortably on his shoulders. He felt a stillness, a suspense in this air, and guessed that a break was soon coming.

Liza came from the house and stood long still, and stared through the shadows at his face. He felt the hot wave of anger flow out of her and roll around him, and suddenly she left the porch and went rapidly over the yard. He lost sight of her on the road but in a little while he heard her half running toward the head of the valley.

He walked on to the mill and stepped on the carriage and put his hands around the carriage lever; the warm smell of the boiler came to him, and the clean reek of sawdust and the leathery fragrance of the big belt on the headsaws. This mill had been a good venture, and so had Colson's, but the whim of a man had cost him one mill and the carelessness of some hunter with his fire had cost him the other.

It seemed to be as Revelwood believed, that a fist reached out of the sky to destroy without purpose. It seemed to be there were currents in which men floated, some of them drawing a man forward to success no matter how much of a fool he was, sometimes carrying him backward even though he deserved better. He stood still and faced this philosophy and had no answer for it; but he hated it and could not believe it, and he gave the carriage lever a quick, light blow of impatience and turned back toward the house.

There was a rapid running along the road and presently a pair came into sight. A voice—Liza's voice—murmured something, and a man answered. They stopped and waited for him to come up. Liza took a step aside. She murmured, "All right, Clyde."

It was the Crabtree boy. That wild, ignorant lad took a shuffling step forward, bent his head and lunged into Sheridan.

Sheridan got his warning too late. Crabtree's bony fists stunned him with the first two blows. He got his arms up but the boy's fists came up through his guard and ripped his mouth against his teeth. He drew his arms together, tripping Crabtree's hands, and he fell against Crabtree and swung himself to avoid the upward ramming of the other's knee. He slid his arm around Crabtree's neck, feeling more punishment in his chest and along his side. The boy hit him hard on the kidneys and the sharpest, most unbearable kind of pain shot through him. He brought his arms tighter around Crabtree's throat, he sidestepped and he threw all his power into a sudden wrenching throw. Crabtree went off balance and began to fall, and as he fell, Sheridan cracked him on the head with his knee, and let him go and stood back. He ran a hand across his bleeding mouth and made a sharp step aside.

Crabtree was instantly up and instantly forward. Sheridan met him head-on and knocked down the boy's swinging fists. He landed his short rough punches on Crabtree's face and came close to breaking his knuckles against the boy's head. He had a moment of advantage and tried to follow it as Crabtree gave ground. He moved forward, missed his next punch and found himself unexpectedly smothered. The boy was a wild and wicked fighter, backing away, swinging aside, coming in. He was a merciless young man, set on to this thing by a woman. Sheridan never fully protected himself and scarcely got in another blow. He was slashed and his senses grew soft and he felt himself hit in a dozen places, and turn as he did to bring up his guard, he could not screen himself. He stood his ground

180

and he swung, and now and then he landed; but he was a chunk of meat on a butcher block and the cleaver worked its way with him. He tried once more to come into Crabtree; he got one arm around the boy and locked it against the other's windpipe and he hit him twice on the side of the head before Crabtree knocked the wind out him and drove him back; one more full-on blow dropped him. He lay half on his side, blinded, and felt Crabtree's boot grind down on his leg.

The girl said: "Clyde. That's all."

She had started something she couldn't stop. The boy's boot, swinging back and forward, struck at Sheridan's soft flank and at his ribs. The girl's voice lifted in alarm. "Clyde!" Sheridan rolled over, away from that battering boot. He reached under his belt and he got out the gun he had carried since the evening at The Dalles. The boot hit him again and unsteadied him, but he aimed low against the ground and let go. He heard Crabtree's short yell of shock rip the night, and the girl's scream. Crabtree turned and rushed away. Sheridan sat up in the dirt and hunted for the boy's shadow. He fired a second time, fully intending to kill; he heard no cry and knew he had missed. He poised the gun, waiting for a third try, but the lust went out of him in that long moment and presently he let the gun sag, and sat still, and began to feel the pulsing injuries of his body. Crabtree's feet were still drumming away along the road and Murdock's voice came roughly from the house.

"What the hell's over there?"

The girl dropped down near him, on her knees. "I didn't mean for him to hurt you that much."

"We're even, Liza. I'm paid off. I guess I had it coming. Why did you pick him for the chore? He's Lily Shottler's man."

"She thinks so," said Liza. She bowed her head and seemed to be thinking. Presently she began to cry. It started as a wavering, sniveling sound and became a case of unlovely hysterics. She scrawled foward until her head was near his face and her tears fell damp and warm on his hands. He held himself still, offering nothing. She reached out and put her arms around him; her lips moved across his face and found his mouth and lay spongelike against it. His face grew wet with the blubbering and his arms, braced against her pressure, felt strain. He had no help for her, yet he had no anger against her. He waited

181

and he held himself still. It seemed a long while later when she drew back. "Oh, well," she murmured, and got up. "No use."

He rose and walked toward the house with her.

"I wish I could go away but I won't. I don't see anything ahead."

Murdock stood in the doorway and watched these two with his prying curiosity, saying nothing. Sheridan went to his room and got into bed. He lay still, one hand over his face, listening to his aches and shifting weight on the bed to relieve them. He heard the girl walking around her room and he remembered Revelwood's words again—that the world was only a thing of accidents. The world had turned out that way for George, certainly; and for this girl too. He grew tired and fell asleep.

Through his sleep he heard the beginning of rain—the first slow rustling of it on the earth and the growing strength of it on the roof; and even in sleep he caught that strong smell of overdry dust turning wet.

Chapter — 18

SHERIDAN turned in the saddle when he got beyond the mill next morning and looked back behind—at the mill itself and at the house and the three Murdocks standing on the porch. It was Mrs. Murdock, always emotional, who raised her hand to him. He lifted his arm and squared himself on the saddle. A quarter mile onward he looked again and found the house hidden behind woolly mists; and in another quarter mile the mill and the valley had also disappeared. It occurred to him that he owed the Murdocks a good deal, and that they liked him and were sorry to see him go; yet none of that had come out in the parting. People were locked inside walls of flesh and bone; sometimes the tone of a voice got a bare message through or the shadows which flitted across a face betrayed a little of it. But that was about all.

Now behind him was no sign of the valley in which he had spent his time; the mists closed down upon it until, in a trick of his imagination, both the valley and his stay there was like the memory of an old man looking far back into his youth, not quite sure which was real and which was dreamed. The raw, fat rain came down on his overcoat and rattled on his hat brim; it soaked his legs, it worked its way along his collar and through his shirt. Earth sent up its exhaled breath in thick crystal sheets of fog, blotting out everything save the narrow lane of road for a distance of two hundred yards before him. The odor of smoke was gone, and what came into his nostrils was the sweetness of a freshened soil. He felt cheerful, he felt whole and strong, and there was no doubt within him; his mind went quickly on from thought to thought. He turned right at the Bright's Orchard store and fell into the main Portland-Forest Grove highway; he passed Hillsboro in the middle of the morning and reached Forest Grove before noon.

He stopped in at the stable of his partner in the stage business, Cray Jennings, and found this beefy, red-faced countryman just returned from the early morning run to Portland. They went into Jennings' small office, a narrow enclosure that had formerly been a box stall, and together examined the bookkeeping of their joint effort.

"It ain't, of course, much of a living yet," said Jennings. "Barely pays me, and nothing for you. What you done about the mail contract since you wrote the Senator?"

"I saw Church in town and asked him to put a shoulder to our spoke."

"My boy," said Jennings, "he'll push no wheel but his own."

"That's what I guess. We need a longer line. If we ran a stage from here to McMinnville, and another back through Newberg to Portland we'd have a loop. Traveling people would depend on it. I'll find somebody in McMinnville to come in with us."

"Spread the starving thinner," said Jennings. He sat back with a smiling, doubtful expression and threw his objections at Sheridan, and listened to Sheridan's answers, and was half impressed. His judgments were cautious and strictly confined to the things he knew about. What he didn't know he put little trust in. "You talk well," he said at last.

"We might hook this thing up all down the valley, west side. The east side stage company is doing good."

"They've got mail and they've got connections to California."

"There's mail to carry on the west side and, so far, nobody to carry it. Put the line together and you've got something to show the post office."

"If it looks good," said Jennings, "somebody's damned sure to smell it and come up with competition. I was the first man around here with a blooded stud for service. Wasn't another one in the state, so I thought I had a natural thing. Six months later there was a dozen. Where they came from, I don't know, but the smell of profit's a powerful thing. Well, you talk good, Mark. Maybe you can make a rich man out of me. Don't object. Find your man in McMinnville."

"I'll find him."

Jennings smiled. "Of course. You got a way of talking about a dollar that makes it look like a thousand." He paused and stared with his kind, close interest into Mark's face. "You believe everything's going to be fine. You got it in your voice, and that sort of makes everybody else think everything's going to be fine. A lot of people don't think that. Most people don't, in fact. So it's good to hear a man that does. It's what we all want to hear, only it takes a special sort of talker to convince us. Had dinner?"

Sheridan took his noon meal at Jennings' and set out toward Colson's with a freshening southwester beating against his flank. Broad curtains of water walked slantingly across the land; the wood culverts boiled under the road, the brush-choked ditches were awash, and ponds began to form on the flat meadows. The earth drank and seemed to swell, and the mountain ridges around him were vague behind the boiling rain mists.

He went steadily along the road he knew so well. When he came to the alder grove where he had found Katherine with her dead brother, a painful feeling revived in him and he visualized her face as it had been that day, and he heard her voice again. She was on his mind all the way; it was in fact the thought of her which brought him here. He had wakened this morning with the sharp wish to see her, not a new wish, not a sudden wish, but one which had come and gone and had come again through the past week

He passed the turn-off which led to his old sawyer's house, and continued to the mill site. He didn't leave the saddle, but walked the horse around the black skeleton of the mill and over to the scar of the Morvain house. The melted washtub still stood in the yard, now filling with rain water, and the iron bedstead sat crazy where the bedroom had been; a mattress lay as a shriveled, half-consumed lump on the ground. He rode along the creek meadows and came to the house, a mile from the mill, where the widow of his head sawyer lived. He thought Mrs. Colson would be there.

He found her finally in the Drumheller house farther on. She hadn't changed; she was as brisk, as pleasant as before. "Now, then, I've wondered about you. Never mind the water. Well, you find the old woman just as she was. Do you know what I miss? Colson's spectacles. I always kept them on the table where his pipe was. I hunted and I hunted, but I never did find those spectacles."

A teakettle sang on the stove, a rag rug covered the floor. She had found lithographed pictures for her walls, and a few knickknacks to occupy the table. She had a huge yellow cat with a hammerhead face. A bowl of peeled apples sat on her work table, that odor filling the room.

He stood with his back to the warm stove and watched her stand by the work table with her obvious pleasure at having a guest for whom she could cook supper. She was thinking about supper at that moment; he knew that from the expression on her face.

"So you've bought another house," he said.

"Oh, no. I rent. What would I do with property? My time's short here."

"You've got twenty years left at least."

"People have got to have use or they don't belong here. I've got no use. Every time I put up a jar of jelly, I wonder what for?"

He walked through to the shed and split wood and kindling for half an hour and brought an armload back to the wood box. He said, "Where are the Morvains?"

She had been slicing the apples. She stopped and turned toward him. "I'm surprised you waited so long to ask. They've gone."

"Where?"

"Just gone. I asked Katherine to let me know where she went. She ain't done it. It was the day after the funeral. It made me so sad."

"That damned Morvain," he said. "He can't stay still."

"This time she was the one that wanted to go."

"Didn't they say anything? Did they speak of a town, or name some direction?"

"Not a word. Katherine's a girl that's afraid of saying much, for fear if she says it, it won't come true. I asked her where she planned to go. I'll tell you what she said. She said: 'People like us don't plan things. Things happen to us.' "

"Somebody along the road will know about them. It's only been a week."

"Or," said Mrs. Colson, "I sometimes think she believed that maybe the bad luck of the family was something that followed them, and that if she could just disappear and leave no trace maybe the bad luck couldn't follow any more."

He said: "If they went out into the valley they'd go on this road and they'd pass Forest Grove. Somebody would have seen them. They'd be camping out. That wagon has no shelter." He shook his head. "Nothing's ever right for her. Rain or fire or misery—they're always in it."

"If that's the way you feel, why'd you leave her after the funeral? I wondered then. I wonder now."

186

He returned to the woodshed and worked on the woodpile. He took the cross-grained chunks and swung on them and broke them, and found some relief. Maybe they'd stop in the valley, since Katherine wanted good land; or they might drift on toward the Willamette. She would be looking for a piece of land that could be rented, or bought cheaply. She would be a close bargainer. Then he remembered she wanted to be in a place where the men could find work. That might be around another sawmill. It might be in a town where rough labor was needed. He worked on, dredging up all the possibilities; he tried to look upon that family through Katherine's eyes and he tried to understand how she would be thinking as she traveled through this wet day. He never included Morvain in his calculations, knowing it was Katherine who would make the decisions—Katherine whose will held his family together and drove it toward security and respectability. It was lamplight time when Mrs. Colson called him back into a kitchen filled with the fine odor of fried meat.

She said: "Sit there." She was happy with her cooking. She had pounded and simmered and fried the steak in flour. She had boiled the potatoes until their swollen interiors made fluffy beads through the cracked skin. There was corn awash in its own milky juices, and small round peas drenched in butter. An apple pie exhaled its spicy fragrance through a slashed crust and her jellies and conserves and relishes—these things she loved so well to make that she made them even when need was gone—made a circle around the castor. She removed her apron, gave the table a moment's glance, and sat down, bowing her head. Since he was the man at the table he understood it was his place to ask grace. He did so.

"You ain't had much practice at it," she observed. "Young man, you'll have to learn to lean on something. Nobody's strong enough to lean on himself, and it won't do to lean on other people. You like chow-chow, I remember. I put it up last week. Couldn't bear going through winter without something in the cupboard."

He was thinking of Katherine when he said: "It would be a good deal better for her if she would lean against somebody. She won't."

"The young," said Mrs. Colson, "seem to think they got it to fight alone. I was like that. I worked hard, I worried a lot, I was always expectin' the worst to happen. Well, it

187

did. Nothing more can happen to me, and I guess I know something you don't. Maybe all old people know it. They get to the point where they know nothing they can do will save 'em—and about that time they discover it don't matter so much anyhow. There's never been a death that's been much of a loss to the earth. Nothing counts as much as we like to believe. But it's the young ones that love to live so much that they're afraid."

"That's no help," said Sheridan, and smiled at this old woman he liked so well. He had his pie and his second cup of coffee; he sat back, half asleep in the room's thick warmth and hearing the steady slamming of hard rain against the house. A little later he helped Mrs. Colson with the dishes, and afterwards stood with his back to the stove to soak up warmth against his return to Forest Grove.

"How's your other mill?"

"Not there now. Owner and I disagreed."

"What'll you do?"

"I've got a shingle mill lined up, over on the Willamette."

"Well, find Katherine." She watched him put on his coat and hat. "I'd like to see her again. Tell her I do miss her."

He said: "Good-by."

She made a gesture with her hands. "Young folks like words like that. Now you'll go off and it's likely I'll not see you again."

"Oh, I'll be back."

"If you come back, do it before spring," she said. "I'm weary of winters and maybe this will be the last I'll care to go through."

"People don't die for the wishing," he said.

"Yes, they do," she said.

Quite abruptly he realized she had made up her mind about it and, understanding that, he looked closely at her and discovered the lines and shadows on her face which he would not otherwise have noticed. He had not come upon such a thing before, but as he stood at the door he knew that probably he would not see her again, and he searched himself for something to say and found nothing adequate. He saw the print of a kind wish for him on her face, and he hoped that she might see some wish for her on his face. That was all he could hope; and said, "Good-by, Mrs. Colson," and left the house. The southwester beat squarely at him, shaking him on the saddle; darkness was a tunnel through which he rode, and a thick rain mist brushed his face though he could not see it.

Reaching Forest Grove he put up at the small hotel and slept. He had his breakfast early on another rough and wet morning. He saw Jennings again and he walked the streets and asked his questions concerning the Morvains, but found nothing of them. Taking another road out of town, he passed through the Chehalem country, along lovely meadows sparkling wet and over heavy-timbered hills gorged with mist and so came into McMinnville. He was there a day before he found a man interested in setting up a stage. His search for the Morvains netted him nothing. At Newberg he was another day on the same business. The third day, moving northwest through little valley pockets and low rolling hills, he fell into the road leading toward the shingle mill.

Early night was drifting in when he reached the meadow and stand of cedar along the river. The mill stood on the river's bluff; not fifty feet from it was a small, porch-surrounded house lying within a young orchard. He dropped his saddle and roll on the porch and let the horse drift toward the good grass while he, drenched as he was, walked on to the mill. He had a quick look at the machinery and walked out to the landing built on the river's bluff. The river made a long bend in front of the mill and vanished beyond cottonwood and willow and alder.

He walked back into the dark mill shed and his mind put it into operation. It gave him a good feeling to stand here and mentally turn this place alive. There was nothing like a beginning; there was never anything so good as a fresh start. This was where he made it, this was where he caught on. He had the best of feelings about this place; it would be the venture that succeeded, following the trial ventures that had failed.

He returned to the house and had a quick look at its half-abandoned rooms. There was a bedstead, a table, a few nailed-on shelves, and a stove. He rummaged up some wood from the shed and got a fire going and stood by it to take the chill from his wet clothes. Night had come on, both black and mist-packed, and the rain drove against the house and water leaked in from a broken roof shingle. He walked to the door and noticed a house light glinting across the meadow. That would be the nearest neighbor, and then he realized he was hungry. He started over the meadow, sinking into its spongy soil; he whistled as he went on toward the house light, his head half drooped against the sharp striking of the rain.

Chapter —19

IT was Katherine who made the decision to leave Colson's. The family had moved down to the house of the newly widowed head sawyer's wife the day following Elgin's funeral; but the evening, walking the road alone, the feeling came urgently upon her that there was nothing here now for the family. She told her father that same night. Next morning they loaded the wagon and set out. Mrs. Colson had protested the move. "You ought not. You're leaving friends."

She was leaving, Katherine realized, the closest of friends; and yet as she sat on the wagon seat and watched Mrs. Colson grow smaller behind her, she found an uncommon satisfaction in the breakaway. In a way it was a matter of survival. This family needed friendship less than it needed to use its own strength. There was nothing much for the men to do in this end of the valley; and once again they might sink to the level of living off the bounty of more industrious neighbors. She wanted none of that.

They skirted Forest Grove and turned to the right toward hills on the southern side of the Tualatin. Her father had suggested looking for work in town but Katherine shook her head, feeling that a town was unsafe for people in their circumstances; firmly fixed in her mind was a piece of good land, a house that wasn't a shack, a school and a job for her father and for the boys. The road crossed the high end of the valley and from time to time came close upon the foothills of the Coast Range. This was the land that the two boys liked best and she saw them quietly talking to her father; it was his land too, in the sense that it seemed to promise the easy, backwoods life to which he was accustomed. She saw the suggestion coming—and listened to him with a cold unfriendliness and shook her head.

The rains began while they moved through the Chehalem hills; the wagon top leaked and her cook fire blew fitfully around her. They touched Newberg and paused here while Morvain canvassed the town with his questions. They turned north from Newberg and on the outskirts of town saw a sign announcing chickens for sale; she stopped, bought twelve hens and a rooster, and lashed the crate to the wagon's end. This road led back to Portland and that gave Morvain a thought. "I can find clerk work here," he said.

He always sought for the work which appeared not to be work, it was part of his dream of being a big man. She had a moment of pity for him, and thrust the pity away and had him turn the wagon into a lesser road. Five days out of Forest Grove—the rain still heavily falling and the world cloaked by fog—they tipped over a hill and came down into a very small valley. Four or five farms lay together here along the bottom of a pocket, and slashing fires burned from stump lands being cleared. They drove down the grade toward a farm—a farm painted white and a barn painted red, and fields set off with rail fences half covered by brush. A lone man stood near the road, tending a stump fire, and gave them a glance as they passed, and stared at them as they went on. The road, having worked its way into the valley went on a short distance and began to climb out.

"Stop here," said Katherine.

They had come abreast a house which seemed to hold no people. Morvain drew in the team and looked at her. "What for? We got to get somewhere, Katy. I'm tired of goin' around like a gypsy."

She put her hands on her lap and looked at the house and at the grove of fruit trees and the land around it. There was a meadow on either side of the house and another which ran back from the house along a hill. On the crest of the hill was a fringe of firs.

"Nobody lives there," she said. "One of those windows is broken in. Go ask that man about it," she said.

Morvain reluctantly got off the wagon and started back on the road. She slipped from the seat and went to the house, cupping her hands beside her face to look through the windows. She circled the house; she opened the top of the well and noticed the cooling shelves built into it. She went into the woodshed, and came back to the front of the house and stood on the porch, sheltered from the rain. Her face had a different expression. She watched her father cross the rail fence and talk to the man who stood by the burning stump. The two of them were together a

192

little while, then the man turned with Morvain and both of them walked forward on the road.

He was around thirty-five; not too large a man, but chunky, with a face reddened by the wind. He had large gray eyes and a pair of heavy lips.

"The place is owned by some people that moved to Portland," he said. "I'm looking out for it. They want to sell, but nobody's buyin'. You want to buy?"

"Not now," said Katherine. "We want a place to move into for a while."

"Well," said the man, "nobody's likely to live in it this winter. Go ahead and move in."

"We could farm it on shares," she said, "or make some arrangement to buy later. I don't think it's worth rent, sitting empty as it's been. We'd keep it up, which is more than it's had."

The man watched her as he listened. He watched her closely. He made a gesture with his hands. "They left it up to me. Your menfolk looking for work?"

"Yes," said Katherine.

"I can use you clearin' stumps and brush. That'll keep you till spring."

"Well," said Morvain, "I don't—"

"What'll you pay?" asked Katherine.

"You can use this place rent free during the winter. I'll tell the owners it's best to have somebody here. Then I'll give these men a dollar a day apiece."

"All right," said Katherine.

He put both hands into his pockets and stared at her. "I'm not married. You want to cook for me? Throw that into the bargain, too?"

"You supply the food for all of us?"

He hesitated, he put his head down and looked at the ground and pursed his lips. "Well," he said, "that's all right."

She looked at her father. "Drive in and unload," she said, and turned back to the house. She walked into the front room, and through it to the kitchen; she opened the rear door and stepped out to the connection between house and woodshed. There was a side room which would be for the two boys. She and Suzie would sleep in the main bedroom; her father could use the front room. The red-faced farmer came into the house. He still had his hands in his pockets. "I think," he said in a careful voice, "I could help you buy this farm at a pretty fair price."

"Maybe," she said.

"You want to cook at my place, or here?"

"Here," she said.

"Take what you want from my kitchen. There's a storehouse back of it. Take what you need." He turned and left the place.

As soon as they were unloaded she had one of the boys drive to the farmer's house for food. Morvain and the boys swept the floors three times, knocked down the cobwebs, patched and washed the windows, scrubbed the rust from the stoves, and got the place warmed up. Arriving for supper three hours later, the red-cheeked farmer —whose name she discovered, was Fred Boxwell—showed his surprise. His glance went slowly around the place, stopping here, stopping there. At the table, Katherine had a better chance to view him. He had not shaved for two or three days and his hands weren't particularly clean. He sat lumped in his chair, half sure and half uneasy, eating with a silent haste. When he was finished he stacked his dishes and sat back, suddenly weary from the day's work.

"You're a good cook," he said. The words were not particularly graceful, nor meant to be; he was simply making a statement. His eyes were red, his shoulders slack, his whole face dull from long labor.

The boys disappeared at once and Morvain went out to the shed. Suzie started on the dishes but Katherine remained at the table with Boxwell.

She said: "Your house is dirty. I'll clean it when we're settled."

He said: "You married, or been married?"

"No."

He opened his eyes a little wider and a slow interest stirred the sluggish weariness in them; he gave a short nod. She got up and went into the kitchen to help Suzie with the dishes and hearing nothing from him, she thought he had fallen asleep. But presently she turned and found him standing in the kitchen, paused behind her and staring at her. He had come quietly.

"Well," he said, "if you want anything more, look around my house for it."

"All right," she said, and watched him go.

She had gotten some muslin sacks in Newburg and,

194

after the rest of the family had gone to bed, she sat by the front-room table and worked them apart and hemmed them. This man, she realized, already had the notion that she might make him a wife. He was being nice to her for a reason. She thought, "What would I do about it?"

She put down the muslin sacks and walked out to the porch, straightening herself against an air so thin that it rubbed her face like fine gauze. Fog solidly packed the pocketed valley and only a faint, shimmering disk of light showed the direction of Boxwell's house. The rain had strengthened, the wind had risen, but it was a wind that, over the pocket, seemed not to come down.

She felt more secure this night than for many years. These round hills created a little world and shut out the rest which had been too large. She got the good feeling that nothing would ever come here to disturb her, that this was a hiding place for the family. Then her mind jumped back to Boxwell—it had never really left him, but—and she remembered that he owned a whole half section in the pocket. He had some good qualities. He was obviously a hard-working man, which gave him some excuse for his slovenliness at the table though she could not wholly excuse him. He was perhaps a close man, the creases of closeness were around his eyes and at the edges of his mouth; even so, he had been kind to them and maybe the kindness was deeper than she thought it was. She let out a long sigh and turned into the house and put another chunk into the stove. The rain pounded on the roof and the night's blackness shone against the window panes like enamel. The room was a wonderfully warm shelter—and she made up her mind then.

Chapter —20

A SNAG, directly across the river from the mill, marked the level of the river in November when Sheridan came to the mill. The steady rains kept on and two weeks later the snag was three feet under water. The steamboat *Drusilla* tied up at his landing that week to take aboard a load of shingles for Oregon City. He had two men cutting logs in the cedar grove at the far end of the meadow, and three in the mill, all of them roundabout farmers picking up winter money. He hauled shingles to the general stores at Wilsonville and Sherwood and Tualatin and had no competition in the region except for a mill near West Linn. It was characteristic of him that after the first week of operation he sat down to his books to estimate how much he could expect of his own mill and what its limits were.

He was back in Newburg and McMinnville as soon as he had the mill shaken down. In both places he had previously talked with livery stable people and on this trip he talked with them again. The Newburg to Portland stage was a slow thing to get started and he left that town with the venture still in the air; but at McMinnville he found his man, and made the first trip with his new partner from McMinnville, through the Chehalem to Forest Grove.

It was then almost a month after his visit to Mrs. Colson's. Beginning again with his search for the Morvains, he visited every house for a mile out of Forest Grove, in the direction of Colson's, and then circled the town and tried every road leading from it, asking his questions at farmhouse doors. He was three days in this search.

The two boys, he found, were not clear in his mind. Suzie he remembered better, and Morvain was entirely clear to him; but it was a curious thing how exact were his impressions of Katherine—how clearly she came to him when, at these farmhouse doors, he painted his picture of her. She was tall, she was dark, she wasn't talkative. She had a face not so much round as long and her hair was full-black, with a shine to it. There was, he remembered, a freckle or two around her nose, and then he usually added in a halting way—the eyes of these farm people watching him—that she was an attractive woman. He meant more than that, but he could not bring himself to add more.

He described her as she might look to others; yet, after the day's empty search when he lay abed in Forest Grove's thin-walled hotel and found her in his mind, he remembered that there was another side to her, the lighter side which she had let him see on the sultry evening of their walk along the road; she had forgotten her troubles, she had smiled—and that was the Katherine he remembered but could not describe.

Four days of fruitless hunting discouraged him; on the following day he changed the direction of his search and took the main road toward Portland. Somewhere near Cornelius a single horseman drew up from the rough rain mist and fell in with him—a tall man, well padded with flesh and swathed around by checkered cloak. The greatcoat's collar covered him to the bridge of his nose and his slouch hat came down to his brows. He hailed Sheridan and Sheridan, looking closely, saw a familiar pair of eyes surrounded by puckered skin. It was Hosea Crawford on his rounds.

"Shouldn't think you'd be hunting lost souls on a day like this," commented Sheridan. "Everybody's indoors."

"Indoors," said Hosea agreeably. "Indoors, restless, idle and ripe for error. Where you bound?"

Sheridan mentioned his reason for riding.

"She was a fine woman," said Crawford. "Much courage—much fortitude. No, I've not seen her."

"If you do," said Sheridan, "I'd like to know. I've got a shingle mill on the Willamette. Wilsonville is the address."

"I'm bound for Murdock's. I feel I've neglected that family. That girl—is she married yet?"

"No."

Crawford's eyes swung on Sheridan, held to him, and moved away. "Wonderful weather. Stirs a young man's blood and makes an old man wish he were younger. Mrs. Murdock, I recall, is a good cook. I turn off here. If I hear of anything, I shall report." He swung into a side road and presently disappeared into the mists.

The middle of the afternoon found Sheridan beyond Hillsboro; and at that point, having found no information along this road concerning the Morvains, he gave up the search for the day and set out for Portland, putting up at the Pioneer near five o'clock. As soon as he had cleaned himself of the mud of travel, he turned to Elijah Church's office. It was near six but Church, in common with the town's leading men, kept long office hours.

"Just dropped in," said Sheridan, "to see if you'd changed your mind about giving me a push with the Senator."

Church played his hands idly across the desk. He had extraordinarily cool eyes; they had a kind of chilly glow, and further the impression of a human bank in which much valuable stuff was safely stored. Probably he was proud of his reputation as a power in town.

"No," said Church, "I've not."

"We're performing on that route. Do you doubt it will be permanent?" asked Sheridan.

"Can you continue?" asked Church mildly. "That's the point."

"We're making expenses, and enough over to keep my partner interested. The contract would make it a very good thing."

"I am glad to hear it," said Church. "I am indeed."

"We've extended to McMinnville and, next week, will probably run from McMinnville to Portland. That gives us a loop for businessmen wishing to cover these towns as quickly as possible."

Church stared steadily at Sheridan. Church said, "I am surprised you've found men to work for you. What do you tell them?"

"Enough to get them interested."

"No," said Church with his interested insistence. "What's their profit in it?"

"A job—and some share in the profits."

"Each driver a share on each run? That's too many partners."

"When you begin a thing," said Sheridan, "you begin it however you can. If I get two or three pieces of this line put together I have got a going concern. These first people are partners. Afterwards, when we extend the line, we will be hiring drivers, not taking on partners."

"It's in the back of your mind to extend?" asked Church.

"The day the McMinnville-Portland stage breaks even, I'll be looking for a man to run from McMinnville to Dayton. And the day that run breaks even I'll start for Corvallis."

Church lifted one hand from the table and delicately scratched his chin. "You must remember that when you start down the valley you'll be in competition with the west side line."

"There's room for both. The west side line cannot serve the east side of the river."

"And yet," said Church, so casual and so quietly inquisitive, "they will see a threat in you. Have you any notion of how to fight them?"

"That's another subject."

Church nodded, made a gesture. "Glad you came in." He was a thoughtful figure at his desk when Sheridan left him and went back into the windy-wet street. He remembered the sudden turn-on of brilliant searching interest in the man's eyes when he had spoken of expanding the line, and he gave that a good deal of thought as he walked up Oak to Tenth, and along Tenth. The blinds of the Revelwood home were up, the lamplight streamed out; he saw Revelwood seated in a chair in shirt sleeves reading a newspaper.

Revelwood opened the door at his knock. He bent his head and gave Sheridan a close, sudden-pleased glance. He reached out and seized Sheridan's arm and drew him in. "By God, I'm glad to see you. Clara!"

She came from the kitchen and stopped across the room from him, giving her hair a swift tucking-up with her hands. Her smile—strong and immediate—came over to him with its disturbing effect. Suddenly moved by impulse, she crossed the room and put her arms around him and looked up and gave him a quick kiss. "Why don't you stay around town?" she asked, and turned back to the kitchen. "George, make a place at the table for Mark."

Sheridan hung up his coat and hat on the hall tree. He stood at the window and put his hands in his pockets and stared out upon the darkening street. Revelwood was in the kitchen hunting extra dishes, and speaking to Clara quietly. Clara's voice came back, equally quiet but with a faint edge to it. Something was wrong in this house.

Revelwood returned to the room. He was, Sheridan noticed, hammered to a wire edge; this man who had observed the follies of other people with a spectator's

199

good-natured contempt was caught in those follies and had no defense against them.

Clara came from the kitchen with supper, laid aside her apron and sat down. She had a long brown scar on her arm, and, seeing Sheridan's eye on it, she said: "George hit me with a stick of stovewood."

Revelwood murmured: "Dammit, Clara, you burnt yourself in the stove oven."

She gave Revelwood a short glance. "Of course. Did you think Mark would believe the other story? Mark—where are you?"

"On the Willamette, west bank, not far from Wilsonville. I've got a shingle mill. Anything new around here?"

"New?" she said. "No. We're quiet married people. George sells his real estate and I knit my wool. Do you remember that Irishman who came off the wreck with us? I saw him on the street the other day. He came up to me and I guess we talked for half an hour."

"Did he ever find his family?"

"His oldest daughter washed ashore. Dead, of course. He never found the others. He wasn't quite sober. He looked as though he was a steady drinker."

"That's one way," said George.

"What about these lots?" asked Sheridan.

Revelwood shrugged his shoulders. "I never was in that kind of business before, but it seems any fool can make a living at it."

"What's become of the gold mine?"

Something of the old flash came to Revelwood's eyes. "I had a nibble the other day. Respectable businessman dropped in to see me and discuss eastern Oregon. I said nothing. He'll be back. He smells money and he'll try to do me, sooner or later." Then the whimsicality died.

When the meal was done, Sheridan made an offer to help with the dishes. Clara said: "That's a country custom you've picked up. Who taught you?"

"A pretty girl."

She gave him her smiling glance and lifted her shoulders. He went into the kitchen and found a towel, and waited for her.

"Where is she now?"

"Still there, I guess."

"Your voice is too casual, Mark. What did you bring it up for?"

Revelwood came to the kitchen doorway. "I'm going downtown for a cigar."

Sheridan leaned against the wall, watching Revelwood leave the house, watching Clara's face. She hadn't answered Revelwood, and when the door closed she looked at Sheridan with some kind of passing expression, and looked down again. "Mark, where are the Morvains?"

"They left Colson's after the mill burned, nobody knows where. The youngest boy died. I can't find a trace of them."

"You're interested in her," she said, a sudden shadow crossing her face. She let her hands lie still in the dishpan and she stared at them. "Have you told her about me?"

"No. Why should I?"

"Because," she said. She faced him and was angry with him. "Because I want her to know. If I knew where she was I'd go tell her myself."

"What would you tell her, Clara?"

"I'd tell her there was a time when I came first with you. I'd tell her there's part of you she'll never get. I can't have that taken away from me, by her or any other woman." She watched him with her intent closeness. "You haven't changed, have you?"

He held down his impatience. "How many men are you claiming, Clara?"

"Oh," she said, "that doesn't matter. You know how I feel about George and Bogart. You know it's not the same thing. We were first. If things had been only a little different—"

He said gently, "If you'd waited a week we'd been married."

She bent forward and rested her weight against her hands; her thoughts were back among those earlier scenes and her face was sad. "I wish I had. Do you wish so, too?"

He said, "God knows what I wish now."

"You see? You were never sure about me. That's why I didn't wait. You don't know women well enough to take them as they are. I knew very well I couldn't live up to what you thought I was. Yet I know if I'd been more reserved, you wouldn't have doubted me. We would have been all right. And maybe, with you, I'd never done any of the things I have done since."

"Well," he said, "it's done now."

201

"When you doubt, your whole face grows cold. That's the thing I couldn't stand. I hate coldness."

He said, "There's something wrong in this house."

She went on washing. "George is miserable."

"So are you."

"Yes," she said. "We're both shriveling up. We're both dying."

He said, "Is Bogart back in town?"

"Yes," she said and changed the subject. "I know you'll get married. I hate the thought, but I know you will. When you go to another woman will you be able to forget me altogether?"

He said, "I won't go to another woman until I can."

"Well," she said, her tone sharpening, "do you think you can?"

"Not now—not yet," he said.

An expression of pleasure came across her face. "You never will," she said, and went back to her work. The pleasure was a brief thing soon turning to regret. "People don't change. Whatever they were in the beginning, that's what they'll always be. And that's the tragedy of you and me, Mark." She looked up at him with her quiet desperation. "What'll I do?"

"Make the best of it."

"Make the best of dying? Life's too short for that."

"You're giving him a bad life."

She shrugged her shoulders. She couldn't pity anybody weaker than she was and therefore had no real feeling for Revelwood, no true understanding of his misery. "He's no worse off than I am. I never promised him anything. He knew his bargain."

They finished the dishes. He put away the towel behind the stove and waited for her to wind up her chores. She took off her apron and turned to him, and it was impulse once more that brought her over the room to him. She laid her hands on his shoulders and looked long at him, her face growing full with the things she thought about him; and she came against him and kissed him and let her lips lie against his mouth a moment, and stepped back with her small, excited laugh. "Don't be solemn. It's no secret to George."

They were in the front room when Revelwood returned with his cigar and his counterfeit cheerfulness. "There's news downtown. Lee's cornered around Appomattox. Grant's just about got him. You know what the end of

202

the war will do for this country? There'll be a lot of soldiers and families streaming out here. It's my notion to buy some more land around town. I believe this country is in for big things, and I believe a smart man can ride on with the tide."

"That's my belief," said Sheridan.

A trace of Revelwood's older manner flared out. "Whoever would have thought that George Revelwood might turn into an honest man of business?"

"Glad to hear of it."

Revelwood's glance lightly touched Clara. "I'm not sure my wife does. I think she liked me better as a scoundrel."

She wasn't amused by his talk. "You must do what you think best, George."

He had tried to touch Clara, to bring out the old liveliness, and he had failed; a shadow went lightly over his face. "Well," he said, "we play it out however we can."

Sheridan got up and went for his coat. "I need sleep," he said.

Revelwood said, "I'll walk back to the hotel with you."

Clara sat still. She said, "When will you come again, Mark?"

"Hard to say."

"Good-by, Mark."

He stood at the door, looking back to her. She had withdrawn into the shadows of her own making and this, he remembered, was the way he had left her on that night of the Bogart tea. She was slowly coming to another desperate break, quite eager for any chance of adventure. He shook his head at her. "Clara," he said, "don't do it," and left the house.

Revelwood, walking beside him, almost at once asked his pent-up question. "What does she really think about me? I can't get it out of her. We're not getting on well—you see that. What does she want?"

"Do you think she'd tell me?"

"Certainly," said Revelwood. "She'd tell you anything. She'd do anything you wished. Anything. I'm not jealous about it."

"George," said Mark, "take a stick of stovewood to her. Go find yourself another woman and make an open affair of it. Tell Clara she's not got enough for you. You're tied to her apron strings and she doesn't respect you for it. Go back to what you were."

"Go back?" said Revelwood and let out a short, strained laugh. "I wish I could, but if I tried to change now it would be only part of a silly chess game and she'd know what I was doing. But what does she want?"

"She doesn't know," said Sheridan, and walked silently beside Revelwood, down the dismal shadows of Oak Street, through the steady rain. He braced his hands behind his back and he felt Revelwood's patient, insistent silence. What was he to say? Whenever he thought he knew Clara she turned upon him with a contradiction. She had been attracted by something in George, and had married him because of it; but she was tired of him now, and no longer wanted what she thought she had wanted from him. She wanted happiness, yet an inconsistency in her destroyed it as soon as she found it. Whatever she touched seemed to grow stale. She expected too much.

George said: "You can't offend me by speaking the truth."

"I don't know the truth. Neither does she."

Revelwood said nothing. The rain rattled on the board awnings above them, splashed into the street, and made a flickering diamond brilliance in the shop lights. They crossed to the Pioneer and stopped.

"No," said George. "She's not that fickle. She wants one thing so much she'd destroy her reputation to get it. It means more than her reputation. I wish I knew what it was." Then, looking at Sheridan, he put out a sudden hand and shook Mark's fist. "I had hoped," he said, "that you might find something from her that would help me. I know she'd tell you. As for me, this hand's about played out. Come see us when you can. Good night."

He turned and walked along the street, in and out of the patches of lamplight shining through the night. He was a small man growing smaller, feeding upon himself and slowly fading. Sheridan stayed before the hotel until he lost sight of Revelwood around a corner; then he swung into the Pioneer and went to the bar. She had about destroyed George, and in time she'd destroy Bogart if she kept up that affair. The truth was, she was stronger than the men she knew.

Chapter — 21

ONCE a week the steamboat *Drusilla* tied to the mill landing and took on shingles for Oregon City and once a week Sheridan freighted a load around to the crossroad stores. The news of Appomattox gave a boost to business and some gold began to drift back from the Idaho and Montana mines to make money a little easier in Oregon. Men were still scarce and wages were high; his mill crew was made up of boys and old men, but at Christmas he paid off his debt to Breckman's estate and owned the mill clear.

He spent most of the month before Christmas tying the loop of the stage line together, and putting the Newberg-Portland leg into operation. He had business in Portland now and then, but he kept away from Clara and George. He wrote another letter to the Senator and he visited the storekeepers along the run and got himself acquainted with the leading people in the communities; a light express business developed between Portland and the lesser towns.

On Christmas Day, riding in from a visit to Cray Jennings at McMinnville, he came to a crossroads store near Sherwood and here he bought a pound of crackers, a chunk of summer sausage and a pickle; traveling on through the cool gray night, he had his Christmas dinner. The rain-soaked land sent up its sweet and moldy odors, the hallooing of nervous dogs were undulating patterns of sound through the darkness, and farmhouse lights lay as shattered stars close upon the earth. He reached a crest and moved into a pocket where stump fires stained the shadows; he passed a good white house with a red barn directly beside it and, a little onward, a gray house sitting to the right of the road. A light shone through the front-room window and from the road he had an incomplete view of people sitting at the Christmas table.

His interest in the mill had stayed alive so long as there was a problem in getting it into operation; having done so, his surplus energy turned him restless. Going over his books he was pleased with the money he seemed to be making, yet even then time weighed on him and he felt its swift passing and his own aimless turning about in this quiet backwater. It was not security he wanted and not a comfortable place with a comfortable living on the banks of a river five miles from a small town.

He had planned to extend the stage line as soon as the Portland-McMinnville section supported itself. In the middle of January, seeing this to be a fact, he rode down to Dayton and spent three days locating a driver, and went on to Amity and Corvallis. By the first of February he had these places connected. Each of these new lines stood on its own feet as the other sections had. The drivers put up their time and some of the cost of the wagons and horses; if there was money enough to pay them day wages, they got it, and if there was some additional profit they took a share. At Corvallis one night he sat down to write a letter back to Cray Jennings:

DEAR CRAY:

Now we can ride eighty miles in our own wagons behind our own horses. That's not bad for a concern which began five months ago as a straight gamble. We could not have done it if we had not interested men to come in to risk their time and to take their chances at a profit. These are the men who will hang on and go through the starving season long after a big outfit, financed from the top, loses its capital and crashes. It is the divided risk and the divided reward which does it. We've got a lot of kegs, but each keg is on its own bottom. The mail contract will make us entirely secure. South of us lies Eugene, and the road is wide open. I am looking for a man. Write yourself a ticket and take a ride on your stage line just for the hell of it.

Then he wrote a second letter, to Revelwood:

I pen this at the end of our stage run which now travels from Portland to this town, either direct or by way of Forest Grove. We are headed south and will get there, sooner or later. How far we get depends entirely on push. Eugene is the next town, but California lies beyond. Convey my regards to Clara.

MARK

These letters he gave to the northbound driver, had his dinner, and circulated about the town to introduce himself and his stage line to the businessmen of the place. He wished to solicit their trade, more than he wished to gain their support on the mail contract. "This line," he said, "builds the west side of the valley as the stage line across the river has built the east side. It is a matter of transportation with you people. The town with the best transportation will turn out to be the biggest town in the state."

That night, after supper in the hotel, he settled in the small bare lobby with a copy of the weekly paper, then three days old. On the inside page he found a brief news item buried between two heavy political editorials

REGRETTABLE OCCURRENCE.—Information comes to us from Salem that a Mr. Bogart, of Portland, was pistoled to death by a second gentleman, one Revelwood. No further details are known. Political sentiment being rampant in that town, it may be the murder was a partisan affair. We have long felt that the air of Salem touched men's brains with its miasmas. In this state we have lost the old virtues. We shall have added news of this affair by the next traveler from that direction.

It was eight in the evening when Sheridan left a livery with a rented horse, crossed the Willamette by ferry, and pointed for Albany, fifteen miles across the valley's heart, through a starlight that laid its misty, crusted glow on these on-running fields and clustered groves of oaks. As he traveled he put Revelwood's story together and had time at last to see that this was a tragedy all of them might have foretold had they not been blind. No doubt the intent to kill Bogart had been on Revelwood's mind that last evening in Portland when he had been so quiet and so depressed. There was an old-fashioned honor in Revelwood which, tortured by the smiles of people at his cuckoldry, could have come to this fixed purpose. He found but one other possible answer, which was that Revelwood, seeing in Bogart only so much more misery

207

for Clara, might have decided that Bogart's death was the cure for it. But why had it happened in Salem?

He reached Albany in two hours, turned north and covered the thirty miles to Salem by daybreak. He had breakfast and went to the town's jail, a low, single-story box of a place half darkened by the thick iron bars at its windows. When the jailer let him into Revelwood's room —a common room for all offenders and now also occupied by three sleeping drunks—he found George concluding his morning shave. Revelwood turned from the jagged bit of looking glass propped on the window sill and showed Sheridan the kind of smile which once had been this man's charm.

"The razor's borrowed and dull. I could scarcely cut my throat with it, which no doubt is what they fear I might do. The water's cold and the light's terrible. When did you hear about this, Mark?"

"Last night in the Albany paper."

"News hobbles around in rustic fashion. The event took place six days ago."

"George," said Mark, "why Salem?"

"They went off together again," said Revelwood. "Here's where I found him."

"Where's Clara?"

Revelwood shook his head. "They were in a house on the edge of town. She came here to see me after the affair. I told her to disappear. I guess she did. She hasn't been back."

"Well, then, she's in Portland."

"If she went there she might get involved in this trial. I don't wish that, and told her so. No, I think she's out of sight."

"Have you got a lawyer?"

"I have," said Revelwood. He put on shirt and stock and coat; he took pains with his dressing and surveyed himself in the mirror and rubbed the shaving soap from his face. "I could wish for a bath. Yes, I have got a lawyer, a sharp old pettifogger who helped draw up the state constitution some years ago. I don't get along with him."

"Better get along with him," said Sheridan.

"Not on his terms. He wishes to set up the ancient defense—the injured husband business. I shan't have it. That's why I wished her to disappear."

Sheridan stood in the room's corner and said nothing. The drunks were waking uneasily; they had slept without mattress or blankets and now they were morose, and acutely miserable. The jailer came in with a mug of coffee and two chunks of bread covering a heavy slice of bacon, and went out again. Revelwood sat on the edge of the bed and began his breakfast.

"Well, you wouldn't use that defense either, would you?"

"I don't know, George. I'm not in your shoes."

"How can I use it? If there was injury in this sorry business it wasn't to me. Bogart didn't steal Clara's love away from me. There was none to steal."

He fell to his breakfast with a good appetite for it, and shook his head over the coffee. He watched Sheridan with his curiosity, making some attempt to follow Sheridan's silence. "Do you want to know why Bogart's dead?"

"I don't see it yet."

"She thought she saw in him the things she always looked for. But I knew he didn't have it. He'd shake her around and use her up, and then he'd drop her and she'd be the worse for it. I didn't want her to go through it. She can be disappointed only so many times, Mark, and then she's lost—and that's the end of the Clara you and I know. That's why he's dead."

"This is no mining camp country," said Sheridan. "It's like New England—these people are stiff. Your lawyer won't make 'em cry and bend the law for you. You've got to show a cause. Did he carry a gun?"

"They found a gun on him. He fumbled around for it, but he was dead before he could get it."

"Your lawyer has got to work on that. You were defending yourself."

Revelwood shrugged his shoulders. "Let him make a case of self-defense if he can, so long as Clara's not in it."

He had thought about it and he had settled his convictions. Cynical and clever as Revelwood was, he had bottom and he grew stubborn when he reached it. It was the same quality he had displayed on the sinking deck of the *Jennie North*. He had touched his bottom then and had made his choice; so had he done now. In his affair with Clara he had permitted himself to believe in some sort of happy ending but this was a philosophy that had torn him apart; and at last he had returned to his belief that nothing was of any consequence and he felt better.

Sheridan turned to the door. "When's the trial?"

"They've got the indictment. I think we start in two or three days."

"You want anything?"

"No. And don't hunt for her. I don't want to see her again. It would even be a better thing if you never saw her again. There's something between you that just starts up a fire when you meet. It's no good." He stood at the door after Sheridan had gone through it; he looked through the grating. "I wish," he said quietly, "she knew what she wanted. Then she'd not need to go through these damned miseries with men like me or Bogart."

Chapter —22

SHERIDAN dropped off the stage at Newberg two evenings later, got his stabled horse, and turned homeward through a thickening dusk. A warm day had sucked up the soil's wetness and this created a gray mist turned rank with the odor of grasses rotted down by winter's rain. The swell of Rex Hill rose before him, and a road bore away to the left, past the red glow of slashing fires. He passed a late-traveling wagon and, a few miles farther on, he saw another wagon before him with its lighted lantern swinging on the reach pole. A prowling cat made a running shadow over the road and his horse threw a whistling breath out of its nostrils.

Bogart no doubt had given her money to live on, but that would not keep her long; sooner or later she'd return from wherever she was to the house in Portland, not to live in but to dispose of it. She couldn't live in Portland any more. "I can't keep a watch on the place myself," he thought. "But I can have it watched."

He overtook the wagon, hearing the dry bullfrog creak of its axles. Somebody's voice—a man's voice—was speaking in a weary, long-winded way. He came up to the wagon, skirted it and noticed the two shadowy people on the seat. He said, "Hello," and moved ahead. The man's voice followed him.

"Nice night."

"That's right," said Sheridan. He rode another twenty feet, then surprised the horse by bringing it sharply around; he wheeled again beside the wagon and looked down.

"Something?" said the man.

The second person on the wagon seat was a woman. He saw her face and he lifted his hat as he straightened back on the saddle. He said, "Hello, Katherine."

"Who's that?" asked the man, leaning over. "I can't see you."

211

Katherine Morvain's voice had a start of surprise in it. "Hello, Mark."

"You live around here?"

"Just two miles. Over the shadow of that hill in front. Why are you here?"

"My mill's on the river, other side of Wilsonville."

She said: "Isn't that strange? People move around and get lost, and then there they are. Are you doing well?"

"It's a small mill," he said. "Shingles."

"Well," said Morvain, "if you're on the river you'll not worry about fires."

Sheridan rode along with the wagon. He found his pipe and filled it and struck his match and cupped it. The light touched her face a moment and went out. He felt suddenly in wonderful spirits and he wanted to tell her how long he had searched for her but he held it back. Maybe that would mean something to her, or maybe it wouldn't; there had been no lift in her voice, no great amount of pleasure at seeing him.

The horse went grunting up the dark slope of a hill and reached the summit. He saw the pocket below, the white house, the red barn, and the gray house farther on.

"In here?" he asked.

"That small house," she said.

"I passed it Christmas night. I saw people inside. I didn't know."

They rolled down the hill and went on to the gateway of the house. Sheridan drew his horse aside as Morvain turned in and stopped. Katherine got down. Morvain called back, "Come in, Mark. Come on in."

Sheridan held his place. He had found her, but she was a stranger who wasn't interested in him—he had a clear impression of it. During his search he had pictured her smile when she saw him but he had forgotten that this girl was afraid of her past and therefore she was afraid of him. He had been foolish to expect a welcome and he would be more foolish to follow her into the house if she didn't want him. Morvain had gone on to the shed with the team. Katherine stood in the yard, watching him through the shadows. She appeared to be thinking; then she made a gesture and spoke with nothing but polite evenness. "Come in, Mark."

He rode to the porch and got down and went into the house with her. He saw Suzie and Suzie's quick recognition; the two boys stared at him, neither friendly nor

212

unfriendly. They were what they had been before—two wild animals uncomfortably penned in the room and anxious to be out of it. Katherine went back to the kitchen to stir up the fire, to fill the coffeepot and place it on the stove. Morvain came in, a physically older man; when he sat down it was with the sudden all-over let-down of weariness. His hands were roughened, his face chapped and there was a grayness to his skin.

"The boys and I," he said, "are working for the fellow across the road. Fred Boxwell's his name—he owns a half section. We're clearing some old land on the hill." Humility unexpectedly flavored his words. He lifted his eyes and managed a reminiscent smile. "Not so much like Colson's, is it? That was too good to last. We're gettin' a dollar a day on this job. If I had a choice, I'd like either to be way out in the hills, or I'd like to be in town. This is sort of in between. But Katherine's hell for havin' a good piece of ground."

She came from the kitchen and set the cups on the table; she poured the coffee and had a cake to go with it. The heat of the room made Sheridan lazy; he sat low in his chair and listened to Morvain's casual gossip. There was no change in Katherine except for a steadier confidence. She had a good deal more certainty, she seemed to be happy with her situation. She knew he was reading her, yet she made no effort to change her expression or to recognize his curiosity by a smile; and this made him realize he had lost ground with her and was no better than any other passing man.

She said: "Did you tell me once that Mr. Revelwood and Clara Dale were married? Where are they?"

"You didn't see the news?"

"There's no news here," she said.

"Revelwood's in Salem. He killed a man. He's to be tried in a few days. Clara's gone—nobody knows where."

"What'd he kill the man for?" asked Morvain.

"It was some sort of a quarrel," said Sheridan.

Somebody walked along the side yard with a stamping gait and in a moment a man stepped through the kitchen door—familiar enough with these premises to ignore knocking. He was short, not quite fat, and had a chest that rolled out from his neck with uncommon depth; his face was wind-reddened and stolid, a face hollowed here and lumpy there, and lightened by a set of odd eyes. He stared at Sheridan.

"Come in," said Morvain. "This is Boxwell—this is Sheridan. Boxwell's got the farm across the way. Sheridan's an old friend."

Boxwell acknowledged the introduction with the briefest of nods. He had, apparently, no sociability in him. He got a chair and sat down, gave Sheridan a second stare and turned his glance to Katherine. The room's heat flushed his face a brighter red. Coarse, cross-grained whiskers glittered in the light; around his eyes was a visible puffiness that squeezed at his lids.

"Would you like coffee?" asked Katherine.

"No," said Boxwell.

A thought warmed Katherine's countenance. "Have you seen Mrs. Colson lately?"

"Last month," said Sheridan. "She asked about you. She was putting up apple butter. She cooked me a meal. You know how she is—glad to have somebody to cook for. I said I'd come back again. She warned me to come back before spring, if I came at all. I think she's decided it's too much bother to live through another year."

Boxwell didn't understand such talk and his expression conveyed a slow struggle with the thought, and an impatient reaction. "The woman must be crazy. Crazy people kill themselves. Nobody else does."

Sheridan shifted on his chair. "She didn't say she was going to kill herself," he answered, and ignored Boxwell. He looked at the girl. "She said she was tired and it was time to go home."

He noticed once more how quickly her understanding surrounded his words, how immediately she knew Mrs. Colson's feelings in the matter. "She hasn't anybody left," she said. "She was so kind to me."

"She wants to see you."

Katherine murmured, "I wish I could. I do wish it."

"Well," said Morvain, "it's only twenty miles or so, we can drive over some day."

The thought of going back was a cool air touching that pliable face and giving to it a glaze of hardness. "No, I never will," she said, and changed the subject.

"More coffee, Mark?"

"Had enough."

Boxwell sat with his head dropped, staring at his loose hands. He ignored everybody. He was wholly still and Sheridan got the impression that this man was silently trying to push him out of the house. It roused his own

214

stubbornness and he thought to himself, "The hell with you," and made a small motion of settling himself in his chair. The two boys got up and left the place, bent on some prowling errand. Sheridan said: "They miss the hunting they had in the hills?"

"They been fishin' the river nights."

Boxwell hoisted himself with an abrupt gesture and turned toward the rear door. He said, "Bedtime." He stood in the doorway a moment, his glance coming back to Sheridan, and then he closed the door and went tramping along the yard.

"Out of sorts at something," said Morvain. "He's a good man, but he works like a damned horse. That's a sure way to get old fast."

Sheridan rose. "You don't get old from work."

"No?"

Sheridan smiled. "It's all a game, and as long as the game is good, no work will kill you. Whatever we pile up, we'll lose some day. We've just got it to fool around with while we're alive. Then somebody else has got it to fool around with. The fun's in what you do with it while it's yours to fool around with."

Morvain was obviously thinking of himself when he spoke. "Some men, Mark, never get started right, and nothing works. No fun in that. These failures in life— they're not all ignorant or lazy."

Sheridan said, "That's right," and looked to Katherine. "I'm glad I found you. You look happy here. I hope it goes on that way." He put on his coat and got his hat and went to the door.

Morvain said, "Come again."

Sheridan let the invitation go by and opened the door. Katherine came after him and closed the door so that they were alone on the porch. Her face, as clearly as he could see it, was solemn and not quite settled.

He said, "I hunted a long time to find you."

"Why?"

He shrugged his shoulders. "It was something I wanted to do."

"You were very good to us at Colson's. I went off without telling you that. If you see Mrs. Colson, please tell her I've only cried once since I've been gone from her place, and that was when I thought of her. I wish she understood why I had to leave."

"She does."

215

"Do you?"

"I think so."

"Well, then, you know why I won't go back until I'm settled and married, and there's nothing more to worry about."

She wasn't the sort of woman to talk unless she had something to say; she definitely wanted him to know she would be married.

"To this man?" he said. "Boxwell? When?"

"When he asks me. It's on his mind. You see that in him, don't you?"

He placed her beside that slovenly unimaginative man, and felt sick about it. "Yes," he said, "I see it in him."

"He's not a bad man," she said, and seemed to be defending herself.

He said nothing. She waited for his answer and he saw the faint settling on her face when she understood he disapproved. "I'm happy here," she said. "There's school for Suzie. The boys are working—they're not running wild. Dad's better off than he thinks he is, and the time will come when he'll not need to work so hard. Boxwell thinks we can buy this place."

He tightened down on the rough answer he had for her. She was still afraid, and fear drove her to make the first bargain that came along. There was no sweetness in her now; she had lost that between Colson's and this place. He said nothing.

Her voice rose with a greater energy. She was explaining herself to him. "We're safe here—and I won't give it up. I won't do it."

He said: "If you can buy this place and feel safe on it, why marry him?"

Clara, with her terrible frankness, would have told him, but Katherine Morvain was another girl. It was not in Katherine to strip her feelings for him to see, nor would she belittle Boxwell by saying she wanted him only for safety. But that was the reason. This little place gave her security, but not enough; she wanted more. She avoided the question he put to her—she was sorry for him and her softer tone came upon him. "I know I was cool to you on the road. I was glad to see you because you reminded me of so many nice things, but when I heard your voice I was terrified, too. It was like everything catching up with us again. I know you don't understand that."

216

"Yes," he said, "I do."

"How can you? You've not gone through it."

"I saw you go through it."

"You couldn't feel it."

"I saw you feel it," he said. "So, I felt it."

"Oh, don't say that."

He turned the waiting horse and stepped to the saddle, more and more cautious in what he said. He didn't want her to close the door of her will against him; it was almost closed now for, without openly saying so, she had tried to tell him not to come again. She didn't want her new life troubled by old thoughts.

"Good night," he said, and moved away. Her answering "Good night" came after him with its falling, uncertain softness and she turned at once into the house.

Chapter — 23

SHERIDAN was delayed at the mill for two days to repair the steam pipes in the boiler. On Saturday he rode to Portland to secure new fittings and to visit Clara's house. The place was locked. Going down to a hardware store, he bought a set of skeleton keys and returned to let himself into the place. A week's dust covered the surface of the living-room table and unwashed dishes lay in the sink, left there by Revelwood during the last days of his batching. It was an oppressive house for Sheridan and, standing in the bedroom, he felt something of that loneliness and frustration which must have finally turned Revelwood's heart cold. To him also came the smell of that loneliness, of the tragedy played out here and still clinging, this dead air, of the woman who had wanted so much and who had so much to give the man able to capture her affections.

There was nothing left of her here, nothing to bring back that warm, impulsive and hungry spirit. He prowled the house thoroughly, anxious to find at least one tangible thing and a last, in the kitchen, he discovered her apron hanging behind the stove. He filled his pipe and he stood with his arms hooked to the kitchen table and stared at the apron. She hadn't been domestic but she had made a good cook of herself, as a matter or pride; having married Revelwood she must have felt the obligation to feed him decently. It occurred to him that she must have hated this house and had left it with the emotions of a released prisoner. It was easy for him to visualize how it had been for her here, she spending the long evenings with a Revelwood turned depressed and silent. No doubt she had grown desperate at the thought of the days running past with their sweetness lost to her, and at last she could do nothing but run. He locked the house behind him and returned to the Pioneer.

He slept, had breakfast and found the fittings for the mill boiler. During the previous evening he had tried to think of some new way of uncovering Clara's whereabouts but could think of nothing. If she needed him she'd send word to him; beyond that there was nothing he could do. He had one more chore to do before leaving town, and went up to the Bogart house with keen distaste for the errand. Mrs. Bogart answered his knock.

On that woman's face, made so unlovely by the suspecting qualities within her, was a kind of settled blankness. All that she had feared had come to pass and nothing was left to either fear or distrust. Insofar as he could make out, she had entered into some kind of bankrupt calm. He said: "I wish to pay my respects to you, Mrs. Bogart."

She stepped aside with a gesture that brought him into the room. She closed the door and took a seat, becoming again an angular, formidable figure. "Would you like coffee, Mr. Sheridan?"

"No, I'm bound back to my mill."

"Another mill? That's fortunate. My husband's mill will not reopen. The lawyer tells me it should be sold for whatever may be gotten. What should be gotten?"

"You'd better have your lawyer get Monastes to make a fair appraisal of the equipment and then take the first decent offer. I don't know of anybody in the locality who could finance or run it. You'd get more in the long run if you got somebody to take it on shares, with a later purchase."

"Would you want to do that?"

"I'd rather not say just now. We're too close to something unpleasant."

She made the smallest of nods and sat still, waiting for him to say whatever he had to say.

"I went to The Dalles," he went on, "as you probably later knew from the condition of your husband's face. It was my idea not to have Revelwood know of Bogart's whereabouts in that affair, for Revelwood would have killed him then. As for this later business, I had no knowledge of it whatever—and should have stopped it if I had known. That's what I came to say. It's a tragedy and it solves nothing."

She said: "It solves one thing. Bogart's dead and will run after no more women."

"Revelwood may die, too," he said. "Maybe you feel that to be just. I don't."

"I'm sorry to hear it," she said. "He was in my position.

219

He had a bad wife—I had a bad husband. I think he did what any man would do. Bogart was warned well enough. He chose to go on with it. He couldn't help it, Mr. Sheridan. He was a bull. I've only one regret. The woman should have been killed, too."

"I don't agree," he said, and rose. "But I wished to express my sympathy."

"I'd accept it," she said, "if I were a hypocrite. But I've got some peace now. If I were a younger woman I might think of doing something with my life, but Bogart had the best of me and all I am now is a rag wrung out. It's queer, isn't it, Mr. Sheridan, how these things happen. I hope it doesn't happen to you. Where is that woman?"

"I don't know," he said.

She shook her head. "You excuse her. That's sentiment. I excused my husband during the first years of our marriage. I thought I could make him better. No, what I thought was that he'd love me enough to quit his hunting. You see what happened. People don't change at all. Your woman is a whore and she'll always be a whore."

He gave her a short nod and walked embarrassed and offended from the house. When he got to the saddle he noticed that she watched him from the window, her hands drawing the curtains toward her so that she was a portrait of eyes spiritually exhausted, of a mouth so long pressed together that it had lost elasticity and was set as it would be when she lay dead. He rode from the town with her remark concerning Clara sticking to his mind.

Mrs. Bogart's judgment would be the judgment of the community. People, as individuals, were not cruel and they were not blind. Many a man in the privacy of his own thoughts would know how narrowly he escaped being a Bogart and many a woman would, to herself, admit that in her breast too were these same greedy longings which obsessed Clara. This was the silent self-knowledge which all people had, and the knowledge gave them some charity.

But it was a charity that died inside them; for people were afraid of the fires and lived in silent guilt, and from this guilt they set up a standard of public morals and all of them bowed to it though they knew it expressed a purity they did not possess. It was not a standard of what they were, but of what they hoped to become. And, since they committed their transgressions in private, they also knew the privately committed sins of others; but these they could excuse because the evil was kept from sight and the law not openly affronted. It was the law that had to be kept pure; if it were not, the law was no good and they were lost. They could give their charity to those who kept their sins secret, but they were cruel to those who were careless enough or indifferent enough to live openly. Knowing their own suppressions, it seemed as though people savagely turned against those who escaped suppression. Clara could expect no mercy.

He went home sorely depressed and cooked his supper, the affair never out of his mind. He crouched by the stove with his night's pipe and tried to find some explanation, and found none. What had begun with Clara as a dream of loveliness, as an innocent search for personal happiness and fullness, had turned into sordid misery. Maybe the community was right. Maybe it had the better knowledge. Maybe there was some race wisdom which warned everybody that human beings could not find happiness by searching for it. Certainly Clara had not found it.

Reaching Salem on Friday, Sheridan went directly to the jail and was let into the big common cell. Revelwood had the room to himself. "I'm an important person now," he said. "They keep the common violators out in a shed." He had gotten a change of clothes; he looked well kept but he was paler and thinner. He sat quietly on his chair, none of his usual impatience showing on him. "Have you got a cigar?" he asked.

Sheridan offered him one. Revelwood lighted it and drew in a long breath of smoke. He rose and walked toward a grated window. "Fine cigar."

"No, a cheap one."

"Matter of comparison," said Revelwood. "When there are only a few cigars left to smoke, each one is a fine cigar."

"I shouldn't be discouraged," said Sheridan. "This thing may turn out all right."

Revelwood said idly: "I guess you've not talked with anybody here. The trial's over. Verdict reached in thirty minutes last Wednesday. I suppose the farmers on the jury wanted to get back to work. Spring's almost here and no doubt they've got to get their brush fires going."

"George," said Sheridan, "I didn't know about it. What did they decide?"

221

"You were right. These people don't cry."

Sheridan said nothing. He stood still and a sensation made its distinct spasm in his stomach and his hands felt both awkward and heavy.

Revelwood said, "There's no appeal. Nobody made any mistakes to make an appeal on."

"Something wrong about that. If—"

Revelwood brought up his head and made a gesture that contained both finality and irritation. "Let it alone, Mark. My luck's out and I know it. I don't want to fool around any more with it. I just want to get it over with. I've made a will. I want you to take care of what I've got. It goes to Clara, if she's to be found."

Sheridan shook his head. "What's the name of this lawyer of yours? I want to see him."

"It will do you no good. I don't want anything done about it."

"You're sick, George. A well man never wants to die."

"That may be right," agreed Revelwood. "But it's not the sickness you sleep off. You don't see that—you can take a beating and get drunk, and forget about it, and try again. That's your way—it's not mine. The only way I can live is to keep the world outside my skin. I did a good job for a while. Then Clara got under my hide and the trouble started. I just wasn't made to wrestle with trouble. It cuts me too deep. The moment I put down my guard I just got the hell beat out of me. It won't do to get my guard up. Can't do it now, and don't want to. I don't want your interference, Mark. Just let it go. My property is for Clara, if you ever find her."

"She won't take it. It would be indecent."

"No, but I want her to know I'm still thinking of her. If she doesn't want it, throw it away. It's nothing anyhow. Just chips and pieces of paper that damned fools waste their lives on. I never knew how to live—and neither does anybody else. There's nothing after death, I'm sure of that. But if there were chance for another life, I'd not want to come back here. Why should anybody want to come back? Why should anybody want to live here very long? We're nothing—we weren't meant for anything. There's no plan, no hope, no future. Even if there were one, we'd ruin it through our own folly. People say God's got a plan for us. Did you ever stop to think if there were a God—and if He had any plan— He'd certainly not send such stupid, stinking bits of animal life down here to carry out the plan. He'd create people intelligent enough to do what He intended them to do. The only person in whom I ever saw hope without selfishness, the only one who wished for no power, who had no desire to hurt, but only to live, and to have sunlight— the only one was Clara." He checked himself, more deeply moved than Sheridan had known him to be at any time; and he stared at Sheridan and the condensed futility and bitterness of this man came up and flung itself out in a flat, hating phrase: "And look what happened to her! And I don't want to live in such a damned miserable world!"

"George," said Mark, "I'm going down the street. I'll be back."

Revelwood shook his head. "I don't want any help and I don't want you to come back. It won't be more than a week or two before they hang me in the courthouse yard. It will be a holiday for the county, of course, and the sheriff will pass out tickets to the favored. His best friends will get the closest view of me dropping through the trap. If they're quiet, they'll even be able to hear my neck snap. Those whom the sheriff doesn't like, will be at the back end of the yard. They won't get so good a view. That's your world, Mark, and you can have it. There's just two people I care for at all—you and Clara. She's a long way from here, I hope. I want you to be a long way from here, too. Give me your hand on that."

"All right, George."

Revelwood put out his hand. "That's a bargain."

It was a quick, brief meeting of hands. Sheridan said: "George, would nothing help you?"

"No. I'm not like you. I wasn't built to want anything or work for anything or fight for it. It's the same with Clara. She got into the wrong world entirely, and so did I. Our tickets read for some other place. Neither of us had any way of making out here and so the sooner we're gone, the better we'll both be."

Sheridan stood before Revelwood, seeking some word which would break this terrible futility within his friend. He found nothing; he could only stand and grope. Revelwood suddenly ended the silence by putting a hand on his shoulder and turning him toward the door. "Never mind. Jailer, there."

The jailer came down the hall and opened the door to

let Sheridan out of the room. He closed the door and walked away, leaving these two men faced together with the barred door between. Revelwood's manner quickened, and a touch of haste came to his words. "There's only two things we need to get out of life, Mark—courage to stand our own troubles, and kindness to help other people through theirs. I had neither, but I think you've got both. If you think good wishes mean anything, I give you mine."

Sheridan put a hand through the bars and laid it on Revelwood's shoulder. "You don't want me to come back?"

"No."

"God bless you, George."

"We had a few minutes of fun, didn't we?" said Revelwood. "Good-by."

Mark nodded and turned away. Near the outer door he heard Revelwood call, and he turned. Revelwood stood with his arm behind him, quietly placed and self-contained. He had no hope and he had no fear, and this was the best picture of him. "Mark," he said, "if you should ever see Clara, tell her not to feel bad—and tell her that although I hadn't enough affection to satisfy her, I have given her all that I had in me. You see, that's her trouble. Few men have got fuel enough to feed her fire."

Sheridan nodded and left the jail. He walked over the yard to his horse and got on the saddle. It was after supper and growing dark, but he turned out along the Portland road and put Salem behind him. It was a soft, mild March night, with a moon low and clear behind him, its long-thrown beams silvering the old fence rails beside the road, giving gauntness to barn and house, sharpening the ink-black density of fir groves. A few miles from town the road swung down into a flat of beaverdam soil which, warmed by the day, now exhaled a heavy mist. The moment he passed into the mist he lost the sky, the stars and the moon; light seeped through the mist and suddenly this mist was a steam rising in twisted, turning, swaying columns. He was surrounded by these gray and sleazy clouds; they ran cool along his face, they laid a sparkling sediment on the mane of the horse, they thickened until road and land disappeared—until he traveled sightless and directionless through a world without

224

substance, supported by the mist and roofed and hemmed in by it.

Near midnight he reached a stage tavern at Aurora and stopped for the night; and by morning he set out again bound for Portland with the hardened intention of once more seeking a trace of Clara Dale. Gray clouds lay swollen in the sky, their edges beginning to shatter with the weight of water within them, and a fine woolly rain rolled along the land. At New Era he saw the Willamette's surface dully glowing, roughened by rising traffic of waters and clothed by drift, and farther on he saw the mists rising from falls and caught its first roaring. When he reached Canemah he saw a group of men gathered at the water's edge, other men running along the shore with a rope. The rope was attached to a row boat fifty feet out in the stream oared by two men who pulled against the current surging toward the lava-black rim of the falls. He thought nothing of that venture at the moment and continued onward. The road lifted to a bluff which skirted the falls and from this point he saw why the boat had put out from Canemah.

A black reef of rock stretched in horseshoe shape, across the river, damming the upper stream into a pond a quarter mile across and lifting it forty feet above the lower river. Over this horseshoe—and through great gaps worn into the rock—the upper river spilled itself in places racing glass-green and narrow, in other places bursting into flashing sheets and shaken into still finer spray and turbulence on the huge boulder chunks below the rim. This picture he had seen before; what caught his eye, however, was a kind of rough raft jammed against a solitary rock in midchannel slightly above the rim of the falls. On the raft sat two men, each one hanging to the rock, and being swayed and stretched by the raft's rising and falling in the swift current. Swept along the upper river's channel, these two had somehow gotten beyond the point where rowing was possible. They had, by a miracle, been stopped by the rock, scarcely more than twenty feet from the lip of the horseshoe. Here they hung.

The boat which had put out from Canemah came slowly downstream, stern foremost, the two men in it both checking its descent and swinging it outward toward midchannel in the effort to reach the raft. The rope which ran from boat to shore—now held by three men on the shore—was their own insurance against being swept over the falls; but as they rowed farther away from shore, the current began to pull against the rope which they were hauling, and in a little while the drag of the river on the rope was greater than their power to pull against it. He saw both men dig deep with their oars, swing far forward, stiffen, haul far back. The boat, surging into the river with these deep strokes, swung immediately back when the strokes ceased. The two men on the raft were still crouched against the rock, holding the raft to it. Sheridan saw the white disks of their faces turned toward the boatmen a hundred yards from them; and over the roar and tumble and reverberation of the falls he caught the thinned-down remnant of their helpless shouting. Now and then some sudden-strong current of water lifted the raft high, ground it against the rock, and threatened to break it from its insecure lodgment. The two men struggled to hold it, the strain of their bodies visible to Sheridan.

The two men in the boat rowed with a full-out energy for at least five minutes; then, obviously exhausted, they swung toward the shore. In slack water they cast off the rope. Other men on the shore coiled it and one man seized the coil and ran along the river's edge until he was abreast the raft. The distance from shore to raft was at least a hundred yards and what the man then tried to do was entirely impossible. Taking a long swing, he heaved the coil upward and outward toward the raft. It fell far short. He hauled it in, coiled it, and poised for another try, and abruptly turned away, realizing his own folly.

The rescue boat touched shore, the men were helped out. One of them walked a dozen feet and sank down and stretched himself full length. A horseman galloped down to the beach and was surrounded by the others. He talked with his arms, waving toward the trapped two on the raft, pointing far upstream, making crisscross motions with both arms. Two other men got in the boat, one man ran toward a house and disappeared, a third man began to coil the rope and to add what appeared to be additional rope. The man who had gone into the nearby house now reappeared with a small round object and dropped it by the rope. Several men worked on the rope and the object, both of which were dumped into the rowboat. The new set of oarsmen pushed away from shore and began to row directly upstream, staying within

226

the shallows. The rope dragged over the stern, being paid out from the shore by a pair of men. They were going to try the same idea again, Sheridan decided.

The boat went upstream for several hundred feet and then the oarsmen swung the boat and shot out into the current with a sudden and tremendous burst of power—trying by this speed to outwit the river's drag on the rope. The current at once took hold of the rope, bending it downstream, but there was slack enough for a little while to permit the boat to go well out toward the river's center; abruptly, when the oarsmen began to feel the strain on the rope, one of the men arose up in his seat, picked up the round object attached to the rope, and flung it overboard. Instantly it went sailing down the current toward the raft.

It became clear to Sheridan what the new scheme was. The river end of the rope was attached to a keg which kept it afloat. This keg, drifting on, might carry the rope against the raft. If this happened, the two men trapped on the raft could seize the rope and be hauled ashore by the crowd.

A pair of men, both hanging to the shore end of the rope, now began to run downstream, paralleling the keg. The keg bobbed along with increasing speed toward the raft, and the two men on the raft turned and were watching it, both using their bodies to anchor the raft to the rock. From his position on the bluff, Sheridan could not be sure the keg would reach the rock; it appeared to be swinging inshore. He sat on the saddle, slowly tightening with suspense, bending forward with both hands pushed down on the saddle horn. All the men on the beach were moving abreast the keg. Out from the raft came a long, odd, meaningless cry. The keg swept on and in another moment Sheridan realized it would pass short of the raft. He saw it from his high place—and the men on the raft saw it; the crowd on the beach did not yet see it. One of the men on the raft turned as the keg came along—he lifted a hand, reached out, made a signal of futility.

As he lifted his hand he shifted the weight of his body, and this shifting was sufficient to change the angle of the raft against the rock. He swung back to throw himself against the rock, and a long and penetrating yell came through the roar of the water; the raft began a slow, wheeling motion, bouncing up and down in the current, and for a series of moments so stretched out by intensity of effort that they were painful for Sheridan to live through, the two men on the raft fought to keep it poised against the rock. It became a thing alive and malevolently bent on destroying them. It pitched in the current eddying around the rock, it flung them off balance; it swayed from side to side, each sway carrying it to a more perilous angle. The two men strained to keep it lodged. Their feet were hooked to the loose poles of the raft, their bodies lay limpetlike against the rock, their arms hugged it, and in this attitude they were twisted and stretched and buckled by the wild contortions of the raft. Even at this distance it was obvious how tortured and frantic were their efforts. They got the raft back on even balance and for a little while Sheridan felt a tremendous relief rush through him, lifted his hands from the saddle horn and wiped away the loose sweat collected in his palms, and he tried to think of new ways of reaching those two.

Then he said, "Goddammit," in sharpest pity. The two men, tiring from the ordeal, had relaxed their pressure on the raft. A surge of turbulent water lifted it, the eddying current seized an edge of it and swung it around; there it hung, half held to the rock and half free, with the two men now again flattened and fighting the river. A choppy roller gave the raft one more blow and it began to slide around the rock and pull away. The men were thus caught in a rack, their toes hooked to the raft, their bodies slowly sliding down the rock. They fought as long as there was power in them or the will to fight, but the current had full grip on the raft and their muscles could not endure the pull; they were slowly dragged downward, their arms and bodies no doubt shredded on the rock's rough surface. It was nothing Sheridan could see; it was something he knew, and felt in a raw and cruel transfer of pain from that rock to this bluff on the shore. He gripped the saddle horn again, fighting with them, and losing the fight. One of the men, quicker of wit and with some tougher instinct of survival remaining within him, unexpectedly released his grip on the rock, made half a turn and flung himself face down on the raft, his arms clinging to it. Without his anchoring influence, the raft pulled farther away and the second man, past caring or past thinking, continued to slide into the water and to suddenly disappear below the river's surface.

The raft shot on across the last thirty feet between rock and rim; it appeared to shoot out into space and poise there, and tip and go straight down through the mist and the ragged spray. Sheridan lost sight of it. He bent forward. He caught it again as it came out of the furious tangle at the foot of the falls—a raft without a man. It came upon the whirlpool below the falls, was caught and pulled toward the center, and sucked from sight. There was no sign of either man.

The crowd on the riverbank broke and began to run toward the road which skirted the falls. Sheridan relaxed and drew a long breath and was tired. He waited until the men got to the top of the bluff.

"Who was it?" he asked.

Somebody said: "Don't know. Couple of fellows who was fishing last night."

"They there all night on that rock?"

"All night," said the man, and went on with the crowd.

Sheridan looked at the falls again, and he thought, "Those men are dead," and rode on.

He reached Portland somewhat after noon. He was tired and hungry, he was dull, he was emotionally flat; he was a piece of rubber which had been stretched so long that it had lost its resilience. Going into the Pioneer's bar he took three whiskeys straight and afterwards sat down in the dining room for a heavy meal. But neither the liquor nor the food lifted him as they should have done. He sat back from the table with his pipe, surprised that the events of the last twenty-four hours had been so rough on him, and presently he left the dining room and turned along Front with the idea of going to Clara's house. At Stark he met Church rounding a corner.

Church saw him, but Church looked quickly aside and seemed not to see him; it was one of those swift, small by-plays but it brought some kind of a distant warning. Then Church, no doubt recovering from his own first impulse, came to a stop. He was affable in his customarily cautious way.

"Glad to see you," he said. "Things going well?"

"Nothing from the Senator."

"I can't speak for him," said Church. "He has his own commitments."

"None prior to this one, in the matter of stages?"

"In point of time, no," agreed Church. "In point of politics, or business preference, possibly yes."

"I don't understand you," said Sheridan.

"Don't be impatient, young man. You're a newcomer.

229

You must bide your time and express your sentiments with some weight and experience, and then may be heard with some respect, and lay your claims with some hope in the proper places. But you are young now and unknown, and unseasoned."

"I still don't understand you," said Sheridan.

"Presently you will," said Church.

"The stages are doing well," said Sheridan. "I expect to extend to Eugene next month."

Church nodded his head and seemed uninterested. He said rather abruptly, "I wish I could be of assistance, but I cannot," and continued along the street. Watching him go, Sheridan felt this meeting to be out of key. He reached for the thing that was wrong and didn't find it, and walked thoughtfully along Oak to Tenth and down Tenth to Clara's house.

It was still empty. He went around it and looked through the windows and saw no change. He crossed to the adjoining house and was met by the woman with whom he had talked before.

"She hasn't returned?"

"No," said the woman. "You've read the papers? She'll be with her husband. Now ain't that a terrible thing? What'd he do it for?"

"Nobody else has been here?" asked Sheridan.

"You mean she might have sent somebody to the house for things? No. I'd know if she had. I been watching. Was Bogart the man?"

Sheridan returned to the walk and moved away, feeling the woman's curious eyes on him. He cruised down Oak to Front and he stood on the levee and stared at the river. She knew very few people. She had some money from her uncle's estate, and she had the house. Maybe she had gone back to California, by boat or stage, but he didn't think it likely she'd leave Oregon before seeing Revelwood. If she had left the state, she'd first sell the house or put it in the hands of real estate people. That gave him a notion and he went back to the hotel and got a city directory and made a list of the real estate people. When he toured these offices he found that none had the house for sale and toward evening he returned to the Pioneer's bar with that possibility exhausted and with no new idea in his head; but somewhere after his second drink, it occurred to him that if she were hiding out in the state, she'd naturally drift to some locality she knew about but in which she was a stranger. That excluded Portland and, because of its painful memories, Salem. There was only one other town she knew—The Dalles. He was on The Dalles boat next morning. Three days later, having searched that town thoroughly without result, he returned to Portland and set out for the mill, going by way of Wilsonville to pick up groceries.

There was a letter in the store post office for him, addressed to him in a penmanship lightly graceful, yet in whose curling, not quite even strokes was a schoolgirl's immaturity. He had never seen Clara's handwriting before but he knew that this was her letter, and before he broke the seal he understood that she was calling for him.

MARK:

I want to see you. I want to know what to do. Go see George and ask if he wants to see me. I want to see him, if he wishes it, and I want to see you, as I always have. I am very lonely here. The place is Albany and I'm at the hotel. My name here is Clara Richey.

CLARA

He got his groceries and rode home and took the letter from his coat and held it before him. Written words were cold cruel things. In this hard form nothing of her spirit was revealed; she had driven the pen across that page with her needs pressing her but nothing came to him from the page but these stilted phrases which seemed like the copywork of a child. A small embarrassment came to him from viewing this pale, inexpressive Clara who could only trace across the page the words, "I want—I want—I want." He folded the page into his pocket, but for a moment he had the traitorous sensation that she was not the woman he had built so round and rich and lovely in his mind.

He stuffed the stove and got a fire started; the river bottom was a channel through which flowed a steady, clammy chill, and this dampness filled the house. Out of hunger he fried himself a heavy meal, still thinking of the trip to Albany. Henry Horsfall, his cutoff man, called through the door and came in, stamping off chunks of sawdust and mud on the floor; his eyebrows were frosted with cedar dust and he brought the smell of it strongly with him. "Thought you said you'd be here four days ago."

"Anything happen?"

"No, nothin's wrong. Man here Saturday wanting to have five hundred squares. I couldn't give him an answer. He left his address. Hear about the two boys that went over the falls? They were fishing past this place the night before. I saw 'em. That's tough on the family."

"What family?" asked Sheridan.

"They've got people a few miles over southwest. They were about sixteen or seventeen, a couple of brothers. Morvain. You better come out and look at the belt. The lacing's going to pull out before long. We better trim and relace."

"Morvain?"

"That was the name. We're running into some punky logs. You want to come and have a look?"

Sheridan rose from the table and went over to his coat and hat; he buttoned his coat against the weather, he jammed his hands into the pockets and touched Clara's letter. He brought it out and found it limp with moisture from his wet coat; and when he tried to unfold it, the page shredded apart under his fingers. He put it on the table and looked around, remembering Henry Horsfall. The man had walked out without an answer, and apparently without noise. Sheridan left the house, saddled his horse again and set out for Morvain's.

It was five miles through a graying afternoon, the early lights of farmhouses glowing through wet windows and the road fences slowly thickening into formless shadows. He came over the hill into the valley pocket, at once noting the light in Boxwell's house, but seeing none in Katherine's. He turned into the yard and crossed the porch. He knocked on the door, listening. He looked in through the window but made out nothing in the room's darkness. He circled the house and went on back to the barn. There was a cow in the stall, this reassuring him. He returned to his horse and rode to Boxwell's.

Boxwell's face, when he opened the door, had a close, narrow expression upon it—the mask of an unfriendly man half expecting trouble. He recognized Sheridan immediately and had no hospitality for him. "What you want?"

"Where's Katherine?"

Boxwell delayed his answer. He was a stubborn man

232

who disliked the question put him and proposed to show it, not openly but in this deliberate impoliteness. "She's gone," he said at last.

"Where?"

"I don't know that I'd care to tell strangers where she went," said Boxwell.

"You know I'm no stranger to them."

Boxwell shrugged his shoulders. "Oregon City. They buried the boys yesterday and they ain't come back yet."

"I'd like a word with you," said Sheridan.

"Well," said Boxwell, "have your words."

"Any reason," asked Sheridan pointedly, "why I shouldn't come out of the weather?"

Boxwell suddenly turned from the door and walked deeper into the room. Over his shoulder he threw his curt order. "Shut the door behind you." Then he turned and stared at Sheridan, and said in grudging civility, "You want some coffee?"

"No."

"Well, then, what you want? I work a long day and I don't stay up late. Was about in bed when you knocked."

He was a queer sort, overbearing, yet not too overbearing; it was as though he brought his bad manners so far and hadn't the courage to bring them farther. He was muscular and young, but his eyes were old, his shoulders rounded, his hands shapeless, his clothes dirty.

"Have you done anything yet about helping the Morvains to get that place?"

"That's between me and them."

"I'm glad to hear it," said Sheridan. "They deserve good luck. I was with Katherine when her brother died. I saw them get wiped out. I followed them here, to see how they were. You understand my interest?"

"If she wanted anything to do with you, she'd send for you. She ever send for you?"

"I don't wait to be sent for."

"Well, then, you're playing your hand too high with me," said Boxwell, and seemed to find satisfaction in what he had discovered. "You came here to say something. It wasn't to scare me, was it? You'll play hell doing that."

"I just wanted to see what kind of a man you are," said Sheridan.

Boxwell's amusement continued. He was on sure ground and knew it. "Not that you've got a chance. I thought

233

maybe you had, but now I know you ain't. When I'm sure of my farm, I don't go visitin' another man's. When I ain't sure, then I go see what he's doin' that I ought to be doin'. That's what you're up to now, but it won't do you any good. You don't like me and I don't like you. That's natural. Now you can go on home and we'll just keep right on not likin' each other."

Sheridan said, "Do you think she'll be back tomorrow?"

"I don't know," said Boxwell briefly. He lost some of his amusement, he turned glum. This was a man, Sheridan at once realized, cursed by some lack of certainty. He could only be sure of himself for a little while; afterwards doubt came, as it came now. "If I was you," added Boxwell, "I'd stay away. If she wanted you, she'd say so."

"Tell her I called," said Sheridan, and turned to the door. He was outside of it when Boxwell came across the room. The man stared through the doorway, sly and suspicious. "Wait a minute," he said. "I mean this. Don't you bother her. I won't have it."

"I'll see you again," said Sheridan.

Boxwell's slow, reserved anger began to show itself. "You like to have your own way," said Boxwell. "I can see you're that sort—just to push ahead and laugh and ride other people down. I ain't that sort. I'm telling you —I ain't that sort. Let her alone, and let me alone, or by God you'll wish you had."

Chapter —24

SHERIDAN rode directly to Aurora and put up at the stage tavern for the night and caught the morning coach south. Reaching Albany ten hours later, he went directly to the hotel and found Clara. She was in her room. He sent word up to her, meanwhile dreading how he would find her. A Clara without a quick and careless warmth was a Clara destroyed—and this was what he feared he would see; yet when she came down the stairs her glance went straight to him and the old smile curved her lips, and she came over the lobby, indifferent to the eyes of the three strangers and put her arms around him.

"I knew you'd come," she said.

This was the old Clara, and it shocked him to know how little any of the past weeks meant to her; nothing seemed to trouble her except the loneliness she had experienced. That was real. It was a feeling in her voice when she spoke again. "I can't live by myself, Mark. It has been dreary. Have you seen George? Should I see him? Does he want me to?"

"I didn't stop in Salem. He didn't want to see you when I mentioned it earlier. But that's no matter. You should see him."

She stepped back to watch him with something like doubt on her face. She looked well, she had taken pains with her appearance. Her brown hair was soft around her temples and her eyes had the same way of drawing him down into her warmth. He didn't remember the dress and thought it was probably new. There was a light dusting of rice powder of her face. "If you think it right," she said, "I'll go, of course."

It astonished him that her response was dutiful, not deeply felt. "Clara," he said, "he'll be dead soon enough."

The phrase was unpleasant to her. "Don't say that, Mark. It makes me shudder."

"I don't think you understand," he said.

"I know all about it. I've lain in bed and thought of it

until darkness came over me and I was in a grave. Then I had to get up and light the lamp. I don't want to think about it any more. I mustn't carry it on my mind. But I want to see him. I don't want him to think I hate him."

They were on the northbound stage early the following morning, and into Salem at noon. She had not said much on the trip; she sat close to Mark, her hand through his arm, her mind busy with its changing thoughts. Once she said, "Does he hate me?"

"No," he said.

"I don't hate him." He said nothing but in that silence she sensed his thoughts and spoke gently at him. "It works both ways, Mark. He thinks I've ruined his life. But he ruined mine, too. I've as much reason to hate him as he has to hate me. Do you see that?"

"You were his wife," he said.

"He knew what he was getting. When I left him, he should have been content to let me go. But he had to kill Bogart. Bogart had done him no harm—not really. Bogart didn't steal me. I went willingly. It was his pride that made him kill Bogart."

"You're wrong. If he'd thought you'd be happy with Bogart he'd not followed you. He saw Bogart pulling you down. That's why he shot him."

She was silent so long that he thought she was grieving over a tragedy newly understood; but when she spoke again he heard only a quiet wonder in her voice. "Didn't he know Bogart could do nothing to me? I'm stronger than George, and I was stronger than Charnel. I changed Charnel. He didn't change me. I took him out of his home, away from his wife, away from his business." She looked at him with that candor he had before noticed; no guilt touched her, no thought of sin or remorse occurred to her. She lived for herself and cared so little for rules, or understood them so little, that they meant nothing to her. Only once had she shown him any feeling that the opinion of others or the beliefs of others concerned her, this when Mrs. Bogart had destroyed her position in Portland. That had hurt her, but when he came to think of it, it seemed to him the hurt was caused not so much by the opinions of other people as by the pleasant way of living from which she had been barred by that incident.

"Poor George," she murmured, "he wanted to protect me. I didn't need it. He wanted to shelter me and I wanted to reach out. But I don't hate him for it, Mark."

He wanted to stay outside the Salem jail but she took his arm, suddenly afraid, and made him go with her. He felt her shrink as she walked along the narrow corridor—the odors, the shadows, the grimed barrenness of this place touching those soft nerves which were so sensitive to ugliness. He stepped back when she went into George's cell, staying outside the grated door and looking on as a spectator. George had seen her in the hallway and was prepared for her; he had risen from his chair and he had made a quick gesture at his clothes and his hair. He had aged, and he seemed absent-minded.

"Well," he said to Clara, "you oughtn't to have come. But I suppose it doesn't matter. You look well."

"Mark thought I should," she said. "I wrote him and said I wished to come—if you wished it."

"Where did you go?"

"Albany."

"Where will you go now?"

"Back to Portland."

"You may find it hard there," he said. "I wish I could know how things turned out for you. That's the only worry I've got left. The only one." He looked beyond the girl to Sheridan. "Mark, you've got to take care of her."

"I can care for myself, George," she said.

He nodded, he stood watching her, not as a man looking upon a woman he loved and would see no more, but with something of politeness. "Yes," he said. "I guess that's right. Is that a new dress?"

She nodded and had nothing more to offer. There seemed no more pity within her than within Revelwood. They were acquaintances, not strongly stirred by each other, and for a moment Mark Sheridan had a gray glimpse at the spiritual destruction of the two people whom he had best known. They had begun with feeling, but the world had beaten feeling out of them. "Well, George," she said, "God bless you."

"I wish you well," he said. Then, after she had left the cell and the jailer had come along to lock the door, Revelwood showed one small pathetic bit of warm memory, repeating to Clara the remark he had made another time to Sheridan. "We had good times for a little while, didn't we?"

"Yes," said Clara, this sentiment inevitably touching her. A film made her eyes brilliant. She turned to the grating. "George," she said, "come here," and when he laid his head at the grating she stretched upward and kissed him, and turned away.

"Mark," said Revelwood, "I'd rather you didn't come back."

"All right, George. Good-by."

"Yes," said Revelwood.

Sheridan walked out of the jail with Clara, holding her arm and feeling the tightness of her body slowly dissolve as they walked toward the hotel. He said: "There's a stage late in the afternoon."

"I had to see him, didn't I? I'm glad I did but, oh God, I wish I hadn't."

"I know," he said.

She shook her head. "You don't. It's so short for any of us, it's so cold and lonely and crazy. Why do they have to make it worse by killing him?"

"Because he killed somebody else."

"That's no answer," she said.

He took her to the hotel and got a room for her and left her; he came again for her at stage time and rode the dreary trip into Portland. They walked up the dark wet streets of midnight Portland and turned into the yard of her house. She had kept her key, he noticed—and he tried to understand, by this little action, what was in her mind. She had run from Portland, but she hadn't thrown the key away. He lighted the lamps and started a fire. She had meanwhile gone into the bedroom and presently came out, walking slowly through the house with a preoccupied air. He heard her open the kitchen drawers and close them. She came back and stood by the stove to warm herself. She seemed calm. The scene at the jail and the dreary ride—these things she appeared to have put away from her. He couldn't believe that Revelwood was not with her thoughts, yet he saw nothing on her face to show that the day had harrowed her.

"Mark," she said, "do you remember the night you stayed—and I wanted you to stay longer?"

"Yes."

"If you had stayed, things would have been different. There's nothing in the house to eat. I wish I could feed you."

"No," he said, "I'll go to the Pioneer."

She made a light, quick turn and sat on the couch and made a gesture with her hand drawing him beside her.

She moved against him and laid her head on his shoulder. "I've thought of the night in the Indian cabin, too. The rain and the cold—that goes away. I don't remember it. What comes back is the nice part of it. You think I don't know what I want. You think I'm not faithful to anything or anybody. But I am. There's only one thing worth anything. It's one certain man and one certain woman— together. There's nothing else. That's what I felt in the cabin. It was just for that little time. Maybe it's never any longer for anybody. Maybe it's a dream that can't last. I don't know, but anything less is like being starved, and if I'm not to have that feeling again, I'd be better off dead."

It was that night, then, he realized. This was the final answer—the night had brought her something. Well, happiness. She was still thinking she could find it again and keep it forever—that she could freeze herself into a moment of wonder which would last as long as she lived. She couldn't face the dust or the bad hours, the work or the crying; she wanted none of the dreariness which lay between these little moments of goodness. All moments had to be good.

"Do you see?" she murmured.

"Yes," he said. "I know."

"It is impossible, Mark?"

It was. The moment was gone, nor could he furnish her with another moment like it. It had been an illusion anyhow, created by misery and rain and darkness. For Clara it had been an explosion which had lighted her world; and here she was running through the darkness in her search for what had been. But it couldn't come again.

He said very quietly: "What will you do now?"

She didn't answer the question. She sat motionless, a terrible disappointment coming out of her. He had failed her again. He would always fail her, for she was faithful to her one wish and could break every rule to have it while he, bound to thoughts he could never escape, would always fall behind her imagination; and quite suddenly he thought he understood her better in one thing. It was the wish for something better than she had which drove her—and that better thing, once she touched it, became something she didn't want and in which she lost interest. Their marriage would have been like that.

She said: "Too much has happened, hasn't it?

"Yes," he said. "What will you do?"

"I don't know. Something."

"Portland's no good for you now."

"I'll go somewhere," she said, "I'll do something. We'll talk about that again."

He shook his head. "Not many more times, Clara."

She showed him an almost helpless, almost frightened expression. "What will I do without you?"

He spread his hands, he shook his head, he was ashamed of this necessary brutality. "It's no good. You want me to stay here tonight?"

"Oh, yes."

"I could give you a little comfort, but it wouldn't be enough. I never was the man you thought and you'd see it if we were together, and then you'd be looking for something else."

She had a rapid thought, and the thought affronted her. "It's another woman."

He rose and put on his coat. "I may see you in a week or so, Clara."

She gave him an absent-minded nod. Her face was loose and preoccupied; she was going through her thoughts and her thoughts gave her no support, for she made a small gesture and seemed to grow small. "I've nothing left," she said. "I depended on you. Do you hate me, Mark? Have I done so much wrong?"

He shook his head. "I couldn't hate you. I'll always see your side of it." He stopped there, for he saw the livening of her face, the flash of renewed hope. This was Clara, so softly loving, so forgetful of the past, so quick to seize upon tomorrow. In this attitude she was beautiful and her willingness came out to touch him and to quicken his wants. She did this to him, she did it to all men, and because of it one man was dead and one was soon to die. She didn't understand how much death lay in her own wish to live. He closed the door behind him, saddened and sensing the end of a part of his life.

Chapter —25

THE early spring rains came up with the southwest wind. Riding homeward next morning he traveled beneath the gorged clouds which boiled and burst and fled raggedly onward, the land crouched before the sudden-violent tempests of rain whose drops, thick as hazel nuts, stung him as they struck, and beat the hedgerow ferns into pulpy brown masses. Hillside creeks rushed yellow between insufficient banks and became shallow ponds on the lowland meadows, and the road was a dark mire wiggling over the flats and through the hills. Somewhere in the upper mists he heard seagulls crying, driven from the sea, and the earth-smell was rank and heavy and fine. He rode through these downpours, soon drenched, and passed through them to come upon calm areas in which the dull pearl-gray air, cleansed of dust, had a magnifying power which brought the far hill crest deceivingly near. In these little pockets of calm he could watch the rain squalls strike near by, the slanting columns of water solid from ragged cloud to steaming earth.

He reached home, cooked a meal and took his brief look at the mill; but the stage lines were on his mind, and, with a fresh change of clothes, he set out again, bound for Newberg by way of Katherine Morvain's place. An hour later, coming down the hill in the fitful daylight, he saw her light shining from the kitchen, and turned the horse around the house into the barn for shelter; she had seen him and stood at the open kitchen door.

"Come in, Mark. It's not a nice day for riding."

He left his coat in the pantry and walked on to the stove; he put his back to it and arched his shoulders and met her eyes. They had something near a smile, they showed him a faint pleasure. She didn't have the effect of grieving on her, but then he realized that so much trouble had gone through her that she had some special way of handling it: The room's warmth flushed her cheeks; she was in a loose dress, low-necked and bare-armed and it astonished him how sharp an effect she had on him. She noticed it, he realized, and perhaps was pleased; she had more serenity about her than he had expected. The ironing board stood in the room, and a basket of clothes.

"Did Boxwell tell you I called the other day?"

"No," she said. "Did you?" She moved around the kitchen to fill the coffeepot and place it on the stove. "Did you meet him on the road?"

"No," he said, "I stopped at his house."

The answer disturbed her. "Why, Mark?"

"I wanted to know about you. Where's your father?"

"In Boxwell's barn, fixing a plow. Suzie's at school."

He filled his pipe and found a sliver of wood and lighted it in the stove. He watched the flame burn over the top of the pipe, growing more and more cautious. She was glad to see him but she hadn't let down her barrier; she suspected he was interfering. He dropped the sliver into the stove and turned his back both to the stove and to her. He wanted to tell her he had seen the boys in the river, but he knew he never would.

He said: "Do you think I've brought you trouble, Katherine?"

"Oh, no," she said. "You've been nice."

"Still, I'm part of the past—and you don't want any more of that."

"I don't want anything to interfere with what I've made up my mind to do."

"I'm sorry about the boys," he said, and was ashamed at the poor, barren sound it made. She had turned to her ironing board. Her back was toward him and he couldn't see her face. He didn't want to leave it as he had said it and he stepped over to the ironing board beside her and drew her around; tears stood thick and shining in her eyes. He put his arms about her; she lay without crying against him, neither resisting nor giving away. It didn't last long; she soon stepped back and walked to the cupboard for coffee cups. She used the end of her apron to clear her eyes and poured the coffee. She got out the sugar and went into the pantry for the cream. He took his cup, still standing by the stove. She walked to a window, looking through it toward Boxwell's. "Did you say much to him?"

"No—not much."

"That was Tuesday night, wasn't it? I thought I noticed something on his mind."

He had an answer at hand. He checked it, growing cautious, and he changed the words before he spoke them. "Maybe he's like any other man in love with a woman. He wouldn't like to see another man come around."

"Do you think he's in love with me?" she asked, and seemed disturbed.

"I suppose so," he said. "You'd know better than I, wouldn't you?"

She shook her head. "I've had no experience. Men have looked at me and I've thought they were interested, one way or another. I never knew which way, or how much You get that experience in girlhood, going with a lot of men. I never did. We were always moving around. One time, when I was twelve, a boy kissed me. I was terrified. I ran home and scrubbed my mouth." She looked at him with a small trace of humor. "I thought it meant I'd have a baby. Suzie's got to grow up in one place. I want her to have boys early. I want her to go to parties. I want her to flirt. She's got to have a nice girlhood. She's got to have a choice of men."

He finished his coffee and took his stand by the stove. She was watching him. "Boxwell doesn't love me. He wants me to take care of his house."

"How do you feel about it?"

"People who want too much always get hurt." She looked through the window again and saw something which put a slight flurry of unrest on her face. She turned toward Sheridan. "You'd better go. I wish I knew what you said to Boxwell. The next day he asked me to marry him."

He walked toward his coat. He said: "Well, what did you say?"

"I'm going to."

He took his hat to the stove and squeezed the water from its rim onto the hot surface. Steam hissed up and made a little cloud in the room. "That will make you secure," he said. "You and your father and Suzie."

She said: "That's not what you're thinking. You're not pleased."

"When will you do it?"

"He wants to fix up the house first. But what are you thinking? I wish you'd say."

He came over to her with a small rough smiling in his eyes. "Do you ever think of him as a man? What do you feel when he touches you?"

"You're different than I am. You want too much. There just isn't that much."

"I expect you'll live another forty years, and so will he." He went to the door and looked back at her. "That's a long time to sleep with a man you don't love."

Her voice, hard and short, went at him angrily. "I know you, Mark. You went to Boxwell maybe to spoil something so he wouldn't ask me. You've got it on your mind now, I can see it. Leave him alone. Don't interfere."

"It's time you stopped being afraid," he said, and left the house. He got his horse and turned westward along the road. He understood then why Katherine had wanted him to go. Boxwell was at the gate of his own house, hatless and coatless and soaked to the skin by the rain driving down upon him. He had been there a long while, watching Katherine's house, a jealous dog guarding what he believed belonged to him. His hair lay lankly plastered to his skull and hung directly about his eyes. He stood still, only his head moving as Sheridan went by. He didn't say anything, but his glance was a savage thing.

Sheridan thought: "I've got to smash that son-of-a-bitch. He's yellow inside. I've got to open him up so she'll see the yellow pour out." The sudden wildness flung at him by Boxwell woke his own wildness. It was the same as Kerby again, or the same as the Crabtree boy who had tried to kick him to pieces on the ground. He had no pity for Boxwell.

By early morning he left Newberg on one of his own stages, bound south. At Corvallis he took up his former hunt for a driver to run on the Eugene, and three days later he took his first stage into Eugene and spent a day visiting the merchants and making arrangements for a ticket and express agent. He was on the return trip next morning, bound back for Corvallis across a valley lying board-flat all around him. The Long Tom was out of its banks, flooding the low meadows a foot deep and crawling over farmhouse porches. Late afternoon brought him into Corvallis and the next morning found him running north again toward Amity. The rain never slackened, for the southwest wind was gale fresh from the sea, sending before it vast, swollen cloud rollers whose spray splashed earthward in crusted gravel-coarse sheets, in ropy gouts, in whirling balls of wind and water that bent the pliant trees and laid momentary furrows in the road's loose mud.

This was early spring, this was a land's storage time out of which the fat and succulent harvest of summer came. Wet as the day was, the odor of growth was around him and the feeling of it was against his skin. It was a pulse in the soil, in the air, in him. He felt fine, he felt young; his thoughts ran quick and there was no sourness in him as the light wagon jolted through the deep mud.

In this closed-down day he thought he saw a dark object in the distance but this was the weather's fore-shortening, for suddenly his own driver swore and hauled the wagon over to one side of the road. The approaching coach wheeled wide, the team traveling at a trot, and the driver—snugged into a heavy coat—shouted a word whose meaning was ripped apart by the wind before it reached Sheridan. The coach was small and new, and so recently painted that the bright enameling glittered against the rain. The weather blinds were three quarters dropped at door and windows, but through one of the windows Sheridan saw a woman's face turned toward him. Across the paneling of the coach's side, in ornamented and gilded letters, was a name: "Portland-California Stages," and above the letters a red and gold eagle spread its sheltering wings.

Foul as the weather was, this coach was in haste, and went by at a maintained trot, bouncing on its leather springs as it surrendered half the road to Sheridan's wagon; and in another moment the rain and mist covered it, and the driver's shout to his horses came thinly back.

Sheridan's driver turned his head. "What was that?"

"Bad luck, I think," said Sheridan. Now he knew why Church, meeting him on Portland's street, had shown a moment of embarrassment. He sat still in the rough beating rain and with an odd detachment he saw his stage venture falling to pieces around him. The Portland crowd, waiting until they saw him demonstrate that a stage line could be profitable, had at last thrown their weight against him. Probably they had the mail contract. It was Church who had no doubt gotten interested in the venture and had gone out to form a pool of Portland's money people.

He wouldn't be certain of all this until he talked to Church; but even now, riding north in the rain, he was thinking of his best way of fighting back. He saw none. He didn't have the chips to play Church's game.

Chapter —26

ON Friday of the week Sheridan had brought her back
to Portland—and on the eve of Revelwood's hanging in
Salem—Clara Dale stood at the rail of the steamship
Orizaba, San Francisco bound, and watched Portland
fade into its mists. Three lonely nights in her house had
been enough to drive her from a town she had not really
planned to leave. The major decisions of her life were all
of the sort reached by sudden impulse, nor was this one
any different. One moment she had been a woman waiting
for Sheridan to return, confident that in some manner
she could still sway him; the next moment her deeper
sense told her this wouldn't be, and then her great fear
of growing old without purpose came upon her and a
desperation stronger than reason came with it, and in
this mood she made her choice.

So she stood at the rail as the *Orizaba* rode down the
river toward the sea, past the rough hills, the little settlements standing by the shore, the flat meadows gentled by
a gray-blue haze, the farmhouses in their groves of cot-
tonseed and willow. For Revelwood she had some regret
and some mild pity; never was it more than that. As for
Bogart, he was nothing but an episode. It was to Sheridan her thoughts returned. Even then, leaving him, she
still had her recurring hope, her little scheming ambition. What closeness to him could not do, perhaps distance would. Maybe her absence would wake him and
make him see her better than he had seen her—and in
case this were true, she had left her address with the real
estate man who was to sell the house for her.

Intolerable loneliness came upon her, not for the town
she was leaving, not for the mistakes she had made or the
tragedies which had come to the two men whose lives
she had broken; the loneliness came only from a wanting
which had not been met, and such was her ability to discard past error and close out past unpleasantness that she
really believed Sheridan would follow her. For a full hour

she stood at the rail of the *Orizaba,* and believed it. Nothing in her mind told her to believe it; the belief came from her wishes—and by her wishes she lived.

The purser had an eye for women, and, to please the captain, put Clara at the captain's table. They had left Portland early to make the tide. Lunch found them well down the river. Descending to the dining room, Clara found herself in agreeable company. The captain was gallant, the other gentlemen—she was the single lady at the table—were young enough to be heavily aware of her. That attention swirled around her with its pleasant provocation; it lifted her and gave her that attraction which never failed to touch men. She was aware of the sudden rivalry between these gentlemen and this took the heavy memories of Portland quite out of her. She was young again, and hopeful, and she looked among the men and picked her choice. Most casually, leaving the table, she smiled at him somewhat longer than she smiled at the others, wondering if he would have the subtlety to understand.

She retired to her stateroom for an hour, then dressed and set out upon the deck. Her man found her within a single turn of the ship. He had been hunting, she understood; that single-mindedness was in him, so easy to read. Faintly she was disappointed for knowing what she already knew about him, from understanding how quickly and with what little delicacy he would seek to master her. He was a man of about thirty, full-blooded, bold, entirely masculine. When he removed his hat his eyes searched her to discover her weaknesses, to weigh her for her innocence or her lack of it. He would not be a patient man; he had a bridling, blunt set of desires and he would tire of a long chase. He was something like Charnel, but younger.

"You don't mind company?" he asked.

She made a gesture of assent. He replaced his hat and fell beside her, opening the conversation with an easy casualness. She wondered if he knew of her history in Portland. Apparently he did not, for he presently asked her name and gave his own, and pressed her concerning her reasons for being on ship. He was, he said, a steady traveler up and down the coast; shipping was his business and he lived in San Francisco. They walked the deck the better part of an hour and when he parted from her, he removed his hat again, and again his eyes searched her and sought for some secret information that she might wish to give him.

She saw him at dinner, and ignored him by giving her attentions to the other men. She had taken pains with her clothes and the excitement of the game she played was an energy filling her, and a confidence which erased her doubt. She had to know she possessed power over men; she had to know that hers was the choice of many men. Ballston—William Ballston was his name—overtook her on the deck after she left the dining room.

"Shall we take a turn?" he asked.

She let him wait a moment, she shrugged her shoulders. "If you wish. I shall need my coat."

He walked with her to her stateroom and opened the door for her and stepped back. She turned into the stateroom and looked at him. Her glance was sharp and quite roused; he strained at the edge of his carefulness, and suddenly she smiled at him and murmured, "I'll be out in a moment," and closed the door against him. She found her coat. She walked to the mirror and looked into it and saw the shining roundness of her own eyes, the full mobility of her own lips and she asked herself, "What does he see there?" and studied her image a long while, fascinated. She never looked better but she knew the origin of that excitement playing over her features and she dropped her glance. The excitement remained. Whatever she wished to say to herself, whatever she wished to recognize about herself—whatever it was, she thrust it aside. She turned to the door and opened it and joined Mr. Ballston.

They walked aft, alternately slowed down and hastened on by the long pitching of the *Orizaba*. Night had closed in fully, broken by a far-off glitter of little lights and the massive shadow of coastal headlands.

"Where are we?"

"Outside the bar, running south," he said.

He took her arm, guiding her solicitously through and around the deck's gear; his big hand's warmth soaked through her sleeve. The night was cold enough and windy enough to keep passengers indoors; they had the deck to themselves, and stood at the stern rail, the throb of the ship's propeller coming up to them and the ship's wake a ragged streak before them.

"Is it too cold for you here?"

"No. What is that big shadow?"

248

"We're off Tillamook Head. There was a sad thing around here last year. A ship foundered just south of the head. Several hundred people were drowned."

"Yes," she said, "I know about that."

"I'm surprised," he said.

She looked up at him, expressing her silent question.

"Well," he said, "it's just a bit of history—just something that goes on. I didn't think charming women bothered themselves with things like that."

"That wasn't a little thing," she said.

"Put it against millions of accidents and millions of people," he said, "and maybe it doesn't mean much."

"No," she said, "maybe not. But to one person it could mean a lot."

"Why," he said, "you are clever as well as beautiful."

The massive hulk of Tillamook brought upon her the memory of the darkness, the rain and the ship sinking; it reminded her of the cold misery she had undergone. He felt the change and said: "Perhaps we'd better not stand here."

"It's all right. That water's so cold. I think of that."

"Think of something warm," he said, and the pressure of his hand turned her toward him. He was a large man and his strength was exciting. She remembered Revelwood and she thought: "If he'd been stronger—"

Ballston, watching her face, suddenly put his arms around her. His head came down and he spoke something and drew her in with a rushing tightness; his mouth covered hers and he held her to the kiss. It was wild and raw and indecent, without any word to excuse it or any gentleness to cover it. Her own impulses flashed up and for a moment she was willing in his arms, glad to have this greedy man's attention. He felt her answer and put so much weight on her that her neck felt strain and the small stubble on his chin pierced her skin painfully. She had to push twice before he let go.

He gave out an erratic laugh—the unhumorous laughter of a man whose vanity has been offended. "Was I mistaken?" he asked, his voice coarse with disappointment.

"What were you thinking?"

"Now come, Miss Dale," he said. "I'm not entirely a fool. I'm willing to pretend with you, up to a point. What's the sense of pretending more?"

"What makes you so sure?" Her tone was small and cold; she laid a hand on the rail, and terror got into her, not because she feared him but because of the way his words ripped through her and destroyed the little walls by which she hid from herself.

"Oh," he said, "you know. I'm acquainted with women. I'm certain you're acquainted with men. You're teasing me and I don't enjoy teasing. Haven't we had enough of it? If you didn't mean to encourage me you'd not have looked at me in the dining room."

"That was only courtesy," she said.

"That was more than courtesy," he retorted. "You understood what you were doing—and I understood it. There is modesty and there is something else. I think I know the difference. I've seen enough of it to know that a woman's glance—if she does not want a man to misjudge her—is one thing, and that if she wishes to play a game, her glance is something else. Don't tell me I misjudged you, Miss Dale. Women are not misjudged. They set the tune as they wish, and men follow. The easiest thing in the world is for a woman to keep a man at a distance. No, I think I read your eyes correctly. It was on your face. You wished me to meet you. Now then, do you think it fair to play coquette?"

She said: "My hands are quite cold. I ought to have my gloves."

"Perhaps," he said, "we ought to return to your stateroom."

"No," she said, "not yet. I wish my gloves."

He was still impatient with her. There was no kindness in him, no sentiment. He had jumped at her callously, knocking aside the niceties. But he still had his hope of capturing her and, with something of an effort at self-restraint, he curbed his irritation. "Perhaps I've been too rough," he said. "You are a beautiful woman and you must forgive me. Do you understand what you do to a man? I think you must. It's your gift, and you use it. I'll get your gloves." He turned away.

He had stripped her of her self-deception, so that she knew what Bogart had seen in her and what Mrs. Bogart had immediately known. Revelwood had understood it but, being weak, had loved her too much to leave her. It was the shadow of that knowledge she had so often seen in Mark Sheridan's eyes, even in those moments when tenderness came upon him; it was her own knowledge of herself which she had so desperately tried to conceal. She remembered how she had looked in the stateroom mirror—that spongy look of thirst, that round-eyed heat from which she had dropped her eyes. Men saw it and women knew it was in her and lifted their fences against her. The niceness was done with, and her appetite would grow and burn away the little covering she had been able to hold up, and men would be less like Sheridan in their slowness to judge her, and more like this Ballston who treated her as a fashionable prostitute. One day she would look in the mirror and the face she saw would be the face of a hag.

Ballston, returning with the gloves, found her gone. He waited a moment, believing she was once more playing a game with him, and he was suddenly furious at her. He made a complete circle of the deck, up the port side and back the starboard. He looked into the women's parlor, he returned aft and rummaged around the shadows made by the lifeboats. Suddenly—quite suddenly—a thought shocked him and he went hurriedly back to her stateroom. There was no answer. He looked both ways along the deck, greatly fearful of being seen; he turned and threw the gloves over the rail and went rapidly toward the saloon. "Goddam her!" he thought. "Goddam her for pulling people down with her."

Chapter — 27

SHERIDAN picked up his horse at Newberg and rode over to McMinnville to give the news to Cray Jennings. Jennings already knew it. "They put a slick and shiny coach on the run from Portland to here four days back. Probably they been gettin' ready mighty quiet. Big money keeps its mouth shut until it's ready. Then it throws all the weight it's got. It's little folks that talk too much and let the world in on their plans. I got no doubt they've had the mail contract in their pocket all this time you was talkin' to Church."

"You want to keep on?" asked Sheridan.

"Who'd want to ride an open wagon with hard seats when they can go in a covered coach?"

"People," said Mark, "talk against monopoly. I've heard a lot of that up and down this state. I think we could appeal to folks to use an independent line against a monopoly line."

Cray Jennings grinned. "People talk, but when it comes to a hard ride or a soft ride they'll take the monopoly's soft ride. They'll still be against monopoly, but just for talk. People's bones come first with 'em. And their pocketbooks come second. Church can cut these fares to half and starve us quick. You think anybody'd ride full fare with us as against half fare with Church? That's sentiment. I have heard this anti-monopoly talk for years, but it don't mean a thing."

"Maybe," said Mark, unconvinced.

"Nothing scares money except money," said Cray Jennings, "and you ain't got it." He gave out a big man's easy laugh. "We didn't lose anything, Mark, except maybe the hope we'd be rich. Well, I'm relieved not to be rich. That maggot's a bad one. It sucks the moisture out of a man, ruins his belly, makes him a poor husband and a father never around his kids. Makes him work when he ought to be loafing, makes his neighbors hate him for havin' more luck than they've got and despise him when he doesn't take over the charity chores they ought to be doing themselves." He laid his massive hand on Mark's shoulder. "You know, we're all little people and we don't like anybody to get too big. It reminds us that we could be big if we wasn't so damned lazy—and that makes us still madder."

"It's agreed, then," said Mark, "that we quit."

"Now," said Cray Jennings, "don't go to Portland and throw Church down the stairs."

"I'll see him, but I won't throw him down any stairs."

"You might," said Jennings.

"And Cray," said Sheridan, "you're wrong. People admire success. It's a sort of left-handed story of their own lives. It's not success they dislike. What they resent is the successful man who forgets where he came from."

"You're so damned convincing," said Jennings, "and so damned innocent. I don't quite understand it. You're a tiger on the prowl. You know there's a lot of other tigers prowling, but somehow you don't ever think anybody's going to get claw-slashed in the fight. I guess you think all tigers are gentlemen."

He spent the night with Jennings and turned toward Portland next morning, traveling through a rainless, clear morning. The air was thick and warm and rich, the sodden fields seemed to turn green with quick growth before his eyes, the daffodils growing hard by farmhouse sills were in heavy bud. It had been his intention to go directly to Church in Portland, but as he traveled along the fair day he began to look at his own beliefs. Church played it rough, but how else ought it be played? If he were Church, with Church's resources, he, too, would play it rough; for it was a game and, like any game, it was a matter of wind and quickness and a smart head. If a men competed, he had to risk losing or else not compete. He had unknowingly challenged somebody with too much power and he had taken his beating. He felt the keenest disappointment at the collapse of this particular ambition, for the picture of that stage line stretched out along Oregon's fields had been so clear to him; the knowledge of his failure at Church's hands prowled through him with its growling, partisan unhappiness. Yet, riding over the Portland hills, through the solid quagmire of Canyon Road, he knew he could not go to Church and complain. Church's solemn, knowing eyes would look upon him inevitably with the contempt that any winner gave to a poor loser.

Thus, he had decided not to see Church; it was entirely by accident that he turned into the Pioneer's bar for his noon drink, and met Church there. Church had the company of three or four others at one end of the bar and gave Sheridan only a nod, which Sheridan returned. He had his bottle and glass when Church came over.

"Expected to see you earlier."

"A drink?" suggested Sheridan and nodded at the bottle. The barkeep laid down another glass for Church. The older man filled it, and filled Sheridan's glass. He tipped his drink at Sheridan, his glance coming across the rim with its thoughtfulness. He took down his liquor and puckered his small lips into a soundless "Ah!" and used his fingers to rearrange his mustaches.

"You're a good young man," he said. "You understand of course you were in something too big for you."

"Was the mail contract in your pocket when I discussed it with you?"

Church said gently, "It was. Will you take a loss on your stages?"

"No loss," said Sheridan.

"You'll abandon the lines, of course?" suggested Church and patiently waited for his answer.

"I've said nothing about that. I've had my experience out of this venture—and my experience tells me to tell you nothing. Have another drink."

"I've had mine," said Church.

"You're too restrained."

"Don't be intolerant," said Church with his austere mildness. "You young men forget that every old man was once young, and saw the same visions in that stuff." He bowed his head toward the bottle. "If there were any dreams left in it, I'd still be drinking. I wish it were that way. It's no particular satisfaction to be old."

Sheridan grinned. He turned from the bar, he tapped a finger on Church's bony shoulder. "Thomas, if you stay in business long enough, I'm going to give you a hell of a beating. That's what I saw in the bottle."

A crusty and autocratic reaction showed on Church's face. He was a better man than Sheridan had thought him to be. He played his game well, and no doubt would continue to play it as long as his fingers could grip and his mind could grasp. Leaving the saloon he felt better from knowing he had not displayed weakness before Church.

Clara's house was empty when he reached it. He circled the place and looked through the windows, and knocked at the door of the neighboring house. The woman with whom he had talked before, opened the door and recognized him. "Well," she said, and watched him with her close and speculative curiosity.

"Do you know where Miss Dale would be?"

"You don't know?" asked the woman.

"I've been out of town."

"So you said before. You certainly travel. Well—" She paused and gave him a closer glance, a changed glance. "Wait," she said and retreated in the house. He heard her speak to somebody else and go lightly into another room. She came back with a copy of *The Oregonian*, and folded it into a fourth of its size. "This was Thursday's paper," she said, hanging it to him. "There."

Her finger touched a small story without a title:

AT SEA. By S.S. Pacific, in today, we learn of the disappearance overboard of one of the Orizaba's down-trip passengers, a Mrs. Revelwood. Porter, master of the Orizaba, put about and cruised four hours in the vicinity of Tillamook Head without result.

The woman's eyes were on him. She had her own suspicion of his relationship with Clara on her face and she watched him for the shock that would verify what she believed. She said: "Poor soul. Both of them—poor souls. It's judgment. I wouldn't have thought she cared enough for Mr. Revelwood, though, to lose her mind."

He brought up his glance to her and found her intently waiting his answer. He gave back the paper and said, "Thank you," and turned from the porch. She called after him.

"The real estate man gave me the key, so I could show people who thought of buying. Was there anything in the house you wanted—anything that belonged to you?"

"No," he said. "Nothing—not a thing." He walked to Oak and turned down Oak toward the stable. She had hated anything cold, anything lonely, anything that touched death. Then what thought or what person had the power to change her? Whatever the cause, it must have brought nothing but full terror to her in the last moment. Her whole world had to crash, and every lovely hope had to die. She had been so quick, so eager, so willing to believe.

He got his horse from the stable and rode from town, saddened and believing nothing unkind of her. She was dead, so was Revelwood, and there was the end of the lodge. Revelwood had not had any hope and she had too much hope of one kind, and both of them had been destroyed. What thing had been great enough to do this to her? He couldn't stretch his imagination far enough to reach an answer.

A rider jogged before him, out along the White House road, a rider with a large and sloping and familiar back, traveling in no haste and now and then drawing a hand across the air as a man will who rehearses a speech in solitude. Coming abreast, Sheridan recognized Hosea Crawford. Hosea looked upon Sheridan with his fisherman's cheerfulness.

"Young man," he said, "it's a fine day, and there's a farm yonder run by a man that knows his trade. Notice he keeps his house as neat as his barn? Where bound?"

"Back to the mill."

"I noticed the death of the two Morvain boys in the paper," said Hosea Crawford. "They must live in these parts."

"Five miles beyond me."

"Then you found her?" said Crawford, and smiled his satisfaction and touched Sheridan anew with his considering look. But he grew sober as he rode on; he dropped his chin upon his breast and fell into his mood of half prophet and half puzzled human being. "She's been tried hard. I cannot say I altogether understand it, but it must be the Lord does not like her pride, which is very strong."

"Katherine Morvain's pride," said Sheridan, "had nothing bad in it. It kept her alive and held up her family. It was all she had—and if heaven's going to punish her for that, I'll stay out of church forever."

"It's not heaven that punishes us," said Crawford, most gently. "We do that."

"As for her," said Sheridan, "she never asked heaven for anything for herself, and never got anything."

Crawford had the air of a challenged warrior rising to buckle on his armor. An enormous, eager dignity came upon him and he sat certain on his saddle. "I wish," he said with deceptive mildness, "that people wouldn't be thinking heaven was a bank they could draw checks on whenever they went broke."

"Hosea," said Sheridan, "did you know Clara Revelwood and her husband?"

"I have heard of them," assented Crawford. "I am sorry for them."

"They came ashore from the shipwreck with me," said Sheridan. "We were good friends. You'd call them sinners and say they had to pay for their sins. I'd say that they were both strangers in the wrong world."

"What the universe holds," said Hosea, "I don't know. Your geography may be as good as mine. But I do observe that a man has two sides and there will never be a world which will please both sides. One side of him is going to be warm and the other cold. Maybe this earth is for right-handed folks, the left-handed bein' miserable. If there's a world of left-handed folks, the right-handed will cry in it." He gave Sheridan his short, sympathetic look. "There is God and the devil in us all, and the struggle goes on."

"That's too easy," said Sheridan. "There was neither God nor the devil struggling in Katherine when she sat in the wagon seat and watched Elgin die. She was out on the road and the sky opened and rocks rained down on her and cut her to pieces. Don't tell me she deserved it, or that she was asking too much."

"What do you believe?" asked Crawford, so soft, so cautious.

Sheridan shook his head. "I'm not wise, Hosea. I'd like to believe something, because a man's no good unless he does. But I can't believe any old story just to fool myself. I can't pray just to be praying. I look but I don't see. The current pushes me one way and the current pushes me another. People cry who shouldn't cry, and rascals pile up money and marry beautiful women. I don't know, Hosea."

The road came to the brow of a gentle hill, one fork running straight down the slope, across a little plain and up another hill, the other fork bending off to the right. Sheridan said, "I'll go that way."

Hosea Crawford said, "When you see Katherine Morvain, tell her I'll be by one day," and nodded and kicked his horse briskly down the other road.

He had offered no advice and no encouragement, very

well knowing that Sheridan, for all his questioning, was at heart a believer. He had been rebellious, but it was not the rebellion of a faithless man; it was the cry of a strong spirit against littleness—and against loneliness. Above all, Sheridan needed a woman, and the woman was over the hill five miles away. There had been, no doubt, some complication in the matter. Hosea guessed that the complication was another woman, since Sheridan had mentioned Mrs. Revelwood. But Mrs. Revelwood was dead, and although Sheridan may have loved her—there was something in Sheridan's manner this day to indicate it— he could not find satisfaction in a memory. Memories were for the old, not for the young. Sheridan might make his everlasting vows to that dead woman, but time would take care of the vows. Hosea had seen all this before; he had seen widowed husbands swear constancy and had witnessed their painful struggle with that announced faithfulness torn between fidelity and the pressures of their own bodies and at last marry again. It was better not to swear. The living could make no contract with the dead.

He rode on through a land suspended breathless and motionless in the calm spell between rains and reached the top of a hill to view a white and angular house in a meadow below him, fire smoke curling from its chimney. There would be supper and comfort in that house, and the voices of neighbors peacefully repeating the roundabout gossip. He loved this land and its people; he loved all of it so well that, going downslope, he thought of Sheridan with envy.

Everything that soul and flesh could wish for lay ahead of Sheridan, everything that Hosea had experienced, had grown rich upon and had put behind him an age—the good carnal pleasure of a man and a woman lying together, the damp hand of a child sliding across his face, the taste of cold water made salty by sweat, the smell of hay rising from the sickled meadow, the sound of strangers coming along a forest trail, the stinging sunshine of an August day burning on his skin, the full storm beating down upon a warm house, the sound of crickets in fall and the smell of fall creeping through the twilight, the flashes of anger and the keen egotism of physical strength, the sounds of a family through a house, the deep midnight silence of that house when people slept in peace, the first stirrings of spring, the fellowship of a pioneer meeting and the loaded picnic tables and the calling of voices long unheard—the list was long and ever-changing through the days. These were the little experiences which, put together, made a life. If a man took them as they came and stopped for them and lived each good moment of them, he was a rich man. It was the great failure of people that they didn't stop. They lived for tomorrow and were impatient with today. They hastened through the day and lost the wonder of these full moments, they starved themselves. On this earth there was but one moment in which to live— that bit of time which was now.

He came upon the house, calling out, "Hello, there!" and waited with some eagerness for what would befall him.

Chapter — 28

SHERIDAN returned to the mill in the gray dusk. He went over to the near neighbor's house for his supper and later returned to his own place. He had looked forward to a good night's sleep, but he found himself restless and dissatisfied with his own company. He walked to the mill. The boiler was still warm and the reek of cedar dust was pleasant to him. A pack rat rustled over the floor, the river made its rippling echoes under the piling of the landing. He walked across the landing planks and watched the water surge past the landing at high stage. Night mists were packing into this crease, given a dull woolly cast by the moon above it. He counted the shingle squares stacked on the landing for the next boat's taking, and he went back through the mill to the house and got a chair and sat beside the stove with his pipe.

Tomorrow, he thought, he'd ride down to see the fellow who ran the shingle mill near West Linn. It could be bought. It was a good location—giving him a close haul to the market at Oregon City. Since it was below the Falls, he could load directly on a steamboat for Portland, which was a better market still. These shingle mills were small enough to handle financially, they paid well, and they built up a nest egg for another try at a sawmill. He intended to have another sawmill, for that was what he knew about, and he intended to have it somewhere on the lower river close by the deep stands of fir, with the river as his shipping bend.

He went to bed with this on his mind and heard a soft beginning rustle in the river willows, and slept, and woke to a clear and riotous day of spring. The wind was out of the northwest, beating back the clouds, tearing them apart and flinging them over the mountains; the air was unshadowed and clean, the earth warm, and spring was a sudden-arrived shock. He cooked his breakfast and went out to the mill. He worked on the deck until noon and cooked another meal, and started back to the mill. Halfway to it, he turned about with a decision coming up from some unknown spot where it had long lain. He was aggressive and impatient, he was hopeful, he had forgotten his failures, and he set out toward Morvain's with excitement running like loose water through him. It was a wonderful feeling.

Coming to the crest of the hill he saw two men plowing a high dry part of Boxwell's land, the furrows as brown and glossy as boot polish against the dull meadow. Washing whipped and wound itself around Katherine's line; he found her in the kitchen at her rub and when she saw him, she gave him a half-harassed glance and laid her hand against the straggling ends of her hair. She was well formed and was physically strong; there was nothing fragile about her. She had the thick and deep tissues of a woman who could receive and withstand trouble and work; she had known nothing but these things all her life and still was not soured.

She watched him and she sensed what he was about; and for a moment the knowledge touched her and changed her face. "Don't do that, Mark."

"What am I doing?"

"You're stalking me like game. I know you."

"No, you don't."

"Yes, I do. You want your way. You make up your mind and then you talk people into doing what you want."

"I don't cheat anybody. When it's something good, it's good for them as well as for me."

"You don't let them make up their minds. You think it's good—you don't know. You argue people around. It's something you want and you fool them into thinking it's what they want."

"Well, what do you want?"

"I've got what I want," she said. "I won't be argued out of it—I don't want to talk about it. You're not helping me, either. You don't mean to help me—you mean to frighten or discourage Boxwell. You think you look innocent, don't you? You're not, and you don't look it. You're scheming, you're sly—you're just terrible, Mark, the way you ride over people when you get stubborn. Let's not talk about it. How's the stageline?"

"The business crowd in Portland sat back and let me get started. When they saw it could be done, they got the mail contract and set up their own line. I'm licked."

She was disturbed and angered for his sake. "That's not right."

"That's business."

"Then business is dirty."

"It's a game. Somebody gets licked in a game."

"You can call it a game," she said. She was increasingly angry at the luck which had befallen him and at the people who had worsted him. The memory of her own troubles came fully into play; she could not look upon trouble with his detachment, she couldn't shrug away injury. "I don't call anything like that a game. Mark, you get back at them."

"No," he said, "that's finished."

"You're through with it?"

"I'll move on to something else." He put up his hands and made a dismissing gesture. "You think I'm stubborn. I am, but only so long as it's wise. If you're licked there's no use staying on to get smashed up. The thing is to forget about it and try something else. I don't learn fast. Last night I decided I don't learn anything—I just go on doing what I've got to do, not for reason, not because I'm smart or because I've got any plans. I just push. I have to do it—I don't know why. But there's no use hanging on to a dead thing, or remembering it, or nursing bitterness about it. People look back too much. When a thing's done, it's done. I believe in forgetting about it, and taking up something else. Never remember the past, for the past will put handcuffs on you, it'll make you small and afraid, it'll hurt you too much."

She said: "You're talking at me. I have to do things my own way, just as you do things your way." She studied him, seeing new things in him that interested her. "You've had a lot of bad luck, Mark. It doesn't seem to bother you."

"Not after the soreness wears off. The thing to do is keep going."

"How can you know where to go?"

"I don't."

"How can you know you're not simply restless?"

"I suppose I am. The fun I get is in working toward something. When I get it, I'm not much interested. I've got a mill now. It's all right. I could make a living from it for a long time. I don't want to settle down on the edge of a riverbank and say I've had enough."

She said: "You're saying something to me again."

"I want you to see what I am. I'll always be trying something, and maybe I'll have a lot more bad luck. That's all right, so long as I can laugh about it, and forget it, and make another try."

She turned back to the tub. "You're holding me up."

He stood behind her, ignoring the hint she gave him. She put her hands on the washboard, waiting for him to go, and when he didn't go, she turned back to him. "It would be better if you didn't come here any more."

"You've got the wrong man, Katherine."

"Don't talk about him. Quit trying, Mark—quit trying! You believe in giving up when there's no use. Well, give this up."

He walked toward her. She saw what he meant to do and she raised her hands, palms against him. "I'll hit you, Mark," she said. He took hold of her hands and pushed them back and saw her affronted self-possession brighten in her eyes and turn her mouth heavy. She turned her face aside when he tried to kiss her. He bent his head and caught her mouth. He held it, keeping her trapped between his body and the tub. She drew back against the tub, she strained against him and tried to get her lips away from him, continuing her resistance so long that he dropped his hands and stepped away.

"Not to me," she said. "Not to me, Mark. I won't change."

"No, I guess not. Everything's happened to you. You want to be safe. Nothing else counts. You think you've got it now."

"I'm not afraid," she said. She put a hand to her mouth, softly rubbing it. She touched her chin. "Your beard's like wire. I'm not afraid. I won't be bullied. I am safe now."

"Look ahead," he said.

"Do you look ahead? You said not."

"I do what I want to do—not what I've got to do."

"I'm doing what I want to do."

"Has he kissed you yet?"

She said: "You'd better go. Don't come back."

"He hasn't kissed you," he said. "When he does you'll know what you've got ahead of you."

"He's a good man. Let him alone. Let me alone."

He stood by the stove, seeing upon her face the frozen intention he couldn't break. He couldn't get inside the wall she had built up since the night she had walked with him across the meadow. He had been nearer to her than he was now. And she was right—he couldn't change her, for her will was as strong as his will, and nothing would ever break her unless she herself wished to break. He got his hat and went to the door.

She said: "You're convinced, aren't you?"

"I'm convinced. I wish I knew you'd be all right."

"I will be."

"No, you're walking straight into trouble. Everybody makes his own misery, I guess."

"Do you think I've made mine?" she asked.

"Not until now. Good luck, Katherine."

She walked toward him, softening as she came. She touched his arm. "Now, you're not trying to beat me. I like you better."

"Well, you know why I tried," he said.

"Yes," she said, and hesitated and for an instant he saw a fugitive indecision run over her face. "I wish—" But she checked it and shook her head.

He went through the back door and along the rear wall to the yard. He walked toward his horse which had drifted toward the road and stood foraging on the grass along the fence line. He heard a shout, a coarse, high, headlong yell and looked across the road. Boxwell, plowing in the far field, had noticed him stop at Katherine's and had left his team; he had rushed on toward the barn and now came away from it with a pitchfork in his hand, running with a rocking clumsy pace. He stumbled on the road and he shouted again as he turned through the Morvain gate. He brought up the pitchfork, the tines thrust in Sheridan's direction. He gripped the handle with his two hands and, twenty feet away, he slowed to a heavy crouching walk.

He was a homely man made homelier by what was on his face—and on his face was the plain intention of killing Sheridan.

Sheridan stood still. He grew cold, he became careful, he lost his decency. He was against Kerby again, against the senseless boy with the gun; he was as unscrupulous as Boxwell. He watched Boxwell's stout body swaying, he watched the fork swing gently in Boxwell's hands. He thought: "There's only one place he wants to jab me— in the guts." Then he thought: "If I slip and fall I'm through." Through this preoccupation he heard Katherine's cry: "Boxwell—put that down!"

He thought: "If she loved the man, she wouldn't call him by his last name."

Boxwell moved on with his crouched care; a great soberness was on him, a narrowed, single-thought concentration drawing his face to a point, freezing his mouth into its rough-puckered line. Sheridan braced his feet on the camp-slick ground beneath him and balanced himself to jump. He saw Boxwell's elbows dip, and his head drop slightly, and this was a warning; but still he stood fast. Boxwell, whose insistent creeping had brought him within twelve feet, made a short jabbing feint, bringing the four points within arm's length with one hand. He touched a tine of the fork, he tried to get his hand around it and swing it. Boxwell jerked back.

But he crept on, his heavy knuckles whitened around the handle of the fork. He had been breathing deeply from his run, and continued to breathe with violent heaves of sound. His lids dropped, his mouth took a new shape, he crouched lower. Katherine cried out: "Boxwell, look at me!" and Sheridan gave ground at last, backing toward the house wall. The look of those steel points was too much. Boxwell, waiting for this break, made a long jump, swinging around to face Sheridan directly on. He rammed the fork full ahead, breast high. Sheridan saw the tines flash directly in his eyes as he reached forward with a sharp sidewise blow and knocked them aside. The weight of Boxwell's body and the power in Boxwell's arms carried the fork points in, they caught Sheridan's hand and clung to it and drove it against the wall, one point scraping bone and going through the hand—all the way through.

Sheridan had his chance and couldn't use it. His right hand was skewered against the house wall and the tines were fast driven into the wood. He used his free hand to seize the fork, he threw up a leg and punched Boxwell in the belly, deep into that tublike flesh. He pulled at his pinned hand to reach Boxwell, and felt the flesh tear, and with his other hand he knocked the fork out of the wall and freed his palm. Boxwell still clung to the fork but Sheridan was inside the reach of the tines and he kept coming in and used his knee between Boxwell's legs. A sickened vacancy came upon Boxwell's face, a chilling agony, a fainting expression. His hands dropped from the fork and he wheeled to put his back to Sheridan, and crouched down and seized himself. Sheridan threw the fork aside. He came beside Boxwell, still crouched, measured the man and hit him below the ribs and above the hip and sent him down. He bent over Boxwell, seized a leg and dragged him face down across the mud and grit of the yard; he gave a hard sidelong pull on the leg and threw Boxwell aside and stepped back. He looked at his hand, at the puncture in the palm and the puncture in back; it had bled a little and had closed against bleeding. He remembered that the fork was out of the barn, clotted with manure; there was lockjaw in that pitchfork. He waited out his violence and he held it in, for he still wanted to kill Boxwell and knew it was an easy thing to do, with the man on his knees and suffering the heat-lightning flashes of pain out of his crotch. There was no sickness like that one.

"Boxwell," he said, "can you hear me?"

Boxwell didn't answer him. Sheridan walked over the yard to the fork and picked it up. Katherine said, "Mark!" and he turned about to find her coming up. "Mark, what are you going to do with that?"

"Give it back to him," he said.

"Don't do anything else."

"No," he said, "I won the fight, so I don't have to." He walked to Boxwell. He said, "Pay attention!" Boxwell still knelt on the ground, his back to Sheridan. Sheridan bent down and caught a view of the man's face, colored like water-slaked ashes, his mouth drawn back until it was twice a mouth. Short sucking gusts of air ran in and out of him. Sheridan gave him a quick, half rough push and knocked him off his knees. Boxwell lay on his face, his legs and his arms and his body caught up by spasms, too deeply buried in his own pain to care what happened to him. Sheridan bent down and rolled the man over on his face; he took a single glance at Boxwell thus sprawled and helpless and a sudden disgust and a sudden pity got the best of him; he reached down and hauled Boxwell to his feet. He moved by Katherine, not looking at her and not wanting to see her face as she watched Boxwell. He was ashamed of himself. He went on to the barn and threw the pitchfork inside. He stood motionless, holding his pierced hand against his chest; the thing began to throb and to send long chills through his body. He tried to forget it, or to make it seem small, but he couldn't stop remembering there was a hole entirely through it, a hole lined with the poisons of a dung fork. "I've got to

266

clean it out," he thought. He jerked his thoughts back to Katherine and regretted what had happened. He ought not to have come here. Now he had broken up whatever security she hoped Boxwell would provide. He left the barn, to find Katherine standing in the same place she had been before. She hadn't moved forward to Boxwell; she kept her distance and watched the man while he stood dumb and waited for the worst of his pain to slacken. He watched Sheridan come up with a complete lack of curiosity.

"Are we through with this business?" asked Sheridan.

Boxwell nodded. He said: "I think you've hurt me."

"I'm sorry for it," said Sheridan. "Think you will want to run a pitchfork through me again when you feel better?"

Boxwell closed his eyes and brought his mouth together and braced himself against a passing wave of pain.

"We can't be going around figuring to kill each other," said Sheridan. "It won't do."

"No—the hell with it. You've hurt me."

"Want me to ride for a doctor?"

Boxwell shook his head and turned; he took a few steps and stopped, and waited a moment, and walked into the road toward his house.

"Mark," said Katherine, "come here." She wheeled and went ahead of him into the house. When he got into the kitchen he found her sliding the teakettle to the stove's hot spot. She straightened and she looked at his hand and stared around the room, her mind reaching out to seize some remedy. "Hot water's not enough," she said.

He reached into his pocket for his pipe tobacco. He gave it to her. "Dump this into a little bit of water. Let it soak and you've got something good as lye."

She put the tobacco into a cup and mixed it with water and let it stand. She hadn't looked at him for a little while, but presently she turned her head and gave him a close glance. She said: "Sit down," and she went to the cupboard to fill the coffeepot. She laid it on the stove and built up the fire, turned and went into the front room out of his sight. Her voice came back to him: "It hurts a lot, doesn't it?"

"I caused the trouble," he said. "I got paid for it."

"I don't like to see people hurt. Was that what you wanted me to see in Boxwell—what he'd do?"

"You saw what I did, too."

267

"But not with a pitchfork."

"If I stood in his shoes—and thought another man was going to take you—I'd use what I had to use."

Her voice came back quietly. "But not a pitchfork." He heard her move around the room; he heard cloth tearing. She came out of the front room and went past him into the pantry and searched for something. She didn't find it, for she came out and left the house. His hand reached a steady rhythm of misery; it was a hammer striking. He moved his fingers and found them stiffened, and could not stretch them full length. She returned with a short piece of smooth wire and stood with her back to him while she worked with it; she made a sudden turn toward him and showed him what she had done. A thin fragment of cloth was wrapped around the wire. She held it in the palm of her hand, looking at him.

"Soak it in the tobacco juice," he said.

She nodded and dropped the wire and cloth into the tobacco juice and left it there; she settled the boiling coffeepot with a dash of cold water, and poured him a cup and handed it to him. "Drink it first. Mark, I didn't know that was in him. Why is it men see things in other men that women don't?"

"You saw what you wanted to see. All women do, don't they?"

"I guess women see something in women, too—that men don't see. Where's Clara Dale now?"

"She's dead. She got on the San Francisco boat and jumped into the sea."

Her face showed the slow, emotional receiving of the news. It was always this way with her, this using of her own experiences to penetrate the things that other people did. There was spongy, luminous light in her eyes.

"She gave up. Why did she give up, Mark?"

"She wanted too much. She hated anything dark or dole or disagreeable."

"Then why did she choose the ocean?"

"I don't know what she thought—or what broke—or what happened—or what it was that she knew she'd lost. I don't know."

She gave him once more a close, prying study. She said, "Did you?" but she checked whatever she had in her mind and took the empty cup from him and turned to the rag-wrapped wire soaking in the tobacco. She dropped to her knees in front of him and took his hand in her own and stared at it; then her glance went to him with its austerity. Her mouth told him she felt his hurt before it appeared. "Don't look at it, Mark. Don't look at me."

He felt the wire probe touch the closed-up puncture in his palm and press tentatively there. The pressure increased as the tight flesh resisted; the probe broke through into the hole and the tobacco was a cauterizing iron that made the previous pain small. His scalp prickled with coldness; he bent over, he put weight on his feet. The probe went on with its terrible severity, the shock rolling up his arm and across his chest. He looked into the front room to the table and saw a small scar on the rim of the table and he fastened his glance to it. He heard her breathing with a shallow quickness; his stomach shook. He felt her turning his hand and he looked around and saw the wire all the way through his hand, from palm to back, with the stained rag protruding.

"Don't look at it," she said. "I've got to let it stay a moment."

His hand was a needle, which she had threaded—that was the idea which occurred to him. Beyond the flaming and crying and creeping of flesh and nerve was the queasiness of having a wire sticking out from both sides of his hand. He remembered the story his mother had told him of Jesus being nailed to the cross. It never had occurred to him before how that might feel. People never knew anything about a thing until it happened to them. He had a short terror of fainting; he felt his head turning and his balance grow uncertain. He heard her say, "It's out." The great chunk of pain had been so great that he hadn't felt the smaller pain of the wire and cloth being pulled back through the hole. Still on her knees she made a few swift turns with a cloth around his palm; she got up and pushed herself against him, taking his head and pulling it against her breasts and holding it there.

"I didn't want to do it. I had to do it."

"Well, it's just another warning."

"Warning of what?"

"We've got to pay the bill some day."

"Don't talk like that. Not you. You don't believe it."

"I believe it, but I don't think of it. Revelwood was always thinking of it—and it killed him too soon. I don't think of it, and maybe I'll last a little longer."

"I don't want to hear you talk that way."

"He was half right when he said there wasn't anything to count on anyway. Nothing but accident, no reward for the good, no hell for the evil, no plans—nothing but a lot of chance, and the sky falling in on us sooner or later."

"I wouldn't have liked him," she said. "He talked like a man who was afraid. He gave up, he never tried. I think the same thing, sometimes. But there's no use talking about it."

She stepped back and turned to the stove and got him another cup of coffee. He wiped away the sweat hanging in heavy drops at the edge of his hair; his whole body was wet. He drank the coffee as fast as he could get it down, and stood up.

"You think Boxwell will trouble you?"

"No."

"Do you think he'll put you off this place?"

She looked at him with a return of her brusque manner. "Let him alone—don't do anything more to him. Don't talk to him. Don't try to help me. I can manage."

He said, "I've done you a good deal of harm," and left the kitchen. The physical exertion of swinging up to the saddle was unexpectedly great, and his hand burned as though it were lying in a fire. He laid it against his chest and rode homeward, self-criticism depressing him more and more. He had failed to change her and he knew he wouldn't try again. He reached home, made up a supper and went to bed to spend a bad night; he closed his eyes but couldn't sleep. The throb in his hand was something like a sea surf; it had a pattern of running out and dying down, of gathering and rolling in and exploding, of running out again.

The thoughts of the night had no such continuity. Bits and pieces fled through his mind, none of them staying long. At one time Clara and Katherine came before him and he saw the difference between the two with as sharp a perception as he ever had. They were not as far apart as he had imagined, for both were pushed on by things they had to have, and for which they were entirely willing to give up other hopes. That was a single-mindedness they shared. In Clara it amounted to lawlessness. In Katherine it was a constancy to the things she believed in. One woman took her pain but didn't change; the other fled from the very shadow of discomfort. He thought of his mill and could find no interest in it, or in any of his plans. He was alone in these ventures—and nothing meant anything to a lone man. A man by himself was a freak, he was incomplete, he had no purpose and no direction.

He sat by the stove with his hand in a pan of hot water next morning, hearing the rig drive in. He saw her leave the rig and stand a moment in the road to look at the mill, at the house, at the meadow and the nearby river. Then she came in bringing freshness with her. She said: "Did you sleep?"

"Not much."

"Neither did I. I thought about you. I knew it would hurt." She looked around the room. "Everything here is filthy."

"I'm not home enough to keep it clean."

"Isn't there some neighborhood woman you could get to keep it clean?"

"Hadn't thought of it."

She went to the window, looking out upon the long meadow running back toward the cedars. "This is a nice place and that's a pretty meadow. You haven't paid much attention to it. The fruit trees need pruning." She was silent a long while. he put her hands behind her, still watching the meadow. The mill's stream exhaust laid its steady "put-put-put" into the quiet morning, the cutoff saw whined through the cedar chunks. She turned and came to him and looked down at his hand, and went on to the river side of the house. She opened the door and stood in it, watching the yellow waters go by in swollen tide.

"Mark, do you have any notion of what you'll do?"

"I'll be running mills here or somewhere."

"You've got a mill."

"Not enough. I've got to shoot for the works, I may have good luck, or a lot of bad—but that's the only way I can live. There's no fun in anything else."

She said: "I want this much. Promise you'll not sell this. Whatever else you do, or however far you go—you'll keep this clear."

"All right," he said. He got up from his chair and found a towel and dried his hand. She turned to him as he came over. She watched him closely. She said, "You think I'm afraid, I'm cold, I won't take chances. You think I'm thinking about being safe now, don't you?"

"My God, Katherine, no!" He stood before her with a

271

tremendous respect. She had made up her mind to throw her security away; she had worked it out in her own mind, she had struggled with her dread of the past and its terrible fortune, and she had abandoned all that with the same single-minded manner by which she had previously set up her life in its narrow pattern. She was the strongest thing he knew, walking directly into the same uncertainties from which she had fled.

"That's good. I'm not. I want to move here today—I want to sleep here tonight. Can we go to Wilsonville this morning?"

"That sounds like something I'd say. When did you decide about me?"

"I haven't had time to think about that. But you know I usually stick to what I've decided, don't you?" She still was troubled by his thoughts of her, she still wanted him to know something she feared he didn't know. "I'm not cold, Mark. Look at me. Do you think—" She ceased to talk and shook her head, regretfully. "You're not the only one who could break law to get what you wanted."

He came to her, seeing the restless flashing of her eyes, the deliberate way she waited to receive him. She was proud of what she had done—and anxious to have his approval. He laid his mouth on her lips and settled and felt the rough force of her wish to please him and to have him. He pulled his head aside and laid it against her cheek. He said: "I don't know where we'll be, or how we'll be. Maybe there's some rules for us, but I can't see them. I don't know about them. Revelwood may be right, maybe not. But we've got to move on and take care of ourselves. If there's something more, I guess we'll learn some day."

"Don't explain. If you'll be with me, I won't be afraid—and when you grow puzzled, I'll make you forget—and that's enough. Could we go to Wilsonville now?"

"You'll have to drive the wagon," he said.

"Then," she said, "we'll go by the other house and begin to move. I love this place. I love you."

"That's it," he said. "That's all there is."